DEATH
OF
DEMOCRACY

DEATH
OF
DEMOCRACY

Barrie Edward

Riverhaven Books

www.RiverhavenBooks.com

Death of Democracy is a work of fiction.
While some of the settings and names mentioned are
historically accurate, any similarity regarding
characters or incidents is entirely coincidental.

Published in the United States by Riverhaven Books,
www.RiverhavenBooks.com

ISBN: 978-1-937588-09-0

Printed in the United States of America
by Country Press, Lakeville, Massachusetts

Cover art by Jay Ardizzoni
www.jardizzoni.carbonmade.com
Designed and Edited by Stephanie Lynn Blackman
Whitman, MA

This novel is dedicated to my wife, Anita, who interprets my scribbling and creates legible transcriptions.

I must also thank my editor, Stephanie Blackman, without whom even a legible transcription would not have reached the printer.

Also written by Barrie Edward

Bequest of a Stranger

A Note from the Author:

The inspiration to write Death of Democracy came from two simultaneous events in 2010, on opposite sides of the Atlantic. In the first a terrorist suspected of planning an attack on the World Trade Center, argued that he could not get a fair trial in New York City. The second was that suspected terrorists, illegally in England, could not be deported because it infringed upon their human rights. The laws that granted these allowances were the very freedoms and protections which these individuals railed against.

Terrorists do not accept the rule of law while planning and committing atrocities but use the law and our Constitution to further their cause.

The characters in this novel are fictitious; the story is from the mind of the writer. The names of famous military leaders include Joan of Arc. The day that the name was chosen, was serendipitously, the six hundredth anniversary of her birth, January 6, 1412.

BOOK
ONE

*"Democracy is the worst form of government, except
for all those other forms that have been tried from
time to time."*

~Winston Churchill

Chapter One

The presidential election was starting out as it had for over twenty years. Two years ahead of the actual voting, there were denials of presidential ambitions. That these denials coincided with an increase in speaking and fundraising activity by the same individuals was, ironically, not thought hypocritical.

Matthew McDougal, known to his friends as Mac, had covered the political beat in D.C. for a variety of syndicated newspapers over the years but, with the success of his novel, was now able to work independently. He had written about a fictitious situation involving political intrigue set within the State House in Boston. The fact that truth in politics, particularly Massachusetts, is stranger than fiction gave his book free publicity. Sales of his work went through the proverbial roof when he was sued by the Speaker of the House's secretary claiming libelous recognition for one of the steamier acts. Mac was surprised by the quick rise of success, but he was not shocked when his editor told him that he was knocked down the best-seller list by the next up-and-coming.

Now, months after the dust of his success had settled, Mac was simultaneously watching C-Span, opening his mail, and talking on the telephone. The television was showing one of the presidential, "I will serve my constituents," non-candidates who was speaking to a half-empty senate. Mac put down a letter he had just opened and jotted a note on the speaker's mode of dress, noting the practiced body language at odds with the vacuity of his speech.

"Yes," he spoke into the telephone, "how many words? Well, one of the Democratic candidates is speaking now on the Senate floor." He waited, glancing up at the television. "Can I name them all? I can name eight without thinking. When do you need it?...For edit, by next Wednesday...Candidates, chance of nomination, dirt. What do you mean by dirt?" He listened to the voice at the other end of the line."Get a shoveller if you want dirt. I'm a reporter and when last I looked, your paper was about news." He clicked the off button, missing the days when one could slam the phone into the receiver cradle to make a point. The letter he had opened asked him to speak at Boston College in the New Year. He reached for a calendar and turned his computer to appointments, ignoring the ringing phone. When he had made his entry on both the electronic and paper schedules, he picked up.

"Mac...Yes, Gerry, I will do the piece and one a month up to the party conferences...No, Gerry, $2,000 per piece. Yes, well you get a famous by-line and then you'll sell it down your chain...Yeah, next time I'm slumming or need a meal you can buy me lunch."

He hung up the phone and made a note of the conversation in his diary and on his computer; he put in a memo of the deadlines. *There's nothing in the world better than being paid for doing what you like and being paid for what you do anyway*, he thought. Mac was already working on a book to chart and follow the upcoming election. He could easily write the first article from his notes.

The Democrats had declared immigration was the number one issue. Mac did not need to hear the senator from Michigan to know what was being said, that "immigrants were the lifeblood of America," and what he would not say, "unless they come to Michigan where unemployment is over ten percent." Scrolling through his documents Mac found his preliminary list of candidates. Looking down the list headed Democrats, the Michigan senator was fifth and Mac had written 'no chance'. To finish the article he would need to get the actual odds from Las Vegas. Picking up the phone he called to see if his list was accurate.

"Hal, Mac here. How's the book on potential presidents?"

"Mac, how are you? I could use your help handicapping these nags." Hal laughed with a smoker's throaty hack.

"Those Marlboros will kill you."

"Not if the IRS has anything to say about it," he choked through his humor, chuckling and gasping for air all at once. Mac tapped his pen as he waited for Hal to speak again. "Book's lopsided, early days; the two broads are both four-to-one if you can believe it, then fifty-to-one Daigle, and hundred-to-one the field, nine other names. Not all starters you know, but we took their money."

Mac wrote down the names, confirming his list, and agreed that there were nonstarters in there.

"Thanks, Hal, I'll stop in next time I'm on my way through Nevada."

Looking at the television screen he could see that the desk reporter was reviewing and retelling the senator's speech. Next would be the analysis with an argumentative counter: a few sound bites, nothing constructive. Standing to go change for dinner, his phone rang; he looked down and recognized that his agent was calling. He ignored the ringing and headed for the bathroom door. After taking a shower, he shaved, looking into the mirror at a strong hard face. *The face of a reporter*, he thought. There were lines there too: lines of skepticism, of a cynic. He was tired from going to too many functions, too many loud meals with indifferent food and a merry-go-round of people saying the same things, and he decided it showed. At thirty-five he still worked out, but not enough to reduce his weight. He was ten pounds heavier than he had been in college, and he carried it reasonably well on his five-foot, ten-inch frame. Patting his stomach he silently promised to take off the additional weight – though he knew he had made that promise to himself before. As he combed his dark hair, the doorbell rang.

Mac looked to see who was downstairs. He saw his agent looking back into the foyer camera.

"I know you're there, Mac. The camera just blinked."

"Come in, Sue; door's unlocked," he said as he pressed the door release. A few minutes later she had arrived inside and closed the door.

Susan Raymond walked toward the bathroom door as Mac, with a towel now around his waist, continued shaving.

"You didn't answer my call so I ran right over here," she teased.

"Sue, I knew you'd take care of whatever the problem was. Or were you calling because I'm your best client? Or maybe you were concerned over my love life?"

"Why can't you call me Ray like everyone else?"

"I've known you for a long time, from when you were called Sue."

"What love life?" she inquired, changing the subject. Sue was dressed in a tailored suit, collared white shirt, and tie. Her hair was cut severely to give the masculine image that she had created.

"Exactly," he responded noncommittally. "Now what brought you to my door?"

"A job: a book signing really."

"I accepted a job today, a speech and book signing, at Boston College next year."

"I mean a book signing that will not cost more in donations than you will make. An event here, in the action, not in the wilderness."

Mac smiled at her reference to Boston, as if it were still roamed freely by cows as in Revolutionary days. But, then again, Susan Raymond believed that everything worthwhile took place in Washington.

"In January there's a fundraiser for the Police and Firemen of D.C., and you will introduce the speaker, then sign and sell a few hundred books. "

"I think you forgot to mention the name of the speaker."

"Marjorie White; there will be TV coverage, press coverage – it'll go worldwide."

"Sue, you know better than anyone in the world why the answer is no."

"I thought you'd be pleased to introduce the Vice President speaking on law and order," she said coyly.

"Normally thrilled, but you know as well as I do that she'll use the occasion to push her aspirations and probably announce that she is exploring a run at the White House. She's already a favorite with those wagering on the election and, since I am writing a non-partisan account of the campaign, you'll understand my reticence."

"You don't know that she's going to run."

"If you don't think so then you're the only person in the United States who doesn't. Can I get dressed now?" he asked as Sue was following him into the bedroom. She backed out, pulling the door behind her.

He came out of the bedroom five minutes later carrying his jacket and tie and found Sue draped across a chair, speaking on her cell phone, angled so she could admire the view of the park from the large picture window. She ended her call.

"Mac, leasing this apartment was genius. Great space, great view, not too many stairs since it's only half a flight up, and the layout is perfect – very open. I'm jealous." Then she asked, "Heading to the Sheraton for the media awards?"

"Yes, starts at seven," he replied.

"Will Helen be there?"

"Probably. I seem to recall she's getting some sort of award."

"Is that the reason you were invited or the reason that you accepted?"

Ignoring the taunt Mac said, "Everyone in the media was invited, and I'm planning to do research, find out what the great minds in the media and politics are thinking. I accepted an assignment for regular by-lines on the presidential race with the Times today."

"What presidential race? No one is committed yet." Then she quickly added, "I'll need a copy of the contract."

Mac smiled, knowing that she was thinking of her commission check.

"Should be on my computer. I can forward it tomorrow together with a first draft."

"That's my boy. Well, got to run; give my love to the delectable Helen."

Mac smiled as he watched the retreating figure. The delectable Helen would be there, but probably in no mood to restart their romance. As usual they had disagreed about politics. Mac argued for the sake of obtaining information, views, current thinking from both right and left. Helen, at the time, wrote slanted pieces for a conservative newspaper. Though she had an upper middle-class background, she had embraced Democratic beliefs while a student at Wellesley College. Her father, an administrator in a large school system, was passed over for a promotion, the job going to a less qualified woman due to equality in the workplace. Then, because he was seen by her as a threat, he was asked to resign and retire early. He had taken to drinking, which resulted in his death. As Helen put it, "He jumped into the bottle and screwed the top back on." Helen blamed the corporate world for lack of moral fiber as she continued to mourn her father and tried to give her mother some moral support.

She and Mac had argued about the rising right-wing swing in the country. He called them fascist and dangerous. She said that the Democrats would protect them from fringe opinions and that it was nothing. When he told her that anyone not seeing the consequences of the Democratic appeasement policy was blind, she left.

Now he stood in the hallway wondering if he should drive or take a cab. If he drove it meant that he would be the only person in the room not drinking. Probably a good thing if he was to talk to Helen. But then, if he took a cab, she might offer him a ride.

Picking up the keys, he looked around and locked the door. Compromise: one beer could last all night.

Chapter Two

Mac drove downtown and gave his keys to the valet. He watched a few moments as most of the other guests came in by cab or limousine with the intention of having a good time or expecting someone else to provide a ride home. He smiled, thinking that neither of those scenarios was likely to apply to him.

Arriving at the bar he ordered and received a glass of soda. Turning, he nodded to a few familiar faces. Since he was working, sort of, he looked for anyone who could possibly have an opinion and, given the relaxed and convivial atmosphere, who would be willing to share any insights. The room was slowly filling. He looked around for those showing signs of a person who was to be the recipient of an award or a presenter. These were the people talking a little bit louder than normal while drinking soda or standing silently with an untouched drink. Mac knew the look; he had been there. His series on the last presidential election had been a new high in his career and, as he looked back, was the start of the book and his independent writing on current affairs. Two years ago he had arrived with Helen and, after the award they had celebrated into the night. Now, two years later, she was the one receiving the award, and she was not celebrating with him. *How could that be?* He had asked himself over and over again. Helen was a good writer, a great writer but, as he had told her, she wrote human interest stories; she did not ask questions that either she or her readers did not want to know the answers to.

Was that why they had been together for so long or why they had gone their separate ways? he mused.

The multi-part piece that she had written was great, covering the presidential visit to Europe; she had earned the confidence of the First Lady and gave behind the scenes coverage to millions of readers. This had led to television talk show invitations. He made the mistake of telling her that it did not hurt that she was gorgeous – her long legs sprung from a torso with all the right curves and her face was made for television. Helen did not respond favorably to that remark, and then she said that she supposed he thought that what she did was not real reporting. He told her that it was not. She had walked away. That was the last time he had seen her.

"Mac, where have you been? My life is empty without you," a deep voice, stressing every word in an effort to sound elegant, beckoned.

"Ann, you're looking well. And my guess is that you have plenty of more worthy admirers."

Ann Gold was a bountiful woman. Gregarious and very astute.

"Where is your beautiful Helen? Important award tonight; she must be writing her acceptance speech, or did you write it for her?"

"Not nice and not like you, Ann."

"Well, the gossip business is slow; just keeping my hand in."

"Gossip business slow, in this town? Give me a break!"

She laughed good- naturedly and nodded.

"Buy a girl a drink?"

"Sure. What's the latest denial from the batch of 'non presidential candidates'?"

"About ninety percent of Washington folk have something to hide. Therefore, by the law of averages, ninety percent of the contenders will not stand up to the close scrutiny that comes with a run for the White House. Take that windbag from Detroit on CNN today; his staff already had a statement for the press before he came off the floor. They stated that he was going home to spend time with his family and that he was going to contemplate running for the White House to replace his good friend and mentor President Watkins. What they did not say was that he sponsored a bill before he left that will give a military transportation contract to his home state. No conflict there!"

"But that's how it's done."

"The cynic in me says that it's a huge coincidence that the recipient of this lucrative bit of business is his largest contributor, legally and ill….and that he has been invited to a holiday party at the mansion by the shore. Naughty that!"

Ann was pulled aside by a small man with a ruffled shirt. Mac smiled, thinking that the man belonged in one of the paintings portraying the signing of the Act of Congress.

"Ann, darling, I really must tell you the most amazing…."

Mac was thinking about Ann's comment on a ninety percent rule. It had not really effected anyone's election had it? He wondered. Perhaps it is a one hundred per cent rule: everyone in Washington had something to hide. Thinking of the stories uncovered relating to those elected to office; it was difficult to remember any that would withstand the current scrutiny. The gossip mill, the tangible reward, and the fifteen minutes of instant fame for the whistle blowers made it a gold mine for reporters, and, he reminded himself, a potential minefield for everyone else.

Surveying the room over the rim of his drink, he saw Helen watching him from a far corner. She looked away. Then, seconds later, she slowly looked back and he understood that, while he may not be forgiven, a white flag had been raised.

Mac bumped his way through the throng, raising his free hand or glass to acknowledge others who were doing the same. Arriving in front of Helen he noted that she had taken a glass of wine and was not drinking it.

"Is Ray here?' she asked in a neutral opening gambit.

"You know she wouldn't be seen dead here."

"But you're here."

"I'm not Ray, and I'm already dead."

She ignored the remark, knew where it was heading, and had no intention of going there.

"Nervous?" he asked.

"Certainly not. I've spoken hundreds of times and this is in front of all my friends."

"Ha!" he laughed. "You have no friends in this room."

"What about you? I thought that we were friends."

"Okay, you have one friend in this room."

"What about Mark?"

"You have one friend in this room, either me or Mark."

She looked gorgeous and professional. It was true that she had many acquaintances and admirers in the room. Mac admitted to himself that her dark green dress perfectly set off her hazel eyes.

"You gave a brilliant speech when you accepted. I've tried to match you," she said.

"That's quite a compliment. I think you might have been the only person in the room to hear it. Everyone else was either looking at their watch to see if their limo was here, or calling for the cocktail waiter, or fast asleep."

"Don't be cynical."

"Why not? It becomes me." He stopped and, in a softer tone said, "I'm sorry – about everything. Good luck and congratulations."

He had seen Mark meandering through the guests with two drinks and preferred to be gone before he came to stake out his claim. Mark Hughes, looking great in a classic tuxedo, was Helen's new escort.

Dinner was called twenty minutes after it was scheduled to begin and then it took ten minutes of utter chaos for everyone to find their tables. The salad had been sitting for an hour and was limper than the handshake Mac had received from the man sitting to his left.

"Name's Horace Wright." Then he said with a gesture to a woman on his other side, "My wife, Lydia." Then, looking around his wife, "Yes, great year for tomatoes," Horace commented, resuming his conversation with another guest at the table who was listening carefully while attacking the salad as though it were the last bite of food on earth. "Lettuce not so good this year. Too hot, needs lots of watering. Squash bit small, potatoes aplenty." He spoke in sound bites.

As the woman to his right finished her last crouton, she noticed Mac who had not had a chance to introduce himself.

"You're Mac Donald. I remember you spoke last year," she said.

"It's McDougal, Matthew McDougal, and I spoke two years ago. But thanks for remembering," he responded in his book-signing tone.

"Don't remember the speech – it was so noisy back here," she admitted, "but I never forget a good looking man."

She turned bright red and, in a quick movement, picked up her husband's hand. "I'm Mary, and this is my husband Bob Merchant; he's an editor."

When Bob turned to acknowledge Mac, his watery eyes were covered by thick glasses, and it was apparent that he would only recognize Mac if he were to read a piece of his prose.

Mac noticed that their table would be one of the last served, judging by the pattern established by the wait staff and the fact that they were sitting in the back. Mac grabbed the arm of a waiter and asked if he might have a vegetarian plate. It was an inspired move as he was eventually served a huge platter of fresh fruit and vegetables with two sauces. The rest of the table looked envious while they were served the sliced turkey with gravy which did not move. The logistics of serving over four hundred people simultaneously is always problematic. It was typically solved, in part, with the bottles of wine on the table.

"Horace, what do you write, gardening tips?" Mac inquired.

"Oh, no, obituaries."

"Obituaries?"

"Oh yes, the most important pages in a newspaper," Horace continued to skeptical looks. "Everyone looks there for their name before going to work." He got the laugh he had intended.

"Seriously, it's a good revenue generator. The casket makers and undertakers take big ads and, contrary to the popular misconception, theirs is not a dying business." He laughed again. The wine seemed to be affecting the whole table except for Mac and Bob Merchant who, Mac decided, was still looking, in vain, for a punctuation error on his plate. Mac excused himself and headed for the bar area to get a cup of coffee.

There was a reward. Standing alone, or rather barely standing with a large scotch, was one of the eight names Mac had written down earlier. A one-on-one interview. Mac would have to rely on his memory and be very careful in quoting anything. He could always call for confirmation later.

"Good evening, sir; a good night for single malt."

"Aye, it is. You are a reporter are you not?"

"Well, this is the annual media awards, so people here are reporters, editors, owners of publications, politicians looking to put in a good word or keep out a bad, or a guest of the above. Which are you?"

There was a silence as they looked at each other. Wariness gave way to peals of laughter.

"John Richards. J.R. to my friends. I think I like you."

"Well, J.R., do you like me enough to discuss your current denial of running for the White House or your current odds of succeeding being one hundred-to-one?"

"Those are the same odds my father quoted when I ran for governor. I borrowed one hundred dollars from my mother. When he paid me the ten thousand, my mother took it from me, saying how would it look, the governor gambling?"

"Sir, your mother was a wise woman. How would it look if a candidate for President of the United States were to appear to have drunk too much?"

J.R. blinked then became aware of the sound from the large room.

"Quite right! George, could you please get me a cup of coffee?"

"George, please get the Congressman's coat and a cab," Mac said.

"Young man, thank you. Here is my card. Call any time."

"Thank you, J.R. Here is my card, in case you don't remember our conversation when I call you tomorrow."

Mac heard a loud guffaw as George steered the governor into a top coat.

A fortuitous and, hopefully, productive meeting. Mac realized that it was time to return to the main room as the awards speeches were starting. He passed a photographer who he recognized heading to the bar.

"Congressman Richards in there?"

"No, he left," Mac replied to a disappointed man.

The President of the Media Association was introduced to rapturous applause. A tall, white-haired man rose from a nearby table and took his time looking around. As the applause started to weaken, he hurried to the podium to raise both hands in mock surprise and acknowledgement.

"Ladies and gentlemen, it gives me great pleasure to welcome you here this evening. This is a special night. It is also a night for reflection, on the future of our industry and our place in the gathering and distribution of information. It is a night of reflections on those members and friends who served so well and have passed on."

Mac had returned to his seat so that Helen, if she needed to look at him, could find him.

Horace nudged him. "Son of a bitch would only allow two inches for the obituary of Paddy Smith, nominated twice for Pulitzer."

"Yes, but he worked for the rival paper," whispered Mac.

The speaker droned on in a predictable manner and Mac was watching the crowd become increasingly restless and he figured that Helen was getting increasingly more nervous.

"....and so to the recipient of this year's award for journalistic excellence. I am sure that all of you turn to the articles prepared by this talented reporter first every morning."

"After the obituaries," Horace intoned sotto voce.

"Her fast moving writing and eloquence of the First Lady's involvement in life at the White House and on the road were enthralling. Please welcome Helen Harvey."

With loud applause, Helen, waiting in the wings, moved forward to accept a commemorative plaque.

"Mr. President, ladies and gentlemen, I want to thank you for this award.

"It is not deserved. I am a fraud. I am not a reporter, but a story teller. A good friend told me that, and it is true. However, I accept this award with humility and remind you all that there is room for a good story in a newspaper, that we sell our wares on the basis of entertainment. A reporter writes the front page; we have reporting on the sports page and reporting fills the gossip pages. A storyteller, however, has a place in the paper and can entertain.

"I would also like to take this opportunity to tell all of my friends simultaneously that today I resigned from the Times and will be taking up a fresh exciting challenge in the New Year. Thank you again for this award, and goodnight."

There was enthusiastic applause as Helen left the stage.

Mac walked over toward where Mark was standing to congratulate her. When she reached them, Mark asked, "When were you going to tell us?"

"I just did."

"I mean, what are you going to do? Are you leaving Washington?" he pursued.

"I can't tell you and, no, I'm staying here."

"You can't or won't say?"

Helen shrugged.

"Then why make the announcement?" Mark pushed.

"Because it will be in Ann Gold's gossip column tomorrow and everyone would then say, I saw her last night and she didn't say anything."

"Congratulations," Mac interrupted and shook her hand.

"Did you know? Do you know where she's going?" Mark asked peevishly.

"No, but I could make a very good guess."

Mark wandered over to the next table, both to get away from Mac and to talk to a friendlier audience.

"Congratulations!" Ann Gold said, propelling her considerable girth between Helen and Mac. "Well, well, well. Very productive evening, including three stories right here. 'Resignation of star reporter and speculation of next position,' 'Sir Galahad saves a certain Congressman from the front page of the tabloids,' and perhaps my favorite couple getting back together."

"Do you need facts? Are you surfing for information or confirmation?" Mac asked smiling, listening, watching.

Ann was a wealth of information, and what she didn't know; she easily created with others' notions. She smiled and replied, "Facts get in the way of a good gossip column."

"Well, you will see that the lady is not talking, a certain congressman has gone home, and Mark Hughes is escorting one of your favorite people."

Ann laughed and her body shook. "Mac, Mac, idealist; the story is in the speculation of where Helen is going, why the congressman left early, and one fact I know is that Helen wasn't looking at Mark during her speech."

"Ann!" Someone was dragging her arm. "The police just made an arrest in Central Park, you will never guess who….."

They moved away. There was no lack of stories for the gossip column

Helen, slightly flushed, was looking at him as he turned. "Mac, would you give me a ride home?"

"But…."

"Mark is being a bore because I won't discuss leaving the paper."

"Okay, but…."

"It's just a ride, Mac," she assured him. As they walked to retrieve her coat she added, "But I'd like to call you tomorrow."

"Anything you say," he said, feeling better than he had for months.

Chapter Three

The next morning Mac was at his computer early, congratulating himself on the previous night's successes. He had not had much alcohol, he had eaten the vegetarian meal, and then there was the bonus of escorting Helen home. *Oh,* he reminded himself, *and I managed to not stick my foot in my mouth.*

He had, by nine o'clock, already finished and sent out his article to Sue to review before sending it on to the Times. Updating his notes and cross-referencing, he was expanding the files on each of his expected candidates. The basic information was generally available: the date of birth, place, parents, schools, studies, and work before politics. There was also abundantly available material on political master strokes, embellished by professionals. Everywhere he looked he could find positive material. Mac was looking for other stuff, in the cracks of each resume.

Standing and stretching, he went into his kitchenette and brewed another cup of coffee, letting the aroma and sound sooth him even before he filled his mug. The individual coffee maker machine had been a gift from Helen who tired of pouring out full carafes of spoiled coffee or replacing the glass dispensers whose bottom had burned out. Today Mac had selected a breakfast blend, strong enough, but not too bold. He savored the first sip, wondering why Senator Carmel

Fernandez had voted against immigration into her New Mexico constituency seven times and then introduced legislation to support immigrants' rights. This would be a good question to ask and then also maybe read the proposed law; check out who really, really benefitted.

The phone rang. He answered, as always, with, "Mac."

"Good morning, Mac; it's Helen. Not too early for you is it?"

"No, I'm just enjoying my second cup of coffee."

"Can I see you today?"

"So soon? Well, you know where I live."

"I was thinking of our favorite Starbucks."

"They're all my favorites. But I know which you mean. Eleven all right?"

"Thanks, Mac. See you then."

The coffee shop was not busy. The morning rush and those with mid-morning cravings were gone, all back at their desks. The lunch crowd was not yet glancing at the clock in anticipation. Helen wore black slacks tucked into boots, a light blue polo sweater, and a grey fleece vest. The clothing emphasized the long limbs and the casual warmth of a sophisticated young woman. Mac stared in amazement, wondering how she always dressed perfectly right for every occasion.

"Hi, Mac. Thanks for coming. I know you're busy. And thanks again for seeing me home last night."

"My pleasure, and you didn't have to buy me coffee for that."

She laughed. "A reminder that I have to pay? Dark roast, milk, one sugar?"

"Yes, please."

She turned and ordered the drinks. He watched and considered that he could easily justify an hour for coffee.

After settling in at a small table by the window, she looked over her cup at Mac.

"Mark called this morning to ask how I'd gotten home. I told him that it was none of his business, so then he again asked where I was going to work. I told him that when I want everyone to know I'll tell him." She mischievously added, "He didn't get it!"

"The job as public relations for Marjorie White's run for the White House is a good job for you; high profile," said Mac.

"How'd you know? Never mind, you know everything. The job is actually media relations, which means the same thing."

"It was easy. If your new position was in the media, then someone in the room last night would have talked to Mark. If it was outside Washington, then a reference would've been asked and someone would have leaked. Therefore it was the President or someone close. Since the President is within two years of retirement, it was someone close. And probably a woman, say a vice president looking to move up a rung on the ladder."

"Very clever, Mac. That's why you're the investigative reporter and I'm merely a story teller."

"Look, Helen, about that," he spluttered, "I'm sorry. I think there's a need for storytellers."

Helen was smiling at his discomfort. "And it sells newspapers, right?"

"Right. Okay. I'm sorry I was a fool, an arrogant fool. I'm sorry!"

"You said that three times. I get it."

"Well then….."

She interrupted, anticipating his words but reluctant to start that conversation. She said, "Maybe; but I'm going to visit my mother and sister for a couple of weeks over Christmas and New Year's."

"In Naples, Florida?" he asked rhetorically. "But they won't have snow and carolers wrapped in warm hats and mufflers."

"No, and no runny noses."

"Well, have a wonderful time. Thanks again for the coffee."

"You're welcome for the coffee, but I wanted to ask you something else."

"The answer is yes," he said.

Laughing, she replied, "That was not the question." Then, with a more serious tone, she added, "You cover the political scene as well as anyone in D.C. The congressional elections we just witnessed, did you see anything of the ordinary?"

"Not really. Usual stuff, some changes, the House stayed the same, Democratic control. There were fewer incumbents returned, but that was due to some whiplash against the President, the war, the unemployment, or the objection du jour."

"But, Mac, you just said two things that aren't consistent: the majority didn't change and there were fewer incumbents returned."

"So what are you saying?"

"I don't know. It may be nothing, but I sat watching the results with a strange feeling that it made no sense."

"Be careful, you may turn into an investigative reporter."

"God forbid," she said.

"I'll take a look. Do they have cell phone service in Florida?"

"Yes. Please call, if only to say Merry Christmas."

Congress was trying to close and leave for a couple of weeks. The newly elected members were moving furniture into the city. Some pork-filled bills were being rapidly pushed through the steps necessary to further line pockets already lined. It was Washington going about its business.

Mac was thinking again about Helen. He hoped that he would have the chance to spend more time with her when she returned. Then he thought about their last conversation. Looking at the results again, there was nothing to see. The races had been won along voter registered lines that had been configured after the last census. Being a thorough investigator though, and also having nothing more pressing to do, he investigated.

In the first few calls he made, most of the former congressmen hung up on him. The fifth might have hung up if he had not been so intoxicated, mid-afternoon.

"Yes, this is former Congressman Charles George, and I recognize your name Macdonald."

"It's McDougal."

"Right! The reporter!"

"Mr. George, can you tell me why after ten years in Congress you decided not to seek re-election after saying that you would be running?"

"It's in the press release," he slurred badly. "Personal."

"I read the release and also the comment that there was some scandal; that it involved kickbacks."

"Garbage!"

"Excuse me? Are you suggesting that there was a different reason?"

"They can't hurt me now. Wife left, children won't talk to me, chucked out of the country club, bank foreclosing. They can't hurt me now; they can't kill me. I am already dying."

"Who are *they*?"

"The ones who planted stories in the newspapers, whispered to my wife in the supermarket, planted drugs on my kids, had the IRS investigate an off-shore account I've never seen before. Them!"

"Mr. George, who are they?"

The former congressman was in tears as he whispered into the phone before he hung up. "I …..don't know!"

Chapter Four

There was something there; but where? Helen was right. How did he and all the other reporters miss it? Or had they?

Mac downloaded the newspaper articles relating to the elections to see if there were any comments regarding strange happenings. It was a monumental task – so many were written as sound bites by reporters tired out from the noise and sanctimonious, self-serving statements. The Union Leader in New Hampshire was refreshing, calling a spade a spade; it asked "how in tarnation a God-loving, deer killing, patriot could be defeated by a baby kissing lawyer."

For another perspective Mac looked at the letters to the editor for the following week, noted the writers' names, and decided that this was a good place to begin his quest for the truth.

Starting with the candidate who had won, Mac asked if he had a comment regarding some of the letters he quoted. The winner stated that he was as surprised as they were with his election since his honorable opponent had served the State of New Hampshire well while in Washington.

A call to the defeated candidate revealed that he was also surprised and was disappointed by the low turnout of his Republican constituents. His campaign had suffered from a couple of mishaps when his super-reliable organizer had apparently booked two events at the same time, in different venues. The customary refreshments had failed to arrive several times. Health issues had been raised at every meeting in spite of his doctor having pronounced him fit as a moose. The missed meetings led to rumors of his being in the hospital. Mac called some letter writers.

"Big Ron, fit as a lumberjack. Saw him last week. Never misses a game at the high school when he is in town."

Another call Mac made resulted in the comment, "This whippersnapper wants to surrender to Commies. Why does he think we fought in Japan, Korea, Vietnam, and Iraq? New Hampshire has been first in a fight since the Revolutionary War. Anderson led the battle every time, and I would have followed any cause he deemed worthy."

"Ron Anderson is the finest American you are likely to meet," a third phone call revealed.

It was unanimous; then why, Mac had asked, had they not voted him in. Each had stated that they did not bother voting when the radio, on election day, had announced that Ron Anderson was in the hospital with serious complications; all had said that they would not vote for anyone else.

Mac called the radio station. Of course they had checked with the hospital and, yes, Ron Anderson had been admitted and, no, HPPA regulations prevented them from giving any more information. The next day it was revealed that a Ron Anderson from Massachusetts had been admitted with a suspected heart attack and released.

Mac had a story, or at least he had the start of one. He needed to talk to Helen. He called Gerry.

"Gerry Clark."

"It's Mac. Hey, Gerry, anyone writing a story on voter fraud and intimidation in the Congressional votes?"

"Usual claims! Disappointed candidates; nothing held up. Not you too?"

"Maybe, when I get more answers. Are you interested or should I go up town?"

"Let me see it first, pay by the word, usual if it makes front page or there's a follow up. We'll put a reporter on it and use your by-line. Okay?"

"I'll call to let you know, Gerry! Thanks!"

Mac sat back in his chair with his hands behind his head. His office was tidy except for a pile of research that sat on the other club chair and the three smaller piles on the floor under the window. The television was off and the computer showed a screensaver picture of him and Helen in front of the Washington Monument. He was thinking and checking mental boxes. Congress, including the new members, would be back in session next week. Swearing in would take place. Now he had to figure out the extent of the damage: how bad it was, if it was part of a plot, if one person or a group was behind it, how that was possible, and why.

He had to write it down, and then he could think and move his thoughts around. Switching off his cell phone, he switched on his computer. He typed in the heading 'why.' Under he wrote: power or money. Looking at the screen he was seized with paranoia. Slowly he backspaced and erased. Picking up a pencil, he found a pad of paper and wrote:

Why:

Power

Money [how much invested?]

[return expected?]

Who:
  Person or group?
How:
  Using media, intimidation, bribery?
Where: State level
  N.H {R} Ron Anderson
  Del. {D} Charles George
Party:
  Democrat
  Republican
  Other

As he wrote down the check list, he realized what he knew was a good start; but the missing information was like the bottom of the iceberg.

The telephone was ringing. Automatically he looked to see who might be calling. It was Helen; he snatched the receiver in case she might hang up. It was silly really because he had the number to call her back.

"Mac," he answered, trying to sound calm and cool.

"Merry Christmas!"

"Is it Christmas?"

"Well, it will be tomorrow, and I know that there will be either chaos or confusion here. The kids are already out of control."

"There will be utter chaos here too as the turkey tries to make another a run for it."

"I thought that you had a small frozen bird."

"It has fallen out of the freezer twice and nearly broken my toe."

"Who are you feeding?" Then quickly, "I'm sorry. I shouldn't have asked; it's none of my business." Helen was genuinely flustered.

"Since you're not around, I invited two women," he teased. "And though it may not officially be your business, I'll be entertaining Sue Raymond and Carol."

"Oh," Helen said with a sigh of relief.

"How's everyone down there?"

"My sister's great; I don't know how she does it. Runs the house, operates a business from home, and manages to keep Fred and the boys in check. Fred is on the road a lot so she's really busy, and yet she still finds time to take me around shopping. And I'm enjoying the beach. Julie has a permit so I can park at Clam Shell Pass free and then walk all the way from there down to the pier and back; must be five miles. How are you?"

"Busy. I've been following up on the congressional election anomaly that you spotted. I spoke with two of the defeated congressmen: Anderson and George," Mac told her.

"Probably nothing," she said.

"Actually it is something; I just don't know what."

"Maybe I can help when I get back."

"I hope that I have it cracked in the next ten days, besides which, you have a job remember?"

"Come down here, Mac. Bring your computer and cell phone; you know that nothing happens in Washington until Congress returns."

"Are you suggesting that……?"

"Maybe. I miss you, Mac. Besides, I really enjoy watching the way you think."

"And I thought that it was my abs that you were admiring."

"Well, are you coming down or what?"

"No, I wish I could, but I sent word I'd visit my mother."

"Oh, okay. I understand." He sensed a sadness in her response, but was it from a need to be with him, a need for intellectual conversation, or loneliness?

After he hung up the phone he sat looking at the receiver. He was lonely too, but their relationship break had taken a toll, his confidence had not yet returned.

He spent the rest of the day preparing and cooking, his thoughts never far from Naples, Florida. The stuffing was prepared, and he was making an apple pie and blueberry crumble. He stuffed the bird, now thawed, and put it back into the refrigerator, then checked again that he had wine, rum for the sauce, and brandy for after dinner. The turkey would be put into the oven as soon as he woke tomorrow.

Sue and Carol arrived on time. Mac met them at the door wearing grey slacks, a white Oxford button-down shirt, and an outrageous tie featuring the Grinch.

"Merry Christmas, Mac. You're the least likely Grinch I know." Carol was resplendent in frills, a stark contrast to Sue's more conservative attire.

"Wait until I've served the gruel, and then decide."

"I can smell the turkey, Mr. Grinch," laughed Sue. "We've brought caviar and champagne though, just in case."

The afternoon passed compatibly as they appreciated Mac's hospitality and gifts. Over coffee and brandy, after discussing the missing Helen, Sue asked how the new book was progressing and if he was working on any other story.

"There may be a story on the Congressional election, but I'm not sure what it is. I've spoken to a couple of former congressmen who lost in bizarre ways, Congressman George from Delaware and Anderson from New Hampshire."

"I know Charles George," volunteered Carol. "A good man, or he was until all the stories came out about him and his family."

"But what if the stories weren't true?" asked Mac.

"They must be. Newspapers, editors, and television producers verify everything these days. The threat of lawsuits is too great for them not to."

Mac told them of his conversations with the two men, his follow up with the media. It was all vague, shadowy, innuendo, easily explained. It was too much of a coincidence.

The next day Mac drove along the Hudson Valley to Upper New York State. The weather was terrible and getting worse as he headed north. Lake effect, the weathermen were saying on the radio, to cover up the fact that they had been wrong again. He would have to stay overnight.

The nursing home had a cheerful lobby. Christmas lights were strung around a fake tree and lighted ornaments hung on the desk inside the door. Some of the staff wore Santa hats and one young woman had a flashing red and green headband. Nothing, however, could mask the smell of old age. Nothing could hide from the outside world the feeling that this was a place where people went to die. The nurses were unbearably cheerful, the visitors duty bound to repeat the same words to the residents week after week: "You're looking better today," said in a tone of mock cheer.

Mac found, after checking at the reception desk, that his mother had been moved. She was on the second floor, right where the elevator opened onto a nurses' station with the obligatory twinkling lights. His mother mistook Mac for his brother and asked about her grandchildren. Mac sat with her for a couple of hours and left. He loved his mother, but this was not his mother. He loved Helen. There was an admission. Had he ever told her that? Probably not.

Mac checked into a hotel and called Helen. "I love you," he said quietly when she picked up the receiver.

"Have you been drinking?"

"No, I visited my mother and a lot of things became clear."

"Like, you love me?"

"Yes."

"Well, I suppose it's never too late for a person to reveal their inner feelings, even if in the presence of their vulnerability."

"You mean like an agnostic praying to God on his deathbed, just in case?"

"Exactly."

"Or a hunter becoming a vegan because he's been shot in the woods? Or maybe a mother having an abortion because she's had an affair and doesn't know whose kid it is?"

Mac was feeling angry and he was not sure why.

"Mac, I'm sorry. Give my love to your mother and I'll see you when I get back from Florida."

"Right. Goodnight." He hung up. Mac looked at the phone, looked around the room, looked at his hands which were still shaking, and he started to cry. He had never felt so lonely in his life.

Finally moving, he went down to the restaurant, then he ordered a beer at the bar while he scanned the menu. There was nothing he wanted and, no longer hungry anyway, he went back to his room and took out his laptop to do some work.

Driving south early the next afternoon gave Mac a few hours to think. This morning his mother had recognized him and said that Roger had been to see her. Mac did not disillusion her but talked of the old times, good times that they had all enjoyed together. The doctor came by and said that there was some congestion; otherwise she was comfortable. Mac, at a loss for questions, thanked him.

Pushing away thoughts of Helen, which were intruding every few miles, he thought again through his gathered facts and the next campaign. Were there parallels? Who was gaining? What was the game plan? Where was he going next? The cell phone rang. Glancing down he saw that it was Helen and turned back to his driving. There was the sound of a message being left. Five minutes later the phone rang again: Helen. A gas station ahead in five miles; it would wait for five minutes.

As he pulled in the phone rang.

"Good morning, Helen. Call to tell me that the weather is fine and our relationship stormy?"

"No, that Charles George committed suicide."

"What? No. How'd you hear?"

"It was on the news this morning. The innuendoes from his campaign were all repeated, also that his wife had left and his family was now estranged. A former aide is on camera saying that George wasn't suicidal but was angry. The aide is denying any wrong doing and is promising to clear George's name."

"Good for him!"

"Her!"

"I should be home in an hour. Let's talk again after I think about it and check my notes." Mac wanted to say more, but he did not trust himself in the moment.

Mac filled the gas tank and set off with a new set of thoughts. As he reached Washington his cell phone rang and showed that Sue was calling. He waited until he had found a parking space and returned her call.

"Mac, where are you, where have you been?"

"To see my mother; we talked about it."

"Oh, yes. Well the police are looking to talk to you about Charles George; they found your phone number in his home on his desk."

"If it was suicide, why do they want to talk to me?"

"What if it wasn't?"

"Then they would want to know where I was."

"Mac, be careful. If the police know that you were communicating with George, and if it wasn't suicide, then anyone else who'd been in his house would know too," Sue warned.

After ending the call, Mac sat and looked around without getting out of the car. He reached for his computer and, finding the notes he had written, copied them to a flash drive, then he erased the notes. The flash drive he used was a gift from Sue and Carol which doubled as a multi-tool, similar to a Swiss Army Knife. He dropped it into the door-well of his car, closed down the computer and, with his computer bag and overnight bag, walked up the street to his apartment. Walking casually, he noted that one of the parked cars, a black Lincoln, was occupied by two men and they were interested in his progress.

When he walked through the door, Mac immediately knew that someone had searched his apartment. Little items were slightly askew – the chairs, the magazines on the coffee table, even his sugar caddy. He was neat everywhere except on his desk. When he sat at his desk, however, he knew where everything was. Sitting now he saw that his calendar had been read, that his recent contacts memo had been moved; looking at his archive of files that sat on the floor and flash drives in his right desk drawer, he realized that they were all in the same order but one; he had not looked at it for months, but it was slightly higher than the rest. Someone had searched, and that someone, he concluded, was not the police. He turned his chair, thankful for the swivel action, and looked out the window. He noticed a white utility van parked directly across the street. It advertised a painting company, but the roof held no ladders and had no rack to put the normal equipment on. It meant nothing, but he was getting paranoid.

Mac made a sandwich from leftovers and brewed a cup of coffee. While eating he called Martin Konrad.

"Technical Solutions."

"Martin, this is Mac. I think I have a virus; can you check it?"

"Virus? Go see a doctor."

"Why is everybody in this town a comedian?"

"Boot up and I'll take a look."

"No, I need you to come here and do it. I think it may invade on my password."

"Wow! That would be new; be right over."

The downstairs buzzer rang and the two men from the car were standing in the entryway.

"Yes?" Mac asked, playing dumb and examining the men's suits – well made, high-end he determined and not bought on a cop's salary.

"We would like to ask you a couple of questions." It was a tall, muscular black man looking back at the camera.

"What about?"

"Can we come in?" There was no courtesy, no please.

"Can I see identification please?" Mac emphasized the politeness.

After two badges were quickly flashed in front of the camera, Mac pressed the door release, then once they were through the door said to their retreating backs, "I'm sure you know the way."

The men were even bigger in his apartment than they had looked in the view of his lobby.

"We're investigating the death of Congressman George."

There was no preamble. This was to be a quick in and out. Clearly they had been the ones in his apartment before he got back and had found nothing or at least not whatever it was they were looking for.

"You think that I can help? I never met him."

"But you spoke with him, just before he died."

The first man had entered the living room and headed towards the bedroom, his companion headed toward the laptop computer.

"I did."

"Why?"

"Why what?"

Mac needed to stall. These men were on a mission, and they were not police or federal agents. Keeping them off guard, distracting them, could lead to more information, although it was doubtful.

"Why did you talk to him?"

"Oh, I'm a political writer."

"What did you talk about?"

"Politics!"

Mac could see the man's carotid artery was throbbing, a sure sign that he was losing his patience. The other man could almost touch the laptop. Mac moved towards the desk.

"Don't touch my computer. All my notes from my interviews are on there."

"So what does it say about George?"

"Nothing; he was so drunk that he made no sense."

"Well, maybe if we looked at your notes we could see exactly what he talked about."

"Do you have a warrant?"

Mac was aware that he was getting close to a point where the men might use force to take his computer and leave him hurt or worse. He was saved by the bell – literally. He dashed over and pressed the entry button for Martin Konrad. The two uninvited guests were taken aback. Mac immediately opened the door, allowing anyone in the hall to see the scene playing out in his apartment. When Martin arrived, Mac placed himself between the men and Martin; his facial expression said, *Follow my lead.*

"Martin, these two men are Curley and Moe from, I'm sorry, what agency are you with again?"

The two men took half a step forward. As big as they were, Martin Konrad was bigger at six-foot, seven, and at two hundred and thirty pounds he looked formidable.

"They're looking for some information about the congressman who died."

"Committed suicide: saw it on the news," said Martin.

"I was going to show them that, in spite of having no warrant, he had nothing to say."

Mac moved to his computer and brought up *Notes* on the date that showed for his phone call. There was a heading *Charles George*, then nothing.

"We're going to have to take the computer," the second man said, speaking for the first time.

"Not without a warrant!"

"We'll be back!" the spokesperson said as they headed for the door.

"What was that about?" asked Martin as soon as they saw the two men leave the building.

Mac held a finger to his lips and pointed upwards.

"Just a couple of policemen who watch too many crime shows on TV."

Mac was writing on a piece of paper: *Wired. I think they will steal my laptop. Can you transfer to somewhere safe?'*

"Want a beer? Watch the game?"

"Yes, I can do that!" said Martin, who hated beer and only watched golf and swimming.

Mac put a college basketball game on loud and made sure that he was seen going into his kitchen area from the white van which had not moved. Martin walked around the room with his equipment, staying out of sight. He then spent thirty minutes with the computer, sending the files to a secure off-site location.

"I can't believe he's a freshman," he yelled. "Is this the best beer you have?" Martin was pointing to the door.

"Wow, free beer and you're complaining. I had enough of that this weekend with my mother. Okay, let's go to the corner, get a pizza and some draft."

"Now you're talking."

When they were outside, Mac started to speak but Martin grabbed his arm.

"And to think, he's only a freshman. What did he have, twenty points in the first half?"

Mac got the idea and they argued about sports for the rest of the way and into the back room of the local bar.

Safely seated with a view of the door, their backs to a wall decorated with a picture of a pizza, a draft beer, and a very large red wine, Martin spoke clearly.

"What did you do?

"The phone is tapped, very up-to-date equipment, only the government has it. No mics, they have very, very powerful directional listening devices. They can hear through walls, cut out extraneous noise, taps running, etc.; could have heard us on the street. If they want the computer, your stuff is saved and I can tell if they send it somewhere else."

"I didn't do anything. They are not police. When they talked about George, they didn't say suicide; it was as if they had been there. Also they had no warrant, they kept gloves on in the apartment, and I think that if you had been five minutes longer, I would be in a pool of blood."

"Bit melodramatic, Mac, even for you."

"Yes, well the guy by the door is drinking with gloves on. When did you last see that?"

For the next half hour they watched the game, aware of being watched.

"I need to sleep," said Mac.

"Need a bed?"

"No, thanks. Then they would know that I know."

Mac's apartment had been entered and his computer discs had been downloaded in a hurry. The black car was gone, but the van remained. He went to bed.

Chapter Five

The next morning he carried out his usual routine, aware of the scrutiny. The van was still there, as were the listening devices. His computer was hacked, so he checked the news which seemed to be spending a good deal of time on the story of a popular congressman committing suicide. There was an interview with a former aide. Mac watched carefully and made a mental note of her name and where she was speaking from. The rest of the news featured unrest in the Middle East, a political scandal in England, and the elections in France. Sitting back, he was aware, as if it were playing across a large screen endlessly, that the major stories were all political. There were no mass murders, no hurricanes bringing destruction, no celebrity scandals, and nothing more worthy than the political turmoil.

The telephone rang. It was Helen. He knew that he could not talk to her, but he needed to answer.

"Mac," he answered.

"It's Helen, about….."

"Listen: I'm in the middle of something; can this wait? How about we meet at our favorite place minus one for coffee?"

This was a sort of code that had been devised as a joke when they were dating. They had agreed to meet at their favorite place and had gone to different restaurants. Helen had insisted that they had a new favorite and that where Mac had gone was the one before. Mac then said that he was at *favorite minus one*. This story they had then extended to all things, and their minus one code meant to take one from every aspect of the conversation.

"On Friday?" she asked. He knew that she meant Thursday as she would be home Wednesday night.

"At ten o'clock," said Mac. "Please have a safe flight; the birds are everywhere."

They severed the connection without further banter.

Mac knew that Helen would replay the conversation in her head, and he knew her well enough to know that she would likely head for the beach where walking and thinking would provide exercise and an uninterrupted study of her present situation. She would wonder why he had not talked to her. He had spoken to her, but he had not conversed. Also he had warned her; he hoped that she understood what he meant.

When he arrived on Thursday at nine o'clock, he found that Helen was seated at the back of Paula's Coffee Shop with a latte and two pieces of biscotti. Even though they had used code, Mac was careful in leaving his apartment, traveling through the corner store and out the back, cutting through empty alleys to cross-streets. He was glad that Helen had heeded his warning; she had positioned herself so that she could see the front door through the mirror.

Mac had been nervous about whether or not both of them would arrive safely. When he saw Helen back in the corner he visibly relaxed, asked the passing waitress to bring him a cup of coffee, and joined Helen.

"So what brings a pretty girl like you out on a dark and stormy night?"

"Mac, it is nine in the morning without a cloud in the sky."

"Precisely!"

"What is going on? Why the secrecy? Codes and stuff – I feel like Nancy Drew."

"But with better legs."

After a reassuring smile Mac described the events of the week: the fact that he was followed, his computer data had been stolen, and his conversations had been recorded.

"You think this has to do with George's death?" she asked when he was through.

"No question about it. They asked about my speaking with him, wanted my notes."

"But why?"

"Well, some people," Mac suggested, "think that there is something strange about it, including me."

"Why kill him? He was drinking himself silly."

"Maybe because when he drank, he talked, and when he talked, he might say something."

"And why does this involve me?" asked Helen.

"Because you and I talked and mentioned some anomalies in the latest congressional election. Which reminds me, how do we know there weren't anomalies, for lack of a better word, in previous elections, or in the governors' races or mayoral?"

"Mac, are you nuts?"

"Is that your answer, your final answer, or would you like to call someone?" Mac did a reasonable interpretation of a favorite television personality.

"Mac, you're scaring me."

"I want you to be safe. You need to have Martin Konrad sweep your apartment, debug your computer, and rekey your locks. Then if you could ask a friend, face to face, if I am being investigated by Delaware or FBI, it will be a start. I'm hoping that since they have found nothing that they will go away."

"I hope so. When I was walking on the beach the other day, after our cryptic call, I swear I was being followed. I'll see what I can find out. I know someone at FBI, actually it's the assistant director; I can ask. How can I let you know?"

"Thanks. I think I'll start having breakfast here Tuesdays and Thursday 8-9."

"Does that mean that this is now our favorite place?"

"No, that is too complicated for us amateurs. I'll think up something more creative by Tuesday."

"Good to see you, Mac. Watch your back."

"Great to see you! I've missed you. When do you announce your new job?"

"Oh, thanks for reminding me. I have an interview tonight for CNN, and I need to leak it to some people before then."

"In order to keep your contacts good?"

"Something like that."

She picked up her pocketbook, kissed his cheek, and left.

The weekend was surreal. Although Mac had become accustomed to living alone, having rekindled the relationship with Helen, he felt that there was something missing. It was like having a tooth out and then the tongue constantly examining the place where it had been.

Absorbed into his work, he completed the next three weeks writing assignments ahead of schedule and brought his book up to date. He declined interviews and commentary after Helen had formally announced her new position.

The television interviewer had been kind to Helen, knowing that there was a potential gold mine ahead for people with access. To be called by name and given first chance to ask questions at a White House or other Washington political press conference was to have the keys to the city and get the attention from the most sought after program managers.

Having recorded the interview, Mac watched it for the third time. He marveled at how well Helen looked on camera, how smart she was, and how adroitly she avoided the obvious question of Marjorie White's ambition to go from Vice President to President of the United States. Helen dragged the interviewer back to her personal reasons for taking the position: to expand her expertise using the knowledge she would gain and Washington media contacts.

"Like Mark Hughes?" the interviewer asked.

"Mark is a dear friend," Helen replied.

"What does he think of your change in career?"

"Ask him," was the response.

"And what other changes in career would you consider?"

"I might host a political talk show on television," Helen replied with a smile.

"On that note, and before my own job is in jeopardy, I want to thank our guest Helen Harvey for being with us and congratulate her on her new position as media relations director for our Vice President, Marjorie White."

Tuesday, Helen sat opposite Mac at Paula's Café.

He was eating homemade raisin bread, toasted with a liberal coating of butter. Helen had ordered an English muffin with a single poached egg, no hollandaise, just coffee. They worked out a code to meet in future. A phrase or word out of context with a P meant Paula's, S meant Starbucks, M was the Monterey Grill. The times were preset: Paula's at eight, Starbucks at noon, and Monterey at seven in the evening.

"It may be moot; as of yesterday morning my surveillance is gone," said Mac. "They were probably bored out of their minds at my miserable life and only stayed as long as they did out of sympathy."

"The assistant director of the FBI cannot find anyone who might have ordered the security. They have closed the book on George and he was surprised at the connection."

Mac frowned.

"What's wrong? I shouldn't have mentioned George?"

"It's done," he replied. "How's your new job?"

"Well, I found the ladies' room."

"Always a good thing!"

"So far I have been meeting the rest of the entourage: chauffeurs, bodyguards, secretaries, beauticians, and also having them meet me. The big test will be her speech at the fundraiser for the police and firemen at the end of January. You will be there, won't you?"

"Wouldn't miss it! Sue wanted me to introduce the speaker, but I declined when I learned who it was."

"It will be media frenzy."

"Will there be a leak of the speech?"

"No! I'll write it with Marjorie, then keep it wrapped. There should be enough speculation without a leak."

Chapter Six

Even though the surveillance appeared to have gone, the fact that it had been there at all gnawed at Mac. He was thinking about Congressman George and lining up interviews with the candidates from his list. Most of the interviews were scheduled with the aides of the potential candidates. It suddenly occurred to him that one of the people defending George had been his aide. Now what was her name and where was she being interviewed? With his near photographic memory and the intuition that he should not appear to show any interest, he had not written it down. Pauline, Pauline, thin girl like a stick, no, like a pole.

Pauline Poles, that was the name; those word association exercises had worked, this time. Not like the time he had introduced a pathologist, Dr. Stark, as Dr. Naked. Pauline Poles, Dover, Delaware, seventy-five miles as the crow flies. The choice was a commuter plane or a three hour drive. He decided on the drive; it was the paranoia. Normally he would have gone for the quick flight in and out or the adventure of a ferry, but these terminals now had security, cameras, and face recognition capabilities. He stood up from his desk and walked to the window; no one was there.Or was some professional watching? Laughing at himself, he almost changed his mind to flying, just to prove that no one out there cared a hoot about Mac

McDougal and his whereabouts. But what about Pauline Poles? Maybe someone cared who she was meeting?

Mac did not mind driving and, though it might be a long day, he decided to leave early in the morning and try to be back the same day. Being a disciple of Murphy's Law, he packed an overnight bag in case of any one of hundreds of reasons that he had to stay overnight.

Finding the right day was simple. He found out through the social network, accessed from a local coffee house, that Pauline would be spending the following week at home, interviewing and waiting for callback interviews from two very interested prospective employers. He decided to go on Friday; nobody interviewed on a Friday in the government, and coming back into the city would be easy because all the traffic would be heading out of town, folks escaping to the shore for the weekend.

Mac did not even tell Helen that he was going; she did not ask his schedule as she was busy promoting sound bites for the Vice President and deflecting interviews prior to the fundraiser next Saturday.

Leaving at six in the morning, Mac was amazed at the number of cars on the road. He headed towards Baltimore, the traffic growing as if some underground garage had disgorged them onto the interstate at the same time. *Where were they coming from?* In between exits there were more. His speed went from seventy-five miles per hour to stopped. *Why?* He was listening to the radio where the traffic report declared the buildup as normal. *Normal! Then what was abnormal? Where were they going at this insane hour of the morning?* He relaxed as he imagined another driver asking him the same question. They all had their own reasons for being on the road.

Reaching Dover, he needed coffee and a payphone. He also needed to walk and stretch. He pulled into a shopping center and parked away from the entrance, then scanned the board of tenants. There were two coffee shops; he chose to walk to the one farthest from the entrance. A trip to the men's room gave him the confidence that he was not followed. He ordered coffee and a breakfast sandwich. It was tasty and a threat to his digestive system.

It was time to make a phone call. He was surprised when it was answered on the second ring.

"Hello?"

"Pauline Poles?"

"Yes, who is calling?"

It was a professional voice and perhaps betrayed a pleasantness that was reserved for a prospective employer.

"I am …. I was a friend of Congressman George and I'd like to talk to you about him"

"Why?" The pleasantness was gone. "Who are you?"

"Can we meet? I need to understand something about his death."

"You mean his suicide?" She was guarded.

"I said his death."

There was a long hesitation. Mac thought that she had not understood and he was about to speak when he heard her ask, "Where are you?"

"At Columbian Coffeeworks in the mall." He instinctively referred to the other coffee shop.

"See you in half an hour, say ten-thirty."

"Works for me," said Mac, hanging up the phone.

This cloak and dagger stuff, was it really necessary?

Mac wandered toward the front of the store and realized that he was conspicuous, doing nothing. There were cameras everywhere. The mall directory was at right angles to the main entrance and he could also see the Columbian Coffeeworks entrance. Mac took out a yellow pad of paper and a pen and started to write down the names of the tenants. He could then tell an inquisitive guard that he was preparing a promotion or doing a survey or something that sounded non-threatening.

A man went by talking on a cell phone, and he would not have been noticed except for bumping into a young woman and not pausing to apologize. When he moved on, the man patted under his jacket. The move was familiar to Mac, and he realized that it was the gesture of a man making sure that a gun was still there. And he knew well enough that these men were unlikely to travel alone. If one man was here, the other must be outside. *Why were they here? Perhaps just to see who showed?* Now Mac had to make sure that he was not seen, not recognized, and definitely not photographed.

Damn! He looked up at the ceiling; every shopping mall in the world had surveillance. If these people were as well funded or as influential as they appeared to be, they would have the tapes before the day was over. He had to start thinking better. He had to start finding out who they were; if not FBI, then who? He needed to start a file with pictures and drawings of the members he had met so far. Taking out his cell phone he walked to the coffee shop as if texting; when the man was facing him, he took a picture and continued as if reading a text, then went back to writing details from the board. This felt dangerous.

Mac physically shuddered when Pauline Poles walked through the door. She was recognizable from the television, but she drew attention to herself by wearing big dark glasses – in January. As she passed, he whispered.

"Keep on walking down the mall and get rid of the glasses."

She turned slightly, instinctively reaching for the glasses. When she saw the speaker, she relaxed a little, vaguely recognizing the face.

The man saw her and realized late that she was not entering the coffee shop. Pauline saw the man and started to run.

What a disaster, Mac thought, figuring that she would head out the side entrance to her car.

He looked after the running figure and decided that she would go right. There was a large black car, dark windows and engine running, outside the front doors. Mac headed towards his car, got in, and drove fast. Swinging through the largely empty lot, he came to the side door as Pauline came barreling out.

"Get in!" he shouted.

Startled, she looked carefully and, with a backward glance, complied.

"Who are they?" she asked.

"That's the question I drove from Washington to ask you."

"How did they know where I was? Why are they following me? Maybe it was you that brought them."

"No, I think not, and they knew because your phone is bugged."

"Why?"

"Maybe because you insist on saying that Charles George did not commit suicide."

"He didn't!"

"There, you just proved my point."

"But if no one listens, why would anyone care?"

"Because someone is listening. I am. They want to know who might listen. Let's go to a suburban housing development where we can park and talk."

"I know you; MacDonald, right? Charles mentioned your call."

"McDougal!"

"Why are we going to the suburbs?"

"Because they have not yet put cameras on the streets there."

"The mall…?"

"Yes, they will know I was there, eventually."

Mac found a street that was quiet, where the houses appeared to be about fifteen years old. He surmised that most would have children in school and two parents, both working. The lack of cars in the driveways seemed to support his theory. Parking outside a house with a for sale sign on the lawn, he turned off the engine.

Turning towards his passenger he saw a very worried expression. Pauline Poles was older than she looked on television – late thirties. Her brown hair framed her face and Mac noted that she was an attractive woman

"Do you live alone?" Mac asked.

"Yes, why?"

"I'm just thinking about the bug in your phone."

"I'll have it taken out."

"They will put it back!" He paused. "How's the job hunt?"

"Good. Several follow-up interviews; I know a lot of people after fifteen years around the political circus."

"But no offers?"

"No. How did you know?"

"I didn't. It just makes some sense for the bug. I think they buy off, or chase off, anyone interviewing you. Is there anyone you interviewed with who you know well enough to ask?"

"There is someone. Someone I lived with before he married; he might tell me."

"Bump into him if you can and ask who and how they applied pressure. Then call my cell number. Do not write it down."

"You think this is about Charles. You believe that he didn't commit suicide. Why?"

"Because I talked with him, and he was afraid, and he was angry that he had been smeared, alienated by his family, accused of having an offshore account of which he had no knowledge, and black-marked about kickbacks that didn't occur. It made no sense. With all that supposed money, why would the bank be foreclosing? And why, after starting to talk to a reporter, having a chance to clear his name, would he commit suicide? Also, I think I found more cases, but they wouldn't talk to me."

"Wow; you did all this for someone you spoke to once?"

"Don't beat up on yourself, Pauline. And be very, very careful."

"I will, and thank you for believing. Charles George was a good man. A bit of a plodder, he couldn't have solicited bribes; he never even got it when someone offered him things. His kids aren't perfect, but they had no access to the drugs that they were supposedly carrying."

"Local police?"

"No. They all knew the family. No, it was…I don't remember. I know they handed the case over to the local police. I will talk to the chief."

"Take care of yourself."

"You've said that, Mr. McDougal."

"Can you take a cab back to the Mall? Go in through the entrance that you came out, put on the glasses, and walk out the front. And again: Be careful. Oh, and send a resume to Helen Harvey at Blair House."

The drive back to Washington seemed to be shorter as Mac tried to make sense of what he had learned. It had been a worthwhile day, though whether good or bad was hard to say.

Driving carefully into his street, eyes peeled for a white van or a black car, Mac found a parking space and picked up the Swiss Army Knife replica with the memory disk. He checked his apartment for uninvited guests before sitting down and writing cryptic notes of his day by hand. His fear was mounting.

Chapter Seven

Helen was absolutely stunning. Mac had the thought for about the hundredth time.

The fundraiser for police and firemen in D.C. was one of the most anticipated events of the year. The mood was buoyant. Many of the guests were associates or friends from the police or fire departments. There would be presentations for bravery; there would be cordiality between factions normally at war. The fight for budget money was on hold, at least for tonight.

In the crowd were politicians promising to be tough on crime and willing to open the public purse for the safety of its citizens. There were union representatives who would be negotiating for those dollars when amnesia would cloud the same politicians' promises. Families of the heroes to be acknowledged were conspicuous in their new clothes and their proximity to the hors d'oeuvres and distance from the cash bar. The bar prices were inflated to recover the huge discount given on the food. An auction was attracting a good deal of money and a silent auction was attracting a generous crowd. Mac gave the firemen $100 for a raffle without asking the prize. It was fun, it was noisy.

"What do you think, Mac?" Ann Gold had moved alongside of him.

"I'm always careful not to think when you're around."

"Well, I see that my predictions were all correct. I see that you and Helen are now taking breakfast together."

"And how do you know that?"

"You just told me." She laughed. "Mac, you never learn. So what do you think of Marjorie's chances in the presidential race?"

"She hasn't declared yet, Ann. Am I learning?"

"You are learning, but I hope that she declares tonight or I'll be up all night rewriting tomorrow's column."

"Ann what do you know of Charles George?"

"Nice man. Tragedy."

"Now tell me something I don't know. Why was he killed?"

"Naughty, naughty, Mac. I invented the bold unsubstantiated statement remember? I don't know anything about his death, but he was framed for some of the things his wife was told. I never printed a bad thing about Charles. I liked him."

"Thanks, Ann."

"For what?"

"Got to go! Be careful!"

The very words that he had spoken less than forty-eight hours ago to Pauline.

Helen came through the throng which was getting louder. Mac watched as Mark Hughes's eyes followed her and narrowed a little when he saw the destination. Mark was the point man and ran a political action committee so he was working very hard tonight soliciting new clients and greasing the campaigns of several politicians. He was talking with a representative of the firemen's union and had clearly given at least one waiter a large tip to keep everyone in the vicinity lubricated.

"You look gorgeous. How am I supposed to keep my hands off of you?" Mac whispered.

"Well, thank you, sir. I think that was a compliment, and me in working clothes."

Helen's working clothes were a simple black dress with pearl necklace and matching earrings, at the wrist was a gold flowered bracelet, the center of each flower was a pearl. The effect was elegant.

"And when can you get rid of those working clothes?"

"Mac, this is going to be a long night and tomorrow will be a zoo."

"Sounds like what I said last time we were together."

"Yes, it does. I am sorry." She was genuinely distressed. "Now I have to go prepare the media for photo-ops with Marjorie bestowing the bravery award. I have decided to do two sets: each recipient separately and then with their families. What do you think?"

"Helen, I think that you were born for this. Marjorie can show concern for crime, for family; a person of the people."

"Are you making fun of me?"

"Not at all. I love you. I love you. Now go back to work."

He watched her leave, a little disappointed, a little jealous; she was so happy and he would apparently be alone tonight.

There was a huge consolation prize as a reward for his attendance; he found himself seated between Helen and Marjorie White. Since the police chief on

Marjorie's other side was a complete bore, after listening patiently for five minutes to some rambling discourse on the difficulty of managing a multi-racial, multi-language police force and population, Marjorie turned to Mac.

"Mac, I haven't seen you for a while. I understand from Helen that you're writing a book on the next election. I also saw that you claimed I might be a front runner."

"Actually you are in Las Vegas. The bookmakers had you as the favorite to win at odds of four-to-one."

"Is that good?"

"It might be for the person who puts a thousand dollars and takes home four thousand when you are in the Oval Office."

"Who do you like for the next President?"

"I am a reporter, not a gambler. The odds-makers think that it will be you or maybe the Attorney General from Texas."

"Ellie May Joseph."

"What would be your platform?"

Mac had an exclusive that he was not going to miss.

"Immigration first. We have to maintain the influx of people; second, support for the military and law and order. What do you think?"

"I think that is the party line and safe with democrats and with your contributors.

"But…?" she added.

"How do you know that there is a 'but'?"

"Mac, I'm a politician. I learned a long time ago that there is invariably a 'but' unless someone is insincere. You don't appear to be an insincere person."

"That is a very cynical outlook on your fellow man. There is a 'but'. A politician who is not listening to the people can't win."

"What are you saying?"

"Listen."

Marjorie sat silently for a while before being spoken to by someone else at the table. The conversation became inane and Mac turned his thoughts to Helen. He was not going to see her much. He was having a self-pity moment when he heard Marjorie White being introduced.

Helen moved closer to Mac and gripped his arm. The words and timing of this announcement were critical. There were several quotable sound bites in the piece and, since all of the networks were represented, they would make the eleven o'clock news all over the country as well as all of the morning newspapers.

The mayor introduced Marjorie White after spending a good deal of time praising his police chief and fire chief to the point of embarrassment for all except the recipients of his praise and their wives. After claiming that the special guest was someone who needed no introduction, he spent five minutes introducing her, finally yielding the podium with the reluctance of the condemned leaving this life.

Marjorie White looked smart. She was efficiently dressed with a little touch of her red blouse showing through the conservative grey suit jacket. Walking with a purposeful stride, the walk of an Olympic Gold Medal winner, she appeared confident in the right to be on stage rather than Oscar winner-unsure, thinking perhaps one of the other nominees had more ability.

She spoke confidently, thanking all of the right people, and in the correct order. Praising the recipients of the bravery awards, she gestured to the tables at which they were seated and thanked their families by name for providing the support and loyalty necessary in a dangerous occupation.

Segueing into law and order, she developed a case for local knowledge, regional backups, national support and international co-operation. It was a very workmanlike speech.

Every time a sound bite opportunity was about to be delivered, the vise-like grip on Mac's arm increased and relaxed only when successfully delivered. Helen was fidgeting, looking at her watch, gauging whether the speech would end in time to make the front of the news. It was clear that she was also hoping that this was a slow night. There was no need to worry. It was obvious that Marjorie had everything in perfect control.

"I'd like to introduce someone special in my life: my husband David."

A tall, handsome, dark haired man had quietly entered and stood close to the podium. He walked forward and gave her a little cheek kiss, making sure no makeup was smudged.

"He's just arrived because he was in charge of making sure that homework was done," she said over genial applause.

"He is also here as, in order to end speculation in the media, I am announcing that tomorrow I shall be assembling a team to explore the prospects of a campaign to run for the office of President of the United States next year."

There was wild applause from an enthusiastic audience with Ann Gold happier than most. Ann was simultaneously applauding and signaling for a gin and tonic. The television crews were frantically calling their producers for a live feed and interviewers were having makeup and hair refreshments while listening to instructions and questions from the studio. They would be going live as soon as an exclusive interview could be arranged. Helen had moved to the back where the on-air personalities clamored for her attention. Mac watched from a distance, observing Helen's ability to listen to their plans and demands, say no to most, and then setting rules that she would need for the campaign.

Marjorie was still speaking as this was where the policy and major sound bite should be, her continuing support for the policies of President Watkins and the Democratic Party. Helen had practiced the speech, knew it word for word, but Mac watched her expression change when she heard Marjorie go off script.

"I support the policies of President Watkins and the Democratic Party. But as I travel this great country, I will be listening. Listening to the people; listening to you; listening and learning!"

It was not what had been written, but it would be the leading comment of every television station and the headlines in every newspaper in the country and in most of the world.

Mac smiled.

Marjorie White was accepting a standing ovation while a stream of well-wishers and others waited for her to leave the podium; she walked through them hand in hand with her husband.

"Marjorie this way," said Helen. "You too, David."

She steered them to an area where a banner advertising the event stood with the hotel logo showing. Mac walked over to offer his congratulations to both women.

"That was brilliant. Why did you change the script, it was designed for solidarity?" Helen asked.

"Your man, Mac!"

"Mac? I'll…I'll…I never should have sat him next to you; he's a bad influence." She gave Mac a dirty look followed by a smile and mouthed a silent thank you.

"Marjorie, I have the networks in alphabetical order, ABC, CBS, FOX, and NBC. Next time I will reverse them. Three minutes max for the first three; we have to lead off the news with a live interview, breaking story, more than ten minutes in and we lose impact. Ready?"

The value of Helen's expertise was immediately evident. Interviews went smoothly. David stood close to his wife, enduring the same questions four times.

"Marjorie, the morning shows are calling for interviews but I have delayed them for a few days. It will give the 'experts' a chance to speak and us the benefit of the reaction. Besides which it is a year before the primaries."

"Good, let's meet tomorrow in the office and decide on our next step, then we can start to assemble a team. Have Martin there and Claire. Can you bring Mac over for dinner to David's parents' house after? They're out of town and the guys are going over to water the plants and watch the game. We can meet them there."

"Why?" Helen asked, looking at Mac.

"He knows things," Marjorie responded, shaking his hand.

"That's for sure," Mac interrupted.

"Show up about one; if we are running late you can watch the football game with David. I think you two will get along. Don't you?"

Marjorie and Helen did in fact run late, about three hours late, so Mac watched the whole game with

David and their younger son Ian. David Junior came down for the second half, when the smell of food overcame his adolescent cool and distance from adults. The smell of kielbasa, boiled in beer and brown sugar, wafted throughout the kitchen. Both boys were excessively polite and as good looking as their parents. The fourteen year old was going to look exactly like his father, while Ian had the softer features of his mother.

Marjorie breezed in, expecting a famished howl of indignation fueled by hunger; she was surprised that with two minutes left in the game the male bodies around the living room hardly acknowledged her entry. Worse, the apologies were wasted. Another tack.

"Helen and I are hungry."

"Offside, he was offside!" David yelled.

"No, he wasn't," Ian said.

"Miles off!" argued David.

"Do you see a flag?" Ian questioned.

"Yes, dear, just two minutes left in the game," David replied. "Wine's in the kitchen!"

The game finally ended. The two minutes having taken fifteen to play.

"Well, you seem to be having fun." Marjorie kissed her husband.

"Yes, and dinner will be served in fifteen minutes."

"What?" Helen asked suspiciously.

"Mac is making steak au Poivre. The potatoes are boiled, the broccoli is ready to steam, and there are carrots for the boys."

"I'm impressed," Marjorie laughed.

"Hold the praise until it is eaten, and hold any criticism forever." With that, Mac shushed them out of the kitchen.

Relaxing over a glass of port after a sumptuous meal that had finished with ice cream, David nodded at Mac.

"Not only do you cook, but you provided my wife with her platform."

"Not really! I think that I was reacting to the status quo, the vanilla speeches."

"Marvin Black?"

Mac was not to be drawn and changed the subject.

"I checked the action in Vegas after the news came out. Sort of an informal poll."

"The odds must've shortened," commented David.

"I don't understand," said Helen.

Mac explained. "A 'book' is made by the bookmaker. He will always want to balance his book."

"The first part is obvious and congress could take a lesson from the need to balance in and outs." Helen was listening, while Mac continued.

"Say someone has one hundred dollars and wants to bet on an event at ten-to-one. If the bookmaker finds someone to bet against the event at ten-to-one then they off-set, book balanced. If no one is willing to bet against at those odds, then the bookmaker needs to lower the risk to say nine-to-one and this is the new book. If too many gamblers like the same 'horse' then the bookmaker will look for another bookmaker to cover some of his risk

"A large number of people wanted to bet Marjorie would be the next President at four-to-one."

"So the odds dropped?" David asked.

"No!" Mac was suddenly very serious. "No David, someone covered everyone at four-to-one."

"A group of wealthy optimistic Republicans,"

"No, it looks like most of it is one person. Someone, who is very, very sure that the next President will not be Marjorie White."

Mac looked at Helen; she was looking back with concern.

"Who is it? Can we find out?"

"The FBI might; give it a try."

Chapter Eight

Boston was always a warm city, even in the frigid cold of February. Boston College had sprung for airfare and a night downtown, so Mac had extended the hotel stay to three nights and took the opportunity to meet some of his friends from college days. Some of these friends, including his former roommate, Sean Lynch, were enjoying a drink at the Boston College Club on Federal Street. Since most were lawyers, it was a testament to Mac's popularity that so many had showed up to share old times. Now they were looking surreptitiously at watches, aware that their continued partnership potential was still dependent upon billing in excess of two thousand hours a year. Juggling this workload with a young family was evident in the manner in which they switched between boasting of kids' achievement and legal conquests.

Mac saved the self-flagellation by suggesting that those who could, adjourn to Locke-Ober for Chateaubriand. Most of the lawyers gave him their business cards and headed home. A few bankers and investment advisors said that they were interested and Bill Fahey, a regular, called and made the reservation. They walked through dark, cold streets to the old wood and warmth of the famous establishment.

The meal over, Sean and Mac sat alone with a brandy each.

"Got to go soon," said Sean. "Good to see you though."

Mac nodded back.

"Do you miss Boston?"

"Yes, I do! The history, the people, the pace of life – sure I miss it."

"I read where you are in with the vice president. Came over to the light side did you?"

"No, I am a political writer which means I have no sides. I am seeing, whenever she is in town, Marjorie White's media person. Some fancy title I keep forgetting.

"You're still voting democrat I take it?"

"Yes, and raising the odd dollar or two for the Massachusetts contingency. I have not yet met the new guy mind you."

"Congressman?"

"No, governor," said Sean.

"What do you mean never met him?"

"Came from nowhere. Didn't ask for money; he added new people all over the place."

"Made it to the State House without the Massachusetts machine? How's he doing?" asked Mac.

"Very well: balancing the budget; raising taxes without fuss; raising productivity at Massport and on the trains without a squeak from the unions. Doesn't owe any favors."

"His opponent?"

"Heart attack; died!"

"History of heart disease?"

"Came out later that she was warned about adding stress."

"Anybody run a book on the governors' race?"

"In Southie probably. You know that in South Boston you can bet on anything"

"Can you find out and get me a name?"

"Sure, I'll be in Suffolk Court tomorrow and I'll call your cell phone when I learn something."

"No. I'll meet you for lunch at the Union Oyster House."

"Okay, twelve noon, at the bar."

Mac arrived early and secured two seats at the bar, then ordered draft Bass Ale.

Sean came in beaming.

"Top of the morning, Mac! Hung jury, how lucky can one man get? Have to try the case again, double fees, one job."

Sean sat, immediately ordering a dozen cherrystone clams and a draft beer. They looked good, so Mac had the same

"Did you ask about the 'Southie' book?"

"Turns out it was in Providence."

"Rhode Island?"

"The same. Seems my client knew and gave me the name and number; he was so happy to be out on bail. I wrote it down."

Mac examined the name and number. The name he knew; the police would give up their pension for the number. Well, maybe not their pension.

The phone was ringing. Mac was at a pay phone in the lobby of a large building.

"Yeah?"

"Guido please."

"No names, what do you want?"

"I'm….."

"No names. What do you want?"

"Did you book the Mass Governor's race?"

"Maybe."

"Balance?"

"Laid it off. Dumbshit took the whole thing."

"And scooped the pool?"

"Yes. A lucky dumbshit!"

"His name?"

"Do I know you? Who gave you this number?"

"No names," said Mac. "A friend."

"Dumbshit had no name; covered in cash, collected in cash. Gotta go."

"One more question. How much?" Mac was listening to a dial tone.

Well, now he knew where the funds were coming from for surveillance, cover-ups, and coercion.

Driving to New Hampshire took about one hour. Finding Ron Anderson took another hour as he was still on the golf course.

"Sorry about that." He greeted Mac with a handshake. "Slow today; would like to blame the women but they are all faster than my partner. For two dollars it should not take five minutes to get out of a sand trap."

Mac immediately liked this solid New Englander, playing golf for two dollars with long-time friends. The friends, after squaring the bets over a good deal of banter, offered to move away but were invited to stay. Food and drinks were ordered. With a great deal of jovial comments to the waitress on the food, they settled to serious conversation.

"From Washington, Ron says. A reporter?"

A man whose name Mac had already failed to catch asked the question.

"Yes and no. I am a freelance writer on political topics, and I work out of Washington."

"Ron here, he likes Washington but prefers where he can see Mount Washington."

"Were you surprised Ron did not get re-elected?"

"Would have been a landslide but for the mix up at the hospital."

"They mixed up before."

Mac was sure the speaker was Bob, or was it Tom?

"They took the wrong leg off that woman, remember? Then they had to take off the one with gangrene."

"She still would have played faster than you today," joked another friend.

"How is he doing, the new man?"

Mac steered the conversation back to his agenda.

"Pretty well; votes with the party line usually," said Ron who had clearly been paying attention to his replacement.

"When didn't he?"

"It was not that he didn't, but it would have been a swing vote on an aid bill, and it was the first vote that he had missed."

"What was the bill? Do you remember?"

"It was 'porked' up to the hilt, but the main part was some planes to Israel."

"Where did his financial backing come from?"

"Nobody knows. Somebody from Concord asked for help bringing their son home for the birth of his baby. He said no, they would serve until he could help bring all the soldiers home. Here's the thing though: the guy sent a contribution; Baker supposedly sent it back with a comment that he can't be bribed."

Back in Boston Mac met Sean in the North End for Veal Marsala, pasta, and a bottle of Chianti.

"How'd you make out in Providence?"

"Very well, thank you very much, and thank your client."

"I would, but he got himself arrested. Seems he went to the track after he was bailed and said how he had 'bought' a hung jury."

"So now it's tampering?"

"Yes, you can't win that; tough to get paid. The tribulations of a trial lawyer."

"Look at all the free publicity. You'll just have to work a couple of extra months to pay off the mortgage."

"Plus the kids' tuitions! Good to see you, Mac. Got to go back to the suburbs. Stay with us next time you're in town."

"With three kids running around?"

"They are house trained. I think!"

"Thanks, Sean," Mac smiled. "Drive carefully."

Chapter Nine

Back in Washington Mac resumed his familiar routine. The spring led to busier schedules for Mac and Helen and those months passed quickly. She was now spending about half of her time at his apartment whenever she was home. The fundraising and constant need to be in the news was keeping her very busy. Marjorie White, having spent whatever time was necessary with the power brokers, was now looking to expand her visibility on the foreign front. The question asked was how deep her knowledge of foreign relations was. Marjorie had persuaded the president that attendance at some of these obscure events could be beneficial. Since President Watkins had no desire to attend the wedding of European royalty or the funeral of a South American president, he was only too happy to agree that she go. Where she went, Helen went. It was also summer and congress was closed. Washington was closed.

All the potential candidates were now in their home states exploring the cost and benefit of mounting a bid for the White House. The extraordinary money necessary was driving this exploration. In that respect it was akin to oil drilling, or mining, or panning for the mineral of access. Mac, having interviewed all of the potential candidates, except one, Ellie May Joseph, was turning his hand to the money issue.

Money: it was costing millions of dollars to run a campaign. Even if someone had a group of volunteers, they had to be coordinated; they needed banners, leaflets, mailings. With people to stuff envelopes they needed postage and, with the door to door canvassers, they needed a story with leaflet, yard signs, bumper stickers – the list was endless. Political advertising was expensive, and transportation and accommodation for an entourage was logistically challenging. Free exposure through sound bites or invitations to speak on national television were nuggets of gold. Media directors, like Helen, were earning their salary by obtaining this free exposure and making the sound bites sound new every time.

He was thinking of Helen when his phone rang. It was her. Wondering if his thinking made the telephone ring, he dismissed that thought since he was always thinking of her when she was not with him.

"Mac….Hello, sweetheart," he answered.

"You probably say that to all the girls."

"Yes, I do. In town?" he asked.

"Yes. I received a resume; you were named a reference. What…"

"I think that Monterey must be suiting the president. Where did Marjorie go?"

"Well, now that school is out, she is going with the family down to the Jersey Shore."

"Great, well, busy now so come by later."

Mac was sure that the message to meet tonight at the Monterey Grill, seven o'clock, had been received. It took a lot of being careful to be safe. They were still out there.

They. No names, no clues after seven months of looking, they were still 'they'. He had just thought of something, something important. What was it? Why had it flown through his subconscious as if not daring to dawdle?

Paper and pencil; he wrote down 'Phone still bugged, no sign of white van or black car, notes offsite, big organizations, big budget, gambling for seed money.'

That was it. That was what he was thinking: money, campaign money. It was available, how much was spent and where. The adage was 'follow the money'.

Campaign contributions, spending, all should be available. Think, think. He could not use his computer or his phone. Mac was aware that he did not want to use Helen. But maybe she could give him an idea of how he should be looking at the issue.

Mac was seated at the bar of the Monterey Grill at seven o'clock watching the crowd. The after work bunch was leaving and the dinner crowd had not yet made it in, so there were plenty of people going in and out. No one paid particular attention to him; a couple he vaguely recognized nodded in his direction. He would have had a hard time putting names to them and, judging by their body language, it was a mutual ignorance.

Helen came in looking like any other office worker with a tan linen suit. The outfit did nothing to enhance her figure or her looks; only the way she walked gave a hint of the healthy sensual body beneath.

Was she wearing lace underwear? *Of course,* thought Mac, *that's why she walks in with that silky smooth stride.*

"Hey good-looking, Can a guy buy you a drink?"

"Why sure," she was doing a Mae West impression. "The usual, and come up and see me sometime."

"That was very good, sounded like you meant it."

Turning Mac said, "Jimmy can the lady have a glass of Chardonnay, Californian, and I'll have another beer."

Comfortably seated very close to each other at the bar, Mac gave one more visual search of the room. Nothing. Helen removed her jacket and revealed a lace backed, sleeveless top.

"Ready to go dancing, I see," Mac said in response.

"Not likely with my schedule," she smiled. "While I was away I received a resume from…"

"No names," warned Mac.

"Okay. I assume you're aware of it then."

"Yes. It's a person who knows the way around the halls of power."

"I don't have an opening at the moment."

"Not important, at the moment. Invite the person in for an interview and let me know when; I'm curious about the person's qualifications."

"A bit cloak and dagger isn't it?"

"Yes, it's a test."

"What kind of test?"

"My kind of test! Shall we eat?"

Mac did not want her to ask why she was not included in the test. He simply wanted Helen to be innocent if anyone contacted her regarding a candidate for a job.

The meal was superb and Helen came back to the apartment and stayed the night. All in all, a perfect end to the day. They did not talk of their concerns, as if by consent they assumed that any conversation was being recorded.

"Where are you off to next?"

"Not sure," said Helen. "There have been some elections in Europe, so there may be opportunities to get in on the ground floor; the Middle East is a minefield. It's impossible to be in the right where they consider you to either represent the devil incarnate or the images of salvation to the population. Sometimes at the same time. I'm trying to arrange a visit with our troops, always a good photo-op, but where?"

"How about the Far East?"

"We have no troops there!"

"No, I meant why not go to the Far East. It is less dangerous, and they are our biggest trading partners."

"But it won't make the best six o'clock news."

"Not everything has to make the news."

"Yes it does, darling. Free publicity, worth a million dollars if it is right."

"Worth nothing if it is Dukakis in a tank."

"Funny!"

The next morning Helen prepared to leave to go to her own apartment.

"Milk is sour. I can't have cereal."

"I'll make you toast with marmalade, fresh coffee."

"Too late, I'm out of here. I'm liberating your last piece of fruit for my journey home."

"Take care, and remember dim sum in Hong Kong is great at this time of year. Singapore Sling, at Raffles, is a must, even if an overrated, drink."

He could not shake off all morning a feeling of dread. There was something in what he had said which was subliminal. There was something in his thoughts but just out of reach. Now that he was thinking it would not come, like a person from the past; a face he could see in his mind without a name attached.

The only cure was work, and he busied himself on research. He looked for the schedule of Ellie May Joseph. It appeared that she was spending the summer on the Gulf, which made sense since her funding was likely anchored in Texas and the oil industry. Mac was reading how she had been a firebrand at college and it looked like a couple of scrapes had been swept under the rug. Looking at Ellie May's background, her father, Jack, showed as a self-made millionaire, a 'wild catter' who had gotten lucky. There were articles showing that he had drilled pretty close to some federal lands. One lawsuit suggested that Jack had moved the markers a bit. Now that his daughter was Attorney General for Texas, it was unlikely that it would be scrutinized too closely. The liberal press was raising the old stories but, since the wells were all sold, it was not selling any newspapers.

Helen called Mac and said that she was heading the next day to the Jersey shore. Marjorie had agreed to play in a charity golf tournament. Some of the other participants were celebrities as well as pro golfers and local and state politicians. It may not make the national news, but it could certainly, with a little help, make the local newspapers and television stations.

Mac, at first annoyed that he was not invited, recognized that this was an opportunity. In his file he had the telephone number and the email for Ellie May Joseph's aide.

"Hi, y'all."

"Sheila Hutchins?"

"Who's calling?"

"Matthew McDougal, I am a political reporter and I am also writing a book on the next presidential election."

"I know who y'are. Ellie May and me were talking on you yesterday."

"Nothing bad I hope."

"Nope! We were saying how ya'll reported on all the other candidates and had not yet spoken to the winner."

"Ms. Hutchins, aren't you about fifteen months ahead of yourself?"

"Young man it's no use coming in second. So I guess you finally figured that you'd like to meet with her? Too bad she is down the Gulf doing a little fishing."

"For fish or contributors?"

There was a guffaw on the phone. "You sound like fun. Can you come down? I'll get you a nice room at the Marriott, then we can go down together. I can fill you in on the campaign."

"Make sure I get the story you want me to have?"

"Somethin' like that."

"Let me get a flight and I'll email the details."

"Good!"

When Mac's plane landed, he walked out of the airport with an overnight bag and his computer. Outside a man was holding a sign with McDougal written on it.

"Who sent you?"

Mac was being careful; even though he was far from home, he had the feeling that the reach was not limited to D.C.

"Ms. Hutchins sent me; said to give y'all a ride to the Marriott. My name's Bobby. They have a shuttle service so figure you're a big wig."

"I am, but until now only my mother would've agreed with you."

"Carry your bag for ya?"

"No thanks," said Mac. "Unless you parked in the long-term parking."

"Nope. Right over there."

The car was indeed right outside the door with a Texas Ranger looking at it with interest.

"Thanks, Roy," the driver spoke to the officer.

"No problem, Bobby; anytime for the lady."

So the car was known, and it belonged to the attorney general. Small town politics on a state-wide scale. Mac sat up front with Bobby, a former All American running back who had blown out a knee, and, in his first game back, blown the other knee. Bobby had completed his degree, but with two blown knees in his resume could not join the secret service or the F.B.I., so he had settled for the Texas Rangers. After twenty years he was now head of security for a contender for the White House and was fantasizing a role directing the service which had turned him down.

Mac learned all this in a thirty minute ride. It was told without boast by a man comfortable with where he was. The conversation also meant that Mac did not need to contribute and, in hindsight, was considerate of the driver to the passenger's privacy.

The hotel room seemed to be of a higher value than he had paid; he hazarded a guess that most guests did not have a bowl of fruit on top of the bar along with two beers cooling in a bucket of ice.

Mac took a shower and then started to enjoy the second beer while watching CNN on television. More unrest in the Middle East, the reporter was saying to a backdrop of flag waving and running men, women, and children. The telephone rang.

"Mac," he answered automatically.

"Sheila Hutchins; is everything okay?"

"Yes, wonderful, being spoiled. Do I thank you for the beer?"

"No, that would be influencing the independence of the press," she laughed.

"Well, it wouldn't be the first time." Mac was comfortable with these people. It seemed a long way from the uptight residents of the eastern seaboard.

"Where can I get a good Texas steak?" he asked.

"Anywhere! Why don't I have Bobby pick you up, make sure you stay safe. Then we can head out at eight in the morning if that works for you."

"I'll be ready tomorrow. I don't want to put Bobby out, but I will agree if he can bring his wife as my guest."

"He'll be thrilled; so will Betty Jo."

The ride to the restaurant was probably half an hour, though it passed quickly as Betty Jo told of her romance with the high school running back, following him to college, and dragging him willingly to the altar.

In the restaurant Mac was the only person without a ten gallon hat. He mentioned it and, after a whisper from Bobby, the waitress came back with a light tan version. The menu consisted of steak: one pound, one and a half pounds, or two pounds; it only came in rare or medium rare with a salad for the table and a bowl of potatoes. Drinks were beer or margaritas and came in pitchers or carafes. Seating was trestle tables. It was noisy, and it was fun. Mac was talking to an accountant and an oil engineer as well as Bobby and Betty Jo. The conversation was on global economics, football, and the predictions of hurricanes in the gulf.

The next morning he spoke with Helen, remembering the two hour difference. She said that she was sorry that he was all alone out west and she

would make it up to him when back in Washington.
Mac took the sympathy without comment.

During the ride down the shore Sheila gave him
some of the promotional material. She also had stacks
of surveys, straw polls, predictions of swing states,
and outlined the strategy. Caucuses were important but
they needed the running start of winning in New
Hampshire. Winning was not enough; annihilation of
the republican competition and intimidation of the
democrats was the plan.

Mac looked at Sheila; she looked like a fifty year
old school marm; she talked like a bull dog. He
mentioned this and her eyes sparkled with charm and
turned a soft light blue.

"Welcome to Texas!" she laughed.

When they arrived at the hacienda which had been
rented to Jim Joseph and his family, Mac was glad he
had brought the ten gallon hat and was wearing blue
jeans and a short sleeved shirt. He was given a tour of
the property on horseback.

Back on the porch he was seated opposite the reason
for his trip while her husband sat at the other end in a
swing chair reading the newspaper. It was
comfortable.

"We need to address the concerns of the people of
this great country. Jobs are the main worry that people
have along with their children's education. Y'all know
that every generation has been more educated than the
last, every generation has been better off financially
than the last. We need to create a generation of
opportunities for the children…" she trailed off."You
aren't taking any notes"

"Actually, I wasn't even listening," said Mac.

"Why not?"

"Because I could have read all that drivel from your campaign literature while sitting comfortably in Washington."

Jim Joseph, at the other end of the deck, snorted. It was a snort of appreciation; someone had spoken up and he clearly agreed.

"You two boys seem to think alike. I paid a lot of money for that literature," she was not angry, she was relaxed. "So what do you want to know?'

"I don't want to know anything. I would like to just talk and find out what makes each candidate tick and why each thinks that he or she will make a difference. I don't care where you stand on abortion for example, or whether I agree, but the reason that you have for the stance is important." Mac spoke while watching Ellie May's body language, noticing that the tension had faded.

"I'm glad you came to Texas, and I apologize for thinking that, like most reporters, you want to write today and be in Wisconsin and Wyoming or Maryland tomorrow.

"Like most politicians, like most people, I am framed by my upbringing and experiences. We led a sheltered life, my father away a lot drilling, but when he was home we were a well off, law abiding, church going family of four.

"With my religious background I oppose abortions, since you bring it up. But my law work brought me into the world, an ugly world, of rape, of poverty, of strange, bad people. Seeing some girl of fourteen raped by family members and crazed with the consequences of a genetically challenged child lose her life, that makes an impact."

"Better," said Mac. "What other issues are of interest to you?"

"Jim, you want to go get something on the barbeque; it looks like we could be a while."

Jim did not appear very motivated to move from his relaxed position, but after Ellie May shot him a look, he got up and headed inside to prepare the food for the grill. Mac laughed aloud.

"Mac, I like you and I know, of course, that you could have direct access to the vice president and that she might be my opposition next year. I'm not worried that you might tell her things; that's not what you're about."

"No," agreed Mac. "I write for me and I write about what I see.

"A presidential campaign costs more than one billion dollars. Is it worth it? What do your supporters ask for?"

Ellie May laughed and flicked a strand of blond hair from her face. It was an extraordinarily simple gesture, likely done millions of times before, but in this moment she looked as Mac imagined she did as a young woman, vulnerable and carefree.

"Is it worth it?" she repeated out loud, as though she had never asked the question of herself before.

"If you win, it is worth it; worth the work, the tears, and the sacrifice to be the leader of the greatest country in the world."

"Do you want me to do my impression of *Hail to the Chief* on my bazooka?" Mac asked.

"No. I'm sorry. Most candidates run on ninety percent ego and fifty percent ability, to paraphrase Yogi Berra. I think that they have well-meaning friends and financial people. A presidential run gives them cachet, a moment in the sun and a virtual shoe-in at their reelection back to the senate or congress or whatever. I think that they believe in the possibility of lightning striking, or of an out of world figure anointing them."

"Harsh."

"Harsh and true."

"Law enforcement; you have a long standing, good relationship with the military and law enforcement."

"It's necessary that we enforce our laws. It's essential that we are strong militarily."

"Global policemen?"

"A trap, Mac?"

"Maybe!"

"It is true that my strong support comes from the defense industry. I also get a lot of support from blue collar America. It reflects my views; it also generates a huge dollar influx in exports."

"And a huge federal deficit when we deploy troops," Mac argued congenially.

"The terrorists want to come here? Then we must go there. The threat has gone from mad Communists having a nuclear device to every tin-pot dictator, every jihadist sheik, and even some screwball democracies threatening these shores with attack."

"Do you think that they might be like the candidates for president: ninety percent ego and fifty percent ability?"

"Touché, Mac!"

"Immigration?"

"Within my presidential term," she paused and smiled to convey some depreciation, "English will be a minority language; Christianity will be a minority religion. Without enforcement, there is no law. Judges are appalled at the cost for interpreters in their courts. Some defendants, criminals in this country, illegally in America for over twenty years, cannot communicate in English. Schools are providing teaching in multiple languages. Illegal aliens are demanding and depleting our welfare services, using their status as illegally in the country to avoid anything they wish not to do – serve in the military, jury duty, etc. They are demanding a seat at the table without paying for the food. They demand representation without voting!" She took a deep breath to calm herself. "Time to eat, I think." Ellie May finished her tirade with another flick of her hair. She did not appear, this time, to be vulnerable.

At lunch the conversation was of family and growing up in Texas. Being outside was pleasant and gave depth of feeling to the spaces. Mac was thinking of spaces: physical, moral, psychological.

The food was excellent. There was a large wooden picnic table, a polka dot tablecloth; there were ribs, corn, baked potatoes, and salad. Ellie May was clearly the center of this world. During the meal her father arrived and was introduced. Obligatory ten gallon hat and blue jeans, he differed only in that he wore a white dress shirt. "Just been to the office," he explained.

Mac decided on a salad and one rib. Later he could not recall how a whole stack of bones ended up on his plate.

After lunch Ellie May and Jim Joseph sat with Mac and told some of their history. Most was information that was readily available, but having the stories first hand gave an authenticity that was important to Mac. Jim was also a lawyer but with no ambition beyond the corporate accounts he represented. Bobby drove Mac to the airport.

The redeye to Washington gave Mac the opportunity to complete a draft of his section on Ellie May Joseph.

Chapter Ten

The summer season was winding down. The days taking a cool turn, football season starting, baseball again anointing a Mr. September. Every year it was the same; every year it was different. It seemed for most that baseball was always the subject of myriad computations. In Washington all of these things were far behind the political machinations. The goal was still the same: the ring reached for, in baseball it might be the World Series, in Washington it meant the presidential inauguration.

Mac was contemplating the similarities in the sports, physical and political. He was looking again at his list of eight likely candidates. Having finished an article which debated the sides of the argument, he knew that the newspaper would have an enormous response. He anticipated that the letters to the editor would be filled with 'How could he compare someone's beloved Redskins, Yankees, Celtics, Colts, Packers, White Sox, etc. with some political bum?' and 'Compare a future hall of famer with a future president?'

Mac was expanding and rewriting the article as a chapter of his book and would enliven it with some of the actual letters; it would be easy to brighten an admittedly dull scene. The political action committees were raising awareness of their own selfish issues; the candidates were scrambling to stay in the race. At this stage a single stupid comment could dry up the funds and scuttle any chance of continuing.

If there was a conspiracy, Mac thought for about the hundredth time, *one of these names could be part of it.* He had interviewed all but Marjorie White, and he knew from Helen and his social meeting that she was not a conspirator. So who? Follow the money! Think of who is being successful.

Nobody.

He looked again. If there was someone there, then he was missing it, or, that person was especially smart.

Especially smart? He was smiling, thinking that this might be an oxymoron when coupled with politicians.

Perhaps that was unfair. Mac needed to interview Marjorie White, still the bookmakers' favorite. Helen would set up the appointment; they had talked about it last night. There was little to learn at this point that was not already either in the media or gleaned from pillow talk. But he needed to do the sit down and eye-ball the candidate.

Fall had come to the northeast and even reached down to the cherry tree-lined boulevard. Few noticed, as they were now drawn into the oncoming cold of winter, quickly forgetting those precious days when bikini clad, or swim suited, they had laughed and splashed through a summer vacation.

The cold weather also meant more indoor events. Fundraising, now in full swing, returned, where those accepting invitations to free drinks found themselves trapped and promising support for political parties of different hues – red, blue, green.

Mac had attended a few of these soirees. The aides of candidates were only too pleased to have media coverage. Thinking again through the meetings with his list of possibilities, he was struck by how similar and different they all were.

Ellie May Joseph had been in town to speak at an attorneys' luncheon. She, at least, was different. Taking the opportunity, while in the capital, she had met with the republican leadership. This had been a private meeting, which meant that it had been almost fifteen minutes before the world knew what had been said. The words she had spoken here were very different: she spoke of reform. This was a change from the pledge to the attorneys that she would keep them in business, with the ability to bring suits on behalf of immigrants, legal or illegal, with changes in the tax law to confuse. The law makers were jockeying for positions in a cabinet or even the vice presidential chair. She was very clear that there was not enough room on Capitol Hill for both herself and any republican member of the house or senate who was not a supporter of her race to the White House.

It was classic; it was great!

Mac called Ann Gold.

"Hello, Mac, where have you been? I thought that with Helen out of town we might have been seen over at The Hayes…"

"That would have sent the gossip writers into orgasmic rapture," said Mac.

"None more than me," laughed Ann.

Mac could imagine her expressive face.

"Ann, what do you have to say about Ellie May?"

"Ah, the delectable Ms. Joseph. Like chocolate caramel; sweet on the outside and hard as rock inside. Very formidable! You wrote a strong article a couple of weeks ago; hit the nail on the head. I think she's a very dark blue, to the right of right."

"But good for business?"

"Very good for business! After last week's performance behind closed doors, word is that money is pouring in."

"Anybody in particular?"

"Not even any industry in particular. The defense manufacturers are swimming in salivation. Mark Hughes has pledged a plane to carry her around."

"How do you know it's Mark? No, never mind. I am sure that I don't want to know."

"Just don't go public with that until I've milked it. Got it, Mac?"

"Yes, Ann. Let's have dinner sometime, somewhere that I can afford."

"Don't be silly. No one goes to any place that you can afford. We'll go Dutch; it will be fun. Next week, Tuesday, call Monday to confirm."

"Talk to you next Monday. Bye, Ann."

"Bye, Mac!"

This was going to cost him big time. It was worth it though; the information was reliable, it was good.

He called Helen next.

"Hi. How are things at the center of the universe?"

It was a theme he enjoyed, reminding Helen that she was sitting next to one of the most powerful people on earth.

"Tiring! I don't know how they keep up this pace. It has been eight months and, if we kill ourselves for another twelve, we can expect to have eight years more. Does that make any sense?"

"Ask the mouse on the treadmill," answered Mac. "Ask the union worker in Detroit, the craps dealer in Vegas, or the fisherman in the Gulf."

"Philosophical. You've been sitting, thinking all day, haven't you?"

"Yes!" he admitted. "Thinking of you."

"Nice try, big guy." She paused and said, "I was going to call you. I met ….."

"Later," Mac interrupted. "Now I need to see you to remember what you look like. Madonna, I bet."

"Michelangelo plus one," she replied to let him know that dinner at the Monterey Steak house was fine but at eight, as she could not make it earlier.

Mac sang through the afternoon, wrote a bunch of e-mails to friends and contacts, mainly to let them know he was alive. He received a reply from Sean in Boston.

"In Washington, next week for depositions. Staying at Hayes. Can we do dinner Tuesday?"

"Expense account?"

"Of course."

"In that case I'll bring someone you'll enjoy meeting."

"Great!"

Mac chuckled; Sean would be thinking that it might be Helen or Marjorie. Ann Gold would not have made a two o'clock drunk turn round. But she was fun.

When Mac finally arrived at ten after eight, Helen was at the bar looking anxious. Part of the reason was a financial analyst occupying the next seat and trying to occupy Helen's seat, or her pants.

"Hello, sweetheart," Mac gushed. He was excessively romantic and knocked into the man as he was taking a drink of his martini.

"Mac, darling, you're so late I think they will have given away our table." Helen stepped on the man's Burberry coat, causing it to fall on the floor, while looking innocently into Mac's face.

Seated in the center of the room, Mac was facing the door. They ordered from memory.

"So what was it that you needed to say before I stopped you?" Mac asked.

"I'll never get used to not having a civilized conversation."

"What is this then?"

"Mac, civilization invented the telephone one hundred years ago. Or perhaps you've forgotten that we now have faxes and emails."

"Perhaps you've forgotten that as soon as we had telephones we had eavesdroppers, then tapping. With computers came hackers."

"Okay, okay. I've got it. Your friend Pauline Poles came to see me today. She's very upset. I know that she's both competent and loyal to Charles George; well, to his memory. When we talked, she wouldn't go into the subject of George's death, apparently on very specific instructions of a Mr. McDougal."

"Good, it will keep her out of harm's way. I hope."

"She said there had been no job offers. She needs to talk to you but was too tired today. Tomorrow morning at Paula's Restaurant at seven; she'll share with you all that she has learned since you met."

"I told her to be careful." Mac's face was concerned.

The food arrived and there was a flurry of activity at the table over wine and then ground pepper, making conversation impossible.

"I have a question," said Mac when attention switched to other tables.

"The answer is yes!" Helen was smiling shyly.

"That's not the question!" Mac looked over his wine glass. "But I like the answer."

"Okay."

"The question is, did anyone pay attention to your appointment today?"

"Funny you should say that. There was no direct attention but lots of indirect negative comments all week."

"Like what?"

"Like did I know about the missing money from Charles George's congressional funds? Like a copy on my desk of a subpoena for Congressman George's aide, Pauline Poles, to meet with a grand jury. Like a blog claiming that George's affairs included one with his former aide."

"Did you mention this in your interview?"

"Yes, Pauline said they were all lies."

"Well, she would, wouldn't she?" Mac could see in his mind the aide's face and understood why she had been nervous and tired.

"She said that she had brought proof for you to see."

"Do you think you might find something for her?"

"I don't know. I can't poison Marjorie's campaign. I can't now put her in fundraising." Helen stopped, seeing the anger in Mac's face.

"That's bullshit, Helen! She no more took money than you."

"I'm sorry, Mac. I'll find something, somewhere. I promise; I'll look."

They finished their meal quietly, the previous mood dispelled.

By the next morning everything was rosy in the garden of joy that Mac and Helen inhabited.

In the shower, a date for Mac's interview was determined, or squeezed into the schedule, whichever way one interpreted the negotiations. It was decided that there was a scheduled meeting for a political fundraiser at the Crab House down on the Chesapeake Shore. Some local democrats were speaking and assuring a good attendance by persuading the leading presidential candidate to join them. Mac, who loved any kind of shellfish, held out for about three seconds.

They drove to Paula's Restaurant, listening to the news on National Public Radio. Nothing new; terrorists in the Middle East had detonated a bomb in Tel Aviv; the Israelis had retaliated. The government of Libya had expelled some American engineers as spies; the American Embassy was closed in protest.

"I thought they were allies of ours in the region."

"Last year they were terrorists, this year they're the elected government," said Mac. "It's also why I would rather Marjorie, should she decide to visit, leave you at home."

"If they are still terrorists, then why accept them at all?"

"Because they are our terrorists and are sitting on our oil!"

"That's cynical, Mac. They want the same things that we want: food, shelter, clothing, education…"

"That sounds too simple. Why then are they fighting? Why not expend the energy farming, hunting, working rather than trying to expel the Jews?"

"Because it's their land!"

"Is it?"

"Probably!"

"So if an American Indian bombed Wall Street he could defend the action by saying that it is his land?"

"Of course not!"

"Why not?"

"Because there was nothing there."

"And did anyone give a damn about the Middle East until Henry Ford. Or whoever it was, discovered that there was oil there?"

"How on earth did we get into this discussion?" asked Helen as they parked.

"American politicians are constantly seeking approval and accepting bad behavior from our friends and allies. As a great philosopher once said, 'Can't buy me love'."

"I thought that was the Beatles."

"Exactly!" Inside he nodded and said, "Coffee please, Paula!"

"What's so funny?" Paula asked the laughing Helen.

"Nothing! No, not nothing, but you had to be there!"

"Usual?"

"Nothing yet, meeting someone, but coffee would be good," Helen admitted. "Mac's out of milk again."

Seated they scanned the room which was busy with revolving clientele, all regulars or faces seen before.

"Are we so predictable?"

"Why?"

"She said 'usual' as if we were an old married couple."

Helen had spoken the 'M' word. Mac decided that it was better not to rise to the bait; he waited until she spoke again.

"What time is it?"

Mac looked up at the clock over the service hatch. "Twenty past. Perhaps you should call in case she's lost."

Helen scrambled in her pocketbook, pulled out her cell phone, and called her office.

"Hi, this is Helen Harvey. Who is this?" A guttural grunt acknowledged someone was at the other end.

"I'm fine, Billy. Billy could you look on my desk? There's a resume with a cell phone number on the bottom. I'll hold."

"Is it okay, his looking on your desk?" asked Mac.

"You had a better idea?"

"No," he admitted.

"Thanks, Billy. No, leave it where it is. See you shortly."

Helen called the number. Her eyes met Mac's when the voice message ran through a cheery greeting to leave a message.

"Pauline, call me at this number. Hope that you aren't lost. We'll wait until eight."

They waited with increasing anxiety until ten minutes to eight then called again; no answer.

"Leaving without eating?" The waitress was obviously dismayed.

"Can I please get a bacon sandwich in a bag and a coffee to go," said Mac.

"A bran muffin and small coffee," added Helen.

"Brown sauce on the bacon?" Paula inquired.

"Of course; it keeps the arteries from clogging," said Mac as Helen grimaced. Mac left twenty dollars by the cash register.

In the car he took a bite of the sandwich and put it down.

"I can't eat," he said.

"Me neither," said Helen, putting aside, untouched, the warm muffin.

"Where could she be?"

"There are a thousand explanations."

"Who else knew she was in town?"

"I don't know. I told no one except you. The appointment only said interview; she had to get a badge downstairs of course."

"Why is every dump truck in the city out on the road today?"

"Take it easy," said Helen, but she made no comment when Mac pulled into the handicapped space next to the front door.

At the front desk he waited while the woman had a conversation which had no end. The name tag said Emily and underneath 'I am here to serve YOU'. Mac stared at the tag on her chest until she turned red and abruptly ended her call.

"Yes, sir, how may I serve you?" It was rehearsed, not sincere.

"You may serve by calling a guest, Pauline Poles."

"Do you know which room?"

"No, but you do." He nodded at the computer console. She started to say something, realized that he was again fixating on her badge, she tapped a few keys while listening to the room phone ringing.

"I am sorry, sir, but no one is answering. Try again later."

"We need to get a key. It is my aunt up from Dover to see her specialist and she's late for her appointment. We've tried to call and now we fear she may have fallen."

"Well, I'll have to speak to my manager."

Emily disappeared into the back.

An older woman came out after a minute.

"How may I help you?" she asked.

"I'm sure that Emily conveyed the seriousness of the situation. Any delay could be critical to someone in her condition."

"Security will be here directly."

An overweight man appeared brushing crumbs from a miserable excuse for a mustache. The procession headed for the elevators.

At room four forty-one the manager knocked loudly, waited, then used a master card key to enter.

It was perfectly tidy, not a thing out of place. All the misgivings seemed to be for nothing.

The bed was neat, except that Pauline Poles was still in it.

Pauline was dead.

The manager screeched, Helen gasped, the security man took one step forward then two back.

When the manager reached for the phone, Mac held her back.

"Touch nothing. Go call the police."

She nodded and left.

Mac whispered to Helen, "Get him out of here."

"How? Why?"

"I need to look for whatever she was going to give me as proof."

Helen turned, then slowly stumbled toward the door and the security man. The man who was already a shade of green caught her as they fell into the hallway.

Mac had to work fast, less than a minute later the manager would be back.

She returned, announcing, "The police will be here directly; they said to touch nothing and nobody leaves."

"Hm...where is the young lady I arrived with?" Mac asked.

"In the ladies' room, just off the lobby."

"Thanks."

In the lobby Mac banged on the door to the women's restroom. Helen came out looking pale but otherwise fine.

"There must be a back door," said Mac. "Let's go."

"But I thought...."

"Let's go! The police will be coming in the front door any second."

Chapter Eleven

"Do you believe in coincidence?"

The question hung in the air as a dark storm cloud.

Mac was seated with Sean, Helen, and Ann Gold in the lounge at The Ritz-Carlton. An earlier call from Sean had asked if the guest that Mac was bringing might be the Helen that he kept hearing about. Mac had answered, "No, but it could be arranged."

It was the excuse that Mac needed. Since the incident he worried all the time when Helen was not with him. Imagination was playing havoc with his typical steady outlook on the world.

Mac had been the first to arrive in the bar, Sean was late as usual. They had a beer and caught up on Sean's family and some of their friends in Boston. When Helen and Ann arrived, almost simultaneously, they ordered more drinks. Ann's eyes never stopped moving. There were several stories in the room; it was the place for the wheelers and dealers of the political circus to meet and be met because an accidental meeting could easily be feigned since everyone in the room was doing the same. A few noticed the moving eyes and nodded.

"So Mac, why are we sharing? I thought that this was our personal rendezvous?" Ann absently asked, stirring the vodka martini in her hand, continuing to scan the room.

"Ann, my darling, I thought that you might have eyes only for me," Mac answered smiling.

"I love dining with my favorite people in Washington. I might even get a snippet of gossip from the White House if I listen carefully. The handsome young man from Boston comes as a bonus." Ann winked at Sean. Her demeanor made her no threat to anyone and, therefore, she was a threat to everyone with her gossip column.

"Sean is a friend from school, and he's active in Massachusetts politics. This week he's blessing our fair city, and he's also taking a deposition."

Ann's antenna turned from the room and Sean received the undivided attention.

"Okay, whose deposition: Hoffa?"

"Why? Do you have him here?"

"If he was in town, Ann would know, Sean," Helen answered, to general amusement.

"Actually, Ann, as you know, Massachusetts has a new Governor."

"Of course, Democrat; where is the news?"

"The news is that this time the Democratic machine didn't get him elected."

"Then my column would ask who did?"

"Thought you might know," replied Mac.

"If I did," whispered Ann, "I wouldn't even whisper it in this room."

They were interrupted by the maître-de advising that their reserved table was ready.

Conversation at the table moved to the specialties of the day, selection of wines and the ordering process.

Sean and Mac had agreed over the phone that Sean would pay for food while Mac paid for drinks. This arrangement was an accommodation of the law firm's interpretation of Internal Revenue Rules and out of control political correctness. Mac was not answerable to a managing partner, although he did respect the IRS.

"Do you believe in coincidence?" Mac asked. "Twice!"

Sean was his best friend, next to Helen; and Ann Gold would do nothing to harm him or Helen. It would be naïve to not believe that this might have to do with Helen's access to arguably the second most powerful person in the country, who might soon be number one.

"As a lawyer I don't believe in coincidence once, certainly not twice."

"Coincidence has been argued successfully," said Ann.

"I didn't say argued. I asked if you believe."

"I am a gossip columnist; I don't believe in anything. Is this about that dreadful suicide last week?"

"Why do you think it was suicide?'

"Well, a little bird told me that Helen had interviewed the woman earlier in the day and that a man and woman at the scene disappeared before the police arrived. It's a coincidence that the description of the missing witnesses matched you and Helen."

Helen had been looking out over the room and her head snapped back to Ann's face.

"Confirmation!" said Ann.

"Circumstantial; no proof," said Mac.

"It will never even be speculated upon by my newspaper," Ann promised. "If you were there then you know that it was suicide; sleeping pills, alcohol…."

"Motive?" asked Sean.

"Three motives," Ann said, holding up three pudgy fingers. "An affair with a congressman, Charles

George, who committed suicide back in the spring, embezzlement of funds from the congressman's re-election fund, and being unable to find employment."

"Not true!" Mac said.

"I would have found her a job," Helen added.

"Then why did she commit suicide?" asked Sean.

"She was murdered," said Mac. "So was Charles George; and those are not the coincidences. The first coincidence is that George spoke to me just before his death and the second is that Pauline Poles was to meet me the morning she died."

"Jesus Christ!" exclaimed Sean. "Why are you telling us this?"

"If anything happens to me it will not be suicide; it will not be an accident."

"You found the body, right?" asked Ann.

"Yes."

"What did you see? Why leave before the police arrived?" asked Sean.

"The police might have asked why I was meeting her. She had some documents relating to George's death that she wanted to share."

"So what were they?"

"Don't know; they were gone! The prescription was filled in Washington at a department store. No one would fill a prescription for someone out of state. I am sure that it will be covered with sworn affidavits at the inquest. Affidavits that say a young woman, matching the description of the deceased, brought in a phony prescription with a phony ID at the time when the department was busy. An oversight won't happen again, person who filled the prescription has left."

There was a palpable silence finally broken by Sean.

"But why?"

"Not sure. Charles George was a decent man who was running for reelection, virtually unbeatable, until a run of bad luck; nothing huge: drugs found on his teenage kids, whispers of infidelity, questionable donors, off-shore funds."

"If true, he shouldn't be a congressman," Sean said.

"But, if not true, should his children be expelled, his wife leave, his house be foreclosed, and the IRS be looking for money laundering? I don't believe that any of it was true. He may have been drinking when we spoke, but he wasn't suicidal; he was going to fight for his reputation."

"Well," Ann inserted, "you certainly know how to give a girl a good time. Next time, count me out."

"I thought you heard everything."

"It's not that. It's that people that you talk to end up dead."

"Who might be behind this?" asked Sean.

"Sean, I love you like a brother. Even if I knew I wouldn't tell you and, even though Ann thinks she might know, it is not leaving her lips."

It was a more somber party that broke up than had sat down to eat two hours earlier. Ann could not resist sweeping the room on her way to the door; gathering information as a vacuum cleaner gathers dust.

Helen, who had taken Mac's hand at the table and held on tight, now reached for his hand again. The act was to give, or to receive, reassurance. Maybe both.

Chapter Twelve

Susan Raymond was sitting with her body sideways on Mac's armchair. Today, in response to the cold weather in the city, she was wearing a tweed jacket over cavalry twill trousers.

"It's cold," she stated unnecessarily.

"It's winter," Mac answered.

"It's winter in Florida, but it's warm," Sue retorted.

Mac was tired; the lack of sleeping and the constant vigilance was taking its toll.

"Then go to Florida!"

"Mac, two things: I live here and like it; secondly, what have I done to piss you off?"

"Nothing, just tired I guess. Sorry, Sue."

"Sorry my ass! I call over here and, if you deign to answer the phone, it's 'what the fuck do you want' and then you hang up."

"That's an exaggeration since I don't often swear."

"But you don't deny the essence of the conversation?"

"No, not really, it's...Let's start again, how can I help you, Sue, or how can you help me?"

"Well, it is what you pay me for. How would you like to cover the primaries for a major network?"

"Since I'm there anyway, why not? Do I get a blazer too?"

"That's more like the Mac I know; trying to double his wardrobe," she laughed."It will be to present an unbiased report daily on the comings and goings."

"All the primaries?"

"Well, I have the contract for New Hampshire to start; then we'll see."

"Sure, make me analyze a hundred candidates and then bring in the eye candy for the later polls."

"You want it or not? Besides you look like eye candy to some yourself."

"I already said yes, so the flattery was not necessary."

"Starts right after the Christmas Holidays."

"Sounds fine. Can I carry my book onto the set with me?"

"That's my boy!"

"Do you fancy having crab for dinner? I'm going to a Marjorie White fundraiser down the shore, then grabbing a crab dinner with Helen, and driving home."

"Sure, that sounds like fun. And I can overlook your being crabby with me all month. I'll just call Carol."

Mac grabbed his black leather jacket and Sue put on her warm fleece vest. On the ride down to the Chesapeake they caught up on the opportunities that might be available for his book. The new book needed a cover design and a title; a presidential seal had already been used several times. After a while, they decided that an artist would be asked to create three or four examples to consider.

The venue was busy and security was tight. Mac used his recognition of a couple of the faces on the detail to get to a small area at the back of a very small stage where the speakers were gathered. The space was made smaller by the large number of people standing there. Helen spotted them and came over.

"Mac," she said, giving him a small kiss on the cheek. She was careful not to smudge any makeup since she expected to be speaking to the local media later.

"Ray, it's a pleasant surprise to see you here. I didn't think you travelled this far from Washington."

"Helen, I just had to come to find out what it is that you see in him. And, of course, for the crab dinner that he promised later."

"I saved you a press seat, Mac. I'll rustle up another for Ray."

Susan Raymond beamed at being included and went off to speak to some media people she recognized. Mac noticed that she received a few strange looks; he guessed that the primarily conservative middle class audience did not agree with her attire.

The local luminaries spoke first. It was easy to see that, with so little to say, they were milking the limelight. The topic, as usual, was the quality of water in the bay and the availability of shellfish. One speaker spoke of the effect of the Gulf Stream and the effect of global warming while the next was concerned about the Pacific Currents and the windborne contaminants. It all went very well and was predictable. The moderator made sure that time limits were kept; this was due to Helen insisting that Marjorie was to speak in plenty of time to make the evening news.

Introduced as a woman who not only understood the global issues, but domestic and even local concerns, Marjorie took the stage, the additional comment being made that she was easily poised to become the first woman president. She stepped forward to warm applause.

"Thank you very much indeed. I promised to listen and would like to address some of the concerns raised this evening. The reason to visit communities all over the country such as this is to hear what you have to say and to see first-hand what is being done. It's amazing to me how similar those concerns are in Miami, Napa Valley, Detroit City, the Texas Panhandle, and here in Chesapeake Bay. Whether we are meeting in large cities, rural areas, retirement communities, or close to fishing beds, the concerns are the same: the environment, jobs, and education.

"I, like you, am concerned with global warming and believe that we must do something immediately to stop and hopefully reverse the negative effect on our lives.

"I was introduced as having the ability to be the first woman president. I would prefer to be your next American President."

In the next fifteen minutes, she adeptly covered her international knowledge, her stance on domestic issues, and her concern for local issues. Everyone was hearing what they wanted to hear.

"....but I am here to listen, and so I want to hear from you, either comments or questions. Yes, sir."

"I'm a local fisherman and want to know what the government is doing about pollutants and run-off into our Bay?"

"We have laws on the books, and there are local laws which should be enforced. Let me ask your name and what you think should be done?"

"Norman Stansfield, and they should stop politicking and pay for clean-up."

"And who are they?"

"Well, the run-off is from the streets up river, sometimes with salt and other chemicals from the freighters. I think if we can just enforce the laws, we'll be better off."

"Then it appears that somehow we have to find, in both our federal and state budgets, the money to hire and train enforcement officers."

"Where do you stand on women's rights and the protection of unborn children?" was the next question, asked by a woman wearing a flowered dress who introduced herself as Margaret.

"This is a question that I hear every time I speak. The question assumes that I have a particular point of view as a woman. I hope that in some ways that's true, but tonight I'm speaking as a presidential Candidate. It is my duty to abide by the laws written, whether or not I agree with them."

"But you can change them!" a voice shouted from the back.

"I can't change them because those men wise enough and strong enough to write our Constitution provided for three branches for the checks and balances. Otherwise the laws would change every few years, which would make following the rules difficult.

There were comments, about jobs and incentives, in which Marjorie engaged the speakers to find that most were personal. The meeting wrapped up cordially and reporters went off in search of those who had been asking questions for their names and additional quotes.

As Helen scooted, she told Mac and Susan, "I reserved a table in the dining room for eight people. See you there."

Susan and Mac were seated alone at the table with a carafe of white wine.

"Is everybody selfish?" she asked.

"You mean everyone except you and me?"

"No, I mean everybody."

"What brought that up? The nature of the questions or the nature of the answers?"

"Everything!"

"You're beginning to piss me off again," Mac said. "Not everybody is altruistic, true, but more also consider their neighbor."

"Especially if it suits their position." Sue was getting the last word.

Later, as they were finishing their meals, conversation started again. Mac was still working and needed a fresh quotation.

"Vice President White...."

"Please call me Marjorie. Some people I don't care for call me Marjorie, but you I consider a friend and Helen's almost family."

"Thank you, but you may think differently when you read what I write."

"It can't be worse than some of the things my staff tried to hide from me." She was relaxing but looked tired. David was sitting on the other side quietly holding her hand.

"Marjorie, what have you learned listening to America?"

"I've learned a great deal about me. When I look out at America, I see myself. When they ask questions, when they give sincere open advice, I see me."

"You don't think America is selfish?"

"Of course it is."

Mac could almost hear Sue smirking.

"We want the best for ourselves, for our children, a better job, more money, less government interference, less pollution. But we also have compassion for our neighbor, for our friends, even towards strangers. How many times do you see when someone loses a home that perfect strangers send them money? How many people, when they lose someone, find a community praying for them?"

"Don't you ever get discouraged, think that half the people approve and half disapprove."

"No, I call it Democracy. When I see a room with split opinions, I see America. As many people support our sending troops overseas as there are people who oppose it, and probably as many have no opinion. It is the same on any hot button: immigration, nuclear power, pollution, high speed transit, anything that you can name. Here's the thing – the percentages probably do not vary over party lines. If twenty percent of Democrats oppose something, it is likely that twenty percent of Republicans will also. The places where they diverge are social service issues and big business.

"That is democracy: the ability to agree to disagree and then selflessly vote for the common good."

"Marjorie, that would make a great speech," Sue commented.

"Maybe," she replied, "but only when I'm elected. Nobody wants to be told how they think; that's American Democracy." Everyone at the table agreed and talk moved on to other aspects of the campaign, Marjorie's stance on the issues, and the competing candidates.

Sue slept in the backseat all the way back to Washington. Helen, who had promised to stay awake, lasted about five miles before she also closed her eyes. Mac, left with his own thoughts, was mentally planning his story and figuring out how to best write a replay of his first article but with the experience of having spoken to all the candidates.

After depositing Sue and Helen at their respective apartments, he realized that he had forgotten to tell Helen that he would be reporting the election for a nationally televised audience from New Hampshire. As he drove home, snow began to gently fall.

Chapter Thirteen

Christmas had again come and gone. For Mac it was merrier than the previous year since Helen was a part of the festivities. Mac again cooked the turkey and invited Sue and Carol. The post celebrations were predictable: Helen left on the next afternoon to visit her sister; Mac headed north to see his mother.

The reception he received could have been a replay of the previous year. His mother thought he was Roger. It was a shame; she was in good physical health, but her mind was obviously unable to cope with the world.

Mac stayed overnight; the next day he took his mother for a ride and lunch. When he left to drive back, he kissed her.

"Bye, Mom."

"Bye, son. I love you."

It was like the clock going back twenty years – he was headed out, knowing that he was loved. He was shaking his head as he started the car. *Not fair,* he thought, *time is a thief.*

Mac was back at his apartment in D.C., studying the candidates daily; he was determined to be ready. He knew that the lead television reporters looked relaxed because they were prepared. The sports announcers had all of the players' names, and how-to pronounce them, memorized. Mac had files which included their wives' or husbands' names, children's names and ages, and most importantly who their aides and major supporters were.

"Mac, how's things?" It came out 'thungs' and Mac recognized the effected drawl of John Richards, the congressman who he had saved from the press at the awards dinner a year earlier.

"J.R., 'thungs' are great," he drawled back. "What's new on the Hill that we cannot see on the internet five minutes after it happens?"

"Trying to get ahead of the internet, eh? Not likely. The bloggers know what's going to happen before we even get to vote most of the time. You know, I was sitting here counting my contributions and thinking on the competition. My team has been in New Hampshire for a couple of weeks setting up headquarters, meetings, etc."

"I'm sure that the New Hampshire economy is grateful for the boost," said Mac.

"The first primary is always a dry run for new staff. It's a gauge of how many volunteers we can count on, how many people we need; it is a great education."

"J.R., as you know, I'm reporting for the television network, so I'll unashamedly use any information you give me."

"Can we meet for a cup of coffee?"

"Sure. Let's meet at Starbucks down the street from Watergate."

"Is that appropriate? Or just convenient?"

"Depends what you tell me; but it is convenient. How about we meet in twenty minutes?"

"See you then."

Seated in the coffee shop with John Richards, Mac was glad they had not continued their original conversation on the phone. It was nearly a year since

Charles George's death and four months since the death of Charles George's aide, both ruled suicide. Mac had found nothing. Pauline Poles had not confided in anyone. As Mac reminded himself constantly, that was the one stipulation that he had made. Trust nobody. But someone had known; known what she knew, knew that she had evidence, knew what and where the evidence was kept. Evidence that was now gone.

"J.R., you look well."

"Stopped drinking after those media awards where you saved me. I feel great."

"I'm glad to hear that. I try to stick with having just the occasional beer myself, maybe a glass of wine when we eat out."

"Mac, when we talked, you asked about odd things happening in the House of Congress."

"And you said that there was nothing you could point to; anomalies abound. So?"

"So, a rookie congressman picks a fight on the most taboo issue, wins against everyone's assessment, scuttles a couple of presidential hopefuls, and the next day he announces that he will run in the New Hampshire primary."

"Anders?"

"Yes." JR was obviously emotional about the subject. He understood that everything in Washington follows an agenda and that everything has a predictable outcome.

"He opposed spending money," Mac said.

"Yes, but he's a Democrat."

"Not all Democrats vote spending, except for social services; this was for defense."

"True, but it was bi-partisan. Additional weapons for our troops in the Middle East. Melvin Black for

Michigan and Carmel Fernandez in New Mexico had co-sponsored the bill in the Senate. There was so much 'pork' in the bill that every state would get something. Black and Fernandez were backing their presidential bids with contracts that would spin into their states. It was a slam dunk. Apple pie for the troops. Jobs to the two depressed states. And cream for everyone else."

"The vote was close though," Mac said.

"It looked to be," said JR "The argument was an old one; stop fighting overseas, stop the pork. Now I grant that the pork was way out of line. It swayed a few people, but this is a presidential election year. Senate races are being run, Congressional races, it's necessary that we show jobs or money to our communities in order to be re-elected."

"I agree that it's strange, but strange things can and do happen in Washington. Besides, from where I'm sitting, Black and Fernandez had no chance anyway. Black is a loser, can't bring jobs into Michigan, and Fernandez isn't sure which side of the Rio Grande New Mexico is on."

"Mac, where is Anders money from? Where's his support?"

"He's putting it all on red; swinging for the fence in New Hampshire. If he does well, he figures money will flow in. Of course he needs a hundred thousand votes." Mac was playing the devil's advocate but was already mentally going back through his notes.

JR was speaking forcefully and pointing a finger. "Anders is running on a 'Bring the troops home and balance the budget platform.'"

"Yes?"

"In New Hampshire! New Hampshire is a right wing, patriotic, right to bear arms, state. Why not wait and run in Massachusetts?"

"Are you saying that people in Boston are not patriotic?"

"You know what I mean," J.R. responded, his face flushing.

"Yes, I do," said a now somber Mac. "Very strange."

They continued to talk on other matters for half an hour, although it was clear that they were thinking about the earlier conversation.

"Good luck, J.R. I'll be seeing you in New Hampshire, and I'll make sure to give you good coverage. When I get home I'll look up the voting on the bill we talked about."

"Thanks, Mac. Good to see you."

When he arrived back at his place, after taking a look to see if anything was askew from uninvited guests, Mac downloaded the voting from the bill onto the flash drive that he kept in his pocket. The bill had been narrowly defeated in the Senate also and was sent on to committee.

Mac spoke to Helen and found that the President had been furious. His legacy was beating back terrorists from our shores and keeping them far away.

Marjorie had taken the practical approach and gone to the political press. On television she had stated that the White House was pleased that Congress was taking the budget deficit seriously and that a veto would have been likely had all of the 'pork' remained. Of course the White House supported our brave men and women in uniform, but it would be un-American to bring them home to a bankrupt country.

"Very nice, very civilized," said Mac to Helen. "But what if it is beaten again and there are no extraneous pieces of legislation hanging onto it?"

"Not possible," was Helen's position.

"Possible," said Mac "With a little help from one's friends, whoever they may be. Remember, Helen, all things are possible in Washington."

Two weeks later the legislation was presented without any benefit to different states and without the attached pet projects of the various influential members of congress. Studies, of intellectual interest only, were cancelled. The final bill culled over one billion dollars of politicking and also reduced the spending on the funds to the military by twenty-five percent. The bill passed narrowly and everyone recognized that a gauntlet had been dropped. The days of special interests were in jeopardy, at least for now.

Mac was as busy compiling vote charts and statistics as he was writing. His desk, previously filled with notes of news, articles, or research, now resembled an accountant's with spreadsheets of voting patterns. There were more Excel charts than Word documents.

Still, he found no smoking gun. Sure there was smoke; just no hand on the trigger.

President Watkins signed the bill and, following the lead of his Vice President, praised Congress for having the courage to delete the pork before handing it up to him.

The President said that the moneys for the brave men and women was less than had been requested; he therefore charged the oversight committee to ensure that every penny was accounted for in a meaningful way.

The telephone calls from a loyal cadre of Democrats were reported to be more than on any other subject in his seven years in office. That the Democratic loyalists were older was no surprise. They had been his contemporaries when he had been a senator. He was at a loss to explain, and they had a stubborn inability to understand.

Mac watched the news. The lead story, played again and again, was a voice recording, a leak from the White House, where a deprived pork barreler par excellence yelled down the phone, "It's not the American Way! It's not right. How are we to get these essential, narrow focus funds back to our constituents? It's expected! It's not even a lot of money."

"It was over a billion dollars," argued the President.

"Well, only one million was going to my state and it would have secured the vote two weeks earlier so that our brave men and women could continue to protect our country."

"Let me get this right, Bob. It's patriotic when we spend money that benefits your constituents but a big business boondoggle if it's not in an election year," the President said sarcastically.

"What the hell's the matter with you?"

"Just politics. After seven years at the White House it gets tiring. You have to be right one hundred percent of the time; once wrong and they have your head. I don't understand what happened any more that you do. You were there; you tell me."

"I don't know, Mr. President, I just don't know."

But Mac knew. Now in New Hampshire, he analyzed the data of the voting and added it to the voting patterns on his desk in his hotel room. The control was there; the bill could have been defeated.

The American people and the world had to be warned. He wrote an article stating the facts and, when he reached the conclusion, it was difficult, even for him, to show how it was a bad thing for the country to save a bunch of money on some of the proposed items. Mac realized that he was writing to an audience, a passive audience, who probably would not care. He reminded himself that Churchill had written and spoke of the threat from Germany for many years and was thought a crackpot. *Well,* he decided, *I'm not Churchill, but I might be a crackpot.*

He called Sue and left a message. When she returned his call he went outside with his cell phone. Even with a sheepskin coat and the phone pushed under his wool hat, it was cold outside.

"Sue, I've written a piece on the Black Bill. Can you put it in a London Newspaper?"

"I can have it in the Washington papers tomorrow. It's the talk of the world."

"Your world: Washington."

"Exactly."

"I want it in a London paper under a different name; then it can be sold to Washington if they wish."

"Mac, are you crazy?"

"Probably!"

"I have much more clout with your name."

"No. Use no name or the name of somebody already dead."

"Like who?"

"Winston Churchill!"

"A joke, right?"

"One I may explain someday."

"Send it. I'll try. You're looking good on television; everyone's impressed with the evenhanded coverage. Speaking of which, how's Helen?"

"Helen's fine, when I see her. Bye."

Mac went back to his room and sent the piece to Martin Konrad with instructions to hide the piece and deliver it to Susan Raymond.

Back outside it was quiet, not a sound. A quarter moon and a million stars looked bigger and brighter than he had ever seen. Was he alone on earth looking at the universe? Was someone in the universe looking down at him? Feeling bare, he let his thoughts wander where they may. Usually they went to Helen; tonight it was the papers on his desk.

Then he knew. It was clear. It was obvious.

It had been a test. But whose test? Someone on the list, or someone out there in the cosmos?

Chapter Fourteen

St. Anselm College was the traditional host of the debaters and the event was televised to ensure that not only the venue was sold out but that all of the voters of New Hampshire and the rest of the country would have a view of the competing candidates.

It was an exciting evening when the Republicans took the stage.

Earlier Mac had briefly interviewed each Republican candidate and these questions and comments preceded their introduction to the live audience. With the withdrawal of Carmel Fernandez and the inclusion of the Republican Senator from Maine just four candidates debated.

The pre-debate interview with Mac delineated their positions. It was clear that the Senator from Maine was hoping for lightning to strike a bus carrying the other three candidates as he had no foreign experience; he also sounded like his political ads: stilted. John Richards was warm and relaxed with Mac and talked of his strong belief in America and his ability to be a leader in the manufacturing of consumer goods based on a more isolationist model. Senator David Daigle had been second in a national poll but had slipped to third in a virtual tie with the Senator from Maine. Daigle had shrugged this off; it was clear that this was not a State in which he concentrated his time and effort. It would be interesting if he were the candidate for President how the voters might react with their long New England memories. He looked great tonight with his west coast tan.

Ellie May Joseph exuded confidence; she had been well received and was the leading Republican candidate. The role was reflected in the crowds at the events where she had appeared and also in the fundraising.

Mac was allowed to stand at the rear of the hall, next to the central camera crew, to watch the proceedings. He was making mental notes of the body language of the four candidates when he became aware that he had been joined by someone.

He turned to see the perfectly dressed Mark Hughes.

"Hello, Mark."

"Mac. What do you think? Are we looking at the next President of the U.S. of A?'

"I'm just a poor pundit, Mark, and I have to remain neutral. Where's your money?'

"Bull, Mac! You're more informed and closer to the election than anyone in the world."

"You flatter me, but then that comes naturally, with the job."

The two men shared more of a mutual dislike mixed with admiration for one another. Both, if asked, would have admitted that the other was the best person that they know at their particular job.

They were shushed into silence, but not before Mark had a chance to suggest, "Drink later at the Sports Bar in Manchester?"

Mac nodded and, watching Mark move on to another target, pondered the motive: was his relationship with Helen to be the topic?

The debate was friendly. Contenders attacked the front runner but not in a vicious spiteful way. As predicted, the Senator from Maine was ill at ease in discussing the foreign situation and completely botched a question on the Middle East by identifying Iraq, which had just been put on the 'watch list,' as the United States' strongest ally in the Middle East. To be fair, Mac considered, the allies and foes were constantly changing. It was also true that the latest change had not yet been clarified by the State Department.

David Daigle had produced a polished performance. There had been little new revealed, and it was clear that his policies were middle of the road and would be brought out over the summer. He was in for the long campaign and was saving his energy and ammunition.

The promise of John Richards to lower the tax rates was well received in a state known for having no income tax. Mac wondered how the Massachusetts newspapers would react to the proposals. There were also incentives hinted: a throwback to the failed incentive zones of the 1980s.

It was interesting how failed policies would reappear, repackaged and recharged, to a new generation. The idea presented anew also sounded as if it were designed for the particular audience. Why would someone out of work in the Northeast think themselves more worthy of a job than someone out of work in the South? How would an incentive like moving manufacturing away from its supply source, always aware of transportation costs, be beneficial? Mac determined that it was not likely to be policy anyway, just political posturing.

The debate ended without changing too many voters' positions. Mac was soon before the camera, giving his point of view after the studio announcer had recapped the debate for the viewers. Reflecting on the body language, his opinion was that only the Maine Senator had looked ill at ease and was the only one to have made a serious error. The studio had additional time and asked Mac to give some advance publicity to the coverage of the Democratic debate. Mac stated that he hoped the candidates would show the viewers more of their personality than the earlier debate had demonstrated.

The theatre at St. Anselm College had emptied quickly. The remaining people were reporters interviewing the candidates, happy to have secured a one on one conversation while the interviewees were in loquacious, positive moods.

Senator Daigle walked past and threw a look at Mac.

"No personality – it's not a Miss America pageant!"

Mac looked at Daigle's retreating back. How on earth did he know of the comment sent out just a few moments ago?

There was little time to speculate on the power of television and the speed of current technology before his cell phone rang. It was Helen.

"Hi, you looked good. The debate was great."

"It was ordinary," Mac replied.

"Well, that's just great for us then isn't it?"

"I suppose you couldn't do any worse."

"We can try," Helen said.

"To do worse?"

"According to my favorite television analyst, all we have to do is show a little personality."

Mac groaned audibly.

"We've recorded the debate and are reviewing the content for anything we might've missed, so we're working late. Will you miss me?" Helen asked.

"Actually, I've been invited out for a drink," Mac teased. "I may be late myself. By the way, skip through anything from Maine on those tapes."

"Is your date anyone I know?"

"Yes," said Mac.

"Anything I should be concerned about?"

"No, it's just business."

Helen was not satisfied with the answer but was being called from across the room.

The sports bar was relatively quiet. There were a few young people around the pool tables and there was a smaller group of four men talking while a basketball game was being shown on the large screen television in front of them. They seemed indifferent, except for the occasional glance to see the score.

Mark, although he did not fit into the scene, did not seem out of place. He was capable of adapting to a situation, of belonging. It was an ability that, had he chosen, would have made him the consummate politician. Was the difference in the amount of money that he earned, the rush that he felt from rubbing shoulders with those who were great and those who believed that they were great, or of having the ability to ask and pay for access and power?

Mac, as he walked across the room, removed his tie. This was definitely not a tie place, though he noticed that Mark had merely loosened his.

"Mac, this is Arabella. Arabella, Mac. Would you like a beer?"

"I just saw you on TV," the waitress stated. "What'll you have?"

Mac glanced across the choices. It was mostly local breweries with a few nationally known light beers.

"Old Thumper, draft, if you have it."

"Coming up," the waitress replied with a smile.

Mark commented, "Interesting choice."

"It's a Portland, Maine, brewery with an English beer recipe; it's brewed carefully and we're less than one hundred miles from the production line."

"You think the debate was dull?" Mark was smiling at Mac over what appeared to be a local lager.

"It was predictable," Mac responded.

"I suppose that you'll have the opportunity to put it right on Thursday before the Democrats speak."

"What did I say that was wrong?" asked Mac.

"First rule of American Television, never say anything negative, second rule always say something positive. I remember Nick Faldo when he was first reporting; he said something accurately describing an errant golf shot and was admonished. Fortunately he changed and is still providing insight, but I think that we lost something."

"Example?"

"Well, instead of implying that it was dull and boring, though true, you could've said that the Democrats will have the benefit of five candidates to bring added spice!"

"That's what I thought I said. But I have the feeling we're off topic. You wanted to talk to me before the debate began. Or did you figure I'd mess up and need a lesson or two?"

"I've been representing certain interests for many years."

"Lobbying, principally for the defense industry."

"Yes," agreed Mark without hesitation or embarrassment. "And I'm quite good at it."

"Although I may not agree with what you do or how, I do believe that you are," Mac answered. He was listening now with a heightened concentration, in spite of the fatigue brought on by the stress of appearing on a live broadcast.

Mark motioned to the waitress for two more beers and a bowl of snacks.

"We're equal opportunity contributors to political campaigns."

"Meaning that you don't care who wins as long as they've received and acknowledged support from your supporters."

"That's true, Mac; a little cynical, but true. The other function though, that we believe benefits everyone, is providing research and information to those members of the government who would like quick answers."

"Those answers may be a little biased."

"Actually no. It's in our best interest and for the running of the government to provide detailed, very accurate information. We don't answer personal questions, you understand."

Mark was coming slowly to the point of the meeting. Both men, by reflex, scanned the room for any changes in the personnel before Mark continued. "First, candidates have refused contributions. Secondly, candidates have refused to use the data provided, and thirdly, data has been subverted."

"Candidates have always refused contributions," said Mac. "And if the information is not pertinent then why is that a problem and what do you mean subverted?"

"The vote recently on the Bill with the liberal attachment of personal favors; the 'pork' bill also was amended to trim a good deal off of the defense budget."

"Your clients must have been annoyed."

"They were, but they'll get over it. What really hurt was that my clients provided a lot of research and gave a synopsis to the members of Congress. Some of the wording was changed and used in opposition to the Bill. And, the amount trimmed was exactly the amount of cushion built into the numbers. Who knew that? Who did that? My clients think that we leaked or that there is a mole in my administration. I've looked; there isn't."

Mac was not ready to share anything with Mark Hughes, certainly not if there could be a leak. He finished his beer and waved away the offer of another.

"Do you have any names, suspicions?"

"Arthur Anders led the opposition. He's refused any contribution, and therefore he wasn't on our distribution list."

"So even if it is Anders, he had help; there was collusion?"

"Yes."

"So what do you want from me?" asked Mac.

"I'm not sure. I need someone else to know. I need someone I can trust outside my own organization to give me independent input."

"Flattered, and I'll give it some thought. It sounds improbable, but that's what makes it sound serious."

"Very serious." Mark said. Mac could tell that Mark was nervous. "Very, very serious."

"Thanks for the beer. I've got to get going; see you Thursday for the next debate. It should be interesting, especially as Anders will be speaking. First time I'll have seen him."

"I thought you'd met and interviewed all of the candidates?"

"All but one," laughed Mac. "Goodnight."

Mac walked through the bar, casually looking around, aware that in the crowd someone might have been interested in his conversation. If he was still being followed, if this entire situation was real, he needed to be cautious.

Stepping outside, it was suddenly quiet. The noise of the bar disappeared with the closing of the door. It was cold and clear. Mac looked around; he was standing in the middle of the largest city in New Hampshire and, in that moment, there was only silence.

There was a late-night frost. As he turned, he heard a foot shuffle. Someone was standing in the corner to the right; his breath betraying his presence, the silence emphasizing his quiet vigil. In the distance a police car siren screamed while making its way to a crime or accident scene.

The mood had shifted from tranquility to disquiet. Why was someone there? Were they innocent and merely enjoying a cigarette, or were they watching? Who? Mac needed to think. No one knew he was going to be there except Mark. Were they watching Mark? Was Mark friend or foe?

Chapter Fifteen

The next day's newspapers vindicated Mac, somewhat. The debate was 'dull and predictable' stated most of them and the polls hardly changed. Even The Boston Globe had difficulty putting a positive spin on the evening.

Mac still underwent a criticism from his news desk for his negative remarks, but it lacked conviction. He was sitting reading the reports and wondering how reliable the polls could be when a debate ended at nine in the evening and the paper had to be completed, printed, and delivered by five. Reaching for his coffee with one hand, he picked up his ringing phone.

"Helen, how did you know I was just about to call?"

"Liar!"

"Honest. I was just sitting, eating my humble pie, and wondering who I should call with my troubles."

"So, you were just about to call Ann Gold."

Mac laughed. "That's very funny, especially for someone up all night trying to figure out how to top that riveting performance last night. Will you spend the day practicing humorous remarks or pithy comments?"

"None of the above. We're off to Laconia for a luncheon meeting, and then I'm free for the day. Thought that we might, you know, get reacquainted."

"Sorry, darling: gotta work," said Mac, genuinely disappointed. "I have to track down Anders before the debate."

"Two birds with a single shot! Anders is speaking in Meredith, at a church hall, five o'clock. I would like to see that meeting myself. Call his aide and see if you can interview him beforehand."

Mac made the call and was rebuffed by the aide. He was informed that the meeting, though sponsored by a group of organizations, was to be at a meeting hall converted from a church. Although he did his best to convince the aide on the merit of an interview, short of begging, Mac was denied.

Rejected but not dejected, he set out with Helen for Laconia. They discussed the strange happenings and resolved to attend Anders' political rally.

"It is atypical for a politician to give up free publicity," Helen stated.

"Unless one is breaking into Watergate."

"But even then, how would he have sold his memoirs?"

"By ending the Vietnamese War, going to China, and talking to David Frost."

"There is that," agreed Helen. "Why are you always right?" she asked sarcastically.

"Don't know; maybe that's my only fault!"

She laughed. Mac changed the subject.

"Write anything new for Marjorie today?"

"No."

"Why not?"

"Since we are democrats in a state with a republican state of mind, why should we shoot all our bullets?"

"You can't go into a debate asking questions. There must be a policy."

"There is, just not honed."

"So what's the plan?"

"Win New Hampshire by spending as little political capital as we have to. Take the delegates; make no enemies, then, when the losers drop out, they'll increase our count."

"Good plan. Sound. Did it take all night to figure that out?"

"Mac, are you Republican or Democrat?"

"Touché. As Bogart said in a movie. 'I am a citizen of the world'."

"I think that it was Captain Renaud speaking of Bogart as Richard Blaine in Casablanca."

"The point is," countered Mac, "that you know what I was saying."

"And that I am right," Helen retorted.

"That too."

They had lapsed into a comfortable banter. Both knew that the other's thoughts were not far from politics.

"I suppose," mused Mac "that made Richard Blaine a Centrist. Centrists elect presidents."Thinking for a few seconds, he added, "Usually."

"So how was your drink last night?" asked Helen.

"Cold."

"You know what I mean. Who….?" She stopped as Mac had a finger to his lips then tugged at his ear.

"A cold beer, then to a warm bed, alone."

The banter had gone and the balance of the trip was in near silence. Mac switched on the radio for the weather and news. According to the report, the temperature was seasonal, meaning that it was up to zero degrees Fahrenheit for a high with brilliant sunshine. The news headlined an ice fishing tournament.

In Laconia Helen went about her business: setting up photo opportunities with local politicians and financial backers; directing the television cameras to the optimum positions; and handing out briefings to the reporters. Mac wandered around.

The luncheon was well attended. Men and women arrived, barely distinguishable from each other due to the layers of warm clothing. It appeared as though those residents not into ice fishing were interested in leaving their homes and participating in life, despite weather which would have closed most of the other forty-nine States.

Mac had secured one of the media handouts and read a soft, vanilla report along party lines. That line was indistinguishable from the party line of the President. Marjorie White was still not her own candidate; she was still a product of the system. This was not quite true, but it was clearly the view that would be seen today. No surprises, no shocks.

Since the event was already being covered by the station he worked for, and since he was not getting paid to cover it, Mac went to an adjacent building and sat at the bar.

He figured that the hamburger he ate was probably an improvement on the campaign food next door. When the meeting concluded, Helen appeared. He wrapped up the notes that he was writing and stood up.

"Writing about Marjorie?"

"Yes."

"Anything nice?"

"No, not really," he said honestly. "Probably just as well; if she ever says anything that President Watkins hasn't said, it'll be news."

"Yes, it will," stated Helen with equanimity. "Shall we go?"

Dressed like the natives, they shuffled to the car and waited for the engine to warm a little before setting off.

"Successful?" Mac asked.

"Yes, a few more dollars raised, a few more citizens giving their views on education, gun laws, and taxation."

"Taxation? They don't have any."

"Of course they do. Real estate taxes are high, but they stay in town so that it is semi okay. But they're scared of a Federal VAT."

"A Value Added Tax would affect everyone."

"It might change the advantage New Hampshire has over those from Massachusetts."

"Does that make sense?"

"No, but it's a concern," Helen said looking around.

"Do you know where you're going?"

"Sort of." Mac stopped the car by the side of Lake Winnipesaukee.

"Let's walk," he said.

"In the cold?" she asked pulling her coat closer to her throat.

"Yes, it'll put color in your cheeks."

"And it's also likely to make my nose run."

Outside the air was crisp, but it did not feel as cold as some damp days where the temperature was fifty degrees higher.

Holding Helen close, Mac pointed across at the White Mountains and towards other landmarks, giving her facts about the area.

"How do you know all this?"

"My grandmother had a summer place here; we visited often."

"Where?"

"Just around the corner, on the lake shore."

"Can we see it?"

"No, it's probably under two feet of snow. My mother and uncle own it now, though they haven't been here for years." Then, changing the subject, Mac said, "I had a drink with Mark last night."

"Is that a secret? How is he?" asked Helen.

"He's great, misses you terribly," Mac teased. "Mark informed me that Anders refuses PAC money and that concerns him."

"I think that refusing PAC is admirable. He just went up in my estimation," said Helen.

"Maybe, but he has no obvious backers and does not come from a wealthy background."

"And he's not spending a lot on his campaign," argued Helen.

"True; he's also not giving interviews."

The sun had retreated behind the only cloud in the sky.

"Can we go back to the car now? It's getting colder."

"Yes, but we can't continue this conversation in the car."

Anders campaign meeting was not as well attended as Marjorie's. Whether due to the location, the time of day, the fact that there was no meal served, or that it was an indication of his place in the polls was open to speculation.

Mac opened his laptop and started making notes on his observations. Other reporters were speaking to the local politicians, some of whom had come directly from the earlier candidates meeting. There had been no handouts and there was very little political literature. The room had been set out with a podium placed away from the audience, giving an impression of distance in contrast to the town meeting style favored by most of the other candidates. Mac noted these observations together with a description of Anders style of dress: Casual, like the crowd, but smart, like an out of towner.

Helen had gone over to talk to the other reporters which Mac thought was a bit mischievous.

The local participants were introduced as they entered and Helen slipped into a chair beside Mac at the end of one of the rows.

While the local sponsor spoke and introduced some of the audience, Mac visually examined the candidate. Anders was taller and thinner than he had expected, dressed in a dark blue blazer, grey slacks, and a plain shirt and tie.

Helen pulled his arm to emphasize that there was a reason to look where her eyes were directed. To the side of the speakers a man stood. Helen's eyes scanned left. To the other side, a man stood. What was he supposed to be looking at? The man was large and now looking at Mac.

It appeared that all of the congregations from the surrounding communities were represented and each was acknowledged. Mac wrote down that perhaps Anders campaign was being funded by grass roots religious organizations.

Finally the speaker introduced Arthur Anders as a man who could stand up to big business and bring back values which had been the basis of the American experiment.

Anders stood to polite applause, acknowledged the speaker and thanked the local congregation for their support.

"Ladies and gentlemen of New Hampshire, my message today is simple. When elected I shall balance the budget, reduce the deficit, and bring our men and women fighting overseas home."

For the next forty-eight minutes he expanded on the basic theme. Big business was the means of bringing in the tax dollars and a substantial reduction in military spending was the means of balancing the budget. The speech was delivered in a self-depreciating manner as if he were talking up to the audience. It was clever as there was no forced humor; there was an amateurish delivery which had been carefully polished. Only people who listened to speeches for a living would have seen the skill necessary to deliver the message without changing the tone from beginning to end.

The applause was positive, different now from the tentative applause at the introduction.

"Questions?"

An older woman in the middle stood up.

"Did you say that you would be bringing my boy home?"

"Yes, ma'am. It is my intention to bring back all of our soldiers, airman, and sailors. What is your son's name and where is he?"

"Tommy Stitt. Sergeant Tommy Stitt in the Middle East."

"Sergeant Tommy Stitt will be home in New Hampshire the day after I am in the White House."

Mrs. Stitt and son Tommy were destined to be front page news, tomorrow, judging by the scratching of pencils and tapping of keyboards.

"What about crime? It's rising everywhere, especially here in New Hampshire," a middle aged man asked. Clearly he had been reading the local police blotter and had obviously not looked at the police reports from Boston, New York, Chicago, or San Francisco, where real crime was climbing. New Hampshire was a place where the doors were still unlocked; the crime was usually domestic or traffic related and influenced by alcohol and drugs.

"When the troops come home to protect their own neighbors, then we'll see a dramatic reduction in crime and swift retribution to any perpetrators."

Mac frowned; he had heard that somewhere before.

"I think that you should stop all of them foreigners coming in and taking our jobs," a man in his thirties with bare arms and a baseball cap said.

"Thank you."

The man was on his feet again. Overweight and underdressed for the weather, he was getting red from his bulbous neck upwards.

"So, what do you say? Just 'thank you'!"

"I was not aware that you had asked a question."

The man bellowed, started towards the podium, then, seeing a large man with his hand reaching inside his jacket for a gun, turned and left the hall.

Anders watched in a detached manner.

"Thank you, ladies and gentleman. I hope that I can count on your support next week as I look forward to serving you all as the next President of the United States.

"Well," Mac commented.

"Well, what?"

"Well, director of media relations, what do you make of that?"

"Extraordinary. He pissed off a voter for no good reason."

"Um, but he worked for Mrs. Stitt's vote."

"Mrs. Stitt and all the little Stitts."

Later they stopped and enjoyed a quiet dinner at a local restaurant called the Lyon's Den. They were seated by a window with a view of the frozen lake and twinkling lights in the distance.

"What was that nudge for, when Anders started to speak?" asked Mac.

"Those men working as Anders's bodyguards – there's no way they're part of the secret service typically assigned to each of the candidates."

"I saw two men, one looked vaguely familiar."

"They were both at Marjorie's luncheon," Helen said softly.

"I didn't go to the luncheon."

"And then they were at Anders's speech. They were also both in the car that followed us from Manchester."

"You're right," Mac said."Now I remember seeing one walk past the bar as I was eating my burger."

Helen said, "One other thing I noticed that's odd: No women; all of his staff are men."

Chapter Sixteen

The New Hampshire Democratic debate was more interesting than its counterpart, and there were a bunch of changes in strategy. Mac was generous to all of the candidates in his description of the talents they brought to the evening. Marjorie stopped asking questions and gave answers. Anders chose not to chase away any votes on national television.

William Ward of Indiana and William Cook, the Attorney General for the U.S., were both strong candidates.

It was easy to confuse the two Bills as they were both political fighters from strong backgrounds. Bill Ward was a former Governor of Indiana, a Notre Dame football player, and a graduate who had worked the family business right into politics. He had a five star resume. A strong debater, he sounded and acted like a president. It was no secret and not a surprise that he was a disciple of John Kennedy who he had met back in 1960 when he was a small boy.

William Cook was Ivy League: Harvard Law School from a line of attorneys. He had gone the route of working in the Federal Prosecutor's Office in New York, prosecuting some high profile mobsters and embezzlers from Wall Street with success. Bright, hardworking, and fearless, he had been U.S. Attorney General for seven years and was still only forty-one.

He was also a great orator, and it was no surprise that he was tough on crime.

After each candidate had given an opening statement which earned moderate applause, it was time for specific questions. Mac determined that it was impossible to gauge any advantage at this point. Marjorie had defended the good ideas of President Watkins and ignored the bad. The three opposing candidates had attacked her, since she was still the front runner. They distanced themselves from any previous involvement in the bad decisions while ignoring the good.

The first question on foreign policy had Marjorie with a clear advantage since she had visited all of America's allies in the last year. Bill Ward was less certain in his answer. William Cook spoke of reviewing foreign aid to countries with poor civil rights records and the commitment to NATO and the U.N. which he claimed was a popularity contest with the United States being a convenient 'whipping boy'. Arthur Anders condemned all foreign aid, allies, and pseudo-allies as either corrupt or unimpeachable. He continued his pledge to bring home all American troops. Since the other candidates had pledged to drastically reduce the troop deployment, he ridiculed them as being no different from three previous Presidents who, having made the same pledge, had increased the numbers abroad by the end of their term.

The question on domestic policy was a plus for Bill Ward who stated that he would profit and grow American industry and have less reliance on imports.

The last question was immigration, and the television cameras focused on Arthur Anders as he listened to the moderator.

Speaking first, Anders said that to exclude immigrants and ask them to return to their home countries would empty the auditorium, since America was founded on immigrants from all over the world. There was no test to take at the gate. It was a masterpiece; well-rehearsed and brilliantly delivered.

Bill Ward said enough was enough; Americans, born in this country should be able to find work. William Cook spoke of legally enforceable quotas, with minimum education requirements, so as not to burden social services. Marjorie White took the party line that properly documented immigrants were always welcome; illegal immigrants must be found and, after due process, deported.

A closing statement from each encouraged the good people of New Hampshire to cast their vote wisely.

Mac was having his appearance checked before giving his expert analysis when Helen appeared.

"That was a freaking disaster!" she fumed.

"Interesting though."

"Bill Ward pushes the domestic buttons, Bill Cook wants to legislate the world, and Anders wants the world to self-destruct."

"Remember: 'the centrist gets the vote'."

"Pig," she snarled as she left, bumping into the producer who was coming for Mac.

"Did I miss something?"

"No," Mac said.

"No," said the makeup lady, smiling.

Mac's summary was complimentary to all and he was able to deflect when asked from the studio if there were any knock out punches or faux pas.

"The candidates were all polished. There are different opinions even within the party, and those opinions may change over the next six months.

Marjorie White is still the front runner, and the other candidates made no mistakes that I saw, nor did they change their campaign strategies."

"Thank you, Mac," the news anchor stated."That was Matthew McDougal reporting live from New Hampshire." Mac remained seated until he was signaled that he was all clear by the producer.

Mac knew Helen was going to be busy with the rerunning of the debate, so when Mark Hughes gave him a signal that they should have a drink, he nodded, and then headed for the dressing room to clean up.

Mark was chipper. The bar was busier, perhaps because the Boston Bruins game was playing. In addition to the pool players there were at least ten people gathered together watching the game and sharing pitchers of beer.

"Good show tonight."

"A bit better," agreed Mac.

"Has Anders any chance?"

"Why, bad for business?"

"Yes, I mean you have to love Bill Ward, all those union jobs, and Cook with his legalize the world. Even Marjorie, Ms. Status quo!"

"Is it always about the money, Mark?"

"When someone says it's not the money, remember it's always the money."

"According to your theory, Marjorie wins, Cook second, Ward third, and Anders last. So why are you concerned?"

"Aren't you?"

"Yes," whispered Mac, involuntarily looking around the room.

The run-up to Election Day was hectic. Candidates were crisscrossing the state, often passing each other on their way to interviews, meetings, and fundraising.

Helen was at the White headquarters most of the time, arranging and juggling appointments for the candidate, providing and orchestrating photo opportunities. She was also looking to the next campaign, the other states, assessing their significance and the ability to provide votes and, just as important, money.

Mac found himself in great demand as he had shown a fresh face with impartial opinions. His articles were being prominently shown, and he was inundated with requests to appear on local and national political shows. Using Sue Raymond as a buffer, he chose carefully those shows where he appeared; deciding only after the other guests had been reviewed for potential traps to his impartiality. The day of the election he was on stand-by all day for up to the minute, on the scene, comments.

The voting was orderly, though there was a lower turnout than anticipated due to a winter storm delivering nine inches of snow. The candidates offering transportation to the polls were busy even though the voters, showing typical independence, often voted for a different candidate.

"Will the weather make a difference?" the anchor desk asked again.

"Not if you are declared a winner," said Mac. *Could the questions get more stupid?* he thought.

Mac then heard the studio personality in his earpiece saying, "Sometime after the polls close at 8pm, we should start some indication of the people's choice."

Mac decided that it was time he put some sense back into this report. "The winner here is only a fraction of the votes needed to carry the convention and, ultimately, the party's flag. The importance here is money; a winner can expect an easier time collecting donations and pledges than a loser."

"It's said that Ellie May Joseph has four hundred thousand dollars in pledges and Marjorie White even more," the studio anchor stated.

"These are pledges, and a poor showing, even a winner may see some of their support evaporate."

"So New Hampshire plays a key role." It was a self important statement. "Thank you, Matthew McDougal, reporting live from the voting scene."

Mac walked back to an area away from the commotion and called Helen.

"Hi. How's it going?"

"Oh, Mac; what a disaster. The voters are staying away in droves, twenty-five percent down from four years ago."

"Thank goodness they're all Republicans," said Mac.

"It's not funny!"

"No, but you are. Relax. If your candidate is the one, then all of her supporters will have voted."

"Got to go!"

"See you in Iowa, or Kentucky, or…" Mac said to a dead phone.

The results followed the polls, and the next day Ellie May Joseph and Marjorie White were declared winners by substantial margins.

The final voting and delegate count read in the papers as votes, percentages, and delegates. Ellie May led the Republicans with 115,941 votes; her closest competition was John Richards who lagged far behind with 50,792. Daigle, Clark, and others made up the remaining votes. Marjorie White led the Democrats with 70,798, followed by William Cook with 27,746, then Anders, Ward, and others.

The coverage and subsequent interviews were predictable. Ellie May Joseph spoke as though already elected. Daigle pointed out that he was a long way from his base on the West Coast. This was true, but he was shaken by the third place showing. Robert Clarke bowed out of the race and went home to Maine, richer in funds and experience.

Marjorie White was more cautious. The voters liked her, but the other three contenders had split the vote. There were no drop outs, and they were all coming for her. William Cook spoke of his long term commitments and Bill Ward promised to do better in states where the labor unions were important. Anders declined to speak and a spokesman said that he had left New Hampshire the morning of the election.

The summer passed quickly. Candidates were crisscrossing the country in efforts to gain votes, delegates, and money; sometimes in that order, sometimes not. The media followed behind them, in front of them, and sometimes alongside. Mac and Helen crossed each other as Mac became media darling, thanks largely to the producers recognizing the women viewers as serious voters. The airports blurred, the television studios faded into one another, and the food eaten while standing, waiting, flying, driving all blended to become indistinguishable. Mac noted to himself that if he never had another piece of pizza, it would be okay.

It was tiring. No: it was exhausting. He was glad to finally have a few days home.

Sue was lounging across a large chair in Mac's living room. "You look like shit!"

"Thanks. Did I need that?"

"You look much better on television."

"The magic of makeup," Mac said.

"So how long are you in town for?"

"Just long enough to get some clean shirts, pay my bills."

"They have laundries at hotels, you know."

"Well they don't do socks."

"Hmm. While you are home, get some sleep."

"I would if people would get out of my favorite chair."

"You really look like hell. How's Helen?"

"Think I look bad, she's worse. Marjorie looks great, so does Ellie May; they're thriving on the campaign trails. I'm home until the conventions start, so I can catch up on my life and also check the heartbeat of the country from a little way off the firing line."

Mac had requested that he be replaced for a few weeks.

"Well, it's a two horse race in the Republican ring. JR dropped out today. He's undecided who to back," Sue said.

"Probably waiting to see if either Ellie May or Daigle need a running mate."

"I'd hate to be running mate with Ellie May. She wears blue jeans and packs a .45 I hear," Sue said with a grin.

"It's a Smith and Wesson 32," said Mac laughing.

"How's the book coming along?" Sue asked. Mac was annoyed, realizing that her visit had not been social.

"I've been working hard on it during my lonely nights and days. The conventions and actual election coverage will be half the book, but the other half is ready for editing."

"Can I take it?"

"Sure, let me download a copy."

Mac downloaded the memory stick and thought of the other file which he had hidden. He needed to update the secret file, though there was less to add than he had imagined. Here in Washington he could tie up some loose ends and try again to find the key.

He could not help but wonder, *Where is this going?*

Chapter Seventeen

On the way back to Washington Mac decided to stop overnight in Boston to visit with his friend Sean from college. They went to the No Name Restaurant where they had fresh scrod, after clam chowder, and then strolled to the North End for coffee and dessert. It was quickly familiar and, since the night was warm, they walked through the Boston Public Gardens and the Boston Common. Although there was crime, as in most big cities in the world, there was something surreal about walking paths lit by the old style lights under the golden dome of the State House. If the lights were still lit by gas, then it could have been 1900; if there had been livestock feeding, 1800; only the intrusion of the twenty-first century automobile, punctuated by the sirens of police cars, fire trucks, and ambulances, gave clues to the present.

Talk, as it always did, turned to politics.

"The new governor seems to be doing well," Sean commented.

"Without direction from the Democratic Brahmins?" asked Mac.

"In spite of, I would say."

"What's the end game?"

"What do you mean?" asked Sean.

"Governor for life? Senator? Back to the bosom of his family, or some cushy role with another pension?"

"Hm," Sean murmured, "tough to gauge. No obvious friends, except your Mr. Anders of course."

In replaying his visit to Boston, Mac played this remark over and over. Governor Flores had not raised funds. He had not used the political machine, which was a fact of Massachusetts politics - had been since John Hancock and friends in 1774 decided to have a tea party.

So Governor Flores of Massachusetts and Senator Anders not only knew each other but were friends. Friends, associates, accomplices? Reporter instinct asked, when, where, and why.

The next day, sitting in his office, Mac took the two biographies and compared age, parents, early childhood, schooling. Then he went deeper: major, criminal records, marriage, children, occupation. There was nothing in common. Nothing!

Anders was five years older. He had been an average student who graduated in the top ten of his class in Naples, Florida, then earned a scholarship to Florida State, Law School. After that he worked in a regional office of a large law firm, where he did not make partner, and then he ran for Senate.

Flores was from Boston's North End and was the youngest of five children. His father was an accountant in the city and sent the kids to Boston University, his own alma mater. Flores had graduated with an accounting degree and had worked for the state where he joined no unions. He attended night school at Suffolk Law and had earned a certificate which he had not used, choosing not to take the bar examination. He was married with two children and lived in Charlestown.

Mac found nothing that explained where they met. Anders did not make partner in a law firm, and Flores did not take the bar examination. There had to be some connection, but what?

He needed answers, but not from his apartment which he suspected was still bugged. Time for a walk.

Mac walked to The Capital Grille and, out of habit, looked into the bar. He was happy to see Ann Gold gleaning tidbits from a junior senator. Seeing Mac, she detached herself and headed toward him.

"Mac, you naughty boy not telling me you were in town."

"Ann, I just got in and came right over." Mac could play the beltway backslapping with the best.

"Dinner, I insist on paying. Is Helen with you?"

"No, Ann, you're in luck. It'll just be the two of us."

"I'll just settle my bar bill."

"Ann, who was the reporter friend you had at the Boston Globe?"

"You mean Virginia?"

"Do you have her number?"

"Right here on my phone." Ann fished it out of her bag and started scrolling. "Virginia. Yes, here it is."

"Would you call her for me?"

"Now?"

"Well, yes."

"Okay," Ann responded, looking somewhat baffled. But her inquisitive nature kicked in. She waved her charge card at the bartender, intent on not missing a word.

"Virginia, this is Ann Gold."

Mac could clearly hear both sides of the conversation as Virginia responded, "Ann, good to hear from you. Anything happening? I'm stuck in traffic heading out of the city."

"Well there seems to be a presidential election, but I think that we can sleep through the formalities. Don't you?"

"Looks that way. What can I do for you?"

"Actually a great hunk of a man wants to talk to you. You've probably seen him reporting on the primaries: Mac- Matthew McDougal."

"Does he look as good in person?"

"Usually, but tonight he looks like shit. I've taken pity and invited him to dinner. Would you talk to him for a minute?"

"Might as well since I'm stuck on the Southeast Expressway with two million of my closest friends."

Ann passed the phone to Mac.

"Hi, Virginia. Good of you to talk to me."

"No problem. How can I help?"

"Frank Flores; can you comment on why did he not take the bar exam?"

"Frank Flores," she ruminated. "Doing a good job. A bit of a surprise for a hack; no visible baggage."

"What about the Bar?'

"Said that he was busy."

"Was he?"

"Working for the state?" she stated rhetorically.

"Then there's no explanation?" Mac asked.

"Not that I know. Maybe next time I see him I can ask what he was doing that was so much more important. I can let you know."

"No." Mac spoke more sharply than he had intended. "It's okay. Next time I'm in Boston I'll buy you a drink."

"Can I wait that long?"

"The Democratic Convention is in two weeks. Maybe we can meet then. Thanks, Virginia."

Mac handed the phone back to Ann.

"You all right?" she asked.

"Fine."

"What's Flores got to do with your book on the election? And why is taking the Bar such a big deal?"

They started walking towards the dining room. Mac turned suddenly, as if he had sensed a presence; there was no one there. No one who seemed out of place anyway. Where had that feeling come from? People talked of ghosts, but he did not believe in paranormal. The supernatural and alien abductions belonged in comic books. The tingling at the back of his neck had a perfectly good explanation, he just could not explain it at the moment.

He was aware that Ann had been talking and he had no idea except that apparently his response had been the wrong one.

"Are you having a gin and tonic with me?" Ann asked.

"Hell no! A draft beer please."

"Mac, you were miles away. Not like you at all. Want to tell me all about it?"

"No, not yet. It may be dangerous," said Mac in a quiet voice.

"You're scaring me." Ann, though, was laughing. "What game are you playing?"

"I'm serious. A lot of people have been hurt in this campaign."

Ann frowned and then said, "Okay then. Let's get some dinner before I lose my appetite. Do you know yet what you'd like to order?"

"Anything sounds better than pizza, or pizza, or pizza."

The meal came and they chatted about local events, people, liaisons – both personal and professional. Mac was finally relaxing. Ann was entertaining, and her profession meant that she constantly scanned the room, giving Mac the opportunity to do the same.

"What has the Governor of Massachusetts to do with the presidential campaign?" Ann asked over an after-dinner cocktail.

"Why do you think he has anything to do with it?"

"Do you always answer a question with a question?" Ann was finishing her dessert. "You're writing a book on the campaign; you have lived and breathed the campaign for six months, and the only question you have is about Francis Flores, friend of Arthur Anders. So what does that mean?" asked Ann.

"I don't know." Mac looked at her and then focused on his coffee. The tension was so thick that neither said anything.

Ann Gold broke the silence. "John Richards dropped out."

"Yes, I'll try to see him tomorrow. Thanks for dinner. I'm tired and promised Sue that I'd catch up on my sleep." Mac stood to leave.

"You're welcome, Mac. Get a good rest; you definitely need it."

"Thanks! Good night."

Mac woke the next morning and looked at the clock: nine-thirty. He had tossed and turned for hours before finally falling asleep. Now he lay there wondering if it had been the steak dinner, or the uneasy feeling that he had been watched, or something else. When he got home his apartment felt like it had been searched. Was that it? The invasion of his space? It was all of those things and also the intuition that he might have missed something Ann had said, or Virginia, or something in the resume.

In the shower, Mac planned out his day. His thoughts were so preoccupied that he could not remember washing his legs and did them again. He would call J.R. and Helen, not necessarily in that order, then he would make an appointment with Martin Konrad to sweep his apartment and check out his car for bugs.

When he spoke with Helen, she seemed crotchety. He hoped that she was missing him, but a more likely factor was simple fatigue.

It had been a grind: initially exciting, then routine with the occasional flash of scandal or the clarification of a misinterpreted gaffe. Now it was tedious. Helen admitted to Mac that the routine was getting to her: she was having to look at the hotel stationary to remember the name of the town, look up the names of the local reporters, set up the same interview parameters, issue the same communiqué in different words. She was exhausted and stressed. The problem was that the convention was coming up and then work began again on the final push to November.

John Richards, in contrast, was happy to hear from Mac and started to tell him of his decision to end his campaign, until Mac stopped him in mid-sentence and suggested that they meet someplace for a bite to eat.

At Paula's Restaurant, they both ordered coffee and both resisted the temptations of breakfast, despite the aromas emanating from the grill.

After preliminary conversation, where they both exaggerated how well each looked but genuinely spoke of the pleasure of seeing each other, J.R., with a glance around, turned to the discussion of his withdrawal.

"I thought I was doing well."

"You were hanging in there," admitted Mac. "I think that the incentive zone proposal was a weak link."

"It is, it was, but unemployment is a big issue. It's a big urban issue. If we don't solve it, we could have riots in the streets. Here's my theory: if we have full employment then we can lower the tax rate, money spent on unemployment benefits can be better spent on job incentives."

"Nice theory," said Mac. "A vote getter!"

"Yeah, I was doing well, raising money, mayors around the country were supporting my campaign. I asked them what they would do with the money. Nothing new: the scheme would fail like the last time without innovative thinking."

"Last time, as I remember, firms hired a straw from the incentive zone, grabbed the incentive money, and nothing changed. No new jobs, or damn few," Mac said.

"I had some other thoughts but was saving them for when I had the nomination," said J.R.

"But you dropped out," Mac said after swallowing some coffee.

"Yes, I dropped out." J.R. looked around the restaurant, which was almost empty, before continuing.

"Once upon a time I could drink with the best of them. Whiskey, bourbon, vodka, gin, martinis, sours. I never met a drink that I didn't like. Then one day, or night really, a young man with a casual comment changed my life. Thank you."

"Me?"

"Yes, you, Mac. When you had me leave that reception that night, I hadn't realized that I had become an alcoholic. The newspapers the next day were confused by my departure. How could a drunken clown run for Congress, let alone the Presidency?" He paused."I haven't had a drink since then, almost a year and a half."

"That doesn't explain why you dropped out of the race."

"No," he spoke reflectively, wondering perhaps how much he could trust a member of the press corps."I owe you, above all, an explanation. As you know, it's hard on the campaign trail. I was in Florida, very hot, very tired. After meeting a civic group, my driver was missing so I decided to drive myself back to the Registry in Naples. Going through Estero on Route 41 I blacked out. When I recovered, there was a familiar smell. It was alcohol. The car had somehow come to a stop with no damage. The police, however, were there taking pictures, taking notes. A witness said that it smelled as though I had been drinking in the middle of the day. The policeman showed me the police report and asked that I sign, then said that his companion would drive me to my hotel. The man who drove me said that there would be a warning issued since there had been no damage."

"Did you tell them where you were staying?" Mac asked.

"I must have since they drove directly there."

"Did you have a drink when you left the reception?"

"The valet gave me a bottle of water."

"Was the bottle still in the car the next day?"

"I don't remember."

"One other thing," said Mac, "where was your driver?"

"In the restaurant; he was told that I'd be another hour."

"You were forced out of the presidential race."

"So you believe my story?"

"Oh, yes. You were set up by professionals; I think you were lucky not to be hurt or killed, or that you didn't hurt or kill someone else."

"Who would do such a thing?'

"Very ruthless people. Very, very ruthless people who were afraid that you might have enough votes to be the Republican challenger."

"Ellie May Joseph?"

"No. She may be a lot of things that you don't like, but she wouldn't do this."

"How can you be so sure?"

"Because…" Now it was Mac's turn to look around the restaurant. "whoever is behind these attacks targets both Republicans and Democrats for the House and Senate. I suspect that you'll be receiving a reminder notice of this event before your Congressional campaign."

"Who are they?"

"I don't know," Mac said as he placed his cup back on its saucer.

"What can I do?"

Mac shook his head, looked around the room, then looked directly into the eyes of J.R. "Not sure. Anyone who tries to expose them dies."

"You're joking, right?" J.R. gave a nervous laugh.

"No," Mac said. "I wish I was."

Chapter Eighteen

Mac walked to the closest subway station where he knew there would be payphones and people. "Ann, would you do me a favor?" Mac had been thinking about alternatives for J.R. that would not get either of them dead.

"Anything for you, sweetheart. Just say you'll be mine."

"Ah, that I could," said Mac in a matching jocular manner.

"Maybe I have a chance now that the delectable Helen appears to have gone over to the dark side," Ann teased.

Mac understood the reference, and he had also heard that Helen had been dining with Mark Hughes. It was true that he had not spoken to Helen for a week and they had not seen each other in more than two weeks. But that was the decision each had made in pursuing their separate careers. "Do you believe everything you read in the papers?"

"Touché, dear boy. What can I do for you?"

"Actually for Congressman John Richards."

"Your lost cause célèbre?"

"You remember that night?"

"I remember because I thought I had an article and because I had to pay the photographer even though he was too late to take a picture," Ann said in mock scold.

"Sorry. But that night changed things. He hasn't had a drink since."

"Not what I heard," said Ann.

Mac sensed an interest in her tone and knew that she was sitting up and paying attention. It was nice to be on the inside."If you believe that he was drinking in Florida, it's not true. I'd like to take the high ground and say which Congressman has been without a drink for a year and a half and see who comes forward to challenge that assertion."

"That's all?"

"Just be careful, Ann!"

Next Mac called his television producer and had John Richards invited onto the network show. J.R. stated that he had not had an alcoholic drink for eighteen months and that he had lost thirty pounds. It was not exactly earth shattering, but J.R.'s idea to kick-start the economy and add to the work force by giving credits for physical manufacturing plants in urban areas was news. The idea was to provide immediate jobs in construction and a return to America's manufacturing years, taking jobs back from overseas. Detroit and Pittsburg were seen as immediate beneficiaries. He stated that he had every intention of running again for Congress and that he would introduce legislation for empowerment zones early next year. J.R. also stated that he would be attending the Republican convention in Las Vegas the following week.

Mac, doing his best to avoid the tourists and the casinos along the strip, took the opportunity to meet and have lunch with Hal, the bookie who gave him odds on the political races.

They were seated at an outdoor table at a hotel where Hal could smoke. There were very few people since it was close to one hundred degrees.

Both Mac and Hal ordered iced tea. Mac ordered a salad with blackened Ahi while Hal ordered *the usual* which turned out to be a Rueben sandwich with an order of fries.

When they were both settled, Mac asked, "How's business?"

"Gambling in general, this establishment, or the political book?"

"All three I guess," said Mac.

"Gambling is doing okay thanks to the slots. The hotel side is down: there aren't as many people travelling. People who come in for the day play the slots or small money roulette or blackjack. The cyber gambling is growing. People will bet on anything. We handle mostly sports: who will score the first basket, the first goal, the next goal. It's sometimes nuts. In England they were betting on who had designed a wedding dress. If that's not open to insider information, then I don't know what is. But then they busted a syndication which was paying off cricketers on when a 'no ball' would be bowled in a cricket match; crazy!"

"That sounds crazy," agreed Mac. "What about the political action?"

"U.S. or whether a certain dictator gets elected President for life?" laughed Hal, choking and coughing as the sudden rush of pure air entered his lungs.

Hal was a small man, thin with sunken cheeks and receding hair. Mac was contemplating Hal's age – he figured that he was about sixty and should be quite wealthy with the skim from several decades of high stakes gambling. Hal was dressed, like many of the citizens of Las Vegas, in dark slacks and a golf shirt which looked as though it had been passed down from a previous owner. He blended in; he was invisible.

"U.S." said Mac. "Do you know who is going to win?"

"Of course," said Hal. "The bookie!" the spasm of laughter and subsequent coughing were louder than previously.

"You know those things are killing you," Mac said, pointing at the cigarette in Hal's hand.

"Yeah, well it's better than dying of boredom."

"You must have enough to retire to a better climate, get out of the air-conditioning indoors, escape the gasoline fumes outside, the entire atmosphere which pervades Las Vegas."

"Mac, you're a good kid, but let me give you some pieces of advice: one, never count another man's money; two, never pay alimony to three ex-wives at the same time; three, don't have children as you'll only disappoint them."

Mac looked into the sad, defeated eyes and had to look away.

"So who's going to win?" asked Mac.

"The book doesn't care. But with the current odds, it's bizarre – strangest thing I've ever seen."

"How so?"

"Marjorie White should win: odds are nine to four. Ellie May Joseph may win: odds are eleven to four."

"Explain what the problem is."

"The book has to balance, or favor the bookie. There has to be vig, vigorish, a profit margin. If someone today takes eight dollars, four dollars each and bets

Marjorie White and Ellie May Joseph, then if White wins he gets nine dollars, a profit of one and if Joseph wins he gets eleven dollars, profit of three. A win either way. Now, say someone bets multiples of four, someone puts up eight million, then they win either one or three million dollars. It's happening."

"So you could lose a fortune," said Mac.

"No. We never lose."

"Then how do you balance?" asked Mac.

"Someone is betting, betting big that they'll lose."

"And the odds?"

"Three to two."

"Walk me through Marjorie White."

"Two people bet; one bets four dollars that she will win, the other six dollars that she'll lose; ten dollars in the pot. She wins we pay out, nine, she loses we pay out nine. We win."

"Who would do that?" Mac asked. He was thinking that he had to write it down to get a better understanding.

"Someone who thinks that the other candidate will win, someone who thinks that both will fail, or some professional doing a 'straddle'. Betting both sides as the odds change – very difficult, very chancy, very unlikely."

"So it's someone who thinks that she will lose."

"They; it's someone who thinks that they both will lose."

"Impossible," said Mac. "Big money?" he asked.

After an affirmative nod from Hal, Mac looked over his shoulder. The next question had to be asked even though the answer could be fatal to one or both of them.

"Who?"

"We don't know. money is wired from some rinky-dink internet bank. It's in cyberspace; except that the money is good."

"Could Homeland Security help? It may be laundered."

"It's laundered, but two things young man: its good money – balances the book, and brings in more money; and two, Homeland Security is never, never going to see my books!"

The bill came.

"Thanks, Hal, for the lesson. Glad to meet you finally. Take care of that cough." Mac leaned forward and whispered, "After the election and you've paid out, be very, very careful."

Hal left in a cloud of smoke. Nobody appeared to be interested. A woman walked by with two energetic children. A worker was checking the status of the rubbish bins, possibly to see if they were full or if they held bombs. His interest, in either case, mirrored the likely minimum wage that he was being paid.

The city was alive with political signs. Throngs of people roamed the streets and hallways of the hotels wearing hats, badges, jackets, and tee shirts, all declaring their affiliation, the states that they represented or called home. Flags proclaimed causes which the new order would champion – overhauling taxes, work programs to assist those on benefits, prolife, prochoice. It was chaotic in an orderly way. It was also noisy.

Mac was busy. Before the mayoral speeches, he was giving a synopsis of the day's events to the network news. It meant sometimes being available for the early news and sometimes for the later programs. The producer apparently had no concept of time zones; the fact that 6 am in New York was 3 am in Las Vegas was totally ignored.

By the time the main speeches were being given, Mac had changed his life to accommodate the will of the viewer and of his producer. He would speak to New York and Washington at 3 am, the West Coast at 6 am and then go to sleep until the evening news began on the East Coast. It was exhausting.

And it did not make for good communication with Helen. The fact that she had been seen with Mark Hughes did not help his disposition. Mac and Helen argued: she said that dinner was business; Mac agreed, but asked what kind of business. Both were on edge from lack of sleep and their demanding schedules.

The convention had very few surprises. The party line was adhered to as Ellie Mae Joseph was known to be ruthless with anyone springing surprises. Her choice of running mate, Paul Merrill of Massachusetts, was popular. He was an articulate, good looking, Yale graduate before joining his father's bank. He was chosen by a committee that interviewed ten candidates according to a press release. The truth, according to Ellie Mae's bodyguard driver Bobby, who Mac had joined at four am one morning for dinner, was that Ellie May said interview anyone you want, but get him.

They all looked great on the platform together. Looking relaxed, Paul Merrill's father, beaming in the wings, had been a major fundraiser for the Republican Party for years and it was clear that he was enjoying the fruits of that commitment. It was obvious that he was into his fantasy, the White House just a few months away.

There was no surprise that the Republicans jumped up in the polls. The blanket coverage by the networks, together with the charisma of the presidential hopeful and her running mate, gave them instant name recognition.

The entourage, now with its own jet plane headed to Boston. It was probably a lost state to Ellie May in November, but nothing could be discounted. A side trip to the other New England states could prove fruitful. That the Democratic Conference was going to be in Boston the following week was another reason to stress the alternatives.

Mac begged off and went back to Washington to work on his book and prepare for the Democrats.

Helen was on the West Coast with Marjorie White, who would make a grand entrance into Boston at the opportune moment.

Mac wanted and needed to talk to Helen. He needed to see her.

Chapter Nineteen

Boston was different but had not changed.

In examining this contradictory statement, Mac admitted, finally, that he had changed. Thinking about those days as a college student when he was not drinking, he was trying to get laid. Actually, even when he was drinking he was trying to get laid. If, in fact, his fantasies and his testosterone had been satisfied, there would have been no time for classes or for eating. So fortunately or unfortunately, his quests had frequently ended like those of Don Quixote, merely jousting at windmills.

The economy had changed too in the past fifteen or so years. It was clear that in order to make money, more was required than just advertising *best hamburger, pizza, fish, meat*, or whatever. There was a more professional air in the restaurants, and many of the places he had gone, had changed names and ownership. The old haunts did not change as much; a person could still be insulted in Durgin Park, get great seafood at the Union Oyster House, or sample delicious Italian cuisine in the North End.

Having the Democratic Convention descend was a windfall for all of the service industries. The moonlight cruises were filled with different delegations, drinking and singing their way around the harbor. The hotels were filled to capacity. And the stores in Faneuil Hall were bustling with souvenir shoppers.

Mac stayed at the Custom House. It was smaller, and it was expensive. But it was out of the mainstream; he decided that he had enough of the limelight during on-camera hours.

On the second day, as he stepped into the elevator going down, he was surprised to find Arthur Anders with 'Tweedle Dee and Tweedle Dum'.

"What are you doing here?" asked Anders.

"Good morning to you too," replied Mac.

"I will not answer any questions."

"So far the only question came from you. I'm staying here, as I am sure you would know if you asked either of the two gentlemen with you. Oh, I do have a question: are they with you?"

The elevator stopped at the ground floor. Anders marched through the door. The two bodyguards followed, but not before the silent one turned and looked at Mac, as though trying to memorize the face and the moment. Mac stared back.

Mac was pretty sure that the Florida delegation was not staying at the hotel, so why was Anders here? Was he staying there or was he visiting someone? Whichever, he came from a higher, meaning more expensive, floor.

"Morning, Mr. Mac."

"Morning, Henry. Cab please."

"Yes sir," he said before putting two fingers into his mouth to summon a taxi.

"Henry, those men who just left, are they staying here?"

"Small guy is; two other guys just pulled up in a big limo five minutes ago."

"Thanks," said Mac, giving him a folded bill from his wallet.

"They don't say much, and they don't tip none."

Mac was an investigative newspaper man, so the next question was out of his mouth before he realized it.

"Anybody else friendly with the small guy?"

Before Henry could reply the cabby interrupted.

"We taking a ride or having a debate?"

Henry was a tall black man. Mac figured that he had probably played basketball at high school but was not quite good enough for college. Henry did not appear well educated, but he did not lack confidence. Mac was impressed with how he handled things.

"We're having a conversation," Henry said to the taxi driver, "and you wouldn't recognize that since nobody wants to talk to you."He turned back to Mac. "No, but those big guys have been here before."

"Thanks, Henry. See you later."

"Convention Center, please," Mac said as he slid into the cab's back seat.

"Okay, boss. Hey, haven't I seen you on the television?"

"I doubt it; I do the news."

The man laughed. "That was funny. I watch the news – see how the Red Sox done."

It was Mac's turn to laugh.

"How's business?"

"Pretty good with the Convention in town, otherwise tough to make a living. A lot of immigrants got a license; got a cab, work eighteen, twenty hours a day. They do it to learn English. Give me a fucking break! How can you give directions to someone who can't understand you? The Convention's good. Thank goodness we got the Democrats, big tippers;

Republicans, well I guess that's why they got all the money." The cab stopped outside the main entrance.

"Thanks for the ride. What's your name? Can I use it and your comments?"

"It's Mike, Mike Curley. Sure, that means I have to watch the news tonight?"

"Why, the Red Sox playing?"

Mike Curley laughed. "Twelve dollars-fifty, boss."

Mac gave him fifteen and waved away the change.

Walking through the door, he showed his pass and gave his computer up to be examined. He was to meet with his producer and examine the layout so he could quickly get around during the speeches. There was a huge information desk set up just inside the door where there was a bustle of activity. On impulse Mac turned toward it where a bright young woman volunteer; who clearly recognized him, came forward.

"How can I help you?"

"Where's the Florida delegation staying?" asked Mac.

"Wait one moment, let me check," she said smiling. She flicked back her hair as she bent to a computer on the desk. Her badge, now revealed, said that she was Mandy.

"Cambridge, Holiday Inn."

"Thank you, Mandy. Mr. Anders one of their delegates?"

"Yes, he is," she said peering again at the screen, after flicking away the recalcitrant hair. "And," she whispered conspiratorially, "he's one of the keynote speakers."

"Thank you."

"You're welcome, Mr. McDougal. Have a nice day."

Mac waved a hand as he left the desk.

The producer was a woman whose age Mac could not quite determine. She wore no makeup and did nothing to enhance an admittedly dull appearance. Tall and emaciated, she looked as though her last meal had been a lettuce leaf three days ago and that it had left her constipated. She quickly went through the walk about. It was clear that there was only one chance to see it all, that questions were unwelcome, and humor was forbidden. She was good at her job, efficient and orderly. Though they had worked together before, she neither acknowledged the fact in a 'nice to see you again' fashion or in omitting any of the instructions. She frowned when Mac's cell phone rang, yet when her own phone sounded with a classical music tone; she turned and left him alone.

Mac retraced his steps in a more leisurely fashion and nodded at sound engineers, people erecting an enormous video screen, and dozens of important looking people with clipboards. It was relatively easy, but when the hall was full of people, he knew that the walking would be a lot more difficult. Stopping at a quieter spot, he retrieved his cell phone and checked his message. He was disappointed. Sue Raymond had checked his calendar and booked a panel on national television and two half-hour interviews with National Public Radio, out of Washington, of course.

The disappointment was his loneliness. He missed Helen; *she has no time for me, but she managed time for Mark*, he thought, petulantly, and he knew unnecessarily.

An early dinner followed by a walk around town, he decided would help him to relax. He could stop in at the usual haunts and gauge the mood of the conventioneers.

It was warm and humid when he wandered around Boston Common, the Public Gardens, and Beacon Hill. Families who had been out for the day were packing up and heading for the train stations or their cars. Commuters and late workers were walking purposefully for their transport home. Those living within walking distance and those taking the train wore sneakers, while carrying work shoes in bags or in briefcases.

Faneuil Hall Market was active and provided a warm after-work atmosphere. It was easy to spot those from out of town as they crowded into the larger areas and looked as if they did not know which direction to turn. They searched either for a familiar face or in wonder at the cosmopolitan crowd in this relatively small oasis.

Mac guessed, rightly, that the Florida contingent would be together in one of the cheaper places. The hunch was based on the train route into the city and the fact that they had opted for a less expensive hotel. He went to the bar, ordered and paid for his beer, and then walked over to the group.

It was easy to fall into conversation as his face, from the television coverage, was recognized immediately. A man and woman were in earnest conversation; the man was looking to arrange a more intimate midnight rendezvous; the woman seemed less enthusiastic. When the man addressed Mac, in a tone which indicated a friendship which did not exist, the woman took the opportunity to slither away.

"Hey, Mac, good to see you again; Norm Harrison," he said extending a big meaty hand.

"Norm, good to see you. How do you like Boston?"

"Great city – always liked it."

"Where in Florida do you live?"

"West Coast, Sarasota. You gonna quote me or something?"

"Why? Do you have something interesting to say?" Mac asked.

"This is going to be a landslide. Marjorie White is a shoe in."

"Everybody says that, Norm; that's not an original. What about your delegate Anders; I hear he's going to speak tomorrow."

"Don't know him."

"Norm, I bet you know everybody in this room; how can you not know your local senator, a presidential candidate, a mover and shaker?"

"I know a lot of people in this room," Norm laughed. "I know a lot *about* the people in this room, but Anders is a mystery."

"He's a delegate, so you must have met to strategize."

"He's staying with friends."

Mac did not enlighten him to the fact that Arthur Anders was in fact staying at a hotel, his hotel.

"Then he's not a team player?"

Norm snorted in reply.

"So who knows him, who is his money man, who is in his organization?"

"Never seen an organization; don't know his money. Emilio might know."

"Emilio Gonsalves?"

"You know him?" Norm was a little peeved.

"Met him once on a panel," said Mac trying to keep his source of information placated.

"Let me reintroduce you," said Norm, gaining some ground. "He's talking to Dot Gallaher, our treasurer."

"Thanks."

The room was crowded and very noisy. Emilio Gonsalves and Dot Gallaher had their heads very close together. Norm touched Emilio on the shoulder. The look on Emilio's face indicated that Norm's was not the face he wanted to see.

"Mac McDougal wanted to be introduced," said Norm, oblivious to the look he received, and nodding to his right.

The contrast could not have been more pronounced.

"Mac, how are you? Long time!"

Emilio Gonsalves seemed to have reached sixty and his appearance stayed there. Certainly over seventy, he was a respected political figure in Florida and known throughout the country.

"Dot Gallaher," he said, introducing an attractive, no nonsense, middle-aged woman. Dot wore no makeup and avoided Norm Harrison with a practiced ease.

"Mr. McDougal, a pleasure to meet you. I enjoy your balanced reporting on television and in your writing."

"Thank you. It's Mac, and I wasn't sure 'til now that anyone was reading my articles." Turning to Emilio he asked, "Can we go outside so that we can talk, unless we were interrupting you, in which case my apologies."

"Our conversation can wait," said Emilio. "It's a pleasure to be able to talk to someone with an unbiased view."

They pushed their way outside. The air felt softer and, even though they had left an air-conditioned room, the breeze was comfortable. Finding a curved bench they all sat within sight of each other.

"Because there is a slight lead in the polls, everyone believes that Marjorie White is a 'shoe in'." Dot was continuing the conversation that had started inside.

"If you don't believe your horse is a winner, why come to the race?" asked Mac.

"I don't imply that we shouldn't be here but that celebrations should wait until November. There's still a tremendous need to raise cash."

"Mac and I were talking about that," said Norm. "Either of you know where Anders got his money?"

Mac was happy that Norm had introduced the subject and allowed him to exaggerate a close, non-existent friendship. These two people knew Norm and his ilk.

"I told him that my friend Emilio would know if anyone did," Norm continued.

"The subject of fundraising is a regular topic, as you are aware," said Emilio. He was being careful; either he did not want to talk in front of Norm, or maybe in front of Mac, or maybe it was just a political non-speech. "The coffers of the Florida Democratic Party are depleted since our senator is never available for our fundraising events in spite of his national exposure."

"Someone should confront him; he has an obligation," Norm said indignantly.

"Knock yourself out," said Dot. "I write and call once a month without success."

"I will," Norm said with vigor.

"Be careful, Norm," said Mac.

The alcohol seemed to be affecting Norm who, after a long look at his empty glass, stood up.

"Another drink?"

Mac, Emilio, and Dot all shook their heads and said, "No thanks." Norm made his way back inside.

"He means well," Emilio said with a smile.

"He raises a lot of money in Sarasota," Dot added.

"They probably give him money to go away," said Emilio. "Dot and I were talking about money and Anders when you came up. I know that you're discreet, but you must recognize that this is a subject that we can't have broadcast, not even that we discuss it."

"I understand," said Mac. "As you know I have followed the campaign for a year and a half and Anders is different. He doesn't appear to raise money. He doesn't spend money on television or radio advertising. The publicity he receives from his positions of defense spending and troop withdrawals seem to be enough. He's the only candidate, other than Marjorie, not to have thrown in the towel."

"He has no chance," said Dot. "It's mathematically impossible."

"You know what they say about those with no hope who stay the course, 'that's why we play the game.'" Mac then added, "Why bother with a convention? As good as it is for the Boston economy, why are all the television, newspapers, and radio shows full of one thing only?"

"Mac, you are a great debater, but on this I have to agree with Dot; Marjorie White is a sure bet and is the favorite to be the first woman President."

"Emilio, you've been to a lot of conventions. I respect your opinion," Mac said sincerely.

"Ten conventions, no nine, I missed one after my wife died."

The conversation for the next half-hour was of the conventions that they remembered and the speeches, good and bad. Obama, Ted Kennedy, the Clintons, Dukakis.

After an hour of good-natured chat, they parted and went back to their respective hotels.

Mac was no nearer to any real information on the enigmatic Mr. Anders. Or was he? A process of elimination was telling him what the Senator was not, therefore that was progress.

Henry met him at the door.

"Your boys came back."

"All three?"

"No, just the big ones. They picked up a couple of people and headed to the airport."

"Logan?"

"No, it must be a private one. The talker called the pilot and said that they had to make a stop."

"Could it still be Logan?" Mac asked.

"I suppose," said Henry, sounding doubtful.

Chapter Twenty

The convention was loud. There was lots of laughter, the kind found in a poor situation comedy show: inappropriate, louder than necessary, confusing to all but the direct participants.

The information desk was mobbed with people picking up identity tags, and replacing lost or misplaced tags. Some were seeking information on places to stay or places to move to. Everyone was being politely directed; calls were made confirming times, places. Mandy caught Mac's eye as she looked up and, with a flick of her hair, gave him a little wave of recognition. He proceeded through the heightened security, allowing his laptop to be examined and then walking through the now accepted metal detector.

Area twelve was the television media section with a mini-studio and rooms to meet guests of the networks. A small food area at the end held a variety of snacks and drinks for the employees. Mac glanced and saw very little with nutritional value but a lot of sweets. It was as if someone thought that an industry driven by adrenaline, ego, and an overly developed sense of self-worth needed a sugar boost. He put a bottle of water in his pocket and picked up an apple.

Walking into 12-D, he was met with a hatchet face, stating, "I've been looking for you."

"Hazel, I could hardly have gotten lost with your excellent directions."

"I wanted to go over the itinerary."

"It's right here," Mac said, pointing to the screen of his computer. "Mayor of Boston, welcome to the city etc, Governor Flores, welcome to our budget booster etc. Press conference, after a while the speaker is the leader of the Congressional delegation from Texas. It's all here."

"Well you are live when we go to primetime coverage, but the network wants you to add a word to the six o'clock news. A 'What to expect tonight piece'. Okay?"

"Got it; taped or live?"

"Live, about six-fifteen, unless there's a weather situation."

"Key note tonight is Anders; do you have his speech?" Mac asked

"No, I do have the Mayor's and the Governor's." She pulled out a bunch of double-spaced sheets and handed them over.

"I've heard Anders story enough anyway. I'll go to the Governor's press conference and can comment on that too."

"Control room not later that five-thirty!"

"Yes, ma'am."

"I am not a ma'am!"

The opening speeches were predictable, as were the press conferences. This was the first day and everyone was still finding their way around. Governor Flores had mentioned that he would be back to introduce his good friend Arthur Anders.

Mac took the chance to put up his hand.

"How well do you know Senator Anders and where did you first meet?"

The Governor stopped smiling and glanced towards the rear door. Mac turned just in time to see a body duck out of sight.

"We're good friends. I think that I met him in Florida at a rally and we enjoyed a meal together." He looked fiercely at Mac. "Any other questions?"

"Yes," Mac said, knowing he was pushing his luck, "who paid for the meal?"

The question, which could have been answered jocularly, caused the Governor to blanch and turn away. He abruptly left the podium.

"What was all that about?" a woman whispered into Mac's ear. "Virginia Black, Boston Globe; we spoke a couple of weeks ago when you were with Ann Gold. You owe me a drink."

Mac laughed. "So I do; met me in 12-D after the wrap-up tonight."

Virginia Black was about fifty years old and spare. It looked as though she existed on cereal for breakfast and salad for lunch after a workout. With wiry straight hair, which she had obviously never colored, she emanated a no-nonsense air. There was no chit-chat, just business.

"See you then." She turned away and was gone.

Mac had less than two minutes. At six o'clock the network showed the Governor speaking, and then making the comment about his *good friend*. Mac used this as segue into the fact that the Governor would be back this evening to introduce Arthur Anders who was due to speak at about nine.

"It's expected that the Senator will cover some of those issues that were prominent in his run for the presidential nomination: reduction of troops serving abroad and reduced defense spending. The main thrust of his speech, however, should follow the party line to show solidarity with the likely candidate."

The studio anchor asked "Is there a chance that Senator Anders could be the Vice presidential nominee?"

"I would think it unlikely," said Mac. "Usually we see a running mate who complements the candidate geographically and mirrors the political positions."

"Thank you. We'll be speaking with Matthew McDougal later tonight, live, during our coverage of the Democratic Convention in Boston."

Arthur Anders, dressed in a pinstripe suit, light blue shirt, and a red tie, appeared completely relaxed. He spoke to Governor Flores and three other delegates as he took his place at the front of the hall. There were none of the usual pins or recognition of the Democrat's logo, none of the waving to his Florida delegate associates. He was received with some reserved applause. No hooting, no hollering.

He spoke as if he were making policy, as if, in January, his administration would be dictating the will of the people. It was high drama; it was received in silence. An hour later he was summarizing.

"The United States of America is insolvent; it cannot pay its bills as they become due. It is a pawn to those who it would oppose. Communist regimes, dictatorships, and hypocrites are its allies. Elected governments are routinely sanctioned, while others with sins and avarice are rewarded.

"We will bring home those troops serving abroad shoring up these communists, these dictatorships, and these hypocrites.

"The defense budget will be less than ten percent of what it is today. A loss of jobs, yes, but a country that can look the world in the eye and say that it did not, provide weapons to both sides of a war in order to prolong it.

"The borders will be open to all who wish to live here. Anyone can apply for citizenship, with the right to vote and participate in the great progress that I expect to see.

"The welfare system will be reformed and provide for only the people who have a genuine need, not a self-imposed need. Those choosing not to work will no longer be provided a safety net.

"With these changes, the budget will be balanced and a surplus generated to make this great country great again.

"Thank you and good night."

There was a smattering of polite applause as he left the stage. Everyone was in a state of shock and, as television employees lost control, the glitches multiplied.

An anchor, unaware that he had been 'miked' and was on camera, gave the global internet a bite which travelled around the world in less than half an hour.

"What the fuck was that about?" he asked a startled audience.

His co-anchor quickly covered the embarrassment by going to a commercial break so everyone could regroup. Television executives were calling to find out what went wrong. Switchboards were lit with callers appalled at the use of the F word; producers argued over the next move.

When some order was restored, the senior anchor chair was empty and the co-anchor announced that they were going directly to the Conference floor where

Matthew McDougal was going to comment on the extraordinary speech that everyone had just heard. Mac heard on his headset that he was to speak for ten minutes, up to the next commercial break, as there was still confusion in the studio.

Mac took a deep breath, looked into the camera, and began. "Arthur Anders has just delivered the most controversial speech of this or any convention that I've seen."

He took his time while looking at his notes to review the speech. Often he paused, and quoted from the speech. Looking up he saw that the time was nearly ten minutes.

"The most unusual aspect of this evening's events is that the speaker spoke of policies not generally on the Democratic agenda. This on the first day of the Convention when the delegates are looking for solidarity."

"Thank you, Mac, and we'll be back shortly with questions for our experts, right after this message."

"Well, well, well!" Virginia Black stood at the door of 12-D as Mac drank water and someone from makeup hovered around.

"Haven't you a deadline?" asked Mac.

"Yes, and no. I have, but I think after we've had a drink I may know what to write."

Before Mac had a chance to comment the door crashed open, knocking Virginia aside. Without apology Hazel gasped at Mac.

"Thank God you're still here."

"What's happening?"

"I don't know, but we had two politicians scheduled to appear, a Republican and a Democrat, and both just walked off the set."

"Why?"

"I don't care right now; America is expecting to hear answers in less than thirty seconds."

"Okay, Hazel, but you owe me. Virginia you primed for national exposure?"

"Sure. Dust me," she nodded at the nearest makeup person.

Walking down to the studio, Mac whispered instructions.

"Virginia, be careful. Follow my lead, say nothing negative. Do you understand?"

"Yes, but….."

"No buts, Virginia."

"We have joining us from Boston the senior political writer of the Boston Globe, Virginia Black." Mac introduced a seemingly nervous but composed Virginia. They had worked out that if Mac squeezed her finger once or used a single finger that he was looking for positive response, a two was negative.

"Were you surprised by the speech given to this audience by Senator Anders, tonight?" One squeeze.

"Yes, on the first day of a convention we see a consolidation of ideas leading to a crescendo for when the candidate shows up for the final day. This…."Mac cut her off.

"Many of the ideas that we heard expressed are in fact new and may not represent the views of the leadership. You were in the hall, what was the feeling? Was there surprise?" asked Mac.

"Yes," said Virginia, looking at the one finger on the table. "The delegates were surprised. They …."

Again Mac jumped in. "The deficit appears to be the number one issue raised by Senator Anders and it is one of the critical issues on the mind of the middle class, but the working class, your typical Democrat is less interested in the deficit than the employment rate. Do you agree?" one squeeze

"I agree, but it is one of the few issues, if not the only issue, that is on the Democratic manifests," said Virginia.

"I haven't seen the manifests, so it's hard to see if this is the only thing, Virginia."

"You think that…" Virginia was sounding annoyed when Mac clamped a hand, hard onto hers. "You are right, having not seen the manifests, it's hard to judge. Marjorie White must have seen the speech before it was delivered."

"We can only speculate," said Mac. "I think that we've been signaled, so back to the studio."

There was confusion everywhere. Mac led Virginia off and held a finger to his lips.

"Thank you, Virginia. Let's go have a well-deserved drink."

At the revolving door Mac looked at the line of taxi cabs; one was not taking passengers. He dropped his bag and they stepped out. The driver put down his paper and jumped out to hold the door for them to get in.

"I left my bag," said Mac to the driver. "Take another fare, I could be a while."

"That's all right, sir. I'll wait."

Mac went back inside to retrieve his bag and stood thinking, realizing, that someone wanted him watched or worse.

When he came back out of the door, he had his cell phone to his ear and was listening. He led Virginia by the arm and she got into the cab with him following close behind.

"Where to?" the driver asked.

Virginia started to answer and Mac interrupted.

"South Station," Mac responded. He held a finger up to Virginia, indicating that he had a plan. She let him take the lead and sat back.

"South Station, okay," the driver was speaking to a dispatcher or other listener.

Mac was listening and talking. "South Station, yes we're on the road." A pause, "No, I clearly said South Station."

The driver was turning for the entrance when Mac said, "Driver, Post Office Square please, a right here, then a left." Back on the phone he said, "A right on High Street; see you in a second."

The meter read seven dollars and eighty cents. Mac was ready with a ten dollar bill as they stopped. Pushing Virginia through the door, he dropped the money into the driver's hand. Walking around the square, Mac signaled a taxi

"Kenmore."

"You know your way around," said Virginia. "Who was on the phone?"

"No one. Just staying alive."

At the Kenmore Square Hotel, Mac crossed the street and led Virginia into the back of Cornwalls. The familiar murals of famous English figures were overhead and other artifacts were in evidence. A dart board was in use in the corner and a cricket bat, together with beer towels, adorned the walls.

A waitress approached and introduced herself as Nicole. She looked at Mac and asked, "London Pride draft?"

Mac was surprised that she remembered his drink of preference as it had been over a year since he had last been into the establishment.

"Yes." Then, turning to Virginia he asked, "What will you have?"

"Same as my host," she replied.

"Two London Pride drafts then," he informed the waitress.

When they were settled with their beers, Mac was ready."I'll try to answer your questions, and if I don't it will be because I don't know the answer or, for your own safety, it's better if you don't know the answers."

"First question then; why all the cloak and dagger to get here?"

"You don't like Cornwalls? Best fish and chips in America; best bartenders in Boston; best waitress in the world." Mac smiled and then became serious."The taxi driver was waiting for us. Either to see where we went, to listen to our conversation, or to take us somewhere that we did not want to be."

"So you pretended to be on the phone so that one, you could change the destination; two, preclude speech between us, and three, to inform hypothetically someone where we were," Virginia speculated aloud.

"Very good."

"Question two. Who and why?"

"Two questions there. I don't know, but it's related to Anders, and I think that they're keeping a lid on something."

"What?"

"Election fraud, if I had a guess." Mac then explained his theory on the election gambling and his conversation with Hal in Las Vegas.

"That raises a million questions, but first why did we say nothing about the speech, on national television, while we had the chance?"

"Trying to stay alive; trying to keep you alive. Too many people have died while getting close to elections in this country; Charles George and his aide, Pauline Poles, that I know of. There are probably others."

"So expose them!"

"Who?"

"Whoever killed them I suppose? You're an investigative reporter, find them."

"I've looked, believe me, but every death was labeled accidental. Every police report is clear and absolutely airtight."

"So, you may be wrong."

"That would be a first," Mac said with a grin.

"Next question. Where does Flores fit in?" asked Virginia, so engrossed that she was completely ignoring her beer.

"I'm not sure. He is Anders's only visible friend and got elected without visible financial help and without the support of the local politicians."

"After we talked I did some more checking."

"Carefully, I hope," he warned.

"Yes, I was careful. The only thing was the two years in the Peace Corps."

"They have records."

"Yes, great records, and very comprehensive. He was in Africa."

"Okay," said Mac, waiting.

"Except that other people assigned to the same village don't remember him."

"So where was he?"

Virginia shrugged. "I can check some more."

"No, Virginia, don't. Oh, oh, time to leave." Mac stood, leaving enough money to cover the beers and tip.

Two men had entered and looked more interested in the people than the beers. As they walked into the other room, Mac, guessing that someone was watching the front, led Virginia through the kitchen. He nodded to the man working the grill. The man nodded back in recognition and acquiescence, and then continued cooking.

"You certainly know how to show a girl a good time," Virginia said, hailing a taxi.

Mac, standing in the shadows, waved and said, "Just let me know when I can buy you another drink."

Virginia was laughing but became serious as she stepped into the cab. Mac knew journalists: she was mentally composing her piece for tomorrow's papers.

Mac slipped into the train station and headed to his hotel. He would walk through Post Office Square since that was where he had slipped the surveillance.

Chapter Twenty-One

Waking the next morning to a warm day, which promised to be hot, Mac automatically switched on the television and picked up a newspaper from outside his door. Then he picked up his cell phone. It was switched off. Thinking through the previous evening, he realized that it had been off when he was on the air and then he had faked that phone call, and later he had been occupied.

He watched the news, glanced at the newspaper and reviewed his missed calls. Five missed calls were from Helen, two from the television producer, one from Sue Raymond, and there were others that he did not recognize. There was a coffee maker in the room and he suddenly needed a cup of coffee.

The television news was highlighted by the previous evening's speech and commentary. There was surprisingly little commentary. It seemed that the newspapers around the world had all headlined with the phrase 'What the f***was that all about?' In the case of the serious newspapers, the speech had then been highlighted in bullet form; in the tabloids, under the same headline, was a debate of how soon the anchor would be replaced and by whom.

Reinforced with caffeine, he called Helen.

"Where have you been?" she asked, though Mac could not tell if the tone of her voice was more anger or concern.

"Boston, didn't you see me on television?"

"You always answer a question with a question. You know what I was asking; I've been worried."

"I took a girl out for a drink and forgot to switch my phone back on."

"Mac, what happened last night?"

"You want lurid details?'

"At the convention! You're so aggravating at times," Helen said. Her pitch was getting high.

Mac pushed on, disregarding Helen's obvious frustration. "Let me see, and I quote from the Boston Globe, 'Senator Anders is a forceful speaker with a strong message. It is hard to see how the American voters will endorse these radical departures from......"

"Mac, I can read; I can hear; I watched the speech from Minneapolis."

"Are you still there?" he asked.

"No, Washington. We jumped on a plane after your empty analysis."

"When are you in Boston?'

"Officially tomorrow, unofficially tonight."

"See you then, Sugar."

"Wait, what happened?"

Mac could tell from the way she asked that she was nervous for the campaign she was running, for everything she had worked for. But there was something more that Helen was not saying. He became indignant and said, "You tell me. Has the party manifest changed?"

"Why didn't you comment on the speech in your analysis? Why not let Virginia Black voice anything of substance?"

"You tell me, Helen, about the Party plans and then I can put it right on the noon news."

"What do you mean?"

"What's the deal? Tell me and anyone else listening."

"I can't; you know that."

"Can't, Helen, or won't?"

There was a silence and in it Mac could hear volumes; he saw something and heard the television replaying part of Anders's speech.

"Marjorie has gone over to the dark side," he said quietly. "Why?"

"I don't know what you're talking about."

"Then I can report on the noon news that I have a story. I can say that the Anders speech was endorsed by the party."

"No! No, Mac, don't."

"Why not, Helen? I don't like being played for a sucker!"

"Wait. You don't understand. Let's talk tonight."

"Meet me at the Convention after my wrap."

"We're not supposed to be in town."

"At the Convention. Be there before I go on the air or I will go public." Mac was angry.

"Blackmail? That's not like you."

"Be there!" He hung up before she could reply.

Mac was putting together his disk with facts as he knew them and speculation of a manipulation that he found impossible to comprehend. There was a look during the speech of the previous night; Mac had seen it before, twice: once in New Hampshire six months ago and then when he was interviewing Flores. It was a confirmation to someone or for the benefit of someone. A glance toward, toward what? He needed to get to his producer, see if he could watch the tapes again.

When he left the hotel, the memory disk was in the lining of his suit jacket, slung over his shoulder.

"Morning, Henry. Cab to the Convention Center please."

"Yes, sir, Mr. McDougal. You looked fine on T.V. last night."

"Thanks, Henry. You're a good liar."

"Yes, sir," he said, opening the door."Mr. Anders, he left this morning, early."

Recognizing the driver from last night, Mac held the door and gestured to a couple wandering out of the hotel.

"Thank you, sir," the young man commented with surprise.

Mac was smiling as he entered the second cab. He imagined the fury that the taxi driver, ordered to escort him, must be venting.

As his present taxi got into South Boston, Mac saw a mobile vendor and asked the cab driver to stop. He had not eaten breakfast. He decided to walk the rest of the way. He walked over to the trailer and ordered: "Bacon and egg sandwich and a cup of coffee."

"Yes, sir. Hey aren't you the guy on television?"

"Sometimes."

"I was watching this morning when I picked up my stuff in Chelsea at five. Where's this guy Anders coming from? He wants to bring in immigrants. Look around, Russians driving cabs, Mexicans cleaning up, South Americans building stuff, non-union see, and nobody on the toll booths speaks English. Look around."

"Thanks, I will." Mac said, handing the man a ten dollar bill. "Keep the change."

As Mac entered the convention site, he was spotted by the reception desk and Mandy called over to him.

"Your producer is looking for you," she said with a warning smile.

"I guessed that she might be."

Heading for the television command center, where he wanted to watch again the tape from last night and to stop it, he bumped into the producer.

"Hazel, I was looking for you!"

"Looking to avoid me, more like."

"What's happening?"

"The network wasn't happy with your coverage last night."

"Which part, my summary which did not transcend the moment or the expert opinion when your experts flew the coop?"

Hazel ignored the taunt. She looked worse than usual this morning. Her gaunt expression was still there, but the fire was missing.

"Commenting is generally easy at conventions and rallies," said Mac. "The candidate gives a thirty minute talk. The theme is always centrist. It never varies from the middle of the party's message. Any commentator can then pick the edges left or right and give an entertaining summary. A speaker who is left and right of the message only leaves the commentator the middle. Otherwise what did the network want? To adopt a right or left position?"

"I know, Mac; it was a difficult speech to follow." There was genuine sympathy in her eyes. "The ratings; you know."

"The ratings will be through the roof. It's all anyone is talking about. The world news is full of speculation.

Was it your idea to have the other anchor use a bad word?" Mac said with a smile.

"Definitely not! I think he's gone home sick."

"Gone, or sent?'

Hazel shrugged.

"What happened to your experts?"

"Funny thing; they both got telephone calls that there was a medical emergency involving a family member and that they should leave immediately. They were told not to worry about the show that the other expert could carry on. A terrible prank since everybody was fine."

"Yes, very funny," said Mac with no humor.

"Well I have to go find some filler to accompany the other anchor who is less than pleased to be on alone tonight."

"Have her interview Mandy at reception and invite Virginia Black on the air; we owe her after she stepped in last night."

"Thanks, Mac."

"Can I look at last night's tapes?"

"Sure, Frank is in the booth."

After forty-five minutes he had confirmed that both Arthur Anders and Frank Flores had looked to the same spot, with the same expression. The look was of triumph. Who was standing there?

He was fast forwarding through the tapes to see if any camera had swept the audience. They had and he slowed them down and zoomed in but saw nothing. It looked as if they were looking at the media area, not at any of the delegates.

So who was in the media area? He recognized many of them and even some of the photographers, then of course there was the foreign press. He stopped the best picture and shouted for Frank to get him a print. Then he could study it at his leisure.

The door crashed open. Hazel dashed in.

"Thank God you are here. We have a breaking story. I need someone to read it."

"Okay, be there in a minute!"

"Now, Mac, now! We're going live in the noon news and it's the lead story."

They walked to the studio, a makeup person dabbed at his face as he took the seat behind the desk.

"Where's the story?"

"On the prompter!"

"What is it?"

"A delegate found dead. Just read it, Mac; they're on countdown."

The screen showed a Washington anchor with a banner which said, 'Breaking Story'.

"We are going immediately to Boston where a breaking story has just come in." The anchor looked down to read, "Matthew McDougal, what do you have?"

Mac was in shock but read as the teleprompter scrolled.

"Earlier today the police pulled the body of a delegate to the Democratic Convention out of Boston Harbor. The statement from the police said that Florida delegate Norman Harrison appeared to have drowned. Mr. Harrison was last seen at a party following last night's speeches. Foul play is not suspected."

Mac was blinking away tears of sorrow and fury as he looked into the camera.

"I'd like to personally express my sympathy to Mr. Harrison's family and to the delegates from Florida. I know from my conversations with them all what a committed Democratic representative he was. Florida and the Saratoga area in particular are going to miss him."

There was a quiet in the room. A monitor still showed the news show.

"That was good, Mac. Thank you," said Hazel.

"Shit! Shit! Shit! I know why he died."

"An accident! The police said….."

"No accident," Mac corrected through gritted teeth. He walked out of the studio, out of the building, and down across the busy street in a daze. He walked until he could see the harbor. It was obvious that Norm, garrulous, friendly, confident Norm, had stopped and asked the wrong person the source of Arthur Anders's campaign funds.

How did he know this? He knew because everyone who got near to that question was dead, except for him.

Why? Why did they die? Why was he still alive? Perhaps he was supposed to have died.

If he died, could he leave a message? A message, to whom? Would they believe or would he die in vain, like the others, like Norm Harrison.

What would the message be? Killed: not an accident, not a suicide. Murdered. By who and why?

Not everyone had been killed. The others, were they bought, threatened, blackmailed? If they were, then they were not going to speak out.

Why not him? Because they thought that he had something to trace back to them. That he had passed it to someone for safekeeping. He did have something; they must not know that what he had was nothing. Or, did he have something that they wanted?

In the meantime he had to stay alive; he had an engagement to fulfill and Helen to meet. It was hardly likely that they would have him commit suicide on the air. But what about the safety of Helen?

Chapter Twenty-Two

Helen arrived at the Convention Center during a routine speech that was being enthusiastically applauded. The delegates were comfortable, well-fed, anticipating a long evening of parties and knowing that tomorrow they would crown a new contender. The audience outfits were more garish; there were more 'Marjorie White, President' signs. The speaker was a political vice presidential hopeful, a worker bee from Montana. Dan Rollins had voted along party lines for over twenty years. He knew everyone, had few, if any, enemies and ran through his political life unopposed. Tall and good-looking, he was a solid speaker. The camera frequently picked out his wife and daughters in the crowd of wildly stomping cowboys and cowgirls from Montana.

Mac was watching and making notes even though a copy of the speech had been delivered to the media earlier.

"Hi," Helen said, closing the door softly behind her.

"Hi." Mac spoke without looking up from the monitor.

"Still annoyed with me?"

"Right now I'm working. I'm glad you showed up though; it avoids a lot of potential problems."

Helen opened her mouth to make a retort, thought better of it, and walked out of the viewing area.

While Mac gave his opinion, he could see Helen behind the cameras. She was not watching; she was thinking, with her eyes on Mac's face. There was no animation, no recognition that words were being spoken: there was no connection.

Mac gave a routine synopsis of the speech. He referred to the close family, the strong family values, the loyal faithful Democrat; the anchor asked the question given to him by Mac.

"Were we looking at the vice presidential candidate?"

He certainly has all the credentials. He's from a Western State, has a strong group of political friends, and is a man who has frequently found the central ground in any debate. Tonight we saw some banners, suggesting that he would be warmly accepted. But there were not enough to suggest that Marjorie White has leaked her choice of running mate. Also Marie Rollins, while happy to see her husband in the limelight, was not showing the pent up excitement that we might expect if her husband had been tapped on the shoulder."

"There are many who believe that he is certain to be chosen as running mate. You disagree, so who do you think that it might be?"

"I don't know, but I expect that we may find out very soon." Mac was looking at Helen who was looking now like a deer caught in the headlights of a speeding tractor trailer.

"Thank you, Matthew McDougal, from the Democratic Convention in Boston. We'll be right back after this message."

Helen had turned to leave when Mac put a hand on her shoulder.

"Let me wash up, then we can talk."

There was resignation in Helen's face and she put on the sunglasses that she had worn even though they were inside. It effectively covered what was in her eyes, but her body language could not hide the inner turmoil.

They pushed their way through the throngs leaving the meeting. There was a happy buzz. The sunglasses had the opposite effect of calling attention to Helen and ensured that she and Mac were recognized by some of the media people.

Virginia Black forced her way through the crowd. Clearly the events of last night had given her a proprietary claim on Mac, and therefore Helen.

"Mac, so do you know who will be V.P.?"

"No, Virginia. Have you met my friend, Helen Harvey?"

"Not formally, but I knew it was someone important by the glasses."

Helen snatched the glasses from her face and stuffed them into her pocketbook.

"I'm not here," she said. Then, she corrected herself: "I'm not officially here."

"Well I guess that means that whatever you tell us is unofficial." Virginia was smiling, enjoying Helen's discomfort.

"No," Helen said and then repeated, "no."

"Then it's official," Virginia stated matter-of-factly.

"No!" She turned to Mac and pleaded, "Please, can we go?"

"Who is going to be Marjorie White's V.P. nominee?" Virginia asked.

"I….I don't know!" Helen said in a voice that was barely audible.

"Impossible; the media director for the Democratic nominee for President has not written, edited, debated, and rewritten the most important speech of the year?"

"I don't know." Helen was coming visibly unglued.

"Virginia, if Helen can't tell you then she won't." Mac put a protective arm around Helen.

"Do you know, Mac? You sounded tonight as though you might."

"No, Virginia, I don't *know* anything. If I did, the one person I'd tell would be you."

"All right, Mac. I believe you." It was said in a way that indicated that she did not believe Helen.

"Let's cross the street to that restaurant and find a cab."

Helen was fumbling with the sunglasses.

"Helen, forget the sunglasses. It's dark. They're a dead giveaway. Anyone following us is smarter than that; they can see you even if you can't see them through the sunglasses."

She stiffened then hooked an arm through his as they crossed at the traffic signal.

Mac whistled a cab that was speeding past. Once inside, he asked the driver to take them to Copley. They walked across the square as casually as the other couples at that time of night and entered the underground station.

There was no chance of being overheard; no surveillance microphone could penetrate the tunnel they were in. Mac chose an outward bound train towards Boston College, his old stomping ground. It was familiar.

"What is it Helen. What's going on?"

"What do you mean?"

"You know damn well what I mean; I had to threaten you to come tonight."

"You mean me and Mark?"

"No. I do not mean you and Mark! I mean Marjorie White and Arthur Anders."

The look came back; Helen looked up and down the nearly empty carriage.

"What do you mean?"

"I mean, Helen dearest," his voice was hard, "Anders delivers a speech which is inflammatory; a speech which is contrary in many ways to the party manifests, and where is Marjorie?" He paused and, although they both could have expected the answer, he spat it out. "Hiding!"

"She wasn't hiding," Helen said with feeling.

"Flew back from Minneapolis, middle of the night, skulked into Boston a day early. Not hiding, Helen? Here is the opportunity to go on every network, give the Commander in Chief speech from the steps of the Capital or Bunker Hill. Why?"

"You know why," Helen whispered.

"Yes, I know why but I want you to tell me."

"I can't!"

"Can't or won't?"

"I can't!"

"Helen, it's me. Remember me?"

"I can't!"

They reached Boston College, walked through the campus, and found an inbound train which was empty. The voice over the loud speaker stated that it would be the last train of the night.

On the walk through the campus Helen had cried. Mac recognized the pressure that she was under and wondered when she had last slept.

"Marjorie White has gone over to the dark side," Mac said again.

Helen nodded. There was a long silence.

"Anders will be Vice presidential nominee."

Another nod from Helen, followed by a wail.

"Why? Why, Helen?"

"Don't ask, Mac. Please don't ask."

"You know that's what I do."

They were back in the tunnel and nearing Copley.

"So?" he asked.

"Nothing," she said, then when there was silence. "It was suggested that he be added to the list of interviewees. The argument was that since he had performed well in the primaries that he had name recognition."

"He did well when the others backed out," interjected Mac. "What was the reaction?"

"Marjorie laughed, said that their agendas were different. The intermediary said that the agenda thing could be worked out. Then his speech the other night wasn't approved. We didn't know what was being said until you did. We jumped on the plane back to Washington where Anders joined us. He had a private meeting with Marjorie which was acrimonious and adjourned until this evening. It was the reason we came in early."

There was more but Mac sensed there was going to be little else tonight as they left the train at Copley.

Walking down the street towards the Ritz, Mac, on impulse, pulled the picture Frank had given him from his pocket.

"Recognize anyone?"

Helen gave a cursory look. "No."

"That's a lie!"

Helen snatched the photo and looked carefully at the image of media people.

"Of course I know Pat from Reuters, Bill Beaumont, an independent, your Virginia Black, and Larry, Trish Elmore, Nick Kidlinton."

"A lot of no ones. Anybody else?"

"I'm tired; I don't think so."

"What about this fellow with the big camera in front of his face?"

"No."

It was a lie, the answer was too quick, the glance was insufficient to have provided recognition.

They reached the Ritz. Before Mac could even think about whether he wanted to spend more time with Helen, she quickly gave him a sisterly kiss on the cheek.

"Goodnight, Mac."

"Goodnight, Helen."

Why, he wondered, *did it sound like goodbye?*

There was a plan formulating in his head. He could not hope to win a frontal assault. Maybe, though, there was a way to warn America. A payphone just inside of the door of a busy bar should screen the conversation.

"Huh! What idiot is calling me in the middle of the night?"

"Wake you?" Mac asked unnecessarily. He firmly added, "No name."

"What's up?"

"Could you put a story into the West Coast newspapers?"

"When?"

"Tonight!"

"Tonight? Send it. I'll try!"

"I haven't written it yet."

"How many words?"

"About five hundred. Why?"

"I'll have to replace something."

"Oh, so you can?"

"Has never been done before to my knowledge which makes it a challenge."

"Encrypted, password, Peter Doath. Destroy all evidence immediately."

"Wow! Now I'm awake!"

"Give me forty-five minutes."

"Why the West Coast? Where do you want it coming from?"

"Las Vegas."

"Las Vegas?'

"Yes, can you go through Miami to Vegas?'

"Sure. Why not the Pentagon?" Mac responded with silence. "Joking," said Martin Konrad, laughing. "You're too tense. Stress can kill you."

"Forty-five minutes," Mac responded and then hung up.

This was what Mac did best. Back in the deadline of the newspaper world mentality he shook off the concerns and went to work. The article was mentally composed by the time he sat to write it.

It flowed in thirty minutes, he had four hundred and ninety words which he encrypted and downloaded; he put on the password and went downstairs. There was a computer in a small room just off the lobby of the hotel. Now, having sent it, two more things; first he snuck out of the hotel, the same way that he had snuck in less than an hour before; secondly he destroyed the memory stick and dropped it into the harbor. Then Mac returned to his hotel by the front door, squinted at his watch which obliged the night clerk to look at the large clock and nod. Mac looked at the clock and nodded; he had established a time for coming in. In the million to one chance anyone found the microburst, they might think it was another guest at the hotel.

He slept.

The telephone was ringing. He looked at the clock; it was just after nine.

"Hello," he said hoarsely.

"Mac, you need to wake up."

"Then why didn't you nudge me, Helen?"

"Did you see the news?"

"What news?"

"The television is saying that there is news out of Vegas that someone put $250,000 at five-to-one that Anders would be the vice presidential nominee."

"Five-to-one? I thought he was a hundred-to-one."

"Everyone here is apoplectic. It must have been leaked. The media is showing up in droves. Television stations are demanding a statement. Demanding! My phone is ringing. Damn, why did I give the number to so many people?"

"Helen, why did you call me?"

"I….. I've got to go!"

Mac sat back and smiled. He had not had his cup of coffee and yet he was smiling. Helen had not mentioned the rest of the article. Switching on the television he made coffee with the machine in the room and sat to listen to the anchors. Who was going to say what, when, and how?

The speculation was split: those who could not believe the possibility of Anders on the ticket, who pointed to the fact that someone with that money might be betting more in hope than expectation. Those believing that the money was always right were using the news to refer back to his speech and the catastrophes that might befall the country. The centrists and moderators were cautious and saying that a statement from Marjorie White was imminent.

Switching channels, a spokesman for the newspapers was saying that they had no information on Peter Doath; he was not a regular contributor. He stumbled, saying, "Yes, we do have a policy of corroborating information." The announcer said that, in fact, the odds were now even money that Anders would be nominated.

"It certainly is looking more like the article is true. The FBI has stated that an investigation into the betting pattern would begin today. A team is already on route to Las Vegas where they will be digging through the evidence."

"Good luck," chuckled Mac. "Good luck on co-operation and good luck on even seeing any records."

He went to the shower, chuckling, but came out in a somber mood. Doing his best thinking in the shower, Mac concluded that the sooner he left Boston, the better. The stealthier he left Boston, the safer. The fewer people who knew, the better his chances of achieving the timeliness and quietness of his escape.

Needing luck, he got it in the form of the doorman Henry.

"Today the last day, then you'll be leaving us," Henry stated.

"Yes, I'll be sorry to go; I like Boston. Henry, I'm going to be in a hurry. Could you have a maid that you trust pack my stuff and put it down here under the name of Smith?"

"Yes, sir, right away."

"No, not right away. This afternoon. I may need to come back." Mac handed him two one hundred dollar bills. "For you and the maid."

"Thank you, sir. Remember that you are always welcome in Boston."

Mac went to work.

Marjorie White's statement was long in rhetoric and short on content. Without specifically denying the article, she managed to mention six other candidates. The interesting part was the strength of her denial of any leakage from her camp regarding the article. This denial reinforced the validity of the information, in that contrary way that denials have.

This, the final day of the Democratic Convention was unlike any other final day in memory. The opening speeches were all delivered competently and to rousing cheers. The President was seen by video link and gave a speech endorsing his vice president and hoping that this meant he would be able to visit his old memories. No discord, no discouraging words, all happiness and light.

The story between speakers and the interviews of speakers spoke not of their speeches or the candidate but of the yet-to-be-named Vice presidential nominee. It was embarrassing; it was relentless.

Marjorie White finally took the podium to the delight of the crowd. There was a long, standing ovation, with horns blaring and a brass band playing at the capacity of their lungs. From the front she personally waved and greeted about one hundred people, with a wave, a mouthed thank you, and blown kisses. It was orchestrated to perfection.

While the delegates and television audience were watching the expected winner of the count, just minutes away, Mac was watching Helen. In truth he was also scanning the throngs for Arthur Anders, but so was every television producer and every reporter.

"She looks awful," was whispered into his earpiece.

He was still looking at Helen and would admit that he had seen her in better days. It was obvious that they were in fact talking about the candidate though. Mac looked down at the stage.

Marjorie White looked ghastly. It was as if she could barely stand. The exhaustion was etched on her face. Though it had been skillfully made up, doing so had created an image that was closer to a circus performer than of a prospective President of the United States.

Holding her hands high, the crowd noise dropped to a few whoops and yells

"My fellow Democrats, you are standing with me on the brink of a new era in American Politics. This year a woman will be elected to the highest seat in this great country."

Mac had a little sheet of paper in front of him next to a copy of the speech. The sheet had a list of phrases on one side and a list of flowery synonyms on the other. He checked 'great country'; there were already nineteen checks to one against 'country'. It was obvious that America could not be described by any politician as a country without the superlative 'great'. The checklist kept him listening to some of the more boring speeches. It was not necessary tonight, just habit. The speech had been written and rewritten and, since he had already read it and knew the content, it was the presentation which held his undivided attention.

He had been asked on air earlier in the evening what his reaction was to the news from Las Vegas and the possibility of Arthur Anders being a running mate. His reply had been that he did not gamble or speculate on political outcomes, just report them. He was asked if he knew Peter Doath and had to admit that he did not. The fact that the name was an anagram would be reported by someone else, not him.

Marjorie had started awkwardly, stumbling a little. The beginning of the speech had fortunately been filled with phrases to bring applause. Every time there was applause, in addition to recognizing it, she took a sip of water and looked at Helen for support.

Now instinct took over; she took the delegates through her campaign mentioning, to great applause, the states that she had won; the states that she had lost came with less applause. She gave her pledge to be, if nominated, the President who continued to ask questions. Her sense of humor, teasing her supporters that she might not be guaranteed the nomination, gave rise to laughter and all cheered loudly to demonstrate their confidence in this woman who possessed the ability to be serious and light at the same time.

This comment also produced the longest applause of the evening and Marjorie gave a long glance to the wings, both sides. Mac's eyes followed. First Marjorie looked at Helen on one side, then at Arthur Anders on the other.

"The question of nominating or recommending a Vice presidential nominee is one of the most important functions of you, the delegates, as you represent the people of this great country. It is a task not taken without a great deal of thought and a great deal of soul searching on both sides. We considered Dan Rollins from the great State of Montana." She paused to allow the loud applause from Montana to diminish. "Dan is a good friend of mine and will be a resource on which I will continue to rely. William Cook, former Governor of the great state of Indiana, is another candidate with strong credentials and a work load that would put anyone to shame. However, I decided that we needed a partner who could balance the ticket, someone close to the people with strong convictions, bulldog tenacity. These are trying times; fighting abroad to protect the ideals of our fellow citizens we lose sight of the sacrifice that we ask our brave men and women to make. We need to address that sacrifice, not recognize it, but address it. The unemployment rate in this country is not what we came here for. We are all immigrants; we came for a better life, the opportunity to work; we, my fellow Democrats must find or create those job opportunities. This great country must be made strong with controls on credit, controls on spending at every level. We must eliminate our dependency on credit."

Mac was feverishly writing; this was not in the notes he had been given.

"So I am asking, and asking you, to ask Senator Arthur Anders to be my partner as Vice presidential nominee on the run to the White House."

There was applause, not enthusiastic, not even from the Florida Delegation as Arthur Anders stepped onto the stage and shook hands with Marjorie. Mac looked over to the other side; Helen was gone.

Mac left his post to get prepared. He knew the next twenty minutes would consist of sweet talk from Marjorie designed for maximum volume of cheers and applause and low on content. She would close by asking her supporters to remind the Republicans that the people to pose their question to were those great people who worked for a living, not some CEO looking for a handout from Congress.

There would be a half hour for commercial breaks and commentary before the delegate count started. The count was scheduled for an hour and could be guaranteed to drag on with fifty spokesmen and women clinging to their time in the spotlight for a lot longer.

"And now for comment live from the Democratic Convention in Boston, we have Matthew McDougal. Mac what are your thoughts on the extraordinary happenings today?"

"You are, of course, referring to the announcement of Arthur Anders as the Vice presidential candidate nominated by Marjorie White. I think that this was less climatic than it might have been twenty-four hours ago."Mac, in a lightweight grey suit, a very pale blue shirt with neutral yellow tie, looked relaxed. He looked more relaxed than he was feeling.

"So what were the surprises?"

"I think that there was a strong move by the candidate away from the middle and toward those views expressed on this stage by Arthur Anders a couple of days ago. I can only conclude that the content had been worked on together and will become the party line. I expect that unemployment, job creation and immigration will be the focus of the domestic agenda, with the armed forces and foreign aid being at the forefront of foreign policy."

For the rest of his summary Mac talked of the candidate and when asked where these policies might fit into the Congressional agenda stayed away from voicing his fears.

Helen was standing at the door as he was leaving. She must have watched the show on the monitor. The cameras were now focused on the floor of the Convention Center and cheering delegates were being lined up for interviews. The noise level was increasing to levels that hurt the ears. She followed him as he went to wash his face.

"You looked good, Mac."

"You look like shit. Marjorie looks even worse."

"Always know how to flatter girls, don't you?"

"Helen, it's a dangerous game that you're playing. Selling your soul to the devil."

"And you're so smart, always right," she snapped at him.

There was a screen in the room and now it showed the nominated candidate with arms aloft gesturing for her family and running mate to join her on the podium. Marjorie, David, and the two boys were folded in upon each other while a beaming Arthur Anders stood center stage arms high.

It was an image that would form a nightmare for the next few months.

"Where's his family?" Mac asked, still looking at the image.

"His wife is very shy."

"Have you met her?"

"No."

"I would say that is more than shy," said Mac snidely.

"Mac, who is Peter Doath?"

"Figure it out and be very careful, Helen."

"You too." Her eyes had filled with tears. It was clear she was exhausted physically and emotionally.

"You need a couple of days rest," Mac said seriously.

"I know, but it's on to Florida tonight, breakfast with the union at the docks. Then....." she broke down in Mac's arms.

"Remember that the graveyard is full of indispensable people," he said.

She shuddered. "I love you. Mac, be very, very, careful."

"I have a vested interest in that." He tried to change the mood. "See you in Washington."

They parted, both thinking of Peter Doath.

Mac was composing a second article when Helen called from the private plane to let him know that she had been pondering his response to her question and that she had solved the riddle. She asked him to hold on and he heard a familiar voice in the background say, "We've been looking for you, Helen. Time to go. The media are asking for access and we have to be in Miami."

"Yes, David," Helen replied. Then, "Mac, I need to get going."

Chapter Twenty-Three

Mac took a cab to Terminal A where flights to Washington originated. He walked through, took a shuttle bus to Terminal D, and then wrote an encrypted article. He sent the file to Martin Konrad under the name Peter Doath and destroyed the evidence. He walked to Terminal E and picked up a phone to call Hertz.

Driving west on the turnpike, he listened to the night talk shows featuring the election. It seemed that the mood was positive and also supportive of Governor Flores. The host, or one of the callers, had early in the broadcast mentioned his friendly relationship with Senator Anders. Mac found that interesting.

Having used a corporate credit card to secure the return of the car, Mac paid in cash. He had shown his license. The clerk, miffed that his replacement had not shown up at midnight, had only done a cursory glance at the inconsistency. Good: he was off the radar temporarily and could easily explain missing the plane and deciding to drive. The deviation was necessary. Terminals, car hire, turnpikes – all have CCTV cameras. He was in plain sight when Peter Doath's article hit the press.

A flashing motel sign read *vacancy, and* Mac was suddenly unable to drive further. The owner was asleep and at first suspicious, but he vaguely recognized the face and cash made him forget to fill out the guest register. The room was small with old beds and carpets; the linens were clean and, if asked to recall the room in later life, Mac would have been unable.

After a short rest, Mac left the motel. When he walked outside, he saw a roadside restaurant, full of trucks and pickups. A large sign advertised *good food cheap*. Eggs, bacon, home fries, beans, and toast came in healthy sized portions. The coffee came hot in a thick mug and was constantly replenished. The conversation among those inside was of the Red Sox losing to the Yankees in the ninth inning after leading from the first.

It was relaxing, it was comfortable, and it could not last.

Mac's phone rang.

"Where are you?"

"Good morning, Helen!"

"Where are you?"

"Why, who's looking for me? I thought you were in Florida."

"I am. Have you seen the news?"

"Yes. Red Sox lost in the ninth."

"Mac, I swear….What's all that noise?"

"Well half is the Red Sox fans and the other half Yankees."

"The West Coast papers have a front page, front page mind you, article by Peter Doath that they are denying."

"Because it's not true?"

"Because they didn't pay for it!"

"They should be happy."

"Their front page picture was changed too, from Marjorie with arms raised, to Arthur holding his arms aloft. The paper has vowed to find the hacker and correct the record," informed Helen.

"Was anything reported that was untrue?"

Helen paused. "No, not really. It says that if Anders is Vice President, he'll have demonstrated his ability to manipulate the voting."

"It says manipulate?" asked Mac.

"No.... But I need to see you. We're back on Sunday; see you Monday. We fly through Pensacola."

"Pensacola?"

"I mean Charlotte," she corrected.

"Minus two. Miss you very much. Bye."

They would meet at Paula's Monday morning at 6am.

Arriving at the nursing home at nine-thirty, the cleaning crews were going through the hallways and bedrooms on the first floor. The sameness of this routine ensured that the same places were missed every day. The smell assailed him as he swung through the door. It was midsummer and warm outside, but it was warmer inside. The décor had been changed, the Christmas lights were gone, and the moth-eaten bunny was put away for another year. Someone had brought flowers, evidently from a back yard, and put them on the nurse's station. Everywhere, there was an air of inevitability, the certainty of death, and there was also an effort to make this respectable. Even as Mac thought the word he wondered what it meant. The manifesto would speak of dignity. The indignation of the process forced the owners and management to seek justification for this warehouse of people who would never again see their 'sell by' date.

Mac approached the desk where a young nurse smiled.

"Can I help you?" she asked with sincerity.

"Mrs. Hough, is she in the same room?"

"Yes and no. We're cleaning, so she's on the verandah."

The verandah was in fact a farmer's porch. The glass had been removed and the furniture looked old but serviceable. The window screens were old, wooden, floor to ceiling, and as old as the house. There were patients sitting quietly, nodding as if to some remembrance. There were others in the chairs dozing.

His mother had remarried and so his name was different. For some reason this fact gave him comfort. He had not really known his stepfather, but Frank Hough had been good to his mother when loneliness had set in with her boys away at college. She, in turn, had nursed him through a severe stroke until a second one had returned her lonely existence. Nursing him had taken a toll and his death accelerated the deterioration of her mind and body.

Not today though. She looked lovely, reading the newspaper through bifocals, her mouth moving as she read.

"Hello Mum!"

"Hello Matthew; I was just reading about you. Well, not really; I was reading about the conventions. I told everybody last night that the handsome man on the TV was my son."

She paused to think of something, the concentration etched on her face. Mac leaned over to give her a kiss.

"Thank you Mum."

"They didn't believe me. Especially that one," she took her cane and whacked the leg of one of the sleeping women.

"Mum, you'll wake her," Mac laughed.

"I want to. I want her to see my handsome son in person."

"You're good today."

"Yes," she said frowning. "I am, but it never lasts."

There was sadness in the acceptance, she was not seeking pity.

Mac was reluctant to leave while his mother was so well. The nurse came by and asked if they would like coffee and cookies. The mention of food opened several eyes and resulted in animation at the word cookies. Mac guessed that those reacting most were among the diabetics.

The nursing home gave permission for them to go out for lunch, but there was a long list of dos and don'ts associated with the suggested fare.

They sat at the local inn and studied an extensive menu. The waitress approached the table.

"A drink with your lunch? Are you ready to order?"

"Yes, please. I'll have the filet mignon and a beer," Mac's mother replied.

"Both of those things were specifically not allowed," said Mac smiling.

"Well, I've managed to live this long without that young woman's help. I'm sure I can still manage a few more days."

"Fries or baked potato?" asked the waitress.

"Fries." Mrs. Hough was clearly enjoying this. "Can't remember the last time I had fries. Of course I can't remember what happened yesterday," she chuckled.

"Steak, baked potato, and a beer, please," ordered Mac.

The waitress walked away and left them chuckling.

"Mum," Mac turned, suddenly serious. "Do you still have the place in New Hampshire?"

"The Lake House? Sure! Why? Do you want to use it? My mother put it into a family trust. It's probably yours now, yours and your brother's."

"You are still trustee?"

"Until I finish this steak, anyway."

"So where's the key?"

"Next door, Chuck Hamilton has it. He must be old now."

They conversed about memories of the house, times spent there when Mac and his brother were young.

Mrs. Hough ate less than half the filet mignon and about a quarter of the fries. She did, however, finish the beer. Then she announced, softly but firmly, "I'm tired. I need to go back now."

Mac drove her to the nursing home and helped her as far as the nurses' station.

"Thanks, son, see you tomorrow." She was already falling into that grey, soup-like existence from which she had emerged for a few blessed hours. The memories had overcome the mind's ability to cope; the act of leaving the facility taxed the body to exhaustion.

Mac decided not to stay another night. Heading south, he was driving by remote control, his emotions still tied to that lady who had carried him to birth, nurtured him, and taught him basic good behavior.

Washington was hot, it was sticky; it was full of tourists. Tiredness made Mac see things, feel things, more acutely. Why should tourists bother him? Why the humidity? Why not?

The reality was that a good number of the people who he knew were not in town. They had escaped to the shore, to the hills, or to foreign lands. His apartment smelled of not having been lived in, of not having the air-conditioning on. It smelled faintly of cologne; Mac did not use cologne. Nothing was missing, nothing appeared to be disturbed, but when he sat at his desk and booted up his computer system things were not quite where he had left them. He mused that every occupant of every desk would know if someone had been sitting there, moving the paperclips, the scrap paper, the quick note reminding the true occupant of a dental appointment, haircut, car service.

The telephone messages were predictable, half were from Sue Raymond: reminders of deadlines, meetings with editors, publishers, and reviewers. The other half of the messages were either congratulatory on his television acumen or solicitations. The congratulatory messages were people emphasizing the fact that they had not left Washington and were therefore available for drinks while also relaying the fact that they were too busy, or indispensable, to leave. There was a message from Martin Konrad congratulating him without leaving his name, he recognized the voice.

The next morning, after a good night's sleep, he made coffee. He thought of breakfast; he had not eaten since lunch with his mother; he picked up the phone and dialed.

"Sue, breakfast?"

"Good morning, Mac. I had breakfast an hour ago, but I can watch you eat if it means that I can finally catch up to you."

"Good; deli on the corner?"

"I'll be there in fifteen minutes."

"I'll be the one with kippers and eggs," Mac said.

"Revolting!" Sue replied.

"What can I tell you? My trip to England last year left its mark."

Ten minutes later Mac was seated in the restaurant behind an order of kippers with eggs over easy, along with home fries and a pile of toast. Sue sat opposite with a coffee mug filled and she helped herself to a half slice of whole wheat toasted bread.

"Sue, can I borrow your phone a second?"

"Sure; you bring me out to use my phone, probably overseas."

"No, but forget the call."

"You didn't make it yet."

"Thanks," Mac said and then he waited for the pick-up.

"No name," Mac spoke before the recipient could greet the caller.

"Museum of Aeronautics at 2?"

"Just a couple of tourists," Mac said disconnecting.

Sue Raymond looked at Mac quizzically. "Not especially illuminating; even given sodium pentothal I couldn't give anyone much information."

"Sue!"

"Okay. How are the kippers?"

"Great. The book is stalled but I will work solidly all weekend. I just need to get in a chapter on each of the conventions."

"A delegate died didn't he?"

"Yes."

"Did you know him?"

"No," Mac lied. It came out as a reflex.

The next hour was spent in catching Sue up to date. She was pressing for some copy for the editor and they reached a compromise. Mac would release all the work to date except for a couple of chapters that he needed to rewrite.

"Why revisit if it's a compilation of the presidential race set out chronologically?" Sue asked.

It was a reasonable question, there was no reasonable answer, therefore, Mac was silent.

It took Mac two hours to get to the Museum. First he went to lunch at an open air restaurant, and then he went across town to the library where he spent time on research that he might just as easily have done from home. Taking the bus back across town, he walked the last mile across the Mall. Standing in line with fellow tourists, he paid full price and went in, walking quickly to the far end and then strolling back.

No one followed him. Even this concerned him. He wondered if this was what paranoia felt like, always looking behind and to the side, always trying to guess who or what is ahead. In looking for familiar unknown faces, he almost walked past Martin Konrad who was dressed in a suit and pushing an elderly woman in a wheelchair.

"Who's your friend?"

"My Aunt Edith loves museums. It's okay; she's deaf as a cod."

Mac greeted her and was surprised at the quick response.

"Hello; I'm Edith Cooper and I read lips, so don't go talking about me!"

"She's a pistol!" Martin said with a smile. "What's happening?" His smile vanished.

"Someone is looking for me, hard. Martin, get rid of your hard drive, change providers, whatever you need to do. These people can do anything."

"Yeah, I figured that's why you were worried about hacking. Thing is, everything looked true. Was it?"

"Yes," said Mac. "These people just have a different agenda and they exercise strict control."

"What is it, Mac? Who?"

"I wouldn't tell you if I knew," Mac said. Then he thought, *I wouldn't tell anyone what I suspect; it's safer.*

"Remember the memory stick that Sue gave me two years ago?"

"Yes, the…"

"Well, what I know is on there."

"You think…."

"Yes. I know that they'll kill if necessary to keep their secret."

Edith was pointing to the older planes so Martin turned in that direction; Mac turned the other way and left knowing that just because he did not see anyone did not mean that someone was not there.

The next few days were work days, with trips out of the apartment only for groceries and meals out. The telephone, mercifully, did not ring, and he was able to ignore the emails.

The news programs were reporting on the mysterious stories of Peter Doath. It appeared to Mac, and to many others, that the attention was out of proportion to the crime. It was as if the news media could not tolerate the invasion. The newspaper industry promised stricter controls which further contradicted their announced impartial reporting of twice checked sources. The hacking of phones and computers was conveniently swept under the rug. An editor said that he recognized the style. Interviewed at length he said that the style was that of a young woman staffer at a large newspaper. A psychiatrist said that the name was an anagram and that the perpetrator was Deep Throat; he then postulated that the person was in the administration and in need of expressing a paranoia, a deep seated fear of government. He also believed that the perpetrator would strike again and come forward to be recognized. A computer and internet expert explained how the message might have been delivered. He tried to replicate the insertion and concluded that the article had been routed through the Pentagon, probably by the CIA.

It was all entertaining, some was actually true. To Mac it was disconcerting that someone was keeping the story in the news. There were several attempts to attack his computer, all, as far as he could tell, were repulsed.

Monday morning he left early to meet Helen. After the weeks of late nights and the days of working at his own speed, having the alarm wake him at five was a shock. When he was showering, he idly wondered if the listeners also heard his alarm. Well the psychiatrist had been right when he said that Peter Doath was paranoid.

Helen was already there, looking as if she had not slept, the dark areas under her eyes, the droop of her shoulders, and her grey pallor attested to the strain.

Mac wanted to take her in his arms and let her sleep, protected from the world.

"Wish you were back at a desk?"

"Why?"

"Regular hours!"

"Mac, why did you write those articles? You took information from me and used it."

"No, Helen, I didn't. First, I am an investigative reporter. Second, I'd figured out the Anders thing; it was merely confirmed by your refusal to deny the fact. Third, someone has to warn the public which doesn't seem to care."

"So put it in the Times."

"It is in the Times."

"And Deep Throat. It took less than a minute to figure that out. Why?"

"Too many people have died."

Tears came into Helen's eyes.

"Helen, why pick Anders from a pack of more experienced more recognizable names, not to mention candidates who might be closer politically? The drop in the polls has reflected the voter's views that this could be a disaster."

"I can't tell you."

"Can't or won't? I'm an investigative reporter. I have eliminated some reasons."

"Mac, don't!"

"Then, tell me. I promise not to use it."

"Money-- he brings money."

"That's true; where from? It's also not the real reason."

"You think that I lied to you?" asked Helen.

"Yes," Mac answered, and he watched as tears rolled down her face. He waited.

When she began speaking it was in a very low voice. "It's not the money."

"What then: blackmail, extortion?"

"No." Helen shuddered. "It's fear."

"Fear?" Mac was surprised. "Go to the secret service."

Helen had broken down crying again and she got up to leave. Mac realized what a mess she looked and touched her arm. She sat down again and cried uncontrollably.

Other customers looked and Mac moved around the table to put an arm around her. Helen slumped against him and continued to cry.

It was clear that she was exhausted, emotionally and physically.

"Come on. I'll see you home," Mac said.

"No, I have to go to a meeting," she stammered through tears.

"Not in this state."

"Not home."

Mac thought.

"We'll go to Sue Raymond's place; Carol will take care of you. I have things to do, people to see, people to be seen seeing."

Carol was surprised to see them, but pleased too. Sue had gone out but the arrangements were quickly made. Mac switched off Helen's cell phone and left instructions: no calls in or out; make sure she sleeps. Then he left.

He would get the story when she woke up; in the meantime he wanted to plant another story, but it would have to be a different route.

Going to a library mid-morning, the computers were all taken by students, so he had to wait a few minutes. He waited until someone left without logging out, then sat down and composed an article which he sent to a London tabloid.

Because students came into the library in droves, the staff barely registered their names. It had been easy to wait until someone left, he only needed ten minutes.

Next, from a pay phone, Mac called Ann Gold and arranged to meet her in half an hour for lunch; public place, public exposure.

"Darling," Ann said, "good to see you again. Dreadfully dull in the city when you're away."

"You were away too, Ann," Mac chided.

"Yes, I suppose, but always working."

"Cocktail parties in the Hamptons work?" he asked.

"Don't you find the wealthy all have the best gossip?" she responded, ignoring the question. "The problem is that it's already old news before one can get to a computer."

"You mean before you are sober and can get to your laptop."

"Yes, well..." Ann conceded. "You're such a pain, Mac; saw your piece from Boston. Not bad, but you could have done with some creative enhancements."

They ordered salads and iced tea. Both claimed that they needed something light due to the hot weather. In truth, Mac noted that Ann had put on weight during the summer season, and he needed to get back to a healthy regime if he was going to be able to keep up with the cloak and dagger routine.

"And how is my favorite newspaper person, Helen?"

"Helen is now in media something," said Mac. "And busy with an election or something along those lines.

Besides, I thought I was your favorite newspaper person."

"Hmm. A little bird suggested that she might be Deep Throat." Ann was looking closely at Mac for his reaction.

"I'd hardly think that she has time or motive," said Mac warily.

"Bob Marchant, the editor, says that he recognizes her style in the writing."

"Bob Marchant is a good editor but it's a stretch that he could recognize an individual hand. Didn't he say on television that he thought that it might be a woman stringer?"

"Yes, that was to avoid a lawsuit for libel. He told me this confidentially."

"Well, *confidentially*, Ann, if he repeats it then it will be more than libel he'd need to worry about."

"Mac, you sound like you know who Deep Throat is."

"I don't know Peter Doath. The fact that what he prints is true seems to be irrelevant; the FBI, CIA, Congress, President, and media all want him found and dealt with. For the truth, Ann? Have we gone so far over that we punish the truth?"

"Or her," said Ann.

"What?"

"It may be a her."

"I don't think so," said Mac. "If it's an anagram for Deep Throat then it's probably a man close to the candidate. Turn it around. What if Anders is throwing up a trial balloon?"

"Interesting thought!"

"Ask him," said Mac. "Next time you see him."

"You know he doesn't do interviews. And he never allows women into his press conferences."

Mac had accomplished what he set out to do. The seed was planted; he had also been seen by most of Washington having lunch with Ann Gold. She was difficult to miss. Time to change the subject.

"Your friend Virginia Black did me a favor, bailed out the interviews."

"My ass."

"Pardon?"

"That was a joke, the two of you dancing around the most controversial speech of the Convention."

"Well, we didn't know he was going to be the running mate. It looked to me as devil if you do, devil if you don't. Frick and Frack, who were supposed to speak, bailed out. Perhaps a gossip columnist might know where they went and who paid? Probably the same person as always: your next door neighbor, your voter."

"Mac, if you knew Peter Doath, would you tell me?"

Mac leaned forward and so did Ann.

"Be careful. Someone asking where Anders was in the Peace Corps drowned himself in Boston Harbor."

It was a lie of course, but he needed the diversion away from Virginia and away from the article currently in print in Europe. Also it could not harm the late Norm Harrison.

Ann's phone sounded and she looked at the message on her screen."Just got an exclusive bit of dirt via text. I love technology. Got to run, my darling. See you soon."

She was gone. And she left him to pay the bill.

Next stop, Mac thought, *Marjorie White's headquarters, then it should be safe to head home.*

Chapter Twenty-Four

Marjorie White's headquarters was six thousand square feet of empty retail space. From two hundred yards it was obvious; the windows were plastered with photographs of the current vice president and the senator from Florida, bound together in a common cause. Bumper stickers, announcing White-Anders, were on every parking meter, on every traffic signal post, and on a number of car bumpers.

Mac noted a solitary Joseph-Merrill sticker on a telephone pole. The sticker was two tones, set diagonally to show that the name was two different people. He smiled, wondering how long before this intrusion was noticed and plastered over.

Inside the building the air was more subdued than he remembered at previous campaign headquarters. There were balloons, about a hundred telephones, television screens everywhere, boxes piled as high as possible, top heavy with leaflets, bumper stickers, banners, and pictures of the candidates; all with a shelf life measured in days. One banner, designed with changeable numbers, now had a large sixty-three emphasizing the number of days until November 5th.

About half of the phones were manned by volunteers, some calling for donations, some taking pledges, some calling to thank people for previous donations in the hope of securing more money. Mac surmised that the other phones might be utilized later as volunteers came from various offices, and calls would increase as the general population finished their regular work day. A different area was set up to answer questions and deal with volunteers in different states. These calls out and in were to bolster morale, distribute more flyers, and organize door to door campaigns. The size of the operation was overwhelming.

In this mêlée Mac spotted the candidate, hands on her hips, listening with only half of her attention to a staffer explain the problems of door to door campaigning in urban areas. Marjorie, when finally allowed a position, told the staffer to find a solution and act on it, she referred to the calendar and the staffer's experience. It was an act of diplomacy that Mac could see was reenacted a hundred times a day.

Marjorie turned, acknowledged Mac, then strode away to the next crisis, touching her husband affectionately on the arm, as she passed. It was likely, Mac determined, as much personal interaction as they were going to get in the coming weeks.

"Hi David."

"Hi, Mac; seen Helen?"

"No, not lately. She was pretty tired, just crashed somewhere probably. I think that your lady, the candidate, could do with a break too."

"We all could, but with sixty-three days left there's no letting up now," he looked automatically at the wall calendar.

"The boys well?"

"Now they are," he nodded to the two boys at the back of the room, one staring desultorily at the scene, without seeing, the other head bent to a message being sent or received on his telephone."Did Helen mention…?"

"Mention what?" Mac asked.

"Never mind. They're fine."

Mac did not press, he knew where and how to get the answers.

"I'll just say hello."

David did not respond, his attention already drawn to another thought.

"Hi, boys. How's it going?"

"Boring."

"Tres boring."

"Well at least you're practicing your French!"

They both smiled, but it seemed like it was dragged from them.

"Mac, can you spring us from here?"

"Yes, Mac, just for a couple of hours, an hour, fifteen minutes."

"Depends what you're doing jail time for."

"Nothing," they chorused, looking at the secret service agent.

"Let's ask Dad then," Mac suggested.

They were animated for the first time and rushed to where Dave White was standing.

Given the request in babble speak, Dave turned to Mac.

"It hasn't been fair on them I know, but…."

"Please, Dad!"

"Where to?" Dave asked Mac.

"Aeronautical Museum?"

"That should be public enough. Take Matt and the car outside."

"Thanks, Dad," both boys said at the same time. Then both started to laugh.

The secret service guard also seemed pleased to have been sprung from the boredom of nothing happening. Matt sat up front with the driver while the boys sat either side of Mac in the back.

"I want to see the space capsule."

"I want to see the Spirit of St Louis."

"I think," said Mac, "that Matt might have flown one of those planes."

"A prop plane, no way!" said Ian with awe.

There was general laughter and it was a convivial party that toured the exhibits for over an hour with Matt sharing his knowledge of fighter planes and surveillance satellites.

Matt looked at Mac and tapped his watch indicating that it was time to leave.

"Let's go," Mac said to the boys.

"Stay close," warned Matt.

The boys, uninhibited, took Mac's hands.

Matt had called for the car and then verified that it was the same driver before waving them down to the back door.

Back at the Democratic nominees' headquarters the boys ran to tell their stories. Marjorie was clearly waiting and cried as she held them.

"Mac…" she turned and ran to the back of the room.

"She's been like this since…." Dave was searching for the word.

"Since we were kidnapped," supplied Ian, receiving a thump from his older brother.

"When was that?" asked Mac.

An imperceptible tilt of the head from Dave suggested that the answer should come in private.

They entered a small office and closed the door.

"We were on the road. The boys were here with a nanny and with the secret service guard. He must have been part of it. The boys left for school, never arrived. A message asking if Marjorie had decided on a vice presidential running mate was received; when told it was none of his business, the man asked if Anders had been considered. I responded, no, he had not been considered. The person hung up. Then I looked at the caller ID. It was my phone. The caller was using David Junior's phone."

"Then what?"

"By then Anders had spoken in Boston. We were aghast. The same voice called Marjorie's cell using David Junior's phone and asked if Marjorie had decided on a running mate, had Anders been considered. It was twenty-four hours. We couldn't tell anyone. Marjorie flew back to Washington and then to Boston early. We had to confront Anders."

"And?"

"And nothing. He said he would be proud to serve his country as Vice President."

"Just like that?"

"Just like that."

"The party line? Canvassing? Fundraising?"

"Not to worry, he knew how to serve."

"Just like that?"

"Just like that."

"The boys showed up at the Convention Center as Marjorie made the announcement. The photographs in the West Coast papers had it right. Marjorie's arms around her family with Anders center stage."

Mac stayed a few more minutes and then excused himself, saying that he had an appointment he needed to keep. To say that he was stunned would be an understatement. Walking down the street his mind was in turmoil and he needed to stop and think. Mac headed home.

It was likely that his phone was bugged, his computer compromised, his every move analyzed, but they could not invade his thoughts. He thought best by writing things down and so he took out a notebook.

What did he know? At first it seemed like nothing, and then as he filled two pages of random thoughts and notes he realized that he knew a lot. But he still knew nothing.

Okay, he thought. *What do I know? End game! There it is, simple. Now, why do I care? Because others have cared and been hurt. Do I want to be hurt? Do I want Helen, Sue, my mother hurt? No. Then walk away be left unscarred. Depending, of course, on the end game.*

But Mac knew something. Something on this piece of paper scared them – whoever they were – and it was keeping him alive. Charles George had died. Pauline Poles knew why and died. Norm Harrison asked about financing and died. Marjorie White was compromised by extortion and kidnapping.

Mac had been watched, searched, had his privacy invaded, but he had not died. Why? Because he knew something and it would come to the surface at his death.

The phone rang, bringing him to the present. He would remember every word on the page. The ability to remember depended upon writing facts down on a sheet of paper. He would then not only remember every thought that he had, but exactly where he had written it on the page. Looking one last time he started to burn the page while answering the telephone.

"Hello."

"Carol here. Ray and I were wondering if you'd like to come over for dinner."

"Delighted, but who is cooking?"

"Me, of course. Veal Marsala all right?"

"Absolutely. I'll bring red wine."

"Great, see you in about an hour."

This was good news as evidently Helen had woken up, had emphasized a need for caution, and was not leaving.

A shower and shave later, Mac left his apartment. He took his computer as he normally would when meeting his agent. It was just another business meeting. Although he had a few bottles of decent red wine, he detoured and stopped at a wine shop to give the person following, if any, a chance to report something like a Montepulciano 2005.

"Mac, I heard that remark about my cooking," Sue said, taking the wine from Mac.

"Sue, I said nothing about your cooking, I was just happy that Carol was in the kitchen."

"We started drinking without you," Carol called from the rear. "There's a beer opened in the living room for you. Ray needs to help me for a few minutes, then we can eat."

Helen was wrapped in a large fluffy dressing gown, pink with pink trim. It was clearly Carol's and designed for cold weather. It was not cold but she held it around her like a comforter, her two hands on a mug of tea or coffee. She looked better, but it was clear that she was far from well.

"Did you hear from HQ?"

"Yes, Helen, I am very well thank you."

Tears welled in her eyes and he regretted the comment.

"I went by HQ," he said, moving close to her.

"How were the boys?" she asked.

"They're great; I took them to the museum."

"You what?"She was confused, concerned, scared all in one emotion.

"David told me what happened. Well, most of what happened. The boys were safe with me. They were a ticking bomb in that room; their parents checking on them every two minutes, an armed guard to go to the bathroom, the mindless monotony of volunteers on telephones saying the same thing again and again."

"Dave told you?"

"Yes."

"Does Marjorie know that Dave told you?"

"Probably not, but they're his kids too."

"I'm sorry, Mac."

"Dinner's served." Sue had quietly knocked on the woodwork and stood by the door.

"I'm not hungry." Helen had shrunk into the dressing gown.

"But you will eat," said Mac. "It would break Carol's heart if you didn't."

Helen managed a smile and slowly stood up.

An antipasto with rolls preceded the veal, served with ziti covered in sauce and fried spinach. It was outstanding; everyone agreed. They were also polite enough not to mention that Helen had hardly touched the salad, had no bread, and had had a taste of each item on her plate then sat pushing everything around for ten minutes. She excused herself and went back to the spare bedroom to rest.

Mac watched her leave. "She'll probably sleep until morning. Sue, when you leave, can you take her with you?"

"Sure, Mac, but what is going on?"

"Read my book."

"Is it in there?"

"No. Don't ask; neither of you should ask."

"Where is the book?"

"In there," Mac said, pointing to his computer. "It'll be on time. If my agent can get it edited, proofed, and whatever else she does, I can deliver two days after the election and it will be on the shelves before inauguration."

"Finished by November 7th?"

"In rough draft. November 5th is generally just a tally, one concession speech which I could write now and one acceptance speech which begins, 'I congratulate my opponent on a well-run race…'.instead of 'This was a forgone conclusion, why did they bother…'."

Both Sue and Carol duly laughed at Mac's performance.

"So, do I get coffee and tiramisu?"

"Of course," Carol said.

Mac felt differently than the bravado he exhibited. He was concerned. Was the concern for himself or for Helen? For any individual or was it for the country? It was difficult to separate; when he thought through one concern another surfaced. Who else cared? There had to be other people; he was not the only smart person in America. Or perhaps he was wrong. Even if he was right there was no way that he was going to alter the course of events. Why not be a reporter and report.

Chapter Twenty-Five

The next morning Mac was up early, still wrestling with the thoughts that had finally tired him into a deep sleep.

"Hi," Mac heard when he picked up his ringing phone. Helen's voice was on the other end of the line.

"Hi, yourself."

"Sleep well?"

"Yes," Mac lied."You?"

"Very. Thank you."

"For?"

"Thank you for being you, Mac. I love you and miss you. The boys think that you're great for taking them to the museum. David was relieved that they'd had a little sanity in their lives."

"You're obviously at HQ."

"Yes, there were a dozen messages once I found my phone and switched it on. The first debate is next week, then there's a vice presidential candidate debate, then another debate – all of this while appearing in every state, kissing every baby, attending media events, fundraising, etc., etc."

"I didn't think they did that anymore," said Mac.

"Do what?"

"Kiss babies."

"I think it's a euphemism."

"Oh, you mean they kiss the other end of the anatomy, and not of the babies."

Helen laughed. "Mac, you make even the grossest things sound professional."

"And accurate. Dinner tonight?"

"Sure, Italian?"

It was clear that Helen was feeling much better.

"I haven't had breakfast yet, but it sounds good to me."

"Are you coming by HQ today?"

"No. Equal opportunity writer. Thought I might look in on the Ellie May Joseph and Merrill campaign."

"Spy for me, let me know what they're up to."

"Want to know what kind of cold pizza they have?"

"That too," she whispered.

"See you later."

"Bye."

The Joseph-Merrill ticket headquarters was in a former car showroom so that it was visible to passersby and everyone there was obviously busy. Inside was bedlam. All the noise and movement usually associated with a campaign was there, in contrast to the previous day in the opponent's place of business. The reason became obvious as Mac watched from just inside the door. They thought that they were going to win.

Ellie May's head of security, Bobby, walked over to and greeted him like an old friend.

"Mac, where've you been?"

"Around, Bobby, and you?"

"Everywhere. We have to take the secret service, but I've seen no trouble."

"Ellie May trusts you and you know the characters."

"Who you looking for? Everybody wants Miss Ellie," he said. This statement reminded Mac of a scene from Beverly Hillbillies, the old comedy show from the 1960s that was still in reruns.

"If she's unavailable, how about Paul Merrill?"

"Anybody is available to you, Mac; just say the word."

"Okay. Merrill, then five minutes with Ellie May."

Paul Merrill was asleep in the chair but woke as they entered.

"This is Matthew MacDougal, Mr. Merrill; he's on the good guy list."

"Thanks, Bobby."

"Mr. Merrill, thanks for seeing me. I'd hate to be on Bobby's bad guy list, and I'm sorry for waking you."

"No problem. I can catnap anytime, anywhere. What can I do for you?"

"Just a little interview if that's all right with you?"

"Shoot."

"First, the obvious. I know that you've been asked many times, but I like to hear things; why you?"

"You mean a well-healed, well-educated Bostonian matched up with a Texas longhorn who's been educated in school and on the range. We have matching philosophies and complement each other."

"To match your rephrasing my question, let me rephrase your answer," said Mac. "You mean that you can capture and raise money from both sides of the Colorado River and both sides of the Mason-Dixon line."

"Okay, Mr. MacDougal. Now that I failed your first question, what next?"

"Call me Mac, please. You didn't fail: I expected to hear the talk show answer. What do you think will be your greatest challenge in your debate with Anders?"

Paul Merrill frowned and thought about his answer.

"I could say that my worthy opponent has untenable positions that we intend to attack, but that's what you call a talk show answer. I think that my biggest challenge is to convince my aides that this is serious. They're of the opinion that Anders's ideas are dangerous."

"Can you be specific?"

"Well, bringing the troops home has repercussions to the economy and to the unemployment rate. Manufacturing will be affected, as will the defense budget, and that is just domestic. On the international level there are commitments to allies, to governments, the supply of military equipment and know how."

"Isn't that dangerous in anyone's opinion?"

"Not if you're a voter serving overseas or a family member of someone in the military. At the end of the day who puts you in office: economists and congressional aides or the voter?"

"The positions taken by Anders then are all vote getters?"

"Maybe." Paul Merrill was a politician, there was no black and white, it was all grey. "That's the real danger; attack on any of these issues and you can lose the military friendly vote, the recent immigrant vote, or the young people's vote."

"You didn't mention the elderly. They vote and there is a real threat to their entitlements."

"True, and they are the most vulnerable to a slowdown in the economy. Interest rates are falling on their fixed income."

"So what are you going to do?" Mac asked.

"Wait. Wait and watch his direction in the next few weeks before the fateful day."

"You also need to lay out your cards in the coming weeks," said Mac.

"Correct, but I just have to stay close to the party line."

"You bet your ass you do!" Ellie May Joseph had entered the room. "Good to see you, Mac. Did my V.P. spill his guts? Did you cut him like a catfish?" She was smiling.

This was a happy camp. Ellie May looked rested and relaxed.

"Not entirely. I was hoping you might fill in the gaps."

"I understand that my opponent does not look well. Is she ill? Are there other problems? Boys well?"

"Call her and ask," Mac suggested.

"Serves me right; I knew you wouldn't answer. Marjorie is a strong, ambitious woman and we are preparing our debate on domestic policy as if she were 100%."

"Good thinking. What are you concentrating on?"

"Why should I answer when you're dating Helen Harvey?"

"Because you know there's no pillow talk and no sides taken."

"I do know that; in fact, I asked that you be the moderator for our debate."

"I know," Mac said. "I declined; I understand my decision was a popular move as a couple of more experienced political anchors were fighting over the primetime slots. Now they will moderate one each and give NPR the vice presidential nominees which may be the job nobody wants."

"Mac, did you see the London piece?"

"Who by? On what?"

"By Leonad Vallice."

"Never heard of him."

"Or her?" asked Ellie May.

"Or her," answered Mac.

"The article suggested that Anders as Vice President would preside over Congress and, as such, would have feet in two sides of the checks and balances, White House and Congress."

"And the third?" asked Mac innocently.

"Well, there's already a seat to be filled on the Supreme Court that Watkins, not wishing to waste his time or political capital, has said will wait for the next President, plus we understand another judge has a tumor," said Ellie May.

"Is this in the article?"

"Yes," Ellie and Paul replied simultaneously.

"Well then," said Mac, "everything in the article is true. Besides, the President nominates to the Supreme Court," his voice trailed off as he remembered the kidnapping.

"What, Mac? What is it?"

"Just wondering what the point is."

"No checks and balances is the point."

"The brain trust thinks that we are looking at another anagram: Linda Lovelace," Paul Merrill interjected.

"The hooker," said Mac. "Sounds like it may be a member of Congress."

"With a sense of humor?" asked Paul,

"Lets out anyone in Congress," agreed Mac to general amusement.

"I'm sure that he, or she, will surface on late night TV eventually," Mac continued.

"It's just strange that with it being true that the person isn't coming forward now," Ellie May said.

"We might not be talking about it if he or she were to come forward," said Paul

"Maybe that's the point, although I'm not sure who else is talking about the facts; all I've heard is about finding the author, not authenticating or disproving any of the material." Mac rose from his seat and shook everyone's hands saying, "Well, I've got to go disseminate this scintillating conversation to the world. See you at the debate. By the way, Helen wanted me to find out what kind of cold pizza you have over here." Everyone laughed and he left through the labyrinth of campaign workers.

It was clear to Mac that the Republican candidates were cognizant of the issues. They were focused on the Democratic nominee for vice president. It was also clear that they had a spy in the Democratic headquarters. They knew some of the problems, some of the angst, and knew that he had spent time there yesterday. Since it was likely that someone was also reporting to the Democrats, it was politics as usual.

The first debate was a resounding success for Ellie May Joseph. It was obvious that the Republicans knew it. Strangely the content of her arguments was not convincing, but the delivery was confident. Immigration was killing the south: Texas, New Mexico, Arizona, California...She was rolling and managed to include the fifty states with a sweep. She attacked the present administration on their no-policy policy and ridiculed Anders's plan to open the gates.

Marjorie vacillated between defending President Watkins and defending her running mate. Defending is being on the back foot and it went downhill from there. Marjorie looked awful, sounded worse, and got pulverized. There was no mercy. She forgot what the

National Debt was and could not recall the balance eight years previously when elected into office.

Mac watched the proceedings from the back of the hall and had been surprised that Arthur Anders chose the same viewing spot. It was odd that he would stay out of the spotlight but be present. When Mac looked over there was a smirk on Anders's face that was hard to define. The two men flanking the candidate looked at Mac, knowing who he was. Mac knew them too.

After the debate Mac went back to the dressing rooms which were on either side of the stage. Both had food and drink available; one looked like a wedding, the other like a wake. He went in search of Helen.

She was entering a room at the rear and, as the door opened, Mac could see David trying to comfort Marjorie who was shaking and sobbing.

"Helen."

"Not now, Mac."

"Breakfast?"

"Maybe."

The newspapers trashed the performance and the odds on favorite Marjorie White slipped to three-to-one, while Ellie May Joseph was accepted as the favorite to be the next President. Mac knew that there would still be some adjustments but he could not see how the Democrats could recover.

Chapter Twenty-Six

The images would not leave, Anders's smirking face, Marjorie crying, David's look of concern, and Helen. Helen, her face, her body language, her voice: all speaking of fear. Then the debate, Ellie May exultant, Marjorie defeated. All of the images were wrong. He said it out loud just to get it into the air, "All the images are wrong."

He woke up; thank goodness the nightmare was over. The light of day gave the lie life. It was true, it had all happened, not in a nightmare but in the glare of lights under the gaze of millions.

"Damn!" he said as he cut himself shaving. "Concentrate or put the blade closer to your neck," he told himself.

The morning news program was advertising that Paul Merrill would be the guest at the top of the hour; in the meantime they showed, again and again, Marjorie White's confusion.

Mac knew how the interview would go just by the tone of the announcer introducing the sound bites and a Republican voice to explain it.

"Perhaps Senator Merrill can explain or speculate on the extraordinary scenes witnessed in last night's debate. We invited the Democratic ticket to join us, but they declined. Next, the weather…."

Mac was in Paula's Restaurant early and found that he had no appetite. He ordered coffee and raisin toast. The newspaper headlines were filled with political news; he found the article attributed to Leonad Vallice on page four.

Reading it again, he smiled, and then saw that it was the subject of the editorial. The editorial was basically that reporters should use their names when writing and not make veiled suggestions that the Constitution was flawed when it set up the balance of power. The article continued in this direction until concluding smugly that the system worked and that the White-Anders ticket had imploded. It seemed to Mac that it failed, by its smugness, to address the question argued. *Well*, he thought, *that should provoke some letters to the editor*. Most would be by someone called 'name withheld on request.' He smiled.

Still smiling, he saw Helen enter the restaurant. She was wearing sunglasses and carrying her computer.

"Good morning. Like to read the papers?" Mac asked waving at the pile in front of him.

"No thank you. I make news, remember."

"Coffee and oatmeal please," Helen ordered from Paula who had appeared at the table. "Marjorie and family went down to her parents at the shore. I have to put out a press release. God, what a mess!"

Mac recognized that she needed to talk and kept quiet.

Helen continued, "She is mentally fried. We practiced the questions, we practiced the answers, and then one little word and she couldn't remember her own name. The kids, she won't let them out of sight, then she looks up, sees them waving and loses a thought mid-sentence. What a mess! Now I have to meet the press and explain. What do I tell them? That she has run away, that her parents are sick, that she is sick, and that she is afraid? What? What a frigging mess!"

The cereal arrived and they stopped talking. When the waitress was out of earshot, Helen stated, "Next debate is Merrill versus Anders. He must be salivating this morning. Anders doesn't want to practice. Says he doesn't care what the questions are, or Merrill's projected answers. He didn't even come by last night; we called him. Then he said everything was fine. Was he watching? Is he on the same planet? How can that guy Leonad think that Anders might have any influence from the last row in Congress? After this he might have his key to the washroom taken away."

"You think that this Leonad is a guy?" Mac asked.

"I know he is, Mac." She smiled for the first time.

The smile quickly left. "What a mess! What do I do?"

"I think it calls for one step at a time. First the press release, then Marjorie strong, third the boys safe. How's that?"

"Thanks, Mac. That's three things and I only need to do one, but you're right; the others intrude. So what do I say? What do I concoct for the great unwashed?"

"I think that reporters now take regular showers. I would suggest the truth. Marjorie was unwell. The combination of stress and lack of sleep may have been exacerbated by a plate of shellfish. She is getting a little home cooking and will press conference seven tomorrow morning; any questions?"

"Seven a.m.?"

"Reporters ask fewer questions while they are drinking their first cup of coffee."

"Mac, I love you!"

"Because of my brilliant solution?"

"No, because of your short fat hairy legs." They both laughed at their inside joke. She continued, "And because I can rely on your support, and for you to pay for breakfast." She flashed him a winning smile. "Thanks for everything. I've gotta go get out a few press releases."

As Mac watched her walk out, he felt like there was a hole in the room. He needed to do his own planning for the day. One, write up his report of the debate; two, find a place for that editorial.

The media tried to keep up the pressure on the White campaign but it soon petered out. They could resurrect it whenever they needed to demonstrate a gaffe.

In the next few days, Marjorie took off, rejuvenated, on a series of huge rallies. It was obvious to some that she was often at the opposite end to the country to her running mate, even if sometimes she and her opponent were in the same city. The boys had been sent back to school. It was business as usual.

The Vice presidential debate was a success for Marjorie. Immediately afterwards she appeared to be congratulating her running mate and the next day appeared on the talk shows taking a centrist interpretation of his wilder announcements. This was helped by the fact that Helen had provided the program announcers with the questions and rehearsed the answers. The question of troop withdrawals was asked in such a way that Marjorie was able to appear statesman-like in answering that *of course we all hoped that the foreign community could enforce sanctions. These sanctions and self-policing would provide a safer world and our troops would be withdrawn*. The follow up question could not be asked because of time constraints, or because the anchor did not know the next question of how we were to get there and when. The issue of immigration was asked in the question of policy and the answer was similarly broad. The answer was that our laws allowed for immigration and also for deportation. These laws had been subject to many tests recently and it was time to bring them up to date. A panel was to be formed immediately to examine a modern approach to this issue bearing in mind that this great country had been founded on an immigration population.

It sounded logical. It seemed like the Democratic camp was a normal family. There was the teenager rascal and the controlling mother. Different approaches but with a common goal.

The Vice presidential Candidate debate had been widely watched and Senator Anders had taken the issues presented and run hard at them. In the area of domestic policy he was forthright, but Merrill, well-rehearsed, had provided numbers and dollars relating to the impact of his positions and thereby appeared to be the more prepared. In foreign issues, Merrill may have had the edge in his portrayal of America as the benevolent uncle of democracy in a world growing used to the influence. He called China a friend and the cameras caught Anders in a sneer. He spoke of Europe as an ally and partner, while Anders looked bored.

Helen was jubilant when she called and, with coded words, spoke of dinner and more. Fine with Mac, more than fine. He was lonely in a city with millions of people. Working everyday on his book, without a break, was tedious.

Dinner was excellent; neither had an appetite for dessert – at least nothing that the restaurant served.

They went back to Helen's apartment. It was a fashionable high-rise with security. The man at the front desk tipped his cap towards Helen and looked enviously at Mac.

The apartment was small, less than one thousand feet, with an open area for kitchen and living space. The kitchen was separated by an island at which there were two bar stools with high backs. In the corner of the living room was a desk with a computer and in the middle of the wall there was a large television screen. Normally tidy, it was an ongoing joke how sterile the room was. Now it was strewn with posters, the desk had a mass of notes and stick-em reminders attached everywhere, even the side of the television had not been left unscathed. The bathroom and bedroom doors were closed; Mac knew they would be neat and tidy.

"Whose place have you borrowed?" Mac asked with a sweep of his arm at the disarray.

"I redid the place to make you feel at home," she replied playfully.

"You did well. I thought it was my place until I saw the pink stick-ems."

"Oh, I forgot that you don't have a sensitive side," said Helen.

"Only for you, sweetheart!" Mac was doing a Bogart impression.

"For me?" Helen blinked her eyes in Vivien Leigh style.

The playful mood ended when Mac, with mime, asked if the walls had ears. Helen shrugged; she had been too busy to worry about it.

"The polls have you moving up again," said Mac.

"Marjorie is doing very well."

"Just a month to go."

"Actually, thirty-three days; then I get my life back."

"Maybe," said Mac.

"Are you going to spoil tonight and talk shop?" she asked.

"I'll take door number one," Mac said pointing toward the bedroom and smiling.

"Oh, Rhett darling, I'm not sure that I should." Vivien Leigh had returned.

There was only one response. "Frankly, my dear, I don't give a damn!"

As they entered the bedroom Helen asked, "Who's Frankly?"

They made love. They slept. They made love again.

Under the covers, wrapped as tightly to one another as they could possibly be, a tangle of arms and legs, they whispered.

"Are you being careful?" Mac asked.

"Yes. Are you?"

"Overly cautious most of the time. I see people behind trees; suspect every phone call; I'm even suspicious of my friends."

"I never thanked you properly for dumping me at Carol's place."

"I think you just did," he said kissing her gently. "Of course, if you want to again, I won't complain."

She laughed. "I told Marjorie about the therapeutic effect it had on my attitude and she did the same thing. Slept it out then had enough time to put goals and perspective together. For some reason Anders was not pleased. I think he thought she might fold or be manipulated."

"But where would he be if she failed to make President?" Mac asked.

"I don't know," she admitted.

They both slept some more and Helen woke to the smell of coffee.

"Good morning," she called out.

When Mac entered, she opened her arms and he walked into them. He was still naked.

"Want cereal and coffee for breakfast? It's about all I can find. Actually, I was surprised to see milk."

"You mean you were surprised to see milk that was not past its 'sell by' date."

"That too."

"Shower first."

"Sounds good to me. Showers are a two person sport."

"Sometimes."

After both were refreshed and redressed, Mac asked, "What's next?"

"You and me, or business?" asked Helen.

"Do you always answer a question with a question?"

"You and me: to be determined after the election. Business: debate on foreign policy."

"Should be good," Mac stated, choosing to focus on the latter response.

"Should be excellent; Marjorie has experience, has knowledge, is on an upswing, and it is likely that the voter wants a person who can be strong with both enemies and allies."

"Too often I think we hold friends and allies to a more stringent set of rules than our enemies," said Mac.

"Are you talking foreign policy or personal?"

"Both."

They were equally quiet, thinking of the conversation.

"You know, Mac, I think you've just given me the sound bite I need for the debate. The American voter thinks in a very narrow way and foreign policy is something that happens in the next country, the next town, the next street. Humanizing foreign policy is a way to get it into the ten o'clock news. Thanks for making breakfast. See you at the debate."

Mac deposited a quick kiss on Helen's cheek and left. Helen was already at her computer typing a memo. She absently waved as he closed the door.

Chapter Twenty-Seven

Helen was correct. The second debate was a direct contrast to the first. Marjorie appeared statesman-like from the moment she set foot on stage. She was simply attired in a pale blue dress with a single string of pearls. Waving to fans and people that she recognized in the audience, there was no apparent tension.

Ellie May had chosen a pant suit which was designed to look professional. Although she looked comfortable in her choice of clothing, the look across at a confident bright opponent appeared, according to Mac's observations, to have made her nervous.

The debate was lively, although it was clear that Ellie May was remembering what she had been tutored. The statistics were accurate, the foreign policy aid and numbers were memorized. Marjorie, on the other hand, knew why the numbers had been increased or decreased; she had spoken with the leaders and understood their needs. She spoke of friends and neighbors, bullies and cheats. It was personal.

The opportunity to sum up in individual five minute speeches was pivotal.

Ellie May Joseph spoke of the need to expand exports to other countries, bring manufacturing and skilled jobs back to the United States. She reiterated the need to control immigration, to secure jobs and profits that would stay in America. When she spoke of aid, it was products, not cash.

Marjorie White moved slightly to the side of the podium. It was a move designed to engage the audience, especially those on television. Her speech, timed to perfection, spoke of the relationships between countries as between friends and neighbors. Neighbors to the north and south, where we should need no fences. Friends in Europe, in the Middle East, and in Africa where, if they were in need, we should provide that support. Enemies and false friends should not be afforded the same generosity. A true friend does not shake your hand and hold out the other for money. Someone who demands money in order to be your friend, never will be. She concluded by saying, *Terrorists will never be asked to eat at our table.*

The centrist message was delivered into the living rooms and kitchens of America. Everyone understood the message. It was a huge success.

In the final days there was very little else on the news. All four of the candidates were followed by armies of media and armies of supporters. There were hecklers who were dealt with according to the mood. Arthur Anders had no time for them and waited until they were removed. Mac, watching him, again saw the smirk. Anders was enjoying himself.

Marjorie handled the hecklers best by engaging them and asking that they come up front so that she could hear their questions and then dismissing those with one issue agendas. When attacked on providing arms that killed civilians, she pointed out that people killed people, not the weapons. She also reminded them that they had the right to vote and to run for office and encouraged them to do either or both.

Ellie May generally did well, although her opinions on guns and immigrants brought several clashes to her rallies. Paul Merrill dealt with the interruptions with equinity and stayed on his subject matter.

The polls were close. The betting money was equally divided.

The campaign funds were rolling in. Each party was anticipating spending over three billion dollars. This was helping the economy but mostly the media. Television revenues were up, magazine revenues were up, and newspapers were never at a loss for material despite the dwindling readership of print versus their electronic format.

There was a steady stream of anti-Anders' writers claiming to be Deep Throat, writing articles and letters to the newspapers and magazines. Probably twenty times that number were sending tweets with the same claims.

Mac tracked some of these for information. One person tweeted that he had been beaten unconscious after leaving the library from which Mac had sent his last article. It appeared that the student who had not logged off before Mac used his computer identity, had claimed to be Deep Throat and had been interrogated by the police then beaten. It appeared that someone was still looking for the source of the article. If the articles were true, then who was looking? Someone afraid of the truth or someone looking to suppress the truth?

One of the few times that Mac bumped into Helen, they had lunch. It was the opportunity he needed to ask about finances since the reports had been in the papers.

"Helen, how does Anders do with fundraisers?"

"Great, I guess."

"You guess? Why don't you know?"

"He never has any," said Helen.

"I'm no accountant," said Mac, "but it appears that a campaign spending three billion dollars must raise money."

"Marjorie brings in a ton; the Democratic Committees around the country have been great."

"Anders?"

"Money comes in, a lot. Bills get paid. Television, radio, and newspapers are good for an enormous amount of free air time because of him."

"So you're working on the theory that bad news is still news."

"Mac, you know how it works. The newspapers, TV, radio, all print or repeat what he says; the Democratic Party is asked to respond; viewers, listeners, readers, call or write in, agreeing or disagreeing, and then he's in another city. Four bites of the cherry."

"I thought cash was king."

"It is, but you can spend or save. He has no ads, therefore, no cost. The transportation and security he pays for himself: no cost. He has no entourage or baggage: no cost."

"He still has to account for it."

"There will be an accounting. Central committee will insist, voting laws insist," she replied.

"So you're thinking that he'll hang himself from his own petard?"

"Something like that."

"Be careful, Helen. Be very careful that you're not the one trying to loosen the jockstrap."

Later that night, Virginia Black called and said that she had been visited regarding the Deep Throat articles. She had called, coincidentally, to ask Mac to reciprocate in a pre-election panel at his alma mater. It was an invitation that he tried to refuse, but the obligation to Virginia and his commitment to Boston College made it impossible.

"You'll have to buy me dinner this time," said Mac.

"You're on," agreed Virginia.

A draft of the book was sent to Sue and the next few weeks were engaged in rewrites, or explanations, correcting punctuation and minor typographical errors. Fortunately Sue had the patience of a saint and, when asked to reread sections for the third or fourth time, never groused and always produced an insight and revision or suggestion without complaint.

"We have the book ready. Do you want to write the last two chapters so we can go to print before the election," asked Sue, a little tongue in cheek.

"Only if you want to tell me who'll win and what the concession speech is."

"You're so good at this, Mac, you must have it already in your head; write the two alternatives then we can pre-edit and be ready."

"Sorry, got to go to Boston."

"Pro bono…again!"

"Well I'll get dinner out of it. Boston College Club is quite smart you know."

"I hope you have travel insurance."

"With you as beneficiary, Sue," he laughed.

The conversations with Helen were getting snappier and shorter as the election date neared. There was little point spread between the candidates and, depending on the politics of the television channel, either could win. Mac kept his own thoughts and tally.

The day that Mac flew to Boston, a bombshell was dropped. Eight days before the election.

Starting as a blog, it circled the globe. News affiliates in Europe picked it up and it started appearing on the airways in America.

It was incredible. There were claims and counterclaims. There were denials. There were threats of reprisals, but against whom? It became a tidal wave; there was no stopping it.

The Republican ticket said that the video was a plot, that the information was fake. Their information and evidence was compelling, but it was too late. The media searched for the source of the blog without success. An old man, who looked a lot like the man in the blog, had died three months before.

Three months: Mac did the math. It was before the Democratic Party Conference. But not before…

Mac went to the blog. It was the most watched video in the world. It was an old man, holding a photograph album. Answering the cameras he said, "Yeah, I know Andy Crocker. Davey we used to call him, like Davey Crocket." He stopped for a wheezing cough of laughter at the memory. "We rode together."

A distant voice asked, prodding "Rode?"

"Yeah, you know, with the Klan."

"The Klan?"

"Yeah, like I told you, we burned out a few nigger houses, drank a lot of moonshine."

"You have pictures?" a prodding, rehearsed question.

"Sure." Opening the book to a picture of five hooded riders and pointing to one on the right side, the man said, "That's him."

"And you?"

"Next to him, see on the black horse with the blaze."

"Don't look like you."

"Does if you know." The wheezing laughter grew."This is me; handsome devil, eh?" He had turned a page. Now four men were passing moonshine; two had their hoods off and he was pointing to one. "That's me. That's Davey there. Made a lot of money Davey did. Never shared neither. Kids went to fancy schools, came up some."

"His granddaughter?"

"Yeah, she's on the television all the time; Ellie May, same name as her grand mommy. Old Davey's wife."

Mac downloaded the blog and watched it several more times. It was a fake, had to be, but how, why, and by whom?

He had to catch his plane. He had to think about it.

It was obvious what the first questions were going to be tonight. Virginia Black met him at his hotel and it was her first question.

"Is Ellie May Joseph done?"

"Give me a chance to catch my breath and then we'll talk."

Mac checked into the Marriott. Virginia followed him upstairs where he shaved and changed into a clean shirt and adjusted his tie. She kept up a barrage of questions.

"Let's ask Ellie, shall we?" suggested Mac.

"She's not talking to anyone," Virginia said.

Mac opened his computer and found the number for Bobby,

"Howdy."

"Bobby, its Mac."

"She's not talking."

"That picture is a fake. I can prove it."

"She might talk with you, Mac. Hold on, it may take a few minutes."

Mac heard Ellie May in the background yelling, "And why should I talk to anyone who is screwing my opponent's media guru?" He heard Bobby say something muffled; Mac figured Bobby had covered the phone so he would not hear anything else inappropriate that Ellie May might say out of her frustration and anger. She came to the phone and said, "What proof?"

"Ellie May, your spy in the Democratic office needs to get a life and a better command of the English language."

"Sorry, Mac. That video has finished me. You have something to make me feel better?"

"The whole blog is a fake. You know I have a photographic memory, that I never take notes because I remember stuff. Looking at the blog on the flight to Boston I remember seeing those photographs before. The two men drinking moonshine were both hanged in the twenties. The man in the video would've been five years old. 'Handsome devil' might have been the man's father, but the other man was not your granddaddy or any relation."

"Thanks, Mac. I feel better than I have all day."

"You're welcome. Good luck!"

"That true?" Virginia was already dialing her editor with a scoop. She had been party to an interview with Ellie May Joseph when no one else could get through and ascertained that she had been framed, just eight, make that seven days before the election. "How do I prove it?" Virginia was all reporter now.

"There's a black studies course here in Boston – Harvard or BU – call someone there to ask them to compare the picture with their archives of the 1920s."

"Thanks, Mac." She was again dialing her cell phone while picking up the hotel phone to get another number.

They walked into the Boston College Club and, since it was early, found a quiet place in the back. Virginia had done all that she could at the moment but was keyed with excitement that is born from a scoop. Not to mention the chance to be the first to break a national story.

Remembering the first and second rule of public speaking, Mac ate lightly and had a nonalcoholic drink.

"Virginia." He broke into her recitation of things to do in order for her story to be heard around the world.

"Sorry, Mac."

"You had a visit from the police?"

"Yes; strange."

"Strange, how?"

"I'm a reporter, a good reporter, and I didn't get their names or precinct number."

"Black and white with identification? Six foot one or two, suits, white shirts, dark ties, military haircuts?"

"Yes, do you know them?"

Mac ignored the question. "What'd they want?" he continued.

"They asked about the articles in San Francisco and in London – said that they were filed by friends of mine. I told them that if they were written by reporters, they were fraternal brothers and sisters in the literary but not necessarily the literal sense and not necessarily friends."

"Did they ask about me?"

"Yes, I told them that we had a mutual friend in Washington, that I had appeared on television with you, and that we had gone to dinner."

"They ask where?"

"Yes. I asked what that had to do with my fraternal friend. I think I asked for their badge numbers and took out my book. The speaker said they were on special assignment and that they'd get back to me."

Mac leaned close and whispered, "Have your place checked for bugs."

"Very boring."

"Remember, Virginia, be very, very careful. Do not call your friend in London again, ever."

"This story okay?" she asked now with real concern.

"Yes, you got it from Ellie May Joseph didn't you? I may have put you in touch but it's your scoop."

"Thanks."

"Who else is speaking tonight?"

"It's a panel actually: a Republican, former congressman Ron Anderson, and Democrat, our new Governor Flores, and you as an independent, neutral observer. Should be a huge crowd, local television is carrying it live. The local anchor is moderator, will try to hog the cameras."

After dinner they took a cab to the Chestnut Hill campus.

When they walked in, the introductions were done and the participants made small talk. Ron Anderson was a likable, typical New Englander. He wore a plaid shirt, slacks, sturdy shoes, and a plain tweed jacket. The tie looked as though it had been picked at random or that the wearer was color blind. Anderson did not notice, nor did he care. The moderator had been at great pains to match tie with handkerchief, both paisley to avoid showing bias. The pale yellow shirt had been favored over the blue for the same reason. Governor Flores arrived with a fanfare, so perfectly on time it was likely that one of his entourage had watched and notified the party to enter just as the moderator looked at his watch. Flores was dressed carefully, just right, light blue shirt with a red tie. Mac, who did not really think about his dress sense, was inwardly pleased that he had chosen the Boston College tie; red and gold just seemed right.

When Francis Flores entered, his eyes swept the room and rested for a few seconds on Mac before continuing the sweep. Introductions were made by the moderator, though not strictly necessary.

There was a break in routine with a small scuffle at the door before Sean Lynch entered, slightly disheveled.

"The rascals searched me," he declared.

"They think they're still working Fenway Park," Mac said.

This remark drew a hearty laugh from Ron Anderson and a glare from the governor.

"A wee drop after the show?" Sean asked Mac.

"Sure; where, the frat house?"

"No, I have clients. They're wearing good clothes; the club I think."

"Expense account?'

"Why not?" said Sean chuckling on his way out.

The interlude had served to take Mac's thoughts off the question of what was happening in the room. He smiled, his mood changing to one where he knew his friend was in the audience, a rooting party of one.

The moderator took a long time to introduce the participants and list their many achievements. Mac drew a few hoots when it was mentioned that he had graduated from these very walls. Mac made a mark, on the pad in front of him when Flores's service in the Peace Corps was mentioned. As he looked up it was directly into the eyes of the Peace Corps fraud. The first question was a warm-up question of each guest's assessment of how the campaign had been run to date.

It was no surprise when the moderator introduced the second question.

"In your opinion, will the unsubstantiated blog of misdeeds by the Republican Candidate's grandfather impact this election? First response from former Republican Congressman Ron Anderson."

This had obviously been discussed in the Anderson household and the breakfast coffee shop.

"In a campaign where the candidates have behaved with such admirable good taste, this is a dirty trick." His face reddened as he continued to postulate, without directly answering the question of the impact on the campaign.

"Our Democratic Governor Francis Flores; what impact are we likely to see on the election?"

Flores had slipped a little crib sheet of notes in front of himself. He glanced up and Mac saw the glimmer of a smirk that he almost recognized.

"That kind of behavior by an American has no place in America. If this took place seventy years or seven years ago, the facts have been hidden. It is impossible to believe that this was not known by the family. Certainly it should be rooted out. How can an American – White, Black, or Brown – vote for a candidate who helped hide this sordid family secret?"

Mac was making notes to himself and missed the rest of the rehearsed rhetoric. The notes, the smirk, the vehemence of the attack convinced him that the question had been written for this response. That the question was at the beginning was designed to put other speakers on the back foot.

The moderator was introducing Mac with relish. There were enough remarks in the program so far to fill the news several times over.

"Mr. Moderator," Mac responded, "I think that I agree with the governor, that there is no room in America for the kind of history on which we built a nation. The slave trade, the Klansmen, the massacre of the American Indians: these were all carried out by our fathers, grandfathers, or their fathers. To the extent they lie hidden in our families we should examine them and live our lives to make amends. The question was, what affect this blog is likely to have on the election. The question should be whether it should have an effect. I believe that the blog is a fake."

There was an audible gasp in the audience and a quickening of attention from attendees and staff in the hall.

Mac continued, "I know both presidential candidates. I have spoken to them both, many, many times. Ellie May Joseph has no skeletons in her closet and Marjorie White is too honest to have known about this blog. The moderator said it best when he called this an unsubstantiated blog. I agree with Ron Anderson when he calls this a dirty trick; I would go further and say that someone has a sick, sick sense of humor. Will this have an effect on this election? Yes; and on every election from this date on. We are no longer the land of the free."

The moderator, in the silence that followed, sensed a magical moment here, that everyone in the room would remember for the rest of their lives. He prolonged the moment and went to a station break and back to the studio. It had been agreed that there would be no commercial breaks, so the improvisation broke into the tension. Mac nodded his thanks. Flores looked at his notes to see what he had missed; Ron Anderson looked bemused.

There were questions on foreign policy knowledge and the direction in which each candidate might take the country. It was no surprise to Mac that Flores endorsed the isolationist that he assumed was the Democratic Party's manifests. Mac stayed in the center, between the hawk policies of the Republican candidate and the vague pacification of the Democrats.

In the summaries Ron Anderson was a gentleman, praising the Republican manifesto. Francis Flores, with notes, attacked with innuendo the Republican candidate. He was making it personal. It was not popular with the audience. The only mention of Marjorie White was as a member of the ticket. His good friend Arthur Anders was mentioned as a forward thinker, a man of action.

Mac spoke in praise of both presidential candidates and said that Paul Merrill was a sound politician and a Boston Brahmin. Arthur Anders may have a better grasp of the foreign policy, particularly with his experience in Africa with the Peace Corps; he made the statement looking at Flores for reaction. He got it.

The debate ended with polite applause and murmuring, then almost a collective gasp as the governor and his entourage swept out of the room without the obligatory shaking of hands. It was a snub. Only Mac knew why.

"Splendid! Splendid!" The moderator slapped Mac and Ron on their backs. "Have to run!"

Virginia gave Mac a quick wave as she headed out the door, phone in hand.

"Thanks, Mac." Ron Anderson said as he stood arm in arm with his wife. "I've been thinking of the trick that cost me my seat. It was the same thing, right? Having people think I was sick?"

"Yes, Ron, I'm afraid that it was."

"Did me a favor really. Don't miss it, not at all. Tonight was fun, but I still don't miss it." He then turned to his wife, "Time to go home, Sweetheart, and take the dog for a walk. Good night, Mac."

"Goodnight, Ron, Mrs. Anderson."

The Boston College Club was unusually noisy. Politics being the bread and butter of conversation in Boston there were added flavors tonight; the debate had sparked an argument over whether the blog was a fake.

"Let's ask the man," said Sean spotting Mac. "Is it or is it not?"

Mac was looking at a message on his cell phone: *Got it: 1921 MS not 1929 TX.*

"I can absolutely guarantee that it's a fake," he said. "I'll have a beer, please."

Chapter Twenty-Eight

It should have been the front page news in every city in the country and most capitals of the world. It was not. In fact evidence of a plot to discredit one of the candidates for president of the United States had been relegated to inside pages. The story barely made the newscasts. The outrage that was anticipated was overshadowed and overcome by a tragic event. The news surfaced while Mac slept, having consumed several beers and finally, after midnight, an Irish coffee.

Mac switched his phone back on. He had switched it off after the text message and had not reactivated it when he meandered through dark Boston streets to his hotel.

There were twelve messages. As he dialed to retrieve them, the phone rang.

"Where have you been? Have you seen the news?" Helen was distraught.

"Boston and no, I just woke up. What's wrong?"

"It's David!"

"David?"

There was a noise behind Helen which was indecipherable.

"I have to go," and she was gone.

Mac switched on CNN and looked at the messages, all from Helen, so he knew what they said. He also understood what they would not say, what they could not say.

"Breaking news this morning is the death of David White, husband of presidential front runner Marjorie White. Police are saying that the single car crash occurred just after one o'clock and it appears to have been an accident."

"My ass," said Mac at the television screen.

"Of worldwide interest this morning are the political implications. It was well known that the candidate and her husband had a strong working relationship. For more on the political aspects, we go to Washington."

The phone rang.

"Hello?"

"Mac, Hazel from the network. Can you get to the Boston studio and comment on the breaking news about the Whites?"

"To tell the world that it was no accident?"

"Actually we want your close insight into the effect on the White campaign."

"So you don't care if David White's death was murder?"

"Let the police worry about that; you're our political expert, our expert on the presidential campaign."

"The show must go on."

"Whatever," said the detached voice on the telephone.

"This time the show must go on without me," said Mac,

"Last chance, Mac; you know I'll have to get someone in."

"Get Francis Flores; even I would watch that interview."

"Good idea," said Hazel, ignoring or not recognizing the sarcasm.

The phone rang again.

"Mac, I have to speak to you; serendipity."

"Thursday?"

"Minus two."

Mac looked at the clock, he was in Boston and Helen wanted to meet today at ten.

"Okay, plus two." He could make two o'clock.

He could hear someone else calling Helen on the cell phone and on another phone. She was up to her armpits in work but needed to see him.

"Gotta go," she said and was gone.

He decided to start the coffee and packing if he was to make it back to Washington. He needed time to think; he started to layout his plan in the shower.

Mac had joined the commuters and the businessmen with briefcases, computers, and overnight bags on the earliest plane. Fortunately he had driven to the airport, so after a quick inspection he had been able to drive directly to his rendezvous. A couple of blocks from his destination, he pulled into a parking garage for the multi-story office park. It would be expensive parking, since his ticket would not be validated by a tenant, but it gave him the chance to check if anyone was interested in his return. No one was; he was not disappointed. Checking over his car at the airport he had been wondering how David might have died. Faulty brakes or faulty steering were the usual suspects, or at least they were in novels. Helen was already in Starbucks when he arrived just a few minutes after two.

The first thing that he noticed was the sticky bun that Helen was eating. She would normally never have ordered anything with that fat and calorie content. But it was already virtually crumbs on her plate. Looking from the door, his expectations gave him the usual outward recognizable signs, up close a different picture painted itself. Dressed in a dark grey suit with a high collared white shirt she was Helen, professional media mania. As he got closer her face collapsed, she stood and fell into his arms, sobbing and sniffling for a full minute. The people around at the time of day studiously ignored the public display of emotion.

Eventually Helen tried to speak. The words were in silent sobs and, since they seemed to be delivered as she breathed in, were unintelligible.

Mac disengaged himself and handed her his handkerchief.

"Everything will be okay," he said.

Apparently that was the wrong thing to say. She looked at him intently and said, "He's dead. Nothing will ever be okay again – not for Marjorie and not for the boys."

This time Mac just nodded and squeezed her hand.

"It happened last night, in Virginia," she continued.

Mac knew these things; he had watched the television monitors in the airport. He had bought newspapers that had the story. He had looked on the internet. It seemed, however, that Helen had to start and finish herself; a catharsis.

"He was going to take the boys to the shore, to his in-laws until next week." She was wracked with another wail which she stifled with the handkerchief. "What if the boys had been with him? We were working on the final week. All the speeches are scheduled, four or five a day. The interviews are mostly set up. We were co-coordinating with Anders and his team. They are very difficult. Someone said State Police, urgent, on the phone, so I picked it up expecting a request for a speech, or something. I told her that Marjorie was in a meeting and I'd take a message. She said, and I will hear it every day until I die: 'There has been an accident involving Mrs. White's husband' and that she needed to get to the hospital right away. Marjorie saw my face and asked if I was all right. How do you say that nothing is going to be right ever again? I remembered and repeated the words; they are the only thing you can say. Marjorie went from animated to deathly still, in a blink. The clatter was still going on around us, but it was like we were underwater, silent, enshrouded in fear.

"We ran out, grabbed a driver and told him to hurry. All the way there she kept saying, 'probably a scratch, he wants a little front page news, doesn't he, Helen. Helen, tell me everything is all right.' Well, it wasn't. Television crews were there before we were. Did you see the pictures?"

Mac nodded and squeezed her hand.

"She's a mess. We cancelled everything. She can't stop crying. I can't stop crying; everyone is crying."

"Helen!" Mac had to get her back to today. "Why did we have to meet today? I would have come to support you anyway, but you used our code, why?"

"He knew, Mac."

"Who knew what?"

"Anders knew that David was dead before the phone call."

"How do you know?"

"I saw the look on his face and then, when I said that there had been an accident, Marjorie glanced at him and I think that she saw the same look."

"You know what you're saying puts you in danger don't you?"

"Of course; and now you're in danger and Marjorie."

"Let's go to the park."

"It's raining," she protested.

"Not much, I need the air."

Mac did not say that he also needed time to think. Walking arm in arm they could walk and talk quietly. Helen had produced a folding rain hat while Mac enjoyed the cool drizzle of the November day with a possible icy mix overnight. The day perfectly matched their mood.

"What will Marjorie do?"

"She goes from defiance, to dejection to tears. One minute she will continue in his name, the next she is going home to New Jersey and take care of her boys."

"So what do you think?"

"Is there a plot, Mac?"

"You know there is; you told me where to look."

"Then why did I not see it?"

"Too close," said Mac.

"Too late." She was sniffling again. Mac's handkerchief was making her nose red.

"In the airport I bought some newspapers, including the London Times. Did you study their recent parliamentary election?"

"Yes, Marjorie's friendly with the new Prime Minister; they spoke."

"I asked if you studied the results."

"Why?"

"Because I think the pattern there is the same as the pattern here. The plot may be worldwide."

"You're joking!" She stopped and looked into his face to see that he was not.

Later, Mac sat in his apartment looking at a blank white wall and a blank white computer monitor. His vision may have been blank white too, but his mind was a kaleidoscope. The images came and went, fading, then rushing toward him. Time passed, the images were no less varied but he had to separate them. He typed into the keyboard: David White, then Charles George, then Pauline Poles, and finally Norman Harrison. Staring at the names he added 'others,' then put accident or suicide next to each name. A line came into his head as he was trying, without success, to see a connection.

'What doth it profit a man if he win the whole world and lose.....' he stopped. These words had been spoken by his father; he could not remember the man but his words had just come to him. If he believed in such things, he would have said that he was here, listening, watching. The thought stopped Mac and he could not finish the line. How could he tell anyone that his father had spoken to him? And what he had said? 'What doth it profit a man...' There was profit. Where was the profit in killing these people, if in fact somebody had killed them? Charles George had proof of a plot; Pauline Poles had found it and would have passed it to Mac. Norman Harrison had said that he would publically question the funds of Arthur Anders. David White was in a position to look at the finances of the vice presidential nominee.

Mac realized, with a start, that he had been here a year ago looking into the money trail and finding none. Just because he could not find it, did not mean that it did not exist.

There were times when elections had been rigged, when evidence of wrongdoing disappeared – Chicago for example. Boston and New York: the teamsters were experts at one time. Even if rumors were true, presidential elections were not immune. Florida ballot counting was notoriously suspect. History is likely to repeat itself, if not analyzed.

The blank white wall and the sparsely written on screen were still in front of him. He stared at the screen and then out loud, he said, "No!"

Picking up the phone he called Helen and then forced himself to think and sound calm.

"Mac, this better be important!"

"Life or death important enough for you?"

"Don't scare me."

"Is Marjorie there?"

"Yes," then whispering, "we're going over for the tenth or maybe twentieth time where we go from here. She's doing everything she can to keep busy until the funeral – says she's doing it for David."

"Bring her to the place we had lunch."

"When?"

"Leave now. Say that you both need a break and some air. Try to lose Anders's goons. But even if you don't, it's still imperative that you both be there in half an hour."

"Now you're really scaring me."

"Good. See you in half an hour, and Helen….."

"What?"

"I love you."

He hung up and typed a couple of lines into the screen and logged out.

Ten minutes later he had changed into a black turtleneck, charcoal grey pants, and a black raincoat with a pull out hood. It was prematurely dark with rain and rainclouds low overhead. There were few people around. A van across the street had windows misted over. Mac stood on the stoop until he saw a van coming down the street. Under cover of the obstruction, with his computer tucked under the raincoat, he headed down the puddle minefield, head down, splashes hitting the back of his legs as he jogged.

He sat at the rear of an empty Starbucks. The only customers were regulars, swiping their cards and collecting lattes or dark coffee with efficient familiarity. Mac stiffened as a policeman entered, but he greeted the server.

"Got something warm to put in my coffee, Penny?" the officer teased.

"Just my finger."

"Later then maybe?"

"Much later! Much, much later!"

The policeman left, laughing and the young server shook her head and rolled her eyes.

The exchange was unnerving. And the fact the Helen and Marjorie had not yet arrived was also bothering him. Mac was about to call Helen again when they arrived almost forty minutes late.

"Marjorie...."

"I know, Mac. Thanks."

Helen came back with two lattes.

"If I had another cup of lousy coffee today I would throw up." Helen sat opposite Mac as Marjorie had taken the seat next to him.

"It's nice to get out and get some fresh air," Marjorie said.

"Were you followed?"

"Mac, secret service goes everywhere with me. They're wired; even I can pick them out."

"What we talk about here must not be repeated. As I said to Helen, I believe that this is a matter of life and death."

Marjorie White stiffened at the mention of the word *death*.

"Look at this," Mac whispered and opened the computer page at the list of names. He had added the quote that had come to him. The page also listed the name of Ellie May Joseph's grandfather and the name of the new British Prime Minister, Claude Kirk.

"These names, I know them," Marjorie said.

"If I'm right, then the first four were murdered and there will be more if we look here and in England. I read the election results in the UK and then went into some of the stories. A number of predicted winners dropped out at the last minute; they were replaced exclusively by men."

"Impossible! More than half of Parliament is made up of women," Marjorie exclaimed.

"Was," corrected Mac.

"So?" This was information that by training she had to see, an aide could confirm this with a few keystrokes. She would call Claude Kirk in the morning.

"I believe that you, Marjorie, were destined to join the top list as a suicide."

The silence lasted for two minutes.

"Impossible," Marjorie's retort was barely audible. "Mac, you're a friend and I respect your knowledge and your investigative abilities. I've never questioned your judgment or your impartiality until now. Where is the proof?"

"You want a smoking gun in the hand of a sole perpetrator? That's only in movies."

"So what do you have?"

"Money."

"Money?"

"The one thing in common for the four names, and the reason that I'm still alive, for now."

"A bit theatrical, even for you, Mac." Helen spoke for the first time.

"I was the last known person to speak to Charles George, Pauline Poles, and Norman Harrison. What do you make of that?"

Helen had reddened at the rebuke but now turned white at the implications.

"Here is the evidence, all circumstantial. Charles George said that he had been ousted, that the opponent had not raised any funds. He was thinking of talking it through; he died. When I talked to him he was distraught, not suicidal. Pauline Poles came to Washington to speak to me, give me information. We discovered her body; there was no computer, no memory disk. Pauline Poles was not suicidal; she was going to be working in Washington again. Norman Harrison, a man conditioned to drink, went to ask where Anders had raised funds to run for senate. He would never have left a party with food and drink. David, I can only speculate, was wondering the same thing."

"And why not you?"

"Because they think that I have the proof."

"And do you?"

"For your own safety don't ask. Another thing happened," he pointed to the screen. "Something else is taking place. The book in Vegas makes no sense even to gamblers, unless you consider…"

"Excuse me, what do you mean by book?"

"A gambler's book has to balance. Two horse race: White and Joseph; if someone bets $100 on White and someone else $100 on Joseph the book balances."

"And if someone bets $200 on White?"

"Then the bookie will offer odds 1-2 on White, 2-1 on Joseph, the book balances."

"Okay. I got it, I think, so what's happening?"

"Someone is betting against the candidates."

"So what?" Marjorie pushed.

"So why not vote for the other candidate?" answered Mac.

"I don't know, why?"

"Because," Mac paused, and took a deep breath, "because neither candidate is going to win."

"Impossible!"

"That's the third time, Marjorie, that you have said impossible. Consider that millions wagered on each candidate finds someone to take all the bets and that person collects. Why would that person need to raise funds. If you know what number will win a lottery, why buy more than one ticket?"

"Does Ellie May know that she's not going to win?" Helen asked.

"While I was waiting for you I booked a flight to Vegas and on to Dallas. She's going to the Cowboys' Thursday night game, speech at half-time, then flying red eye back to the East Coast. I think that I can hitch a ride."

"What if….." pointing to the screen, "…. her plane is due an accident?" Marjorie asked.

Mac shrugged.

"What can we do?" Marjorie was half-convinced and now looking for action.

"How about a statement? A written statement that you are of sound mind and not suicidal," Mac suggested.

"And will she be believed?" asked Helen.

"Let's have Penny, the server, witness and the secret service guy outside."

"What if he's one of them?"

"Even better; then they will know tonight instead of waiting to get the official word, composed by Helen, in their morning newspapers, and on the morning shows."

"And the election?"

"Can you wait until I get back from Vegas Friday morning?"

Chapter Twenty-Nine

Mac stopped into the lobby of The Hay-Adams and made two calls before taking a cab to the airport. He was tired; all of these cloak and dagger maneuvers were wearing on him. He fell asleep in the cab to the airport

When had he ever slept in a car? Probably not since he was a toddler.

The driver woke him as they stopped at the British Airways check in. Mac decided that he would take the shuttle over to Jet Blue. Why was he doing this James Bond stuff? Part of the game was his answer. Anyone with the kind of influence that he had seen could easily check airline manifests. Would they involve him in an accident? If they brought down the plane just to make him disappear, that showed the kind of despicable people he was tracking. But he already knew the kind of people he was dealing with. And who could he tell from a grave?

Tiredness overcame him on the plane and he slept the whole way to Las Vegas. Sleeping, he was smiling. He was thinking of the phone calls, just before he passed into a beautiful unconsciousness. The first to Hal ensured that a recognizable driver met him at the airport; the second call he made was to Ann Gold.

Using his handkerchief to muffle his voice a little, he affected a Southern accent.

"Miss Gold, I have a snippet of information for you."

"Who is this?"

"Aren't you a trifle interested in some scuttlebutt on the race to the White House?"

"Of course, but I like to know who to credit and to whom I may owe a favor."

She was good, and Mac was going to give her names, but not until she had worked for it. Things you got cheaply were not worth much.

"No credit needed, no favors expected."

"Well, what can I call you then?"

"Miss Gold, are you trying to trace my call?"

"No, I wouldn't do such a thing." Her tone made it obvious that she was indeed using a feature on her device to bring up a caller ID or telephone number.

"Good. I wouldn't want to have to call your competition."

"Listen, Mister, whoever you are, I have enough for my by-line for tomorrow."

"And a funeral helps."

"Yes, a nice man, unlike yourself."

"Miss Gold, my name is Peter Doath."

"Pull the other leg."

"You want the story or not?"

"Okay, let me get a pad."

The delay was a ruse as the conversation was being recorded, so Mac ignored the request and avoided further delay by starting to talk. He had rehearsed it several times so the Southern accent was working just fine.

"Miss Gold, I believe that David White was murdered."

"That's ridiculous, go to the police."

"Listen, he might not have been the target. If you hear that Marjorie White has committed suicide that will be a lie. This call and your reporting will likely save her life."

"I don't get it," Ann Gold stated, sounding bemused.

"Y'all are smart. Just think about it. Love your column, give me credit or yourself. Bye."

Hanging up the pay phone, he headed out to his flight.

Mac awoke to pitch black and figured that they were flying across the desert; then the sky lit with a halo of light over a city with dark secrets. The rumored visitors from a distant planet must surely have seen this incandescent oasis. This is the place most likely for an extraterrestrial being to touch down. But what would he or she think? The shear hubris of a place that catered only for pleasure. Twenty-four hours a day, energy was expended by the inhabitants to match the wattage on the streets, the buildings swathed with spotlights.

Hal was not working since it was close to midnight and the book that he oversaw was mostly East Coast money, so his busiest time was in the morning. It was fine with Mac; he would catch a few more hours sleep and be ready at eight when he was expected. It was tempting to play a little blackjack, but prudence suggested that he stay out of the ever vigilant camera's eye.

After a few short hours of restless sleep, Mac went down to the hotel lobby for his meeting.

"Morning, Mac. Sleep well?"

"Not really, but thanks for the pick up."

"All part of the service."

"Why? I'm not a gambler. How can I repay?"

"We'll think of a way, one day." Hal wheezed, the perpetual cigarette hanging from one side of his mouth.

"What if I don't?"

"It's just a joke, Mac It's like gambling or running a book, not everybody loses; but we don't know who the winners and losers are until the end. With relationships, if we show respect to everyone, then one of these days some may be able to help us. We don't know who."

"Speaking of winners, the book on the presidential race, have you found out anything?"

"Yes and no." Hal coughed and lit another cigarette.

"Illuminating," said Mac sarcastically.

"We got interested ourselves so we pulled a few of those favors that we talked about. Seems that this is one elaborate scheme. The betting appears to run to billions."

"Who the hell has that kind of money?"

"Government."

"You're saying that the U.S. Government is funding gambling, extortion, intimidation, blackmail, and murder?"

"Well, hell, yes. They have been for hundreds of years. But, in this case, not knowingly."

"Explain from the beginning please."

"I have to start from the end. Money is being placed against both presidential candidates. The money is coming through the Bahamas. We traced it through Vanuatu, the Maldives, and Malta back to Turkey."

"Turkey? All of the other places are tax havens and probably money laundering centers. How did you do that?"

"Who can beat us at money laundering?" Hal laughed and had a coughing spell; it was a deep chesty cough that wracked his body. It occurred to Mac that the expression 'died laughing' could actually happen one day to this grey emaciated figure.

"We had a few computer geeks in the IRS, isn't that ironic, Homeland Security, and the CIA help us out."

"So now you're in Turkey, now what?"

"We have temporarily hit a wall. The wall is a Muslim group close to the government."

"Since the US sends aid to Turkey, you're suggesting that the money may be laundered back in here to fund these activities."

"Or it may never leave."

"You lost me," Mac said.

"We don't understand that bit ourselves, but some of our brightest economists sat with our foreign brain trust and came up with a Dr. Strangelove scenario. Someone in the States is making money; someone in Turkey is making terrorists."

"Terrorists?"

"That would be bad for our business, very bad. We should be the bad boys in America."

Dallas was hot even though it was November. A call to the Joseph camp had produced a driver at the airport. Not Bobby, but his wife, Betty Jo, who had been brought in to help with the campaign. It was also the only way she could see Bobby in this sprint to the finish.

At the Dallas Republican Headquarters it was mayhem. The frenzy, the palpable energy in the room, was similar to Las Vegas but with much less laughter. This was serious; no one was not totally focused.

There was a line of people shouting questions at the candidate. The phone chief would call and Ellie May would turn, look at the scribbled note, and her tone of voice would change in the instant.

"Hi, Mrs. Temple, thank you so very much for your generous support. Now, please make sure all of your neighbors go to the polls next Tuesday. Thank you and God Bless."

Instantly back to some other speaker, snarling, "No. There is no way I can be in Phoenix on Monday; I don't care how big the shopping mall is."

"Mac, how y'all doing?" Ellie May had stopped, excused herself for a minute, and then took a seat. Having taken off her shoes, she was trying to have a few minutes out of the maelstrom.

"Fine, thanks. You looked worn out."

"Well, I figure you're a long time dead and you can get all the rest that you want when you are on the other side of the grass. I sent Bobby out for Chinese food. He'll bring enough for a regiment. That's okay 'cause if I see another pizza, ever, I swear someone will wear it."

Mac chuckled, comfortable with this all-American, with the warmth of welcome which she managed to exude to everyone.

"Y'all didn't come out here just to see my Cowboys beat your Redskins though. Ain't that as anti-P.C. statement as you've heard today?"

Although political correctness was not high on the things that Ellie May concerned herself with, she knew that she ignored it at her peril.

"Five bucks says Washington wins," Mac said.

"You have a wager, my friend."

"I came from Las Vegas. Interesting conversation, but before that I was on my way to warn you. I needed to speak, face to face, in private."

Bobby entered the room with a huge plate of food for Ellie May.

"You want a plate of this, Mac?"

"No, thanks. Can you join us for a couple of minutes?"

"Sure. Just let me grab something to eat."

Bobby was immediately back with a plate brimming with food. They started to eat.

"I believe that someone killed David White."

"So does Ann Gold in the Post and Peter Doath who seems to be close to the candidate. Did you see the article?"

"Yes, and I believe it's true. I also believe that you will also be targeted."

"Good luck to someone trying," said Bobby. "This is Dallas and we remember."

"It won't be assassination, Bobby."

"Mac, have you warned Marjorie?" Ellie May asked. It was interesting how her first thought was of her rival.

"Yes."

"It's not possible."

"It is possible." Mac found himself repeating the same argument to people who were convinced that what was seen was how things were and would be. There were new rules, new money, and new players. The internet and global business made it impossible for America, or any country, to proceed with business as usual. Major car manufacturers in America were making foreign cars, supermarkets were owned by European conglomerates, American computer companies were invested in the Far East. America, still dependent on imported oil, was selling bonds to pay for it to other countries.

"What if I said that someone has wagered heavily that neither of you will win on Tuesday?"

"Impossible."

"Wagered over a billion dollars at four-to-one"

"Impossible; we would've heard."

"How?"

"I don't know," Ellie May admitted.

Bobby interrupted. "That story about yo' granddaddy was a vicious attack."

"That reporter woman spotted that pack of lies." said Ellie May.

"Please, please take care. I'm serious," pleaded Mac.

"See you at the game," she responded. Ellie May was putting on her shoes. "Time to go back to the race." And with that Ellie May was gone.

"I'll bring in even more people," said Bobby.

"Watch the inside too."

"You mean spies?"

"You know that they're here," said Mac. Then he abruptly asked, "Can I catch a ride back East with you?"

"Sure, Mac," replied Bobby. "No problem."

"Make sure someone you trust thoroughly checks out the plane and that you recognize the pilot."

Chapter Thirty

The trip back to the East Coast was calm and smooth with a nearly full moon dancing alongside, then above, before settling in behind clouds and shyly disappearing.

It was quiet, most people were sleeping or snoozing, already weary and aware that there were five days ahead that would be more hectic than any they had yet experienced, and then they could rest.

Toward dawn, as they approached Washington, there was a commotion that woke Mac who was instantly attentive to the verbal exchange. One of the reporters on the plane rushed forward to the place where Ellie May and family were sleeping. A secret service agent stopped him.

"I must see Ellie May," the reporter stated, holding his telephone.

"They're not supposed to be switched on in flight."

"Yeah, I know," he shrugged. "She has to see this before we land."

"I'll check." The agent discretely looked through. "Sheila, man here says it's important."

Sheila Hutchins came out.

"Sorry to disturb you, miss."

"It's okay. I was working on the speech for when the plane lands."

"Then you'll want to see this," said the reporter hitting play on the video message.

"I'll get her," Sheila said with a sense of panic.

A few minutes later a tousled, hastily dressed Ellie May appeared.

"What have you got, John?"

"Video came through, thought you should see it." He repeated the playing of the video message and Mac looked over his shoulder.

"Similar to before, this has been denied and proved false, so what's the difference?"

"This video has gone viral; I checked before I came up here; also, it's specifically targeted."

"Okay, let's go in and sit down. Sheila, Mac, can you join us?"

Seated around the room were six people. The table in the middle had been ignored as people roused from sleep sat or slumped in the chairs, pushed to the walls. Someone came in with a tray of coffees in paper cups which rapidly disappeared. The video had been connected to a large screen television monitor. It was now played for everyone.

The movie showed Klu-Klux riders dragging three black men to a tree, throwing ropes over a branch, and with the ropes tied to their saddles, backed their horses up until the legs left the ground. The men on horseback, six in all, then passed around a jug of moonshine. As each man took a drink, he lifted his head. There was an intake of breath as one of the men bore an uncanny resemblance to Ellie May Joseph's father. As the picture froze in close-up a voice said, "Do you want this family in the White House? A place for whites, not for people of color. Vote no to this affront to our freedom; remember all that we have fought for. Vote Tuesday to send this family away."

The video concluded with a picture of Martin Luther King.

"Comments?" Ellie May asked.

No one spoke.

"Mac, you think that this is part of what we were discussing last night?"

"Yes, I do."

"We were able to refute the charges last time," said Sheila. "We need to forcibly deny and prove the fraud."

"John?" Marjorie looked at the reporter. "You said that this was targeted."

"I did a little research when this came into my phone. It appears that this video went viral throughout the Black and Hispanic communities. Someone blasted this simultaneously through the Southern States and urban communities, you recall this is where there has been a push to increase voter enrollment for the last few years."

"Is this bad, Mac?"

"Yes. It's too late to find proof. And proof won't sway many of this targeted group; they've never seen a reason to believe middle-class America. And, unless I am very much mistaken, there will be more of these videos over the weekend."

"Like what?"

"Well, since you've made a stand on immigration, it will involve abuse of immigrants. If this is a sample of their work, it may involve more murders."

"Murders?" Ellie May was shocked.

"Sure, this video was made recently and probably used real people."

"No, you must be wrong."

"See if three youths are missing from the Delta region, probably big city."

The conversation was interrupted by the captain.

"Prepare to land, please take your seats and make sure that your seatbelts are properly fastened. Also, the tower has advised us that there is a reception of reporters and television crews in the airport."

"Okay," Ellie May said, "reconvene here when the seatbelt sign is off. Mac, sit with me please; you too Sheila." The other people returned to their seats. Mac could tell by the look on his face that John, the reporter who had brought this to Ellie May's attention, was obviously disappointed at being excluded. Ellie May did not seem to notice anyone else; she was focused and said, "Mac, you are one crazy, scary cowboy. What was the last comment about?"

"The kinds of trees in the picture are in the Delta; the black youths, one wearing high top sneakers. I'm sure that a forensic team could come up with a lot more, but you're out of time. Whoever planned this picked the optimum time to put this out. There's a weekend coming up just before the vote; every channel will make it the number one story, every weekend family gathering will discuss it."

"What can we do?" asked Sheila.

"Pray," Mac said.

"What if we go down South and plead our case?" Sheila was anxious.

"I believe that the organization that put together this video could organize a riot if you were to do that. I'm sorry that I can't help more. I'll tell everyone that the video is a fraud, beyond that I'm a neutral observer. Good luck."

"That's not a lot of use!" Sheila was exasperated that there was apparently no magic wand, no easy fix.

"Thanks, Mac," Ellie May said, recognizing the reality of the situation. "I appreciate your honesty and respect your opinion. Come on, Sheila; we have to prepare a statement. Let's look at the video again and then turn it over to the FBI with Mac's comments."

The plane taxied, but only Mac and a couple of crew members deplaned through a sea of cameras, microphones, and klieg lights. There were a few shouted questions. Mac pulled his rain jacket hood over his head and strode through the gauntlet.

There was a row of telephones and, with a twinge of conscience at the early hour, Mac dialed Helen's number. To his great surprise it was answered immediately, snatched up.

"Hello."

"Morning, Helen. You're up early."

"Or to bed late. I thought that it was Marjorie again."

"Tough?"

"Uh-huh!"

"Potomac?"

"Need some of that now!"

It being resolved that they would meet at Paula's for breakfast just as soon as they could get there, he hung up, hitched his overnight bag back onto his shoulder and picked up his computer.

He arrived half an hour later at his destination.

"What a mess," Helen said as he sat.

"Are you referring to the breakfast? The political scene? Or life in general?"asked Mac. "It appears as though the breakfast is the only good thing about today. The political scene is chaotic and life is lonely."

"Have you seen the KKK video?" Helen asked.

"Yes, a real killer, in more ways than one."

"Marjorie had nothing to do with it. We were as shocked as everyone else."

"I know. There are dirty tricks and spies in each other's camps, but this is so despicable that it's below the level of civilized behavior or common decency."

"Is it true?"

Mac was surprised at the question. "No, it's a fake. Made for an audience, for a purpose."

"Do you have proof?"

"No, but I have about a million reasons." Mac recounted the betting scenario and the implications. "If neither Marjorie White nor Ellie May Joseph wins, then there will be a huge pay day for someone."

There was silence, each with their own thoughts. Mac was thinking how to prove the video was a fake. The more he thought of it, the more convinced he was that everyone involved in the production of the video was probably dead. Except perhaps the person paying for it. He also knew from experience that the proof would take weeks or months to track down and then corroborate.

"A statement must be issued denouncing the video," Helen said. "But then what? Marjorie has more problems to deal with than to spend a lot of political capital on sending aid and succor to her rival. I mean, the poor woman has to bury her husband today."

They were interrupted when Paula turned up the volume on the television set nearby to hear a news bulletin. Ellie May's team had left the plane and they were standing shoulder to shoulder and facing the barrage of reporters.

"Let me make a statement, then I will answer questions. Perhaps my statement will satisfy you." It was spoken jocularly, and since nobody could ever remember reporters not to have some mundane, sometimes irrelevant question there was a smattering of laughter.

"Just before we landed I heard of a new attack on myself and on my family. I was shocked, I was dismayed. This had been a hard, fair fight to represent this great country, to take the seat as the head of the leading democracy in the world. I do not believe that Marjorie White knew of this attack and I will say publicly that anyone capable of such a deed is not a person anyone would want to see in the White House. The video is an obvious fraud. We have asked the FBI to investigate. We have passed to them all of the reasons that we believe are proof that it's fabricated. Anyone, running for any office in the government must be sure that there are no skeletons in his or her closet. I have examined my closet, and the closet of my Daddy and the closet of my Granddaddy; there are no skeletons, there are no white sheets hung there. Anyone running for office should not be beholden to individuals or to foreign governments. I am not beholden. Questions? I have time for three, and then I have an appointment at the White House. Yes," she said, pointing to the senior reporter from a large television network, whose hand stood among a forest of hands.

The question was actually a statement for his own television audience. The ramblings mentioned the earlier tape and finally stated the obvious worst conclusion. "Isn't it often true that where there is smoke there is fire?"

"Sir, if you play with matches, that is very likely true. But if someone intends you to see smoke where there is none, will you shout fire? Next?" she pointed to a young attentive woman at the front.

"Do you think that a foreign Government is involved?"

"Whoever is involved will be determined by the FBI. I am determined to work hard for the next few days to become the next President of the United States."

Pointing to another hand.

"Which foreign Government?"

"I suggest that you check notes with this young woman. Thank you and God bless America."

With Bobby in front, she weaved her way through the flashing of lights and additional shouted questions. Her sights were focused while she waved, still smiling, from the waiting car.

"What do you think of that Helen?" Mac asked.

"I think that Sheila Hutchins and her team did a hell of a good job. Very professional, slick, nice timing, just three questions and she practiced the answers to those asked. Great."

"The content was good too?" Mac asked.

"Oh, I suppose so." Helen looked down, "Marjorie has phoned three times since I've been sitting here."

"How is she?"

"Fine," Helen replied looking down.

"Helen, how's Marjorie?"

"She's a freaking mess; we all are. I can't remember what I came into a room for, and then I can't find my way out. It's brutal. We're putting out statements because we can't speak. The funeral is today at two. You'll be there," she added. It was a command; it was a plea.

"Of course."

"Some wanted to wait, some wanted private, some wanted network coverage; it was a nightmare. Television will find a way to cover it; the politicians are off campaigning, so it will end up being semi-private, family and some gaping ghouls."

"I'll be there as a friend."

"Thanks, Mac. I have to leave. See you about one then."

"Sure. I'll pick you up at your place."

Chapter Thirty-One

The funeral was unreal, influenced by media frenzy outside the church. There was an unseemly scene when the hearse carrying the coffin tried to pull into a space set aside for the purpose. A television reporter was standing in the space with her cameraman setting up opening remarks. After waiting a minute for her to move, and in spite of others shouting and pointing, a funeral employee approached and had to physically move her aside, over indignant protests.

The paparazzi had largely ignored requests for privacy. A cacophony of clicks and barrage of lights accompanied Marjorie, David Jr. and Ian into the church. Helen and other aides followed. The secret service detail had moved ahead and formed a wedge, a phalange of black suits and ties, dark glasses and earpieces.

Marjorie looked pale, hidden behind large black sunglasses. The boys, either side, held their mother's hands. It was difficult to see who was taking the greater comfort: Marjorie or the boys.

Behind the first sad group was a crying trio, his parents and sister, Angela. She supported her mother on one side while her father supported the other. They were obviously distraught that they were attending David's funeral; Mac wondered if they had started yet asking why.

It was against the rules; the old died, the young attended the funerals. The news and subsequent questions had taken a toll. They had aged overnight and it was an aging that would not reverse itself, not ever.

The service passed in a blur. Helen indicated that Mac should sit with her. She tightly held his hand, her nervousness and anxiety palpable. Marjorie had written a eulogy and Helen delivered it to the large congregation, silent but for the occasional audible sob.

As the congregation was filing out, the front seats first, Marjorie was stoic until she saw her rival, Ellie May Joseph, who had silently entered the church late. It was a moment of anxiety for everyone.

Ellie May held out a hand, slightly upturned as if to demonstrate that it was empty, that the gesture was of friendship. Marjorie blinked, stopped, and then embraced Ellie May.

Outside the reporters were quieter. Somehow during the service the acceptance of a finality that only death produces had imposed itself on the group.

The procession went back to Blair House, family only. Others leaving the church found cars or cabs and went back to lives that had not changed.

Mac went back to Blair House. Helen excused herself to the bathroom, the need to recompose herself of more immediate importance than to use the facilities. Mac, waiting nearby, was surprised to find Arthur Anders at his side. He had been at the church, but anonymous, in the middle of a pew, not at the end.

"Sad day." Anders was starting a conversation. Mac did not want to talk to him.

"Your wife here?" Mac was bringing up the subject which had ended so many interviews.

"Flying in today."

"That will be nice for you."

"Yes," without enthusiasm. "Why do you think Ellie May Joseph was in the church?"

This, then, was the reason for the conversation.

"How would I know?"

"It's well known that you are friendly, that you know her campaign better than anyone."

"You are kind. I arguably know more about most of the current and former candidates. The exception might be you. Is it possible that we can remedy that hole in my education?"

"H'm. I think that you know enough."

"But you don't know everything that I know about the campaign. Do you?" Mac was trying to bait him.

"I think that I know enough of what you know."

Was this the admission that he was responsible for the surveillance, or just that he knew, or was it a knee-jerk reaction to the baiting?

"Murder?" asked Mac.

"Singular or plural?"

"I thought that we were talking of David White. In the plural we would be talking a conspiracy; you could not possibly be referring to crows."

"We might have been referring to the exhaustion of the campaign trail, or are you a disciple of Peter Doath? An associate perhaps?"

"A journalist reports independently and hopefully neutrally. There is money to be made if one is right, but sometimes it is difficult to know where money comes from; don't you think?" Mac was pushing hard now. "I do know that the Joseph video was staged and that they have no intention of blaming that on Marjorie White."

"You didn't say the Democratic Committee."

"No, I didn't," agreed Mac pointedly.

"I would believe that you might go to the police if you know the source of a fake video, or if the perpetrators have infiltrated. I believe that it is a federal offense to subvert the course of political elections."

"Yes, it is," agreed Mac. "But impersonated policemen, then where would one go? I rely on the power of the word over the sword."

Anders was confident. The look was there, that look that he had seen in Boston. Mac remembered now that when talking with Ann Gold about the leaks to the press by his alter ego he had remembered a glimpse of Frank Flores's face. The look was the same. When he was debating in Boston, Frank Flores knew of David White's accident before it had happened.

Anders and Flores knew each other from their Peace Corps days. They had used the volunteer organization to pad their resume and to disappear for a year in Africa; in North Africa, Sudan, Algeria, Libya, it didn't matter where but he was willing to bet that there was a Turkish connection there, and someone who was in the British Parliament. What about France, Germany, Spain, Italy, Russia, the European Union Parliament? Well, maybe not Russia, Mac thought to himself.

The look on Anders's face said more clearly than words that he knew what was going to happen next. It also said that it was going to be soon. Was there time to intervene or was all that was left just a rattling of cages?

"The Peace Corps," he began, "appears to have been a pivotal point in your life."

"Yes, great experience."

"What country?"

"As you know from my resume: the Congo," he said with his trademark smirk.

Mac saw a flash, a map, a guess. Then he took target and said: "Sudan."

The smirk vanished. Direct hit.

"Congo." A snarl now.

"Were there Turkish missionaries there?" Another direct hit.

"Nice talking to you, but I have to go. I have a campaign to work."

"And a wife to meet," said Mac, now the one smiling.

"Yes," Anders agreed, walking away.

"That looked cozy," Helen said. "I waited until he left."

"Um. Where's Marjorie?"

"With the children in the library. Why?"

"I'm not sure."

"I think I'll go check," said Helen and turned toward a room closed off by curtained French doors.

Mac wandered over to a table laden with food that nobody would eat. He picked up a sandwich and some fruit and retreated to the corner of the room. He poured a cup of tea and stood with his thoughts.

"You're one of those damned reporters." David's father had stopped at the beverage table.

"Well, yes, I'm a reporter and, yes, likely to be damned, but I hardly think that the judgment will come this side of the divide."

"Sorry, but the stories go on and on. Leave it alone; let us grieve in peace."

"Sir, I considered David a friend. He was an outstanding human being, and everyone knew that. If the press is still carrying stories then it is an effort to explain such a tragic loss."

"I can't stand it. His mother..." he paused. "Eric couldn't make it back, Istanbul. Eric is Angela's husband," nodding toward his daughter."David called Eric the same day he died."

"Is Eric in the Foreign Office?" asked Mac.

"Bureau chief. David had asked what he knew about the Muslim Brotherhood. Eric told him that they were the quasi-government in Turkey. Does that make any sense?"

"None at all," lied Mac.

He had the pieces; he had the tiger by the tail. Now what?

Mac asked for and wrote down Eric's contact information.

Later, Helen relayed in detail the events and conversations that Mac had missed. Marjorie had taken a telephone call from Ellie May Joseph and, after the greetings and condolences, had a cryptic conversation. Mac guessed that Marjorie was aware of the likelihood that the telephone was not secure.

Ellie May had asked, "Can we meet?"

"Where and when?" had been Marjorie's response.

"The White House, one hour."

"Okay," Marjorie agreed."I'll clear you in."

As Vice President, Marjorie had access to the quiet room in the basement since the President had gone home to California in order to vote on Tuesday.

Helen continued laying out the events to Mac. "If the secret service folks were surprised at the strange happenings, they said nothing. Though one did make a phone call," she said. Ellie May showed up with three advisors: her press secretary, Sheila Hutchins, chief of security Bobby Williams, and her chief of staff,

Alistair Kirk. Marjorie took me, her chief of staff, and Matt, from her secret service detail." She went on to explain how Marjorie started the meeting by saying, "The reason that we are together is that we have a common cause while on different courses. The reason that we are here is security and privacy. Nothing of this meeting should ever leak. Questions?"

She added quickly that she had asked for and received permission from both parties to discuss the meeting with Mac.

Helen went on to say that Alistair Kirk had been seated defensively on the last seat on the Republican side. He had said, "The press probably knows of this meeting. The whole world probably knows of this meeting. How can we keep secret the subject matter?"

"Heads of state of all countries routinely have, behind closed doors, meetings with other heads of state. The press secretaries issue a statement that there was a meeting where progress was made on mutual issues…or some such nonsense," Helen had replied.

"Let's do it and worry about the real things. Not the press," agreed Sheila Hutchins. "Helen and I can deal with them later."

Helen went on, telling Mac that Ellie May had asked, "Why is Matthew McDougal not here?"

"Because this is political; he's a reporter and it reduces the speculation on the reason for the meeting," said Marjorie.

Mac commented, "The consummate politician."

Helen went on. "She gave you full credit. She said that if both of our campaigns have been targeted by ruthless, desperate people, as you believe, that we need to combine our forces and our information to determine, who, why, and what we can do to take back our lives, our campaign, and our dignity."

"Sounds like a nice plan in theory," Mac said. "Did anyone dare to answer those questions?"

"Yes," Helen answered. "Marjorie went on to say that we do, or at least we think we do, know who is involved. She flat out named the Muslim Brotherhood and explained who they are."

She continued by telling Mac that everyone had tried to speak at once. Marjorie stood and held up both hands. When quiet was restored she suggested that they make a list of issues, then a list of solutions.

"Sounds like Marjorie is going to make a great President if she's allowed the opportunity," he said.

"She will. I projected what we know and what we think on the big screen. I was scared as all hell, Mac, when I saw it so large. It's overwhelming.

"So what were the questions?"

"Who is behind the Muslim Brotherhood? What do they want? Where do they get their money? Who benefits in the U.S.? Why had this not been in the news? And what can we do?"

Mac was pleased that they had been listening to him, but it was frightening to consider the outcome if they could not put a stop to all of this.

"We went over what we know: The Muslim Brotherhood is a quasi-government group about which we know little. The CIA is actively watching and examining the work of this group. It appears that they get their seed money from the aid sent by the United States to Turkey, or maybe other Middle East countries. They then speculate on an election and, with the winnings, after paying the costs of manipulation, they fund the next round of elections. Alistar Kirk then mentioned that the only problem with the theory is that it's against Islamic law to wager."

"It's probably not wagering if you know the result beforehand," Mac replied. "There's always a loophole, Helen."

"And the scary thing is that it appears the beneficiaries span from U.S. politicians to the Senate, the House, governors, and other posts. Incidentally the pattern seems to include the UK, Germany, France, Italy and probably the European Union," Helen said with exasperation. "And the people who get hurt are initially other politicians. Some like Charles George and..." Helen hesitated, "others die; some have spurious untruths printed or broadcast about them," like Ellie May Joseph, and some are personally threatened. We also believe that there could be tampering with counting votes."

"How was all of that information received by those at the meeting?" asked Mac, always the reporter.

"Well, it was definitely questioned. One person wanted to know how we could be sure you were the last person to speak to Charles George and Pauline Poles before they allegedly committed suicide. But since neither were suicidal and evidence that they had of voter fraud vanished, and since someone has been betting heavily that neither of the candidates in the room would win, no one could come up with another plausible theory. I also informed them that the money is being laundered into the U.S. through several tax havens."

"Sounds like you about covered everything."

"I think so," Helen replied. "And, finally, it has not topped the news because who would believe it? There have been some articles by Peter Doath and Leonad Vallice which should have led to the story, but a strong lobby killed the story and attacked the messengers."

"Anyone ask who Doath and Vallice are?" Mac wondered aloud.

"Yes. Sheila asked if anyone knows the reporters. The resounding answer was, 'No'," said Helen. "Oh, Mac, this was the most stressful meeting I've ever attended. But I have to tell you that upon revealing the anagrams Deep Throat and Linda Lovelace, poor Bobby had asked, 'What's a stripper got to do with it?' It broke some of the tension when the rest of us laughed. But poor Bobby looked confused."

Mac smiled and asked, "So who broke the news to him that her nickname was Deep Throat?"

"Alistar. I swear, Mac, I'm not sure that man has a heart."

Mac laughed.

"Marjorie got everyone back on course though. She went over how the reporters attacked the messenger and expended energy in trying to find the reporter. All of the talk shows speculated on the anagrammatical connection or the benefit to one party or the other. None, not one, invested in the content. There had to be interference."

"So, what did everyone decide to do?"

"That question was put around the table. Not surprisingly the two chiefs of staff focused on gaining enough time to get through the election on Tuesday. The security people were talking access, control, locks, and shoring up the defenses. Sheila and I spoke of information which could or should not be disseminated. Marjorie disappeared into her own self. She was observing as if from on high, hearing without listening. She was aware of time passing while she was standing still, marking time, and treading water."

"Marjorie's had a rough week to say the least," Mac sympathized.

"Yes," Helen agreed. "Ellie May brought everyone back to the present problem by banging on the table. You should have heard her, Mac. She said, 'Enough of this partisan, defensive posturing shit. We need a plan!'"

Mac laughed again. "I can envision that. I always did like Ellie May's direct handling of things. She doesn't mince words."

"The CIA is looking into the foreign connection. The FBI is looking into David's death. Marjorie told everyone that we have to stay strong for three more days. Then she was defiant and said, 'What can they throw at us? If we go together to expose this plot, what are the consequences?'"

"I'm glad the meeting was secret. If Anders had known, he'd likely have blown up the entire White House. The CIA and FBI are likely too late; they would have to go to an oversight committee in Congress and there is at least one member of the benefitted politicians on each of those committees."

"I know."

"Democracy!" Mac said out of frustration. "The very thing that is supposed to protect us is making us prisoners."

"Marjorie suggested a frontal attack. Tomorrow morning we'll meet with the press and then hit as many morning and evening and weekend political talk shows as we can between now and Monday night."

"It seems that's the best that you can do," agreed Mac. "Ellie May is going to have to face the onslaught of seeing that doctored video a million times, but hopefully it will put a stop to this madness."

"Mac, do you have any advice. What evidence do we have to show the public?"

"Nothing. None," said Mac. "You'll have to rely on the goodwill and trust of the American people that all the campaigning has engendered. If they believed you then, they'll believe you now."

"What about our Vice presidential nominees?"

"Your judgment. I like Paul Merrill and think he can be trusted. I guess you have to leave that up to Ellie May."

"Sheila and I worked on a joint statement for the press. When we did, Sheila asked me if Marjorie trusts Anders. I hesitated out of loyalty before responding, 'No'."

Chapter Thirty-Two

Mac watched the breaking news on CNN. It was a strange sight. Three days before the election the competing candidates stood together, their chiefs of staff stood together, and their media relations directors stood together. The network had been given little notice. Reporters were falling over each other trying to get seats; most Mac recognized as stringers and figured it was because the principal White House reporters had taken the day off or headed to California. A few, alerted by their contacts at the White House, were baffled by this unprecedented press conference.

Helen Harvey and Sheila Hutchins approached the microphone.

"Earlier today," Helen began, "we asked President Watkins if the candidates representing the Republican and Democratic Parties might meet and discuss a matter of national security. A short while ago we shared the results of these discussions with the President. We are going to read a statement. The candidates will then each make a short statement. It is our intention to give you all that we know or suspect. Therefore there will be no questions."

Mac thought that Helen had done an outstanding job setting the ground rules. He was now on his feet, watching the television. He waited with trepidation.

Helen continued, "The CIA and FBI are investigating whether a foreign terrorist organization might have attempted to control the election of politicians both here and abroad. Questions have been raised and since it might appear that dirty tricks were emanating from the opposition, both of the candidates met here today to clear the air."

"Good, good," muttered Mac to himself. "Stay alive, sweet Helen." There was more to the statement and it concluded with a reference to the ongoing investigation and there being no further comment at this time.

Sheila Hutchins took the microphone.

"Ladies and gentlemen, I am here to endorse the previous statement and to confirm that we believe that the fabricated videos circulating were part of this plot which the FBI is investigating. We never believed that the Democratic presidential candidate had any involvement in this scheme. Let me now introduce the Republican candidate, Ellie May Joseph."

Mac frowned, "Sheila, Sheila, be careful!" She had not exonerated the Democratic Party, just the candidate.

Ellie May Joseph's statement was that this was not the time to talk about politics but to show a strong face to those who would oppose or suborn the American Democratic process. "If, please God, I am elected President on Tuesday, then I will seek out the perpetrators, root and branch. God bless America!"

Marjorie, in the black of the mourning, was finally showing the strains of the day as she took the microphone.

"I thank my opponent for agreeing to meet today at short notice. I have every intention of being counted and elected next Tuesday, and I promise that I will defend these shores as vigilantly as any previous President. Thank you all for your thoughts and messages of sympathy during this period of mourning for my family. I look forward to continuing to serve you all. God bless!"

In spite of the previous statement, a cacophony of questions were directed at the retreating backs on the podium.

Mac had recorded the press conference and was about to watch it again when his phone rang. He looked at the number and was tempted not to answer it as he recognized it belonged to Mark Hughes, then he thought Mark might leave a message that he did not want others to hear. He snatched the phone and spoke first.

"I know, I owe you a beer."

"This is…"

"Good time for me too. How about the Flying Shamrock just around the corner?"

"It's the…"

Mac cut him off before he could reveal the real name of the proposed rendezvous. "I know, how about fifteen minutes?"

"Okay, but Mac…"

"See you then!"

Twenty minutes later they were sitting in a crowded Irish bar called The Plough and Stars. They both ordered a Guinness draft. It was exceedingly noisy and most people were speaking directly into the ear of their companion or bellowing as loud as they might to be heard. The bartender was taking orders by hand signals and, since the predominant drink was beer, it was generally just a number of fingers in the air.

"Nice to see you, Mac; thanks for coming. We could have talked on the phone."

"Just a little paranoia. I was sure that you wanted to discuss something other than your seeing Helen while I was away."

"Just a lucky guess or are you clairvoyant?"

"The press conference had been on television, and then my phone rang. You had to be calling about something important triggered by today's events."

"Very good, Mac. Dead on." Mark paused and seemed to be organizing his thoughts. "It was the foreign government bit that had me thinking. Remember I told you that research we did was subverted; well I looked at the trend and it was Middle Eastern."

"Turkey?" interjected Mac.

"Yes, mostly. How'd you know?"

"Never mind; carry on."

"Turkey is in NATO."

"The eastern most member."

"When they were looking for planes, the Brits gave them Harriers, used of course; the Americans gave them F14's…used. The Turks, being Middle Eastern, accepted with both hands, and then held out their hands for money to maintain them, train pilots, and update the avionics."

"And who gave them the money?" asked Mac

"As usual only the U.S. agreed. It was part of the aid package anyway. The argument was that most of this work could be done by U.S. companies."

"Your clients."

"Mostly," agreed Mark.

"So where does the subverting come in?"

"We provided a report that less than half of the money allocated had actually been spent."

"The other half?"

"Disappeared. There seemed to be the usual fees paid to the politicians, but the work was never done."

"So, the planes?"

"Gathering dust. A few were refitted, a bunch of pilots trained in basics, no advanced training. The money disappeared: billions."

"What do your people in Turkey say?"

"The government office says that it's spent and accounted for; please send more money."

"Mark, I think you should document your story and then hide it after sending a copy to David White's brother-in-law in Istanbul. I'll get you his contact information. Let's meet here tomorrow at one, should be noisy for the football game."

Mark Hughes nodded. "Is there anything that I need to bring?"

"No, I have a good memory; just be careful and bring yourself, safely."

"Thanks, Mac," Mark said as he stood. He left cash for the drinks and made his way out of the crowded bar.

Mac watched Mark leave, then he watched to see if anyone followed Mark. After another fifteen minutes, Mac swallowed the last of his beer, added a few dollars to the money Mark had left, and went home.

The disaster struck like a train wreck the next day.

The world awoke to find negative stories in every major newspaper, ignoring the previous day's joint press conference. In spite of the denials and the doubts cast by the foreign media, it was a blitzkrieg. The television news highlighted the funeral footage and then gave twice the coverage to the claims and reclaims against Ellie May Joseph and her family. She was due to appear on a mid-morning television political talk show. In spite of the proximity of the election, the talk show pre-views highlighted the issue of the effect of social email. Mac thought it a strange topic, but he figured why not. It was denied, proved false, and was blatantly a fabrication. His fear, however, was that it was an ambush.

Mac tuned into the station where Ellie May would be appearing. The television announcer introducing the show warned viewers that there was developing news that would stream in as new information came to light. The talk show host introduced Ellie May Joseph as the Republican candidate for the White House and then, after pleasantries, showed the video footage which had been posted recently and asked for comment from Ellie May.

"This footage was seen by us yesterday and was denounced as fabricated. The scene may be real, but obviously not Texas and definitely not my Daddy."

"We want to switch live to Lubbock, Texas, where our reporter, Alex Rooney, is standing by with the family of Tyrone Jones, an African-American teenager who has been missing for a week."

There was an introduction by Alex Rooney, standing outside a run-down tenement in Lubbock, Texas.

"This is the home of Tyrone Jones, who has been missing since Saturday when he left to meet friends and go to a movie. His mother…"

The camera panned to an older woman, surrounded by three other women. All three were visibly upset.

"Mrs. Jones when did you last see Tyrone?"

"Last Saturday. He was on his way to meet friends then go see a movie. He's a good boy," she moaned.

"He was gonna start college next year. He was murdered by them night riders," she said, her pitch rising. "They strung him up like meat."

At this pronouncement she collapsed into the arms of the three other women. One of the women, who looked about twenty, shouted at the camera, "My brother Tyrone deserves justice."

"This is Alex Rooney from Lubbock where the police declined to be interviewed regarding this case."

The television host turned to face Ellie May and said, "Mrs. Joseph, you've watched this with us and I am sure that you, along with the rest of us, send sympathy to Mrs. Jones for her loss."

"Hogwash!"

"I beg your pardon?"

"First you ask me to appear, knowing that this unsubstantiated footage was going to be aired. Secondly, there is always a police response in Texas, even if non-committal. Thirdly, those third rate actors could not identify that which has not been identified. Police and FBI have been searching the lower states for missing persons. All accounted for so far. That your reporter not only found the family but that they are now identifying a body not yet found is a new low in reporting."

"Then you accuse this grieving woman of fabrication?"

"Can we talk politics? The election is three days away," Ellie May said in an attempt to redirect and gain control.

"You haven't answered my questions."

"The FBI will handle your questions."

"So you categorically deny that your father and grandfather were and are members of the Klu Klux Klan?"

"Many times."

"In spite of this strong evidence?"

"This is not evidence. There is no evidence. This interview is over." Ellie May Joseph stood and left the studio.

A camera crew followed her. Mac watched as Bobby fell in step beside her, and the microphones picked up pieces of their conversation.

"You want the Rangers to arrest her?" Bobby asked.

"Find her, arrest her, her crew, and the television reporter. Identify where they were filming and log any requests for comment."

"Yes, boss."

"Unfortunately, Bobby, that means they've succeeded. I'm sure that asshole in there is showing the tape of that swearing woman again and again to fill his space."

Mac, sitting a few miles away shook his head, knowing that clip of Ellie May swearing would also be replayed. The television personality had gotten the exact reaction that he had been told to get. The smile showed that this was a big pay day for him. The women were obviously actresses. He knew when he looked at the clock: nine in the morning in Lubbock, Texas, and they all had fresh hairstyles and makeup.

The camera crew had followed Ellie May outside the television studio. She was met by a hostile crowd yelling accusations of *murderer, liar,* and *cover up*. A few people even had signs.

The secret service detail ensured that Ellie May and Bobby got into their car. The final shot was Bobby looking out the back window as the camera crew turned to get additional shots of the mob.

"Spontaneous, my ass," Mac said aloud. He phoned Bobby and had him ask the driver how long the crowd had been there.

"They started arriving half an hour ago," the driver replied.

"Before the live broadcast?" Mac heard Bobby further probe.

"I guess," was the response.

Mac hung up and made a call to Helen. She was across town and said she was "…watching in horror." Even though the Republican challenger was the opposition, there was something primal, primitive, about mobs. They belonged to a culture seeking fifteen minutes of fame before slipping back into the mud.

Mac asked Helen if there was anything pressing for Marjorie that day. She replied that there were no interviews or statements due until the next day. Marjorie needed to regroup, refocus, redirect. It was going to be hard. Helen reviewed the agenda for Sunday with Mac, looking for traps, looking for the ambush. Neither saw any, but then obviously the Republican candidate had not seen this coming either.

Mac sent Helen a text from his cell: 'Wife fill bride tent.' An anagram. He was reading her mind. He figured it would take her less than five minutes to unscramble and reassemble it to his intent: 'it will be different.'

Yes, Mac thought to himself, *it will be a different attack.*

The more he pondered the question, the further he seemed to be from an answer. Security was the first step, and Mac suggested that she raise this issue in the strategy meeting. Helen was anxious how the agents assigned to Marjorie would react; she was concerned that they would be furious that she did not completely trust them to keep this candidate safe. She said, "Mac, the tension is beginning to fracture the team."

Marjorie was scheduled for a Sunday morning television show in New York, then she was to fly to Chicago in the afternoon and then onto Indianapolis in the evening. Monday's schedule was just as grueling before being back in New York to vote on Tuesday.

Mac watched the next day as the television show in New York passed without incident, principally because Helen had chosen the show, the interviewer, and had supplied the questions. There was a moment when Marjorie was asked to comment on the woes of her opponent. It turned out to be the highlight of the show as Marjorie, showing unscripted fire, said that she did not generally comment on ongoing FBI investigations but wanted the country to know that were she to be in the White House for the next term, all of the perpetrators of the fraud would be arrested, charged, and tried for tampering with an election. As an afterthought she added that she was referring to any and all election tampering.

A few minutes after the show, Mac received a frantic call from Helen. She informed him that on the way out of the studio a little girl handed flowers to Marjorie. They were spring flowers and so different from the autumnal colors that were everywhere. Helen, however, had quickly taken the flowers from Marjorie and headed to the cars that would take them to the plane and on to Chicago. It was a flurry of activity as the schedule was tight. The small motorcade sped through the tunnel to Teterboro airport where a private jet was waiting.

Her voice sounded frail as she relayed, "There was an envelope with the flowers and a note that read, 'DO YOU KNOW WHERE YOUR CHILDREN ARE?' Mac, I couldn't believe that someone would use a child like that. That someone would use Marjorie's children like that. Hasn't she been through enough? I asked the agent who was riding with me where the flowers had come from, knowing full well that they were from the little girl, but I didn't know where she had come from, who she was with."

Mac said, "Have the FBI meet you at Teterboro."

He heard Helen relay that request to the agents.

"When the cars stop," Mac further advised, "hand the evidence to the FBI agent waiting at the terminal. Don't give them a statement. Just move on to the next venue. Tell them you'll do it by phone if needed, and then wait until you hear from me. Instruct the staff not to accept any more flowers, and have Matt find out who the detail with David Jr. and Ian is. Ask if they can be supplemented with local police. Tell the others that you have something to take care of and will rejoin them in Indianapolis. Don't get on the plane." Mac knew that under normal circumstances Helen would have known to do all of this, but with the onslaught of ambushes and emotional attacks, she was stressed to her limit and in no condition to make decisions.

Mac determined that this was the attack. If Marjorie had received this note and no response from her parents, she would have been frantic. That was the objective. Both candidates were having their families assaulted from very different angles.

Helen called him after the plane had left. She quietly relayed, "Local police are on their way; the FBI is half an hour by helicopter. Mac, hold on a minute. The agent is here; I'm going to put you on speaker phone."

"I'm Agent Lisa Devony." Then the security agent asked, "What's happening?"

"Election fraud," Mac replied.

"Ellie May Joseph?" the agent questioned.

"Hell no. She's a victim too," Helen said.

The agent completed the statement and was called away. When she came back it was evident that it was not great news.

"Helicopter finally got there, after being delayed. Two policemen, two secret service agents...drinking tea in the front. Family playing scrabble in the living room."

"Did the agents identify themselves?" asked Mac.

"Yes, Alveres and Milan."

"So what's wrong?" asked Helen, sensing a question in the agent's voice.

"Maybe nothing, but it just seems neat, too neat. Teenagers playing scrabble with their grandparents when there are college football games on television."

"Can you get me to Newark? From there I can fly to Indianapolis," Helen said.

"Sure, I have your contact information in case anything comes up."

Mac waited just over an hour for Helen's plane to land in Indianapolis. She called to let him know she had arrived and had a dozen calls to return. Each one she listened to, she told him, caused increasing concern. She was first meeting with Marjorie's chief of staff who knew the whole story. He would already have her checked into the hotel.

"Okay," Mac said. "Ask him to get you two into a conference room. It's unlikely to be bugged, then call and put me on speaker again."

"He's right here, Mac. You might as well hang on," she told him.

Mac could tell from Helen's tone that something was wrong. Helen calmly said, "Excuse me, could my colleague and I use one of your conference rooms." There was a pause, then Mac heard them walking and a door opened and closed. Helen said, "Start at the beginning."

Mac heard the chief of staff say, "You said no flowers, no notes. Well the make-up woman commented to Marjorie, 'I have two boys, I know where they are.' It was an innocent remark… or was it?"

"Did anyone ask her?"

"She said she was talking to someone with a security badge of some kind and that he had said that Marjorie didn't know where her boys were, that it was a shame, a mother should know where her boys are."

"Then what happened?" asked Helen.

"Marjorie was a little shook, called the boys," the chief of staff continued.

"She talked to David Junior?" Helen asked.

"No, Ian. He said that his brother was watching the game."

"What time?"

"About 1:30 I think."

"When they were reportedly playing Scrabble. Then what?" Mac asked.

"On air the interview was about education. Marjorie was asked about the Joseph's campaign promise to require that high school students wear uniforms. After she answered, the interviewer asked, 'Do you know where your boys are?' Marjorie lost it on air and said that yes she did, and where her husband was, and that she was going to bring accountability to the people responsible. The interviewer was Jim Skelton, do you know him?"

"No," Helen and Mac said simultaneously.

"Well Jim Skelton said that he was asking where her boys stood on the issue of school uniforms and was sorry if there had been a misunderstanding. The rest of the interview was a disaster. Off air Marjorie called the house again. She has called the house every five minutes since; spoke to the agents mostly who are showing some frustrations."

"Where is she?" Helen asked.

"Holed up! The press believe she's resting, but they have questions; they'll be looking for blood, I think."

Just then Mac heard the door to the conference room open, and Marjorie's stressed voice asking, almost pleading, "Helen, where the hell have you been? Never mind; I'm up to my armpits in reporters and my media director takes a sabbatical."

"Marjorie, calm down; we only have a couple of hours before a large reception and dinner."

"I'm not hungry. Do you know what they're saying?"

"Who?"

"You know who, Helen."

"If we give up to conspiracy theories then we might as well give in," Mac said.

"Not theory, Mac. Fact: there is a conspiracy and they can win. I don't give a shit. I just want to go home."

"Marjorie, this has been grueling. I know you're tired, and you miss David. Just three more days to go," urged the chief of staff.

"Don't patronize me; you never have before. I miss my boys. If I win, can you imagine what their life will be, can you imagine what my life will be, without them, without David. Can you, Helen? When David was here we could do it. Not now, not now," she said, her voice beginning to fade.

"I'll go talk to the reporters. Then one way or the other we need to prepare for this evening," Helen stated.

"Give me half an hour, then gather the team together in my suite," Marjorie said resignedly.

By the bits of news he saw, Helen had placated the reporters and just had time to freshen up before the meeting. Mac hated not knowing what was going on. He needed to talk to Helen, but it was not safe.

*What a frigging mess! H*e thought.

Three hours later, the major network news stations carried Marjorie's speech. It was confident and well received. A cynic might have credited the food and drink, which, according to Helen, was acceptable for a change. There was a small shadow when Marjorie mentioned her family. A general misunderstanding, that she was thinking of David, not her boys, resulted in sympathy. The issue had to be dealt with head on so she referred to an ongoing FBI investigation, as both a reason and a challenge, for not discussing the issue. She promised to spend all holidays and vacations with her boys who would be going away to school.

This was a surprise to Mac and he wondered what the boys thought of that. Unfortunately a reporter wondered the same thing and asked at the press conference if Marjorie had spoken to the boys. Marjorie's eyes widened and then she sat down; Helen was left to wrap up the evening with the reporters.

Chapter Thirty-Three

Sunday morning was dark and raining; it seemed to sum up everyone's attitude. The newspapers were full of doom and gloom, the talk show hosts snapped at their invited guests. It was as if the world had switched itself to slow. Weather forecasters, unapologetically, were describing the obvious and forecasting without their usual false convictions. Mac decided that nobody was watching, nobody cared.

Mac tuned in to the station where Marjorie was appearing on an early show in DC. She and her team had flown in at five; the time difference had for once helped. While waiting for her slot, Mac read the newspapers. The arrival of Arthur Anders's wife onto the campaign had been relegated to page two or three, depending on the paper. The continuing accusations of racism against Ellie May Joseph and a questioning of the mental state of Marjorie White were the lead stories. The articles were all credited to men; Mac wondered if anyone else noticed. The photographs of Shirley Anders showed a small ordinary woman, wrapped against the cold. The accompanying article spoke of her shyness. Since there were no interviews, there was nothing to like or dislike. The reporter had determined that her maiden name was Serat. A quote was attributed to her, in which she stated her support of her husband, his campaign, and a pledge to be involved in humanitarian work. The statement was, to the professional eye, a press release prepared by her husband.

The phone rang during a commercial and Mac picked it up without looking at the caller ID. He was tired of always being worried. Marjorie and Ellie May had given the world a story, and no one cared. Why should he?

"Mac," he answered.

"Morning," Helen replied. She sounded as frustrated as he felt.

"No good in front of that morning?" Mac asked gently.

"What's good about it? Anders's wife arrived, but he didn't bring her to headquarters. We're no more informed than the general public. We don't know what she looks like, don't know what she sounds like, or where she came from," concluded Helen. "The only item that might be interesting is that it appears that they married abroad."

"Why is that of interest?" Mac asked.

"Anders went abroad for a year or so and came back married. And no record of a marriage in this country."

"Do you think that we might find a Shirley Serat at any college?"

"No. We looked; no high school either. What's really funny though....." she trailed off.

Mac finished the thought. "Nobody is looking."

"No," she agreed. "I just wanted to hear a friendly voice. I ought to get back to work, and I want to see how the rest of this interview goes. I'll talk to you a bit later, okay?"

"Absolutely," Mac said. He hung up, turned the volume up on the TV, and then went into the kitchen to make himself another cup of coffee.

The interview with Marjorie was sour. Everything had been covered ad nauseam; the interviewer was saturated, the interviewee was saturated, and the early morning audience was saturated. The questions referred back to the newspaper articles. Marjorie refused to heap onto Ellie May Joseph, abhorring the medias' interest in something so profoundly nasty and false. Her mental fragility they should understand and she tried to redirect them, tried to talk about the political issues that were polarizing the country, especially those issues which related to terrorists and allies.

Asked to sum up in the thirty seconds left, she was defiant. Ignoring the time limit, she challenged them to shut her off. She said that this country had to elect a President; this was a long-term political discussion. The country was not interested in a cat fight. Those that were, obviously, were selling advertising and newspapers, but doing a grave disservice to our country and to the free world.

Mac watched in amazement. He was not surprised at how the interview had gone but rather his lack of shock. He guessed that the host was likely not happy about the conclusion of the interview, especially when the producer seemed to cut out the thirty seconds that had been assigned to the host in which to pontificate.

The phone rang again. He let the machine pick it up.

"Mac, Marjorie had me cancel the next meeting. We're going down to the shore. She wants to go to church with her boys. We're leaving now."

"Shit!" Mac said. "She knows better. Why did she tell them where they're going?" Mac hurried and got dressed. He calculated how long it would take for the entourage to speed down the turnpike. And then he wondered if they would be too late.

The end of the street to the beach was blocked by a large black car and a man emerged as Mac stopped.

"Everything quiet?" Mac asked.

"Very."

Just then Marjorie's black SUV pulled up. Matt got out and said to the guard, "We'll pick up the family and head out to church."

"They went already. The grandparents and two kids said that they were going to church."

"Your orders were that no one went in or out."

"We heard you were on your way to church and it looked right." The security agent was now on the defensive.

Matt signaled to the second car that one of his agents should join them.

"Get out an all cars bulletin, then interview this cretin and his partner. Do not let them leave; they're suspended."

"You don't have that right," the man protested.

"No, but the Vice President does, and she may just rip out your throat when she finds out that her family is missing."

"They're not missing; they went to church with Milan and the other guy."

Matt was already walking back to the two cars. This was looking bad, very bad.

Mac got back in his car and followed them.

Reaching the house, Marjorie was out of the car before it stopped. She ran screaming into the house.

"David, Ian!" She paused. "Mum, Dad!"

The front door swung back with the kind of noise that signifies an empty house. The usual sounds of television, radio, running water were all missing. What came back was silence. Silence and the panicked footsteps of Marjorie running from room to room screaming.

The house was not empty. The body of agent Alveres was found in the basement, tied to a chair, mouth taped, shot once execution style.

There was a message typed 'SAFE-FOR-NOW' on the kitchen table. Marjorie saw it and threw herself at the wall with enough force to be bleeding. Then spinning, she ran from the back toward the beach screaming again, "David!"

The car had, as expected, found no sign of the family at the church. The town had no surveillance cameras. The weather and the lack of summer visitors made it impossible to know where they were.

"What a frigging mess!" Matt sat at the kitchen table. "What do we do?"

"We need to keep a lid on it," Helen said.

"How? We're two days from an election. We have a candidate who needs to be sedated to prevent her from running into the sea. We have a kidnap situation and no clues, not one, nothing. And you say keep a lid on it!"

"Sorry, Matt. I know that you blame yourself; I blame myself for not following my intuition, the information. We were so busy watching the front door that we missed the obvious."

Mac added, "Also, you're wrong: we do know who and we do know why. We have to keep our heads. Have you swept the house for bugs?"

"Yes. Nothing. Damn it. How did they know we were coming?"

Mac gave Helen a quick glance and she looked away. She knew.

Matt continued, "I knew Alveres, good man. This is what we have pieced together. Alveres, Milan, and maybe another man were down here with the family. Later a road block was set up; they saw two agents and the family. The family was intimidated, probably with threats against Marjorie or against each other, maybe a demonstration, punching or cutting, against the grandfather or even Alveres. They were coerced, cell phones confiscated, cut off from outside." He paused, thinking. "What were they waiting for?"

"Timing is everything," said Mac. "I think they thought it would be sprung on Marjorie either on air or at a press conference, probably timed for today."

"So we disrupted their timing," said Matt hopefully.

"I don't think it matters, do you?" Helen gestured upstairs. "I'm going for a walk," she said.

Mac let her go alone, but he watched her. Helen walked down to the water. It was peaceful. A few gulls wheeled above the sands; sandpipers skipped in and out of the waves, oblivious of the dark rainclouds scudding across a steel grey sky.

Mac's thoughts were of the future, taking the present and extrapolating each piece. He looked down at Helen and could tell that she was sobbing. Was she sobbing for Marjorie, for the boys, or for herself? Strangely, Mac decided, she was sobbing for America. What had become of integrity, loyalty, goodness? It had to be still here somewhere. Their crystal ball, the future that they had been so sure of, was cloudy. Like today, November third, the day the music died, he thought, out of nowhere.

Helen came back up to the porch where Mac was sitting, watching her and trying to figure out a plan.

"Mac, this is a frigging nightmare! I hope that someone is listening because this is a warning. I am coming after you bastards and I will not stop until I die."

"Helen, what are you saying?"

"The bastards that we've been talking about have kidnapped David Junior, Ian, and Marjorie's parents. All I can figure is that they're holding them ransom until she drops out of the race."

"Why do you think that?" Mac asked.

"Because there can't be anything else. What other reason is there?"

"About three billion dollars, twice. Between us, Helen, we have the whole story. But, as you know, timing is everything, and it may be too late."

"We need to do it anyway."

"Okay, Helen, I'll follow your lead for now. You have obligations to Marjorie, and I understand that, but we need to move."

"As soon as I'm no longer needed here. I have a job until the end of the year anyway. Then who knows."

"I'll be waiting. Tuesday morning at the latest. Has anyone checked on Marjorie lately?" Mac asked.

The door from the house creaked open and soft footsteps came out onto the porch. Helen and Mac looked up in surprise.

"I'm awake," Marjorie said.

The Vice President of the United States, a candidate for President, looked small. Sunken eyes stared unblinking, at a spot on the horizon; hair that had been perfectly placed just hours before gave the impression of the mad woman in *Jane Eyre*.

"How are you feeling?" Helen asked, then instantly recoiled.

Mac understood. They all knew how Marjorie was feeling: helpless.

"I'm sorry," Helen said quickly. "It's an impossible conversation to start. Let me start again with updates."

"No, Helen, there are no updates. If the update I'm waiting for had happened, I would've heard it."

"Then what, Marjorie? What can I do?"

"Pray, Helen. Pray with me for strength."

"I want to kill!"

"Won't help! Give them what they want."

"Give in to terrorists?" Mac asked.

"Not good for a Commander-in-Chief is it?" Marjorie replied.

"It's a direct choice: America or your family," Mac agreed.

"If that's the choice," said Marjorie vehemently, "then America is on its own!"

"You can't give up," Helen cried. "It doesn't have to be one or the other."

"It does, Helen. I can't concentrate on running a country if I'm constantly worried about my family. Even if I think that, how can I serve, how can I be an effective leader? Why should I even try?"

"So people get the elected officials that they deserve?" Helen suggested.

"No, they elect people who say they'll change and then disappoint when they don't. So I can tell them I'll change; I can make a deal with the devil and then say that I would be tough on terrorists. What does that make me?"

"A politician," Mac added wryly.

"Not this politician. I've given enough; I want my boys back, now."

"There has to be another solution. Marjorie, you're sedated, give it a couple of hours," Helen pleaded.

"I am sedated; I'm out of my mind. How will that improve? By hearing that a body shows up that police are trying to identify. Think about it, Helen. The bastards' timing couldn't have been more perfect. We're out of time, out of options."

Helen was beaten. Mac sat silent.

"Gather the team in an hour," Marjorie whispered.

"I'll put it together," Helen said.

"Include Anders. I want to see his face."

"Then it may take more than an hour," Mac suggested.

Mac told Helen that he would prepare a story for the media. When Helen had chided him for now writing stories instead of investigative reporting, he had admitted his failure. The problem was that his investigative piece which he would also submit would require verification by the editorial staff. The story would therefore not make the news before the election. Similarly, even with influence, a talk show host was unlikely to present anything controversial so close to the election.

Mac felt like a coward. He was making excuses; worried about his personal safety or about his professional integrity. He decided it was time to get off the fence.

Mac spent the next hour calling in favors, contacting friends and associates to use influence with everybody they knew. It was Sunday; he was only slightly successful. Success, if any was limited to those few who believed there was a problem and those even fewer who might get involved. He secured a talk show interview, as one of three guests so that his time on camera was likely limited. The European newspapers would take a story with a strong disclaimer.

Over three hours later a group of twelve met in the living room where the day before a family had reportedly played Scrabble. With twelve people together, there were twelve different emotions, from apprehension to anger, acceptance to wary and weary. Some closed their eyes, either in badly needed rest or to shut out the scene before them; others looked nervously from face to face, a weak smile if they made visual contact. Helen examined the floor, the grain in the hardwood taking on an importance previously ignored. Helen, along with most, stood as if flight might be an option.

Marjorie entered the room, not like the presidential candidate, but quietly. She was pale, her hair tied back in an untidy ponytail, with slacks and a sweater; she might have been a suburban mother on her way to pick up her children from soccer practice.

There was movement as eyes lifted, feet shifted. Two people stood, one proffered the vacated seat. With a slight shake of her head Marjorie declined. Arthur Anders remained seated.

"Marjorie, you look tired. Is there a problem?" Anders asked.

"Where are my boys, Arthur?"

The shrug could have been intended as 'I don't know,' but it looked to Helen as 'I don't care.' Either way it was an acknowledgement that he knew that they were missing.

"I have an important decision to make, Arthur; it's hard to think when the unthinkable is a possibility. Perhaps your pal knows," she suggested, nodding at the man standing implacably behind Anders.

"I think not, Marjorie."

The two looked directly at each other.

"We're here to decide the best direction for this campaign. I would like everyone's input."

After a silence, in which the rain could be heard, Marjorie delegated.

"Helen?"

Helen looked at Marjorie with defeat. "I already gave my opinion to you, which I'll reiterate. I don't believe in negotiating with terrorists. I realize that we all have to make individual decisions in our individual circumstances. I can't believe there are people who would murder for political gain."

Mac realized that Helen was looking at Arthur Anders and the man behind him during her last sentence. In a flash she understood the mistake of her assumption. Flashing through Mac's mind was a picture of David Jr. and Ian, then a picture of the crash site where David White had died.

The chief of staff said, "I agree. We take our oath seriously. The FBI and police are looking and I'm sure we'll hear very soon that they're safe."

"Realistically, it could take a few days," Matt said. "Even if they knew where to look, they would need evidence before getting a court order to enter."

Someone else, who Mac did not recognize, asked, "Even in a life or death situation?"

"We don't even know that they're missing. Has there been a ransom demand?" the chief of staff asked.

"Not this time," Marjorie replied.

A multitude of questions were thrown at her. "You mean it's happened before? When? Why didn't we know about it?"

"We don't have time for this," Marjorie said bringing back order. "Assume it is credible, assume that these terrorists want Marjorie White out of the presidential race, and assume that if I go ahead that my children and parents could be murdered."

"Who would do such a thing?" a man who Mac did not recognize asked.

"We know," Helen said. "But right now Marjorie is asking for your input."

"If you know, denounce them and arrest them. Ask Congress to delay the election until these allegations are proved and the perpetrators jailed."

"We don't have the votes," Helen said with a realization that was confirmed by the smirk on Anders's face.

Mac wanted to wipe it off. Without thinking he blurted out, "Arthur Anders would be the beneficiary of Marjorie White's withdrawal."

The smirk disappeared.

"I don't recall you being part of our official group, Mr. McDougal. Marjorie, you believe that I could orchestrate this scenario for my person benefit?"

"Yes,"

"I'm shocked. I hope that you have something substantial to back up these scandalous accusations."

"The proof is in the hands of the world media as we speak," Mac said.

He understood that this conversation was being heard elsewhere and that the veracity of each statement was being confirmed. *At least the smirk was off Anders's face*, he thought.

"Marjorie," Anders said, "it's a decision that even with the input of these great minds, ultimately only you can make. I will support you in any way that I am able. I am confident that you will make the right decision and that your family will be home soon, safe and sound. If there has been any wrong doing then I shall support the investigation and prosecute those responsible." He rose to leave. "Let your conscience guide your actions and let me know what you have decided."

"You'll be the first to know, Arthur," said Marjorie.

"Asshole," Helen said under her breath as Anders went through the door.

Into the silent void a young woman whispered, "I think that I would die if anything happened to my little girl."

"Denounce them, Marjorie," Bill said. "There would be no way they would carry out any threat."

"How do you know they're not already dead?" Marjorie asked somberly.

It was a question everyone had been thinking but was afraid to voice.

"It's the hope that we live in a just world," she answered to her own question.

"Then why, monthly it seems, is there an act of genocide, good people mugged, burglarized, people just disappear?" an aide asked.

"It's not a just world. We still have hope that it will be," Marjorie responded.

"Take care of yourself, and your family. Does it really matter who's President?" Matt said despondently.

"It matters a great deal," Mac said. "On a personal level, on a national level, and on an international level."

Everyone had a different opinion; everyone was talking now at cross purposes.

"Thank you, everyone. Bill, Helen, Mac, can you stay?"

When the others had left, Bill started to speak. "I think….."

"Let's get some air," said Mac.

"It's raining and cold," Bill protested.

Helen was making signs that the walls could be listening. She opened the door and spoke to Matt, asking that he get coats and umbrellas and that he follow them outside.

"This is not happening," said Bill.

"The rain, the extortion? What?" asked Marjorie. "It is happening. Let's look at the alternatives. One, they're alive because if they were dead, as their mother, I'd know; I'd want to die myself. I'd want to take a gun to every terrorist, to every murderer; what kind of life is that? If they are alive and I fail to save them, the first scenario is doubled. Bill, Helen, convince me that if you were in this position that you would make the sacrifice."

"Let's look at it the other way. Can you work from outside the government for justice or against injustice?" asked Helen.

"Probably not! I will be a pariah. Either way I will be in danger for the rest of my life. A retired vice president doesn't get a security detail," Marjorie said sardonically. "Not that it does much good."

"What a nightmare," Bill muttered.

"Helen, you said that the media has proof. Was that true?" Marjorie asked.

"Yes, unlike that self-serving 'I didn't know' of Mr. Anders, Mac has provided the press with all the proof."

"Mac, you may have endangered yourself for nothing; it may end up on page two. Speaking of danger, it seems like you've angered Arthur with your accusations, Helen."

"Screw him! He never liked me, and I bet it had more to do with the fact that I'm a woman than anything else." Helen's eyes were on fire with anger.

"Bill?" Marjorie asked.

"I've been in politics all my life. Governor had its problems, but nothing like this. Politics is a dirty business and this is dirtier than anything I've heard. Is there anything Watkins can do?" Bill's reference to the President was a change in direction.

"He's looking forward to being out. What would he do now, withdraw the U.S. Ambassador from Istanbul? Complain to the UN? Hugh has used his influence with the FBI and even the CIA is involved because we suspect foreign intervention. My brother-in-law has called in favors. Informers have been promised huge cash rewards. It has reaped only silence."

On the way back to the house Marjorie asked Matt for an update.

"Nothing, Ma'am."

"It will be dark in an hour. Helen, prepare a resignation speech. Let's release it just before the news at ten." Marjorie walked away, her body language showing her resignation.

Stunned, Helen followed with a steely look; her tears would have to wait. Mac watched as Helen went and sat down at the computer, looking hopeless and without words to enter into the keyboard.

Chapter Thirty-Four

Mac arrived at the television studio for the talk show. They were running late. Between the football game going over an extra twenty minutes and the breaking news about the resignation of Marjorie White, Mac knew they would be at least half an hour later starting than planned. His comment to the young lady greeter about telling the National Football League to finish on time or be cut off was treated with a one word renunciation: *Heidi*. He chuckled, remembering the uproar that had occurred when a switch to *Heidi* had enraged the country's red-blooded sports fans and had lit up the studio lines for hours after. His comment that maybe they would finish on time with fewer or shorter television commercial breaks was treated as though he had dropped from another planet. But one thing was for certain: No television station was ever again going to switch early from a football game.

Mac watched the resignation speech, recognizing that Marjorie was reading verbatim Helen's script. She cited personal reasons which everyone should understand, thanked her supporters and the President for their efforts. After a short rest she would fulfill her obligations as Vice President until the end of her term. Marjorie was effusive in her respect for the Republican candidate and the responsible campaign in

spite of the false, spiteful allegations which would
have forced weaker people from the race.

What was missing was an endorsement or any
mention of her running mate. She finished with God
bless America.

"Amen," Mac muttered.

It was no surprise to Mac that the show, now
running an hour late, featured not two celebrities but
one politician. The politician was a Congressman from
Delaware, Adam Fox. Mr. Fox had taken the seat from
Charles George after George and his family were
smeared.

The host introduced the two guests to the studio
audience and the nation.

"Good evening, ladies and gentlemen, and welcome
to our show. Tonight we witnessed the astounding
resignation of Marjorie White, for many, the front
runner in the presidential race. To try to make sense of
the why and wherefore, we have invited a leading
member of Congress, running unopposed in Delaware,
Adam Fox. We also have in our studio Matthew
McDougal who has been covering the campaign for
two years and knows the candidates. First, what do
you both make of the news today?"

"It was a great surprise to me," Adam Fox said with
a smile."I thought Marjorie White could have made a
great President."

"Liar! It wasn't a surprise to you or your backers."
Mac was trying to kill the smile with little success.
"Marjorie White would have made a great President.
She resigned due to extortion and the threat of
murder."

"That's a little theatrical, Mr. McDougal, and what's your source for this extraordinary claim?" Adam Fox asked, still smiling.

"You tell me the source of your campaign funding. It may be the same," said Mac, and then realized that he was losing the thread of his argument. "The information that the governing of their country and other countries has passed into foreign, not friendly hands has been provided to the media. Your own campaign, Mr. Fox, was the tip off, actually. The murder of Charles George, after he spoke to me, and Pauline Poles after she and I spoke were all I needed to obtain the rest of the information."

Bingo! The smile was gone from Adam Fox's face.

"My predecessor, Congressman George, committed suicide after information came to light of his improper financial dealings and family issues, which included drugs and infidelity. Ms. Poles also committed suicide as she had been having an affair with the Congressman."

"Untrue. I have the proof that none of those statements are true."

"That's preposterous!" Fox was now standing.

"This is interesting. But we must go to commercial break," said the host. "We'll be right back."

As they went off the air Adam Fox, red in the face, turned on Mac as he prepared to leave.

"You'll hear from my lawyers who will be suing you for slander."

"Add libel as this information will be in the newspapers tomorrow. It'd be easier if you were able to claim that I committed suicide. By the way, were you aware that your partners were going to have a grieving Marjorie White kill herself? You may want to be careful who you're friendly with."

Back on the air the host announced that one of his guests had a previous engagement and, as they were running late, he had to leave. He was left with only Mac to examine the circumstances of an election fraught with unusual happenings.

"Before the break you made three extraordinary assertions: that the Presidency was being hijacked, that Congressman Adam Fox was involved in a murder conspiracy, and that this is worldwide. I would like to examine these three comments. The first and easiest would be that Adam Fox could have been elected on the back of a felony."

"Adam Fox sold his voting powers for a seat in Congress. There was a conspiracy which targeted the popular incumbent. Charles George was accused of having an offshore account, he did not. His children were accused of having drugs; they did not. He was accused of infidelity; it was completely untrue. These charges were brought to different jurisdictions, by the same men claiming to be law enforcement officers; they were not."

"You mentioned proof?"

'Yes, I spoke to Charles George. He denied the charges and told me that he would fight back, that he had proof. He was not suicidal, twenty-four hours later he was dead."

"Then he gave you the proof?"

"No, but the perpetrators made two mistakes. First, as an investigative reporter I took note of the death, secondly, they searched my apartment and tried to coerce me into giving them information on George."

"But you didn't have it."

"Correct. Pauline Poles found and delivered it to Washington. She was murdered and they did not find the information."

"The world wide conspiracy theory? How does that fit into the picture?"

"An examination of voting trends in the UK, Germany, and France has shown similar behavior."

"For example?"

"For example politicians who should have been elected had defamatory material appear in local newspapers just days before the election. Too close to the election for evidence refuting the claim to be presented."

"There is a correlation?" the host was seriously interested.

"One, Charles George I have mentioned. Ellie May Joseph is an obvious example."

"Which brings us to the hijacking of the presidential election?"

"Extortion and harassment have been used on the two leading candidates. Threats were made against Marjorie White and her family; David White was murdered to further their ends. Attacks against Ellie May Joseph, including obviously staged outrages, were coordinated by dangerous, committed people. Other candidates have left the race after spurious charges were levied or with doubtful claims threatened to be released if they failed to acquiesce."

"Is there proof, or can it be put into simple terms that a poorly educated talk show host can understand?"

"Have you ever made a wager?" Mac asked.

"Not a winning one," the host said to general amusement.

"What if I said that I could guarantee a winner?"

"My new best friend," he said laughing.

"Someone bet millions of dollars that neither Marjorie White nor Ellie May Joseph would win the presidential election. Someone will collect billions of dollars if he is right. The bets were made with money that they stole from the Federal Government."

"Who would benefit, and are you sure?" asked the host looking at his timer.

"Senator Arthur Anders, and I am positive."

"Our guest is Matthew McDougal, the reporter and an author who has accused elected officials of fraud, murder, and mayhem. I'm sure that some of our viewers may not have been surprised by allegations of skullduggery in Washington. This close to an election of a new President, the election of Congressmen and Senators, it's shocking to think that as we cast our ballot it may be that we have little idea of what or who we are electing. Mac, any final words?"

"I have spent a great deal of time this year with two wonderful women politicians. Either one would have made a tremendous President. Depending upon your political views, either would serve the United States honorably. If we elect, influenced by innuendo, people who owe their place on the ballot to coercion, extortion and murder, then we lose. America loses. Thank you and good luck."

The major news was Marjorie White's decision not to continue her campaign. Mac's statement about the extortion was largely ignored when the missing members of her family appeared and explained that they had travelled to New York; an error in communication was blamed.

Mac challenged Helen on the obvious lie and was told to drop it.

Monday brought indignation from the major cities of Europe. The implication of ballot fraud brought out previous opposing factors in mutual condemnation of the charges.

In England the outcry was pushed to the interior pages of newspapers and to the end of the television news behind the adoption by Parliament of legislation giving broader definition to the rights of illegal immigrants. The armed forces budget was also slashed without debate. In France the right to have religious schools funded by the State was passed. The fact that this benefit was for immigrants was lost in the small print. The cost was to be funded by scrapping the development of a new supersonic bomber. In Germany the Bundt agreed to a long-term financing of new manufacturing plants in Turkey. The terms of the deal gave the downside risk to Germany and the profits to the host country.

Monday brought pariah status to Mac. The first call, predictable, was from Sue Raymond.

"Mac, are you nuts?"

"Good morning, Sue."

"Everybody in the world has your name on the front page."

"That's good, isn't it? You said that any publicity is good publicity."

"Yes, I did, but I wasn't representing a serial killer, a Bambi barbecuer, and a Benedict Arnold all rolled into one."

"It was important. When I agreed to go public, I had no idea that Marjorie was about to fold."

"Mac!" It was an exclamation which was to remind him of their relationship, based on honesty.

"Okay. Maybe I suspected her withdrawal. Okay, okay. I pushed my way onto the program in an effort to persuade her not to quit."

"How can we spin it to sell books?"

"Re-title the book 'Mad Mac and his feeble mind,'" said Mac.

"Not funny. I have to go."

Other calls were from friends and acquaintances who said the same thing in different ways. Mark Hughes called suggesting lunch. Mac turned off the phone, picked up a sheet of paper, and listed the alternatives. He wrote two words then stared at them for maybe an hour.

Capitulate: Fight.

Capitulate to whom, or over what? Or was it a capitulation of ideas, ideals? Fight, who or what and how?

Lunch with Mark sounded like a good idea. They met at Mark's suggestion at a small deli with a seating area which had room for only about six diners.

"Not your usual meeting choice, Mark."

"No, but I'll have to get used to it."

"Because?"

Mark looked much older. He had not dressed with his usual care. Clean and tidy but not crisp. The eyes betrayed a concern that his weak smile did nothing to dispel. This was a man who could easily be suicidal.

"Because….." again the weak attempt to smile "…. my clients have all abandoned me. I've made commitments, they made commitments. They…." He spat with contempt reserved only for those who have been betrayed. "… they have refused even to pay those pledges for which I have put out money. In a word, I am bankrupt, or will be when I add up all of my bills. A corned beef sandwich is the 'new' banquet."

"I'm sorry, Mark."

"Mac, the reason I asked you to share my misery is because, in all the world, you're the one person to understand. In spite of your not agreeing with the work I did, there was never a criticism or a judgment. My clients believe now, as you have been saying, that there is a conspiracy. The monies that they pledged were for a kind of status quo to their contracts with the government. It looks as though, if Anders is successful, there will be no more contracts. The defense industry will be decimated, no new business and maybe a cutback on current orders. Defense stocks are 'limit down' on the New York Stock Exchange. So many of these executives are selling out their bonuses and then selling short, except that there are no buyers."

"What about section 144, that prevents insiders from selling without notice?"

"The accountants had twenty-four hours to come up with strategies to circumvent the rules. More directors resigned before the opening bell than on any other day in history. They then sold out, if they could, and will fight the SEC with cash in hand. It's a bloodbath."

"Sorry, Mark, what can I do?"

"Nothing, I just needed to cry on someone's shoulder."

"What will you do?"

"I could apply for a directorship," he said with a wry smile. "After the lawyers have had their pound of flesh in liquidating my assets, I may go back home, get a teaching job, bag groceries or something."

"Keep in touch."

"I will. And Mac, take care of Helen, I think this whole thing will blow up in her face too."

"It has, Mark, and in ways that I can't tell you."

"I believe you laid it out last night pretty well. Too bad the rest of the country, particularly your associates in the media, have their heads so deep in the sand."

"Human nature, Mark. Something you don't like will go away if you ignore it long enough. Then, when you re-examine, it's harder to see with sand in your eyes."

"See you around?"

"Not for long. I think that the climate may be too warm. If Helen agrees, we may head to friendlier climes."

"Overseas then?"

"Maybe."

Mac found that his apartment had been examined again. He knew where the evidence was now, finally. It had occurred to him in the television interview. Charles George had it, then Pauline Poles, now Helen.

Pauline had found that George had hidden it with her and she had done the same thing. It was easier than carrying it and could be passed in person. He had to get Helen back to Washington, and then they could plan their future.

Mac called her cell.

"Helen, are you coming back tonight in order to vote tomorrow?"

"Marjorie needs me; I was thinking of staying here."

"Not a good idea. The boys are back, their strings are cut. It's time to think about Helen."

"Mac you know…."

"Okay, then. Time to think about Mac. Come back, we'll get married, go on a nice honeymoon, never return home."

"You're such a romantic," she said sarcastically. "I'll go talk to Marjorie. You're right: she has her boys back. There's nothing more for me to do here. Looks like I need to get home and re-create my resume."

It was late by the time Helen arrived at Mac's apartment. She had been unable to get a flight out of Newark until eight, and then the taxi from the airport had been slowed down by an accident on the beltway.

They had talked about plans for getting away. Mac, ever aware that there may be people listening, did not reveal his destination.

When they were lying close to one another, Helen whispered, "Mac, do you really have proof?"

"Yes. You'll see it tomorrow, after we've voted."

"Let's vote at six then."

"Let's wait until they open at seven." Mac stifled a laugh and pulled her closer. "It'll give us another hour in bed."

"Busy day today. License, schedule a wedding, invite friends, etc, etc, etc, etc.," said Mac over a shared cup of coffee while wrapped back in the warm blankets and Helen.

"We could have more guests if we invited your enemies based on the articles in the paper," Helen replied. "I can't believe that so many people without a positive thought between them could have so many negative opinions."

"Well, when they're savaging me, they're leaving everyone else alone," Mac said, unable to hide his disappointment in mankind, especially reporters. His integrity, his veracity, and even his having a father, had all been challenged.

"The truth should somehow shine through," she said. Then, touching his cheek, she smiled, "Well, it cut down on the number of invitations. Even some of my closest friends and associates have joined the negative bandwagon."

Outside the poll station, Mac called a cab.

"Blair House please."

"Mac, I thought that you were going to show me proof."

"I am."

In Helen's office Mac asked, "Is this where you interviewed Pauline Poles?"

"Yes."

"She gave you her CV on a disk?"

"How'd you know? I asked if she had a resume and she gave me a disk."

"What else was on the disk?"

"I didn't look." Helen's eyes grew wider. "You mean that she handed over the proof, and then all she had to do was tell us where it was?"

"Exactly. Except that someone killed her before she told you where to look. Let's copy it and get out of here."

"It's locked."

"What?"

"Password protected."

Mac rubbed his forehead and then said, "Okay. Copy something else on the front, Replace Pauline Poles with Helen Harvey resume, re-label the file, then we can have Martin open and transfer it. Nothing is easy."

This being Election Day, everyone was busy and Mac and Helen were able to run around town without interruption. Martin opened the file and transferred it onto a different file with a new password. The people who wanted the information did not need a password since they just wanted to destroy the information and anyone who might have seen it.

Helen and Mac planned to have an early dinner then a nap before watching the results come in. That was the idea anyway. The information that they read, however, with dates, names, amounts of money, and names of conspirators was foremost in their minds.

On television, the attacks on Mac were designed to make the viewer believe that the views that he presented would be assumed false or part of his unwarranted attack on Arthur Anders. Mac mentally compared the names on the disk with the names that he had compiled. They matched except for a few that were new and a few that he had wrong. The amount of money was staggering. Where had Charles George found this information? He must have been involved and then gotten cold feet. It made sense: first they would approach incumbents; if they were unwilling, then they removed them and brought in someone new.

The early results and predictions were preceded by endless drivel with computer models predicting everything except the end of the world. There was a section devoted to Mac's quotes of the previous night with his antagonist, Adam Fox, now smooth and prepared, dissecting the points made by Mac. It was masterful, professional. Mac and Helen enjoyed the drama as they understood and recognized the lies.

The news mentioned riots at polling stations in Mississippi and Texas. New Mexico and Arizona had peaceful demonstrations against Ellie May Joseph. The participants were members of the minority or immigrants who may or may not have been eligible to vote. The theme was the same, their particular understanding of the racism of the Republican candidate. It was a case of election, or in this case non-election, by social media.

Early voters in New Hampshire and Maine were for the Republican candidate. After that the Eastern seaboard went Democratic. The South was for Anders, or perhaps they were just against the Joseph ticket. The North was mixed again: the urban areas were anti-Joseph. The weather outside of Detroit and Chicago kept many people indoors. Buses to the polls with food packages swayed the vote: Democratic. Indiana went Republican, as did Wisconsin and Montana, but it was, by then, all over. Arthur Anders would be the next President. Democrats made inroads in both the Senate and the House. Governors would be predictably mostly Democrat.

The final news of the day was that Arthur Anders would ask his good friend, Francis Flores, to be his Vice President. This was delivered in his acceptance speech which was not well attended nor was it raucous. The majority of workers on the campaign had been Marjorie White's recruits and therefore were home crying into their hot chocolate.

Ellie May Joseph had conceded with tears. Her final speech of the campaign praised Marjorie White and sent her condolences to her and her family. There was pointedly no mention of Anders. Ellie May pledged to return to Texas and serve that state.

The media, predictably and without foundation, patted themselves on the back for their coverage of the elections. President Watkins finally surfaced in California and pledged his support of the transition process. He also spent more time in his praise and sympathy for Marjorie White. Marjorie White was unavailable for comment, as was her media director.

It was always a strange time, between election and inauguration. This time it was surreal. In previous changes there was a transparent, palpable excitement; who was coming, who was going. Previously there had been speculation on promotions, cabinet members, and heads of committees. The new Congress would invite speculation among the pundits revolving between the studios of major television networks. This was different though. The news hosts were soon sick of hearing 'I don't know'. Anders and Flores kept their own council, and if plans were afoot then none were leaked.

Helen and Mac were married quietly. There was a gathering after the ceremony at the Monterey Grill.

"Bad, bad, bad, Mac," Ann Gold scolded. She was wearing a large gold caftan which was not, in Mac's opinion, very flattering.

"Are we talking weather, politics, or religion?"

"No; you rushing into marriage with Helen and leaving me to cry into my martini, regretting my lost loves."

"Oh, that. I thought you were talking about something serious. In this life, Ann, you have to be quick or you're destined to be disappointed."

"Speaking of politics, your friend Anders was neither quick nor was he disappointed. And speaking of other things, there is no, I mean no gossip in Washington. I'm so desperate that this wedding will be my major story tomorrow. Unless..." she wandered off having seen Mark Hughes talking to a young aide who had worked on the White campaign.

Sue Raymond came by holding Carol by the hand.

"It's so nice to see that finally you came to your senses."

"You mean having submitted the proof of my book or marrying?"

It was amazing to Mac how, since they had announced their wedding plans, each of their friends had decided that it was a good move for him. The congratulations, however, had a tone of 'good for you, not for me' about them.

"The editor loves your proof," Sue said. "He sent a preview up to the publisher with a suggestion for pre-publishing."

"What is pre-publishing?" Helen asked.

"You know, coming out January 15th: the long awaited saga you will not want to miss."

"I still need to include the inauguration. Though I don't expect to be invited to any of the inaugural balls. Speaking of which, there has been nothing said about venues."

"Not likely that you'd be on the list anyway, Mac," Sue replied. "I couldn't get you in with a crowbar."

"Umm, Ann would know," Carol suggested.

Before he could find Ann, Helen came up behind him.

"Buy a married woman a glass of wine?"

"It's an open bar, and I'm a married man you know."

"I know." She leaned in and kissed him suggestively.

Mr. and Mrs. McDougal honeymooned in Naples, Florida, staying at the Registry. They remained to spend Christmas Day with Helen's sister. It was the best time that they could remember.

Each day they would read the newspaper and then walk the beach. They talked about their alternatives. Mac voiced his concerns for their safety once they were back in Washington. Since neither had jobs, there were other choices. Mac was asked daily to write or comment on some aspect of the transition. He told Sue that they must be desperate to need something from an old married man. She assured him that indeed they were desperate as there was a wall of silence surrounding the transitions; the outgoing administration had very little to add and the incoming had even less. Meetings on foreign policy and alliances were attended by Flores, who asked no questions.

Their morning walk often ended with a swim in the gulf. The water was too cold for the natives. Alert to any stingrays that might be on the sandy bottom, they would swim parallel to the beach. It was during one of these swims, just after Christmas, that someone tried to run them over. Turning to swim north, Mac had noticed a couple of boats coming out of the inland waterway: one went south, the other north. It was unlikely that they would come close. After a few more minutes he stopped to look around and saw that a boat had accelerated and was headed for them. Mac shouted at Helen to head for the shore while he headed out and yelled at the oncoming boat, waving his arms. The boat veered toward him and he dove straight down. Helen had reached shallow water and was standing, yelling at the retreating boat. The bottom of the boat caught Mac's foot, but it thankfully left only a bruise.

The police listened, made out reports, and ultimately did nothing other than admonish the stupid Yankees for swimming offshore in the middle of winter. There were lots of thirty-five foot Sea Ray boats up and down the coast; there was no point in looking for a needle in a haystack.

Helen was concerned for her sister and family. It was time to return to Washington, carefully. The next week was spent in a paranoid state. The friends who knew stayed away from them. If they drove, Mac inspected the car for tampering before he started it and then opened the door. He did not know what he was looking for, but he needed to do something. They went to busy places, they met associates in shopping centers, and business meetings were in public parks.

Mac ran into the back of a car which had stopped suddenly. The car in front had two men who both got out to examine the damage. Mac recognized them, backed up and, with a squeal of tires, sped away.

It was exhausting.

They had to have a plan.

Cash was king. He had heard the expression many times and now he started to turn investments into cash. Since the Patriot Act, transactions of five thousand dollars or more were tracked. A series of transactions totaling that amount were reportable. Mac spent every day for a week moving money, taking cash less than five thousand and each time giving a plausible story. He bought gold. He discreetly transferred money into a trust to pay for his mother's nursing home. Finally, he purchased a trip to Las Vegas. Discretion was the hallmark of Hal the bookie. Mac wondered if it was wise to 'Invest' in someone with a death wish, smoking endlessly. He determined that it was probably a better bet than abandoning it as he took up a new identity. Besides, Hal had made a fortune, thanks to Mac, on the elections. Having the edge, he had placed bets in Europe on Anders to win at two hundred-to-one just one week before Anders had in fact won. They set up a code and put money into Mac's new name. It had been so easy. The man took a photo of Mac and an address. When he came back he had a driver's license and social security card for himself and another for Helen, now Peter and Ellen Howe of New Hampshire.

Mac studiously ignored the notices to declare cash in excess of ten thousand dollars and carried the cash in various sections of his computer bag which he trusted would not be opened. His explanation of a lucky streak might just see him through. One hundred thousand dollars might have to last a long time.

Chapter Thirty-Five

Inauguration day was the most important day in many people's lives. It would change the face of world politics. This was not the most important thing for Mac and Helen as they prepared to disappear. It was important that none of their friends and associates knew of their plans. It was critical that none would be implicated in their relocation, not even Helen's sister.

They had chosen Inauguration Day as they were sure that anyone following them or attempting harm would be tied up in the security. Even though they were confident, Mac had carefully moved their clothes to a storage unit.

Mac and Helen were at the airport watching the swearing in ceremony.

"Does something look odd here?" Mac asked.

"You mean all the dark suits or the fact that there aren't any women?" Helen asked.

"In this day and age there has to be a least one woman. Hell, they make up the majority of seats in Congress."

"Past tense, Mac. No women were seated in the last election, from presidential election on down to dog catchers."

"Seriously? I didn't check dog catchers," he said with a smile.

"There are two women present. Must be Mrs. Anders and Mrs. Flores."

"They're tough to see under those clothes and scarves."

The two women were dressed identically in black. They both had black Astrakhan coats with long black scarves over their hair and black gloves. One was carrying a black book.

"That must be Shirley Anders with the family Bible," said Helen.

"What denomination?"

"I don't know. It's been don't ask, don't tell since JFK was the first Catholic in the White House and Obama the first black."

The oath was always taken on a Bible. The Chief Justice, soon to be retired, spoke slowly as one who recognizes that this is his last act of public service. Anders repeated the words with authority. In less than a minute he would have the key to launch the might of the United States of America on any square mile in the world. Francis Flores stood behind and to the side in full view of the cameras. Mac noted that his wife stood slightly behind him; they were not touching. This was not an important day for her, but it was for the man who was, obvious to Mac, struggling to keep the self-satisfied grin from his face.

The weather was not bad for January; damp, dark – it had briefly rained on the waiting crowd. There were few in attendance. People who had been to several ceremonies before were attending to say that they had been there. Buses had brought people from generally poorer neighborhoods; why was not yet evident, but they were all men. These men waited, patiently, in quiet expectation. Arthur Anders was left with the podium. He had turned, shook hands with his Vice

President, ignored his wife, and then returned to the microphone.

"Fellow citizens, I am here today to reaffirm my campaign pledges. I am not a politician who might say one thing on the run to the White House, the run for any political office, and then do something entirely different. Today, just one hour ago, I ordered the Chief of the Armed Forces to bring all of our brave men and women serving in the Mediterranean countries home. He refused and I accepted his resignation. Admiral Wallworth replaced General Lloyd and is complying with that order. I take this pledge to you seriously and therefore General Lloyd will be arrested and charged with refusing a direct order from a superior officer."

There was a gasp around the airport. Helen tightened her grip on Mac's arm. The audible shock at what had just been said and heard around the world began with whispered requests to repeat what had been said by the new President.

'I have pledged to end the contribution of aid to foreign countries, particularly those to whom we have pledged military aircraft and equipment. Entitlements will be examined by Congress and cut to not only balance the budget, but to build a surplus. All social programs will be under scrutiny."

"Are you sure he's a Democrat?" asked Mac.

"He is when he talks about taxing the rich and increasing estate taxes. The entitlements have been generally untouchable and it's hard to see how he can push them through Congress."

"He owns Congress, remember?"

"We believe he does," said Helen.

"And we are never wrong," he said with a wink. "It's probably time that we started moving. No one is paying attention and we want to be in the crush leaving the city."

The plan was to change, transfer the bags that were packed into backpacks and their appearance from respectable professionals to respectable students. The students would then catch the shuttle back into the city and mingle with the crowds leaving. A train to Baltimore, then a bus to New York, and transfer to another bus to Boston.

When Mac came out of the men's room in a sweatshirt and blue jeans, baseball hat and sneakers, he glanced back at the television. What he saw riveted him to the spot. Anders was now brandishing his 'bible'; the crowds were now cheering wildly and Mac could not see why. Then Anders was speaking again.

"This is why I pledge these things. I pledge my life to this country and my people, but most of all I pledge my life to Allah."

The noise from the crowd was now deafening. When it abated slightly, Anders continued.

"And that is why with the Koran in my hand I change my name to that of our greatest prophet. My name from this day will be Mohammed Al Adana."

"What is it?" asked Helen.

"Adana? A place in Turkey. The announcement: the end of the free world. Time to leave."

BOOK
TWO

"Dissent is the highest form of patriotism."
~Unknown

Chapter One

The night was clear, cold, and crisp. A white mantle stretched as far as the eye could see. The snow was fresh and remained on the branches of the pine trees; no animal had tracked through it. As a breeze came across the lake, the higher branches released a little snow onto the lower branches, silently, then, the accumulated downward fall resulted in a 'plop.' If there had been traffic, the noise would have been muffled. No one was out.

The solitary figure was standing, looking north, recognizing stars and drinking the silence. Behind him, but out of sight, was a solitary light. He thought now of the lack of wind. As a child he had been mesmerized by the word zephyr because of the grouping of unusual letters. When he thought of the wind tonight, he imagined that a zephyr could set the whole silent, unmoving landscape into motion. Much like life.

Mac's thoughts frequently went back to that inauguration, almost two years ago. The day he went from reporter to whatever he was now. The day he left city life for a life in the country; left friends for life with Helen. The day he went from law abiding citizen to fugitive, from patriot to terrorist.

The introspective examination continued as he touched the face, the beard of 'Peter Howe'; he examined the sturdy boots and quilted jacket over lined blue jeans and a tight wool cap.

Mac had been standing for almost an hour, not feeling the cold, feeling instead a familiar self loathing. It was the long winters, people said. Winter brought on depression; it resulted in an increase in alcoholism.

The thought of alcohol worked as a catalyst to his memory.

It had taken them three weeks to laboriously work their way north from Washington. They had left the Boston-bound bus before its final destination, at a terminal that had no cameras outside. Their days involved slipping out of the public gaze, exciting no interest, staying in guest houses in anonymous towns, catching rides or buses in a serpentine route. The benefit had been that by the time they had reached Lake Winnipesaukee, Mac resembled the bearded photograph of Peter Howe, the man who he had become. Ellen Howe, likewise, had the bleached blond hair and contact tinted blue eyes that still surprised Helen whenever she looked in the mirror.

When they arrived, Mac went and knocked on the neighbor's door.

"Yes, son, how can I help you?"

"Mr. Hamilton?"

"Yep! And you are?"

"Peter Howe. My mother said that you had the key to the house."

Mac had pronounced the name on his driver's license in a close approximation of his mother's new married name. It was good enough, as a smile of recognition came to the old face.

"Mother!" he called into the house. "Look who's here."

Mac saw the apprehension on Helen's face as she was anticipating the appearance of someone twenty years older than the old man in front of them. The woman who appeared was clearly his wife. His wife of many years, they had grown to look alike. Never tall, they had both shrunk to about five-foot, three inches, and had the dried look of people working outdoors, but with a genuine smile and bright eyes.

Mrs. Hamilton was wiping her hands on an apron as she walked through, evidently from the kitchen, to meet them.

"It's the Howe boy and his wife," he completed the introduction.

"Come in, have a cup of coffee, just took a cake out of the oven. How'd you get here? Staying or just visiting?"

Mrs. Hamilton commanded and talked, the questions falling like rain. Was she expecting answers, being polite, or just being neighborly?

As they entered a comfortable open room which served as kitchen and living room, it was clear that they did not have many visitors and obvious which two chairs they usually occupied.

Mrs. Hamilton kept up a one-sided conversation as Mac and Helen were directed to the two favorite chairs. Dropping their bags, they instead sat together on a small sofa with a homemade coffee table in front of it.

"Nice weather, above freezing I think; cold tonight though." Mrs. Hamilton kept up a monologue as she made cups of strong hot coffee. She served the coffee with huge wedges of cake and sat expectantly.

"We thought that we might stay in New Hampshire a while. Got laid off, no jobs in Albany. We needed to get away." All of these things were true, even if misleading. Mac changed the subject. "The cake is wonderful; maybe you could share the recipe with Ellen."

"My pleasure," smiled Mrs. Hamilton, obviously pleased to be complimented on her cooking.

"I remember your mama, a wonderful woman; still alive?"

"Yes, she doesn't get out much now."

"I remember the first time she water-skied. We had just moved in here, Mother, hadn't we? 'Bout sixty years ago must have been. She skied every day that summer, she'd go with anybody with a boat. Then a bit later she babysat for us to go to the movies, remember that, Mother? Must be…."

"Chuck, these kids got to get set before dark, get a fire. You can talk tomorrow."

"Ay," he said getting up, putting on boots with practice, and taking a large coat from the back of the door as he went out.

It felt colder outside after the warmth of the house, and it seemed colder still when they arrived at the small house about a hundred yards down the road. It was assumed to be a road, probably dirt, though it was covered in snow. The door closest to the road was blocked with snow, drifted in by the wind. Walking around to the front, or lake side, they stepped into a screened porch. Snowflakes and ice had accumulated on the Adirondack chairs and on a small table. The key went easily into the lock and, with a shoulder charge to dislodge ice around the edges of the door, they were in.

The thermometer showed that the temperature was lower inside than out, if that were possible. The lack of light penetrating did not help.

Chuck Hamilton, with the benefit of over sixty years experience, started a fire. First, he burned paper in the chimney to dislodge any animals that might have made a home there.

"Should be a woodpile out the side. Take a hammer or ax and try to get enough for tonight. Tools are in the lean to."

Mac went out, glad to be doing something. When he came back in he found Helen moving throughout the other rooms, touching the unfamiliar furniture, opening stiff drawers, looking into dark foreign closets. It was dark in the house, and he knew she was tired, she was very cold, and she was crying. He could tell what she was thinking: Was this dark, cold, place, to be her home?

It took several days for the house to warm. The first thing Mac did was to put fresh gasoline in the generator. The next chore, he quickly realized, was that wood was needed daily for the stove. It was an old fashioned stove and it took a day to clean all the rust from the burners and oven. It doubled as the heating source for the house and, with the drafts, it had an insatiable appetite for fuel. Wood cutting and splitting had the benefit of being a warming exercise. The downside was that for a week Mac could feel pain in muscles that he had not known existed.

They had an enormous learning curve. The nearest store was a mile and half away. It carried basics - no garlic or asparagus or paper tissues. Also, Mac and Helen quickly learned never to forget something or it was another three mile walk and that a twenty pound bag of potatoes seemed to weigh forty pounds after a mile and a half. They also figured out to watch the weather as it is harder to walk through a blizzard.

The water came from the lake. If the pipe from the lake froze then a hole in the ice was necessary to fill a bucket for drinking and washing.

A fishing license was another necessity. Chuck, who naturally knew everyone, facilitated the license at the general store.

"Need a license, Bob." It was a statement.

"Never fished before?"

"Need a license. Give him a license, Bob."

"Need to see identification, fill out a form," said Bob.

"I didn't bring identification, next time I'm in perhaps." Mac had the driver's license but was reluctant to show it without thinking it through.

"We know who you are, where you live," Chuck replied to Mac. Then he turned back to Bob. "He don't need to show you some identification, like some flatlander. I know you done it for the Gillespie kid, Bob – kid who don't know his own name, don't know his own daddy. You did it for him."

The knowledge and threat of exposure had Bob return from the back room with a form and a permit to fish.

"Thanks, Bob. Thanks, Chuck. Now I need to wait until spring."

"Hell, no," said Chuck. "We'll cut a hole this afternoon. Gonna need a bottle of that cheap, gut rot, whiskey you sell, Bob."

The hole cut, the lines set, the bottle drunk. It was a man feeling no pain and no cold who triumphantly presented Helen with two bass for supper.

"What do you expect of these?" Helen was not adjusting to life without supermarkets, without television, telephone, and internet, or to a life without restaurants.

"Just gut them and put them in a pan with wine to poach."

"One, I do not 'gut'; two, we have no wine." She left the room, slammed the door, then opened it again as she realized that a closed door would admit no heat.

Mac went in and apologized.

"It's hard. We knew it would be."

"I miss my friends. I miss going to a restaurant. I even miss the goddamn television." Tears ran down her face.

"We'll go out this weekend, walk to the nearest restaurant. Maybe they'll have a television signal."

"They'll probably be showing an ice fishing derby," said Helen.

They both laughed.

"I'll clean the fish, pan fry some potatoes and defrost some peas," said Mac.

"I know I said that I would follow you to the end of the earth, Mac. Well, I have! Any place where defrosting peas means bringing them in from the porch is the end of the earth."

The nearest restaurant was in fact a bar. It did have a television and, being February, it was showing ice hockey; University of New Hampshire was hosting Boston University. It was not exactly an ice fishing derby, but the irony caused Helen to have a fit of the giggles. The stares from the regulars were as much for the interruption as for the sight of strangers.

"You the Howe's?" a woman tending bar stated, more as an announcement to the other patrons than as a question. "Cousin Bobby told me you were up for a while."

It took a minute but 'Cousin Bobby' had to be Bob who issued fishing licenses and ran the store.

"What'll you have?"

"Beer and white wine."

"Bud or Miller?"

Mac looked around at the bottles in front of the regulars.

"One of them!"

She came back with a bottle of Miller Draft and a glass of white wine.

"Why didn't she ask what kind I wanted?" asked Helen.

Mac was laughing. Helen realized the obvious limitations of the local inventory. All the women were drinking beer, and Helen started giggling again.

"Can we get something to eat?"

"Sure," the woman said, pointing to a board announcing specials.

"A menu?"

"Just the board. Everything is special here." She laughed, as did some of the men at the bar.

There were a few whispered remarks, and then attention went to the television as UNH was on a power play. The hard skating BU players with the one man disadvantage held UNH for the two minute penalty; this received groans from the partisan television audience.

Walking home after a passable chicken pot pie and a couple of drinks, they were friends again. The only sound was the crunching of snow under their boots; their breathing could be seen in little clouds which dropped to the ground as ice.

"Dinner out and a hockey game for twenty-four dollars." Helen smiled.

"I did leave a tip."

"I know. She fainted when she saw that you didn't want change from your five dollar bill."

"A mistake." Mac was serious. "We have to fit in."

"We should have stayed to watch the news. The Union Leader is okay, but it's a little bit to the right for me."

"It's the only paper they have; that and the Laconia Sun."

"Hunting license." Chuck was again at Mac's elbow in the general store.

"I never hunted, never had a gun," Mac confided.

"I got a gun; Mother says no more days in the woods, I may get hurt, have a heart attack or something."

Mac learned to hunt as 'Mother' was happy to let her husband Chuck out in the company of their neighbor.

It turned out to be a win-win situation. Mrs. Hamilton invited Helen to spend the day with her, cooking and braiding rugs. The Hamiltons had no television either, as the reception was impossible because of the mountains and the cable company saw no merit in bringing technology to such a small number of people. Chuck had put an aerial on a very high post when their children were growing up, but when it blew down in a storm he saw no benefit in replacing it. When the grandchildren visited they were shocked but quickly found other things to do.

In the general store one day Helen, during a conversation with Bob, found that the eggs came from a farm nearby and that the farmer would also sell chickens. There had been a conversation at breakfast that fish from the lake and venison from the woods, while nutritious, was getting repetitive. Mac reminded Helen that chicken pot pie was also available if one was willing to brave the elements.

The farmer agreed to sell a couple of chickens, one dollar each.

"Help yourself."

Helen looked in dismay at the heaving, cackling mass of Rhode Island Reds.

"But...."

"Any two, don't matter to me. Just help yourself."

Eventually, sensing her dismay, he pulled out two, expertly broke their necks, tied their feet together and handed them to her. It was obvious that the plucking and cleaning was her job.

"You're Mrs. Howe, right?"

"Yes. Why?"

"Your husband, is he looking for the odd job?"

"Maybe, like what?"

"Some days we get busy. Day after tomorrow I need a truck driven to Boston. Can he do that?"

"Sure."

"Okay, five o'clock, day after tomorrow."

"In the morning?"

"Well, got to be there seven-thirty."

"All right."

Helen was excited. Mac, spitting feathers from the bird he was plucking, was a little more cautious. Was he ready for Boston? Were people looking for him?

"It's been ten weeks; we should at least find out. I could change some bills too. The bank clerk looked so long at the last hundred dollar bill I changed that I almost left. What did the farmer say was the pay?"

"Didn't ask. Perhaps he has some stuff he can pay you with, like potatoes, vegetables, and such."

"It might be a lot of chickens at one dollar each," said Mac, spitting out another feather as he plucked. He had yet to learn that dunking the chickens in hot water loosened feathers and kept them from flying.

Chapter Two

Mac walked to the farm through the dark night, leaving before four-thirty. He was surprised by how many people were out already and by how many houses showed lights through the bare trees.

The truck was next to a diesel tank. The farmer was already filling the vehicle from the tank which said 'Farm Use Only.'

"Bring these to the meat market." The farmer handed Mac some paperwork which included an address. "Straight through Boston, watch for the sign. Get a check, then go to the grain store. They should have an order for me. Give them this envelope. It's a check for them. Okay?"

"Tolls?"

"Oh, yeah." He fished in his pockets and handed Mac a ten dollar bill.

The load was quiet but as the engine started with a backfire seven hundred and fifty chickens squawked and jumped up. The truck left the yard trailing feathers.

Driving down the highway, Mac stayed within the speed limit. Mostly this was through necessity as it was doubtful that the truck could exceed the limit. Mac's senses were alive. He watched the sun rise in front and to his left. He noticed that the snow cover was diminishing as he drove south. In Washington they would be talking about the arrival of the cherry blossoms. Cherry blossoms, the everlasting, annual harbinger of spring, courtesy of the Japanese. A policeman briefly showed interest as the truck passed through the toll booth, then returned to his coffee and newspaper.

At the entrance to the meat market, a mob manned a checkpoint. They were demanding tribute. A load of chickens was of interest.

"Inshalla!"

"Inshalla!" Mac said automatically, greeting the man as he had been greeted. With a full beard and wool cap, he might have been a member of the similarly clad mob.

"We are accepting contributions for our brothers and sisters."

"These are not my chickens. I am just delivering them."

"Then we are going to take them," said the man, suddenly angry. The snap in mood had been instant, probably drug related. The man shouted and a teenage boy jumped onto the back of the truck and threw down a box of chickens from the top row. As the box hit the ground it split open and the chickens escaped in a hopping tangle. Some had broken one or both legs in the fall and lay, or hopped, and fell in an eruption of sight and sound which had the mob frantic with shouts. They were clearly unable to hold onto their weapons and catch chickens. Mac took the opportunity to put the truck in gear and drive away.

"So what did they get you for?" the receiver at the loading dock asked.

"One crate of ten chickens."

"Lucky. Your boss got a hiding and most of his load disappeared while he was on the ground."

"Probably why he sent me."

"Probably. Go get a cup of coffee while we unload and tally you."

"Is there a bank here? Can I get breakfast?"

"Yes, bank is next to the breakfast place. Bank opens at eight."

"Thanks."

Over breakfast he heard stories of the mob rule. The police could do nothing as the perpetrators were quickly released to continue the harassment. No business was immune. Banks were a favorite target; those going in and those leaving were robbed in broad daylight.

How had this happened in ten weeks?

Breakfast was wonderful: eggs, bacon, and coffee had never tasted so good. Banking was a challenge. Mac wanted cash, in twenties. He was warned of the mobs. His bearded, unkempt appearance, with broken fingernails and evidence of hard manual labor, resulted in a fifteen minute wait while the manager did some checking. Mac thought that the draft from Hal could not be verified in Las Vegas, as it was still early there. Finally everything was all right. Probably more than all right, judging by the reception from the manager, who, once again, warned that anyone knowing that he had four thousand dollars in twenty dollar bills would be willing to kill for it.

"Then let's just keep it between the two of us," said Mac.

He intended there be enough menace in his voice to convey that his relationship to the Las Vegas 'settlor' of the account was very close.

When Mac had collected the check for the chickens, he went to the grain store and presented his envelope. The shipper went over the order with him. Mac asked for an empty sack and put his brown paper bag of twenties into it. The sacks were all loaded and the chicken crates, now empty, folded, and covered in chicken excrement, were put on top and tied down. At a pay phone, with a fist of quarters, Mac called Sue Raymond. Carol answered the telephone.

"Hello?"

"Is Ray there?"

"Who is this?"

"Carol, is Ray there?"

"No, they took her away."

"Who, why?"

"The police had questions. Who is this?"

"I'll call again," Mac said as he hung up the phone.

He made two more calls. The first ascertained that his mother was unchanged; the second was local.

"Virginia Black, please."

"Speaking."

"I was calling to see how your former governor was doing and how your studies of 1921 Mississippi were progressing?"

"If you remember, there was an invisible man on a white horse. Well, the horse is dead and the man should remain invisible." Virginia Black hung up the phone.

Mac drove to Harvard Square. He double parked and went into the book store and bought Washington, San Francisco, Boston, and London newspapers. He picked up a Time Magazine, a copy of Barrons, and the Wall Street Journal. He got back to his truck as a crowd was gathering. There was a policeman talking on his walkie-talkie while taking out his book.

"Inshalla!" Mac said as the crowd backed away.

The policeman put away his book and dispersed the crowd.

The ride back to New Hampshire was without incident. The farmer was pleased with the check and made no comment of the tally being less than shipped. He agreed to paying Mac in kind; he gave him two dozen eggs, a couple of chickens, and a shoulder of pork as a start.

"Thank God you are back." Helen still could not call it home. "Any problems?"

"No, I missed you. I got a couple of newspapers and a pizza." Mac would tell her about the phone calls later. "Warm the pizza and we'll read the papers."

Later Mac and Helen were seated amongst the litter of newspapers. They had initially started reading interesting bits to each other. Then, as the articles were showing a pattern, they read in silence.

It was clear that the problems of America had been increasing from the day of the inauguration. Troops returning from their overseas assignments had added to the already dangerously high unemployment rate. The cancellation of defense contracts had closed Boeing plants across the country and had closed truck building plants in Detroit. The knock-on effect had created layoffs in every section of the economy. In less than three months the unemployment rate had risen to twenty percent. It was still rising. The record keeping could not keep up with the claims. Money was flying from the Federal Reserve. Immigration applications and claims of naturalization were overwhelming the system. Claims for housing, claims for benefits, medical care, and food created lines at government offices, at shelters, and food banks.

The next phase of this tremendous increase in unemployment was foreseeable: crime escalated. Some areas became war zones at night, inevitably there were places where it was unwise to go out in the daytime.

Mac's experience in Boston and Cambridge were examples of a police force unable, or unwilling, to provide protection. Courts, with no cell room, were routinely returning criminals to the street.

The President was still talking of his achievements and promising legislation very soon to address the crisis in the country, created by the former President and by those who would oppose the government

"Did he mention crime or unemployment?"

"No; the editorial says that law enforcement agencies are still looking for radicals who tried to subvert the election."

"They mean us?" asked Helen.

"You don't look radical, well not to me."

"Things aren't any better in Europe. Britain pulled back troops at the same time as the U.S. Some U.N. peacekeepers were massacred. Israel is on high alert as threats of violence from their neighbors went without condemnation, or comment, from the West."

Mac had recounted the words of Virginia Black, and the panic of Carol. Helen went quiet; finally, she raised her head from an article in *Time* about the new First Family.

"Next time you go to Boston, I want to go with you."

There were volumes in the statement. Did she want to see for herself, communicate with family, or just get out?

There was only one answer "Okay." Mac did not say 'if there is a next time' or 'it may be dangerous.'

The weather improved. The ice broke up with creaks and cracks that, at first, kept them from sleeping. Fishing was more of a challenge and hunting season was over. Mac discovered talents for repair that he never knew he had. Drafts were addressed; windows were caulked, drapes were made and hung. Log splitting was still a daily chore. The line from the lake bringing water was now free and Mac had installed, with supervision from Chuck, a heat wrap to be activated when the ground next froze. With the warmer weather came longer days, an uplifting of spirits, and black flies.

Mac acquired Chuck's pick-up truck by default. One day Chuck had skidded into a ditch; the truck needed a rebuild that was not worth the money. He gave the old Chevy to Mac and asked in return that perhaps he could sometimes get a ride. The Hamilton's daughter lived not too far away and was asking her parents to move in with her. Mr. and Mrs. Hamilton were resisting. The Chevy also gave Mac an additional headache as he added car mechanic to his rapidly expanding resume.

Mac and Helen kept a low profile but, as the black flies and summer began, the increased volume of people moving back for the summer, visiting for the day or for longer, gave them freedom to move further afield. They went one day to Meredith, another day to

Wolfeboro. They went to Portland. The truck broke down, the clutch, already rebuilt, had burned out.

"Why not buy a new vehicle?" asked Helen.

"Because car dealers will want information, identification, mail addresses, email addresses, etc. We would be on someone's radar."

"How do we know that anyone gives a jot where we are?"

"Remember what Virginia Black said, that the invisible man should remain unseen and that the white horse is dead."

"That was months ago."

"True, but is only a blink in the memory of most."

"I'd like to check on my mother and sister. Let them know that I am okay. Well, at least alive."

"You're not happy here?"

"No, I'm a city girl. Mac, don't get me wrong. I love you. I just can't see living this way forever. We should be doing something."

"What?"

"I don't know. We now read newspapers regularly, we see what is happening. It's awful."

The price of gasoline soared. Mac, following the lead of his neighbors, bought five gallons at a time. At twelve dollars a gallon many gas stations went out of business. The vacation industry disappeared, creating more unemployment. Anyone with a generator was buying fuel and storing it for the winter months. The conversation at the store was generally on ways to save. These were careful people and now they were cutting back further.

It was late summer when the farmer asked Mac to again drive to Boston. Helen assumed that she was going and could not be dissuaded.

They set off at four-thirty, through quiet streets, with their squawking load. There was a road block at the toll station. A tired policeman looked inside the cab, scanned the load, and passed them through.

"What are they looking for?" asked Helen, who had agreed to wear a head scarf hiding her lower face; Mac had said that he would not take her without precautions.

"I think that they are looking for someone," said Mac.

At shortly after six in the morning the encampment at the food market had not come to life. A solitary man held up his hand to stop them; a small boy held a large gun at the side of the small barrier.

"Inshallah. We need food to feed the poor."

"Inshallah, This is not my food."

"What you do not give, we take."

"You and the boy?" asked Mac.

"My son," with a wave of his hand, "and others."

Helen pointed Mac's gun out of the window at the man's lower extremities. "He will be the only son you have if you don't move."

"I have many sons. You shoot, in five minutes you will be dead."

Mac put the truck in gear and accelerated past the man who had jumped clear. He was now shouting and men were pouring out of the makeshift tent city.

"Why, why Helen?"

"He pissed me off. Using his son, what, nine or ten years old, teaching him to steal, armed robbery. They are not poor. Did you see the gold chains? Even the boy was wearing a gold chain. I am dressed in old clothes; they have designer jeans and gold chains."

Mac looked at his wife. He could understand her frustration.

"He pissed me off!" Helen exclaimed.

They followed the routine and, after a large breakfast costing twice as much as six months earlier, Helen went to the pay phone with a handful of quarters.

Mac retrieved the truck and a much larger check. He had already been to the grain merchant, who had his shipment on the dock. He wanted to get, or to check on, his money but needed Helen first.

Driving across the street, he could see and hear a commotion at the entrance. Mac blew the horn and indicated that it was time to go. Helen seemed reluctant and was walking, without urgency, to the truck when Mac shouted.

"Get in! Now!"

"Why?"

"Get down; we have to get out of here."

At the entrance there was a truck with armed men. The leader was clearly setting up rules for in and out. Mac was stopped. The armed men looked in the cab, under the truck, and in the back, and then waved him through. Helen crawled out from behind the front seat. They had been looking for a woman. They had a picture of Helen.

"How did they know?"

"Your sister's phone must have triggered the alert."

"So they are still looking for me, or you, or both of us?"

"It looks that way," said Mac. "Let's see if Sean can speak to me."

Waiting outside the office building on Federal Street, there was a contrast to just a year before when the Democratic Party Convention had been taking place. The Conventioneers had seen a Boston bustling with people, bursting with self importance. Now the streets were quieter: less traffic, fewer people.

Everywhere the signs of unemployment were obvious: "For Lease" signs were on half of the retail stores, while office towers had signs with "Space Available". On the benches secretaries ate lunches obviously brought from home, while they were badgered by beggars of all ages. The beggars asked for food, money, and clothing.

Sean finally came out and they almost missed him. He looked much older and did not have the 'bounce' that confident people exhibit. He found a seat and opened a sandwich. Mac and Helen approached him.

"Go away; I have no money for you." He had barely glanced at the poorly dressed people in front of him.

"Not even for an alumnus?"

Sean now looked up. Recognition, then panic, then thoughtfulness were expressions crossing his face as he searched for the right reaction and words.

"I am supposed to report contact of any kind."

"To whom?"

"FBI, CIA, Secret police, Gestapo."

"Oh, them. Well then, you didn't contact us."

"Very good, Mac; still quick." He smiled as though he had not smiled for a very long time.

"How is the family, Sean?"

"Good, I guess. We're not making the money we used to, but hey...." he gestured to the two of them, "....who is?"

"Why us?"

"It's everyone who might dissent. Marjorie White is a recluse, probably under house arrest or something. Ellie May Joseph, she's something, goes around with an armed posse. They've backed off, for now."

"What are you doing?"

Abruptly Sean shoved the paper bag at them.

"Here, take my sandwich. You put me off my food anyway." He stood up and left.

Without turning around Mac whispered, "Put that head scarf around your lower face before you move."

They both stood and moved away. When they rounded the corner they looked back at the two men who had stopped Sean. Both were bigger than he was.

"Gestapo," Mac whispered, grabbing Helen by the elbow and leading her back toward the truck.

When they were finally on the road, Mac was in deep thought. There were many things to think through on the day. He had not taken out any money or checked on it. That was not a huge problem as the farmer was supplying them with eggs, pork, chickens, and seasonal vegetables. Helen had started a garden, and, after feeding most of the squirrels, rabbits, and chipmunks in the village, had gone on an offensive that would have routed Patton. Now she had lettuce, tomatoes, potatoes, cabbage, and squash. They were living rent free and chopping down trees for heating fuel. Mac was still fishing, and hunting season was coming up. He mused that if his friends could see him now, they would not recognize the man who used to eat at restaurants half the time.

Mac's thoughts went to the road blocks.

"I think that we'll take the scenic route, just in case. A farm truck looks out of place on the Interstate."

Helen had been deep into her own thoughts.

"Fred was laid off," she said.

"What will they do about the mortgage?"

"Mum will help. She moved in with them and feels responsible. Julie's still working for now."

"How are they all?"

"Worried. Julie said that friends of mine call her regularly to ask if she has heard from us. Too many to be a coincidence; she asked where we were."

"Did you tell her?"

"No. She asked if we were coming for Christmas or mum's birthday."

"You said no?" He asked.

"I said I didn't know; that we were in Boston today.

"Sorry, Mac."

"Not your fault, but we cannot make any more mistakes. Sean looked tired. I think that he's worried too. Speaking of Sean, did he leave any potato chips in that bag?"

"I'll look." Helen rummaged behind the seat for the brown paper bag. "Yep, you're in luck. Also…" she pulled out a piece of paper. She looked at it for a long time.

"This may be why Sean was worried," she said.

"What is it?"

"A meeting notice, 'Sons of Liberty', next Wednesday. Do you think that he meant to give it to us?"

"No," said Mac. "I think that is was for someone else. I think that the 'someone' else told the Gestapo, who planned to pick up the notice and Sean."

"So he dumped it on us and ran."

"He warned us and…"

"Mac, think very, very hard before you say one more word."

Chapter Three

Mac had thought very, very hard. It was a Gordian knot. Helen, who was not in favor of staying in New Hampshire, was afraid of moving back to civilization. Mac, whose whole being had been centered on the takeover of the White House, the U.S. Government, and almost certainly the British, French, and German Governments, was content with his new life. The consequences of being found were difficult to imagine, and probably painful. The choice of doing nothing, while others led the opposition, was against everything that he had argued. It was too late to say that he should have done things earlier or better. Now he was married and had to consider Helen as well.

The answer came, as answers generally do, from the furthest thing that can be imagined. Israel bombed the Iranian nuclear bomb making facility. The reaction was swift; a condemnation from almost every country in the world, including the United States. Pakistan, goaded by the Muslim Brotherhood, threatened nuclear retaliation against Israel. The Israelis promptly bombed Pakistan's nuclear facilities. The Arab League massed troops on the desert borders of Israel.

The news item that changed Mac's mind was that Israel refused to back down. Prime Minister Tishman said that they would protect their piece of the earth to the last Jew, and that Arabs would return to oil fields that would be contaminated for a hundred thousand years.

David versus Goliath.

Helen cried and finally agreed that Mac must, somehow, be at the next meeting of the Sons of Liberty.

Mac went to five gas stations to fill the truck and a spare container. He would leave early in the morning, stay on the back roads, find a place to park without causing excitement and walk. It was likely that he would stay overnight somewhere or in the pickup truck.

They went over the plan again and again. Helen wanted to go with him but finally agreed to stay in New Hampshire. Mac read the notice one more time and burned it.

The Sons of Liberty were meeting, not at the South Meeting Hall where their namesakes had plotted the original tea party in 1774, in a town house on Beacon Hill. It was close to the State House, a bit too close for comfort.

Mac knocked at the door five minutes before the advertised meeting time. A keyhole lookout asked his business.

"Sean Lynch."

The keyhole closed. He stood and watched, the keyhole reopened

"Your business here?"

Mac took a deep breath, "Sons of Liberty!"

The door opened, he stepped into a dark entry hallway. The door closed behind him and a light shone in his face as a wand was waved over his body. The examination for electronic devices complete, another door opened off the hallway and he entered.

"You were spotted half an hour ago, walking past and paying too much attention to this house."

"How? I was being careful of a trap," said Mac.

"Sean was questioned by the police. If he said anything about this meeting we could expect a raid."

"Is he all right?" asked Mac

"We'll know if he shows up tonight. I hope so."

The spokesman was tall, athletic looking, about sixty years old with a mustache. "Benjamin Franklin."

"Really?"

"No, we use different names. What would we call you?"

"Peter Doath," said Mac without hesitation.

"Let's join the others, Peter." He gestured as doors slid back showing a room that was twice the size of the one he was in. The other side had eight people, men and women. One man was the person who had been walking the dog; the person, Mac assumed, who had spotted him on the street.

"We have two people upstairs, front and back, who will watch and then rotate into the meeting," explained Benjamin Franklin.

Everyone was seated and the meeting began. The leader of the group stood and introduced himself as John Hancock. He was about fifty with short hair and spectacles. A professional appearance, Mac guessed that he might be a lawyer, an accountant, or banker.

"We have a new member, perhaps?" He looked at Mac who instantly felt out of place and somehow naked.

"I don't know. A flyer with the meeting information was put into my hand, apparently by a member. That member is not here, so I cannot ask why."

"You took the name Peter Doath. If you have the political acumen of a writer by that name, then you are welcome. Do you have any questions?"

"I expected more people."

"Well, there has to be a start. The original Sons of Liberty were a group of nine. The nine grew to thousands and had groups in every State."

"What are the goals of this group?" asked Mac.

"A return to Democracy," an angular young woman, probably just out of college, said with passion.

"America is the leading Democracy in the world." Mac said argumentatively.

"Past tense! You need to read the articles by your namesake," she shot back at him.

"Paula, everyone needs to introduce him, or herself, as they speak," said John Hancock.

"Okay; Paula Revere. Since we have a Benjamin Franklin and since my fellow members recognized that I was a woman, it just fit."

John Hancock further explained, "The return to Democracy has to be a non-violent response to the attack on the Constitution. The original Sons were printers and related tradesmen. We loosely fall into that description. If you were to work with us, it would be to use your writing expertise and your contacts to spread the truth."

"My writing expertise?" Mac was aware that he was wearing working clothes, a beard, and a carefully cultured new identity. It had been seen through or had his choice of pseudonym given rise to the comment.

"The articles by Peter Doath, and the article by Ann Gold of an interview with him, would be admired only by a fellow writer." There was a glint in Paula Revere's eyes.

She knew but would not call him on it, not jeopardize his cover.

John Hancock asked the members to discuss the latest news from the underground. Benjamin Franklin spoke of how Old Macdonald, who was supposed to have been here this evening, had seen pending legislation that would give militia rights to certain groups. Mac assumed that Old Macdonald was in fact Sean.

"I am concerned that he did not show up tonight," stated a large woman who seemed to have overpowered a deep chair. "My name is Betsy Ross, and I am also concerned that this man shows up when Old Mac is seen with the authorities. There have been too many of us interviewed."

"Are you suggesting a mole?" John Hancock asked.

"John, you were stopped."

"I think that they were stopping everyone better dressed than they were. When they ascertained that I was a…. teacher, they lost interest."

Mac realized that he had seen John's face on a book on economics. He was a professor at Harvard.

"What do we have planned before our next meeting? Is there any way to influence the sanctioning of militia? We also need to link with groups in other cities."

"How do we know that there are other groups?"

"The Secretary of State referred to a group in New York who had produced and distributed a newspaper as terrorists."

"What happened to free speech?" asked Betsy Ross.

"Well apparently there were a couple of articles that were reprints of Peter Doath and there was a discussion regarding the television appearance of Matthew McDougal which was mentioned. According to the Secretary they were not protected by free speech because those acts incited action against a legally elected Government."

There were a few snorts.

Benjamin Franklin spoke. "I can go to New York, sniff around."

"Father!" Paula Revere blushed as she realized the error. "Benjamin, you are not to get excited; you are supposed to have an operation."

"Paula, I have waited this long, what with the chaos in the hospitals for lack of funds and their being overloaded with welfare cases, a few days in New York won't matter."

The date and place of the next meeting was set and Mac promised to bring documents and present an article for distribution. Paula, now on lookout, called down that all was clear. A dog appeared from under a chair, his owner claimed him and they left. A couple left, then Benjamin and Paula left by the back door to melt into the back alleys of old Boston.

"I hope that your friend is all right." John Hancock shook Mac's hands as he was leaving. "I'm glad that you are all right. We had heard rumors that your friends were all questioned regarding your whereabouts."

"You know me?"

"I bought your latest book, before it was removed from the bookstores. It is a bit of a 'bible' to our group."

"I need to stay hidden for now. I need to know what happened to my friend."

"I understand. I'll try to have information in time for our next meeting. That is if you make it to the next meeting."

"May I bring my wife?"

"This is a dangerous business. You must decide for yourselves. Be careful."

It was late when Mac arrived at Sean's house in the suburbs. He drove past and found a house being renovated about half a mile away. Parking the pickup truck next to a dumpster, it looked like it belonged. Mac slapped mud on the New Hampshire plates, and then walked back. He left the sidewalk and took to the back yard of the house before Sean's.

The light startled him. "Shit!" he said in surprise as he realized that he had set off, by his motion, the security light on the back of the house. Fortunately everyone was asleep.

There was a light in the study which Sean used to work on legal cases that he brought home. Mac tapped on the window. Nothing. He tapped again rhythmically. The light went out and Sean peered through the window. Recognition and then a nod of the head toward the back door.

"What the hell are you doing here?"

"Pleased to see you too. You weren't at the meeting."

"Shush, everyone's asleep. Come in here."

"What happened to your face? Were you in an accident?"

"Sort of. I told Trish," he nodded upstairs, "that I was mugged. Completely believable in these times."

"But it was the police?" Mac said rhetorically.

Sean gave a nod of confirmation. "You went to the meeting?"

"Yes, interesting. Not particularly illuminating. What did the police want you for? Something serious by the look of the questioning."

"They asked about my friends. They asked about you, Mac. I told them that I had not seen Matthew McDougal in over a year. They asked who the man was to whom I gave my lunch bag; I told them that it was a hungry panhandler. They asked why I was asking questions about proposed legislation. I guess that the bottom line was they don't want people looking and asking. I decided that they might be following me, so, since I couldn't lead them to a private meeting, I came home."

"The group is smaller than I thought that it might be; pretty smart people though. I said that I might have some documents that could be used and that I would write an article for dissemination."

"It's dangerous, Mac, especially for you. The new government doesn't like dissenters. There was a protest walk in Chicago, crushed, never made the news."

"How can it not make the news with all of the social media activity?"

"Social media activity in Chicago went 'postal' for a week. By then it was deniable."

"There is proposed legislation for a militia?" asked Mac.

"Yes, scary as hell. The press release, prepared for the media, says that it is temporary, to help the police combat crime. The inside scuttlebutt is that it is a private army. A right to arm certain people in an emergency has been around in Massachusetts for several years. This is why it is to be tried here, before transferring the idea to other states."

"Whose army?"

"It will be funded and administered by the ghost police force. The same people who questioned me."

"Funding?"

"Off the books."

"You're right, scary as hell, material that I can use for my first article." Mac was suddenly very tired. "Can I crash?"

"Trish can't see you." Sean was scared and worried.

"I'll leave at sun-up, before five."

"Thanks, Mac. Oh, I should use your pseudonym."

"Peter Doath."

"I might have known." Sean smiled for the first time in the last hour.

Chapter Four

The winter months passed more quickly as there seemed to always be something to do. Hunting, fishing, and keeping a warm fire were required regular activities. Mac was now an expert on all three, so he was much more efficient. Keeping the pickup running was a challenge, also keeping it full of gasoline without arousing suspicion took planning. Mac was also writing, so was Helen.

They had missed two meetings because of the weather and one because of mechanical problems with the pickup. Their articles had resulted in more exposure for the Sons of Liberty. The resulting exposure had swelled the ranks of the organization and also brought attention from the authorities. A number of printing establishments had burned or been raided. The one used by the Sons of Liberty remained undetected on the campus of MIT. The social media was spreading the word across the country. There were attempts weekly to infiltrate the group or to suppress criticism of the administration. So far all had failed. The core group of twelve continued to meet, gather information, authorize and organize its distribution.

Peter Doath had become public enemy number one with Leonad Vallice a close second. Mac and Helen used these names for the articles. Helen had had to choose a pseudonym. She had toyed with Queen of Troy, but since that was obvious she settled on Scarlett O' Hara.

Summer came, along with protests and riots. The protests were broken up with violence. The militias were being directed by their handlers and the police were then coming along to arrest any who had been leaders of the protests while ignoring the brutality of the militia.

The riots were a result of unemployment monies having dried up; there were families with nothing. The federal government had stated that single parents no longer had rights to housing. If the single mothers refused to leave, their children were taken into care and the women thrown into the streets. The apartment was immediately occupied by families. A few single mothers, who quickly married, were forced to prove that the husband was the father of the children and was spending all of his nights at the house. It was then assumed that he would support his family and benefits ceased.

Helen, in addition to the newspapers, was spending time at the local library using the computer. Mac had emphasized the use of caution, reminding her of what had happened after she called her sister.

She had called her mother twice since that first time, each time from different locations in the Boston area. It was difficult to find a pay phone and harder to find one not under the scrutiny of a closed circuit camera.

The price of gasoline went to twenty-five dollars a gallon with the crisis in the Middle East showing no signs of lessening. The Israelis, under increasing pressure and provocation, kept the possibility of a nuclear destruction of the oilfields as an option. It was clear that they were reluctant to use the threat. As the threat receded, the provocation increased. They hit a small refinery in retribution; they used conventional weapons. The Arabs retreated, for now.

"We need to get first-hand information to and from Washington." John Hancock was speaking.

"Peter knows his way around there," said Old MacDonald.

"I'm also known there, and I'm public enemy number one."

"We'll go," Scarlett said.

Two things helped make the decision final. The first was that with the high price of fuel, virtually every automobile in New Hampshire was for sale. Mac found a diesel pickup truck, cheap. The second was that he had seen a conversion that would fit on the back. The conversion could convert to sleeping quarters and hold cooking utensils. Diesel fuel was still available for transport, so he could find fuel at any truck stop along the way.

The journey to Washington was fairly uneventful, keeping to lesser roads to avoid cameras, the New Hampshire plates had them stopped twice, both times in small communities. The explanation that they were heading south looking for work was believable. When Mac asked if there was any work locally he was told to move on.

Washington was at first eerily quiet. They had become accustomed over the years to traffic noises, truck and bus airbrakes and diesel acceleration; cars and taxies with hand-on-horn, jumping amber traffic lights.

There were fewer vehicles on the road. Cars and taxies negotiated with care, a timid approach to the streets at odds with recollections. Mac, wishing for anonymity, looking for changes, showed a care previously missing in his trips through the city. They drove past his apartment. It looked older than when they had left, just a year ago. Maybe it was always old looking, but when it was home it took on a countenance that was friendly and comfortable. They drove to the apartment that Sue Raymond shared with Carol. His agent should be able to bring them up to date and perhaps suggest a place where they could stay.

The last time they had been here was when Helen had come close to a breakdown through exhaustion. This time they parked a few streets away and walked toward the familiar door. It was decided that Helen should go first, as a woman she would elicit less interest. If all was clear, she would appear at the front window.

Mac watched from the car as Helen rang the bell. He watched her speak into the intercom. After a couple of minutes he saw her open the door and go inside.

Down in the street Mac was getting anxious; almost half an hour had passed with no signal. He was feeling conspicuous. Finally he saw Helen and cautiously crossed the street. In the apartment Carol was seated on a sofa with both hands wrapped around a mug of tea. Another mug of tea was on the table.

"A cup of tea?" Helen asked.

"Please." Mac had a questioning look.

Carol had not moved. She had not looked up as he entered, not stirred from that place that she had gone to when he had walked through the door and dropped his backpack.

Helen returned with the tea for Mac.

"It seems that Ray has gone. From what I gather, she has been arrested. The charges, if any, are vague. That is all that I've found out."

"Ray's gone; they took her. What am I supposed to do?" Carol looked pleadingly at Mac.

"Carol, who took her and when? What is she in trouble for?"

"The police came a week ago. They took her computer. It must be the same as last time. They were looking for Matthew McDougal, Peter Doath, Leonad Vallice, and Helen Harvey. She didn't know. I told them that I didn't know. They hit me anyway, but I still didn't know."

"Where did they go? Did you go to the police station?"

"Yes, they said that I had made it up, that she had left me, gone away. She didn't, did she? She wouldn't! What am I to do?"

"You said, 'same as last time'; when was last time?"

"They came in January, stayed for about two hours and asked about you; they came again, it must have been right after the book came out. They confiscated all of the author proofs and other copies and then they took her for three days. She said they kept asking where do you send the checks? How do you get instructions? Where's McDougal? Where's Peter Doath? Over, and over, and over. They hit her; they hurt her bad." Carol cringed at the memory.

"The police took all of the books? Did they give you a receipt?"

"No and no. They said that the books were to be burned, but I had one that I had been reading; it was under my pillow."

Mac took Helen aside.

"Not police. I need to go meet some people. I'll try to find out about Sue; I'll be as quick as I can. Will you be all right here?"

"Why can't I come with you?"

"Because I think that Carol will do anything to get Ray back, including calling our buddies to tell them we're in town. Be careful."

"You too. I love you."

They kissed passionately.

Mac left.

The meeting with George Washington and a bunch of characters named for famous generals was interesting and informative. The group was pleased to meet Peter Doath, whose writings were copied into their own literature. This group was non-militant, and although they were sharing ideas with each other and with other groups, it was clear that they were looking for a plan of action.

"We're picking up new numbers every week, but without a direction it's hard to see them staying."

"Do you have someone inside the Government giving you previews of legislation?" asked Mac.

"We did," said George Washington.

"He was arrested, beaten, and fired," continued Dwight Eisenhower.

"Is he still a member?"

"Sort of. We're not sure that he's not providing information to the police. He misses a lot of meetings."

"The arrests, beatings: is this commonplace?" asked Mac

"We're not really sure since no one talks about it. What we need is someone inside the police or FBI," said Joan of Arc, a large older woman belying the chosen name.

"Can anyone think of where I might find a literary agent, Susan Raymond, supposedly taken about a week ago?"

"What offense?" asked Joan of Arc.

"None. It would seem that she represented some undesirable that they would like to talk to. She has no idea where he is."

"She may just disappear," said Dwight Eisenhower.

"This is not a third world country; people don't disappear," Mac said.

No one agreed with him.

"Try the armory. We've heard that it's in use. It was rumored to be the headquarters of the militia."

"So militia is an issue here too," stated Mac.

"They're saying that the right to a militia was granted by the first Congress and never repealed. They may be right; it makes no matter since the present Congress could reinstate. The most immediate concern is the arming of the militia. Take the National Rifleman's Association, with its right to bear arms agenda: an armed militia formation, the twenty-five percent unemployment, fifty percent of the people speak a different language from the other fifty percent of the population, rampant inflation, and what does that add up to?" Joan of Arc was quivering with righteous indignation.

"Not good," admitted Mac. "So what should be done? Why is this being allowed?"

"A better question might be when have we seen this before," said George Washington.

"I don't think that these are National Socialists," said Joan of Arc.

"Maybe not, but their tactics are similar to those used in Germany in the 1930s," argued George Washington.

"What should be done?" Mac asked again.

"Watch, it is all that we can do. Watch and document for the day that this thing passes."

"If ever."

"If ever," agreed George Washington. "We don't have enough members to organize a sit-in. Most of our members are too old to fight the police, or the militia, or even a strong-willed meter maid!"

They exchanged means of communication, pass codes that hopefully would prevent infiltration, and Mac departed. He was depressed by the encounter. The group promised to see if Sue Raymond was held and in good health. A meeting was scheduled for two days hence; Mac would then immediately leave Washington.

Helen was pacing when he returned and confirmed that Carol had the contact information and would have used it to call, had she not been there.

"She's sleeping, but I think that we need to stay here and one of us should remain awake."

"I am dead beat from driving. Could you do the first few hours?"

"My favorite thing is watching you snore."

Mac relayed the meeting details in a whispered conversation. She asked a few questions; Mac knew more would come later.

The next morning they cooked scrambled eggs and toast that Mac had bought. There was very little food in the house.

"Listen, Carol, we're going out to see if we can help Ray. It won't help if you call the men who took her. Do you understand?"

"But they said to call if I heard from you. The last time you called I told them and they brought Ray back home."

"I didn't say who I was," said Mac.

"I know you though, don't I?"

"Well this time don't tell them!"

Outside, they put their things in the car.

"Do you think that she'll call?" Helen asked.

"Fifty- fifty."

"Then we have to find somewhere else to sleep."

"Let's make some calls from the train station. It should be busy enough there to make us anonymous."

Mac called Ann Gold.

"Hello, Ann."

"Is this…"

"Probably!"

"Well, well, well, how is half of my favorite couple?"

"Well thanks. Can you switch off your phone tracer?"

"For an interview with you, dear boy, of course I can."

"Sue Raymond was arrested because she doesn't know where we are," said Mac. "Be careful what you know or ask."

"True, true. So tell me what you want me to know."

"That Sue Raymond does not know where we are. That I am a patriot, not a terrorist, and we are perfectly happy out of sight. I will say nothing of the circumstances or geographic location as it may help someone."

"One man's patriot is another man's freedom fighter. It really depends who is in the seat."

"So, since I am opposed to the seat, it makes me a terrorist?"

"Afraid so."

"Ann, what can you tell me?" asked Mac.

"I miss you both. There is little that I can write for the newspaper that won't get someone into trouble. If I name the person who may have been naughty, they are dragged in off the street. If I withhold the name, I am visited and dragged off for questioning while they raid my office."

"Next time they drag you away, ask after Sue would you?"

"I'll try. What else? The federal budget won't balance, even with no military to speak of, no defense spending, no foreign aid, no money for the United Nations, NATO, or NASA. Know why?" she asked, and then answered. "Because there are no taxes coming in; corporations are losing money: no taxes; individuals are out of work: no taxes; no one is buying gasoline. Do you get the picture? Money spent on social progress is running out; the states are sucking fumes; Medicare is drying up."

"How can this be in just one year?"

"It was precarious before. We depended on fairness, we supported each other, and we were living on a knife edge that only needed a push. Bringing home the military was the push. The idea was good: save billions a year that we could not afford. The practical application shut down millions of jobs around the world which added to our unemployment. General Lloyd opposed the President and was executed last week."

"I didn't see that. How do you know?"

"Obituaries said he had a cerebral hemorrhage. His wife told me that it was because they lodged a piece of lead there."

"Horace Wright was correct."

"Horace....?"

"The guy who writes the obituaries says that everyone reads his column first."

"The militia will report to an old friend of yours, Adam Fox, and is to be headed by an FBI man called Melvin Milan."

"The son of a bitch who killed Charles George and the bastard who kidnapped the White kids, probably killed David White, and definitely killed agent Alveres. What a lethal duo."

"I have to go Take care; give my love to your wife."

"Thanks, Ann."

Helen called Marjorie White; Mac shared the earpiece with her but remained silent.

"Hello, Marjorie. How are you and the boys?"

There was a gasp at the other end of the telephone.

"Helen. Where are you?"

"It's better that you not know."

"True. We're terrible; never know when we are followed, harassed. This phone is hacked so don't expect privacy, and don't visit unless you are prepared for a full body search. The boys are as fine as can be expected. I found a good private school down here and they are coping. What about you, a married woman for about a year, any children?"

"Into this crazy world? No. Marjorie, are you still in touch with your team?"

"No, most are out to pasture, some, like Matt, are in jail for something that was cooked up. I can't think of what it was at the moment. Did you see that David's murderer is now Home Security Czar? He's going to have his own army."

There was a clicking on the line.

"Hang up; someone has a trace on this call."

Helen hung up and called the FBI. She eventually got through to her friend who had been demoted.

"Helen, you're wanted in connection with terrorist acts and to explain your connection with the Sons of Liberty. If you give me your location, I'll pick you up and bring you in. Do you understand this message?"

"Perfectly. Goodbye." Helen hung up quickly.

Mac and Helen stayed in the pickup truck overnight. They were parked close to an area frequented by the homeless. They were safe since a good number of the homeless also sleeping in their cars were ex- military. They did not sleep but talked in the dark.

The meeting with the Generals, as Mac insisted on calling them, was well attended and included the man who was a potential mole. The suspected mole was Ulysses Grant, who was quiet and attentive.

"It has occurred to me," Mac said, "that the primaries might be a way of getting our message out."

"It would be a death warrant," said George Washington.

"What if it were a different candidate in each State?"

"The point being?"

"A unified message: awareness. The candidate's health and campaigning would be the responsibility of the Sons of Liberty in the state in which they appeared. The candidate should be Democrat, I think; then he or she can request that the President debate the issues."

"It would be a bloodbath. They would have the militia intimidate the candidate and the audience," said Joan of Arc.

"Do we want to do nothing?" asked Mac.

"We have a year in which to come up with a strategy," agreed George Washington.

"New campaign laws will limit spending," said Ulysses Grant.

"What new law?" asked Joan of Arc.

"Limits spending, the bill requires lists of every donation plus having the candidate making a non-refundable deposit in every state."

"Will never pass," Joan of Arc predicted.

"Already did," argued Ulysses Grant. "Quietly passed through House and Senate last week, signed yesterday."

"How did we not know?" George Washington asked.

"Because we use bush telegraph and the media is scared shitless," Grant stated.

A number of conversations started, with everyone conversing with his or her neighbor.

George Washington slowly quieted everyone.

"Do we have questions for our Boston emissary or messages to our northern comrades?"

"Yes, we're as clueless as they are," said Joan of Arc. "But Peter is correct; we must do something, anything. I think that the primaries are still a way off, but Congressional seats will be contested next year. We should test our mettle in those."

"A great idea. Each committee should field at least one candidate to contest a seat which went over or is likely to be compromised."

"Thank you all; that's the message I'll take back to Boston and pass along to any groups with whom we have contact," said Mac. "Now we must be on our way."

Outside was a beautiful day. It was difficult to imagine that there were dark clouds over Washington.

Joan of Arc had arranged for Mac and Helen to have the use of a health club in order to shower and change. A meeting with Martin Konrad was next. The middle of a crowded Starbucks, where most customers were taking advantage of the Wi-Fi, was as safe as anywhere.

"How's Martin?"

"Good, and yourselves? You both look different from the last time we saw each other. Safer, I'm sure."

Martin looked older, considerately older.

"Martin, seriously, how are you?" Mac was concerned for his friend.

"Having my business disrupted on a regular basis means that even those clients still in business can go elsewhere with less hassle."

"Because of me?" asked Mac.

"Probably. Although your two friends came to see me and one of them needed stitches right afterwards. So I guess that I did nothing to help myself. They take my computers, download my programs, and copy my correspondence once a month. It's hard. I've been to the armory twice to answer questions. *Where is Mac? Who is Peter Doath? Where is Peter Doath? Where is*

Helen? Who do I work for? I think I have a cracked rib for every stitch that he needed."

"I'm sorry."

"For what?"

"For involving you," said Mac.

"Don't be sorry. I'd be on the opposite side to those thugs anyway."

Mac gave Martin the means to access George Washington and told him that he would need to watch and check out Ulysses Grant. They worked out a way of keeping in touch and went their separate ways.

"Mac."

"I think I recognize that tone of voice. What do you want, Helen?"

"Since we are half-way there, can we visit my mother?"

"I don't think that Washington is halfway to Naples."

"It is from somewhere."

Since it was hard to argue with this logic, they were soon headed south.

Helen was reading the newspaper that they had bought. There was a nice article by Ann which asked why Susan Raymond, agent to the famous, was being held even after the confiscation of the book written by her client Matthew McDougal. "Listen to this, 'If I don't know where to find this man for an exclusive interview, then Ms. Raymond doesn't have a chance'."

"That's nice," said Mac.

"Hope it helps and doesn't get Ann into trouble," Helen stated, truly concerned.

She read the article again and turned to the international news.

"Ha!" she said. "It seems as though the Muslim Brotherhood have ousted the government in Turkey. And guess who was the first to recognize the new government?"

"Our Muslim President?"

"None other." She continued reading. "It looks like the new head of the Turks is his father-in-law, Abdul Sirlee Serat."

"Her name is Sirlee, not Shirley?" said Mac.

"In the old days we might have sent the Mediterranean Fleet."

"On which side?" asked Mac.

It took three days to reach Naples as they kept to lesser roads, endured further police harassment, and, being ultra-careful, went south as far as Miami, then west across Alligator Alley.

Watching from down the street, they followed Julie to the store where Helen confronted her.

"Hi, Julie."

Julie gave a little shriek and then, recovering, she slowly recognized her sister.

"You scared the crap out of me."

"How's Mum?"

"As well as can be expected with the weekly inquisition regarding your whereabouts." She realized that she now knew where Helen was. "What do I say next time?"

"That you have not seen anyone who looks like your sister."

"Well that's true; you look awful."

"I feel great."

"I'd invite you back, but if the kids see you, who knows what they might say and to whom."

"Bring Mum here tomorrow, this time."

"Okay. We heard that you were in Washington, heading to Boston."

"Where did you hear that and when?"

"Two or three days ago. It was on the news that the police had utilized a new militia group to set up road blocks on every road north to capture a ruthless and dangerous husband and wife team of terrorists. It was you because they said that there were ties to Marjorie White who was placed under militia protection as a precaution."

Mac suppressed the urge to swear. "Shows how wrong they are. We've been down here, working on our tan."

After meeting twice with her mother, it was time to leave. It took four days to drive back to Boston. They were silent for huge stretches of time. Silent, each of them thinking their own thoughts. Helen thinking of her mother and sister, that she had probably seen them for the last time. Mac going over and over plans for combating an assailant that was never there; hitting at shadows.

Chapter Five

The summer turned to fall. Fall, in New Hampshire, was spectacular. The trees of summer were, in September, blushing scarlet across the mountains and soon the birch trees, jealous of the riot of colors from the maples, showed their own vivid yellow garlands. The air was crisp, the days warm, and the nights cool. What visitor activity there had been was gone.

Sponsoring candidates for Congress had been taken up by all the Sons of Liberty groups contacted. It was hard; it was dangerous and exposed all of the members to identification. It was important to immediately refute bad publicity. Fundraising was a challenge as the competition seemed to have endless monies.

The results were mixed. It produced winning candidates in rural areas, but the urban mobs overran the rallies without police intervention. Candidates dropped out, two of them from hospital beds. These stories, all authenticated, were used in articles by Mac and Helen and distributed, now to all of the known groups. It was exhausting. Emilio Gonsalves had won in Florida and had a broken leg to take with his defiance to Washington.

Helen had participated in decorating the church for the holidays and they were invited to a few house parties. Ever careful, they had declined most invitations. The one party invitation that they had accepted was from the farmer, Randolph Scott, and his wife Patricia. Farmer Scott said that his name came from a crush that his mother had on the film actor, but that he preferred to be called Randy in spite of the connection.

They had become friends with the farmer, since Peter Howe and his wife now regularly drove to Boston to save him the time and trouble. There was never a problem with the money, the delivery, or the merchandise that was picked up. If they left early and came home late he pretended not to notice. If, as part of their barter the diesel fill ups were increasing, he asked no questions.

There were three other couples at the Scott's farm and lots of conversations revolved around the cost of farming and inflation. The cost of fuel was driving up the cost of everything. The increased value of food was making it the target of crooks.

"I heard that the Federal Government has taken over some farms and let the unemployed move in and operate them."

"Like a co-operative?" asked Randy.

"Like in Zimbabwe," said Bill Murphy.

"That didn't work," added his wife.

"Except that a lot of farmers ended up dead," said Randy.

"Then putting up with the cold has its rewards," said his wife. "I was wondering why we put up with eight months of winter and three months of black flies."

"It is for the one month of summer," said Bill Murphy.

"Peter, how about setting up a trucking business; take my stuff to Boston as well as Randy's?" Ted Knight asked. Ted was a healthy, heavy man, with a healthy, heavy wife who farmed over in Gilmanton.

"Sorry, Ted, not right now. The price of fuel, then gangs in the street, sleet, snow…." Mac shrugged; he needed to think through every move he made. "Besides, so much work to do at the house – keeps me busy all the time."

Mac liked Ted and his wife. They had met at church a few times and always seemed affable.

"I agree with you, Peter. I don't like Ted even going to Manchester and would never go to Boston," said Kate, Ted's wife.

"So, where do you get your money?" The question came from a man introduced as Joe Sykes.

Mac was instantly wary. He had never met Joe before and had a sense that he had been watching Helen and himself.

"Savings, redundancy pay that I set aside."

"Won't last long at today's prices."

"No, I suppose not."

"What did you do?" Joe asked. He was getting too interested.

"Accounting, accounts receivable at G.E."

"Boring," Patricia Scott interceded "What's everyone doing for Christmas?"

"Chicken for us again," said Randy "Again."

Everyone joined in the fun as they knew that he had a barn full of the birds. The subject changed and the discussion of local people, unknown to the newcomers, gave Mac the chance to indicate their intention to leave. Joe Sykes was still watching them carefully.

"Good night and thank you," Helen said to her hostess and then to the group, "Merry Christmas!"

A chorus of similar greetings came from the other guests.

"What was it, Mac?" asked Helen once they were alone.

"I don't know. It was either the mention of driving or the questions that Joe Sykes asked. I just got a little spooked. This is a lousy way to live. It was not what I had envisioned for us. I'm sorry, Helen."

"Mac, you didn't make the world the way it is."

"No, but I can change me."

"Ha, you think so? You are who you are. If we had stayed in Washington, you would have been muzzled or put into jail. Either way you would have been unhappy. And so would I," said Helen, looking into his eyes,

"We're all prisoners: Marjorie White, Ellie May Joseph, Congress, the American people. Even, I suppose, the President."

"How do you figure the President is a prisoner?"

"I'm sure that his reality is not what he dreamed would be the result for his actions," said Mac.

"Interesting. You mean when he went to the Middle East for training that he expected to strap twenty pounds of explosives onto his back and blow something up?"

"No; I think that he was recruited, together with a number of other likely international candidates. I think that the Muslim Brotherhood knew that they could take advantage of the Democratic Constitutions of the civilized countries."

"You mean we were gullible and/or civilized. Since only civilized countries were targeted, would we have been safe from attack if we were uncivilized?"

"It's really a common trait among people of every nationality: they want more. Unfortunately, when it comes on a large scale and countries, nationalities, or broad groups want more, it often leads to war. Civil war in the case of African nations, nuclear war if it is the Israelis, religious war in the Middle East, and wars of ideology in the Far East."

"That will make a great article, Peter Doath, but does not answer the question of how we get our lives back, miserable as they seem to our righteous enemies."

"What if this is it?" asked Mac. "What if the American Empire went the same way as the British Empire, the Roman Empire, the Ottoman Empire, etc, etc?"

"Is this the return of the Islamic Empire or the Ottoman?"

"Take your pick."

"The consolation I get is that each succeeding 'Empire' lasted less than the previous one. So this one may be over in a few years."

"Or last a thousand years," argued Mac.

Christmas came with snow. The trip to Boston had showed fewer lights than in previous years. The stores did not have the busy shoppers of the past. If there had not been holiday music, it would have been difficult to see the difference from a regular week. The unemployment figures were blamed. There was also a sense of lethargy and also wariness. Petty crime was rising; anyone carrying a parcel was a potential target.

The mob at the market was larger, hungrier, and more aggressive. Mac, having given a virtuoso performance, donated a box of chickens; the mob took another box. As he drove away, he was feeling that he had been lucky. His luck was confirmed by the buyer in the market; two truck drivers from the previous day were in hospital. The early hour explained his good fortune.

Mac and Helen met with the Sons of Liberty and learned that the nearly total blackout of news was the result of a standoff in Texas.

Anders had denounced Ellie May Joseph as a traitor. He had claimed that she was the first female member of the Klu Klux Klan and also a member of a terrorist group, the Sons of Liberty. The claim accurately quoted some of Mac's writing but attributed it to Ellie May Joseph; the President called for her arrest and transportation to Washington for trial. Ellie May had made the suggestion that Anders should personally come and try to take her in.

The government had put a block on any news from Texas while continuing to assert that the FBI was looking for Ellie May Joseph. News was coming out of Texas through the Sons of Liberty organization. With the active social media network, it was impossible not to know what was happening, even if there were active attempts to prevent the truth being heard.

"We understand that the National Guards of neighboring states have been sent by the Federal Government to the border of Texas. The guardsmen have no stomach for a fight with the Texas Rangers," Paula Revere said, standing next to her father.

"Then they will have to send in regular troops," said Helen.

"They'd have to be pulled from the riot control in LA or San Francisco, which is unlikely. The unemployed are still roaming, looting, and pillaging," said Paula.

"Proper twenty-first century Vikings!" said Mac.

"And just as much fun for the victims," said Benjamin Franklin.

"We should go and show them that there are others in the country with concerns. It will be like the Alamo," said Mac

"I think not." John Hancock had been listening, thinking. "Peter, you have to do what you do best, and that is to write. We have to stay here and wait for the opportunity to open a second front. If the Sons of Liberty were all in Texas, we would be playing into their hands. They would bus in the militia and crush us. If we stay at home in Boston, New York, Chicago, etc., they have to respect our growing strength. We wait and watch."

"Some of the college boys are going to Texas," said Paula. "Youthful disobedience; I hope they learn something and then come back."

"Can we have them take messages?"

"I think it might be helpful as introductions for them to take messages. Write a message now as they are leaving soon," John said.

Mac handed over an essay that he had written on the election of Emilio Gonsalves and how Norman Harrison had not been suicidal and had not been accident prone. It was written as Peter Doath. He was pretty sure from the information in the piece that

Emilio would recognize the writer's real identity. Mac was also one hundred percent certain that there was no torture capable of extracting Matthew McDougal's name from Emilio's lips. This piece should, however, show that Emilio could be trusted by the Sons of Liberty and vice versa.

Helen had written an essay on the subject of global war against terrorism as Leonad Vallice. It was a complicated treatise and ended with the quote from the Revolutionary War, that 'dissent is a form of patriotism'.

It was sure to engender conversations all along the Sons of Liberty pipeline and in those hard to reach places in the hearts of the uncommitted. She was an expert in writing a political argument, then answering it.

They had stayed late, as Mac wanted to try some ideas for opening a 'second front'. Sean had shown up late to the meeting to the relief of the five or six members still there.

Mac suggested that they discuss alternatives. It was to be a 'Blue sky' list. List everything, regardless of the absurdity, then go through the list and give them priorities from the most promising, to the most absurd, Once they were prioritized, feasibility was to be discussed. Every piece of paper was to be shredded and put into the open fire as soon as it had served its purpose.

The ideas, after the first thoughtful few minutes, flowed until they had nine and had begun to repeat variations of those listed. The final seven included everything, from assassination, to secession, dirty tricks, open rebellion, and accumulating weapons and money.

Assassination was low down the list due to those present being unable to visualize pulling a trigger. The additional argument was that an assassination attempt was expected and, even if successful, would produce a martyr. Secession was a choice, if other like-minded states followed. It was not on the immediate 'to do' list. Dirty tricks found favor and would be investigated by Sean.

Open rebellion was out of the immediate question, while the support of Texas or any other state with propaganda and intelligence gathering was popular. Accumulating weapons was already taking place but needed a focus and a leader. There was a heated discussion and during the debate it was Sean who said that he understood that General Lloyd's son lived in the area. There had been wide spread fury after General Lloyd had been charged and executed for disobeying the President's demand for immediate repatriation of troops without discussion in Congress.

John Hancock volunteered to find, approach, and recruit Joe Lloyd as he had once taught his sister Sylvia Lloyd. This was therefore the unanimous number one choice of action. Number two was the raising of funds. Mac volunteered to lead, as he mapped a strategy to have the Sons of Liberty funded in a similar scam to the one that had been used against their political opponents by Anders and others.

"Good night, Peter and Scarlett. This was by far the most exciting and productive evening of my life." John Hancock had seen them to the door. They could hear the excited voices still talking in the other room.

"Thank you, John. Maybe next year we can have a Merry Christmas."

"Thanks to both of you it will be an exciting New Year."

Planning for funding the money for the Sons of Liberty had been easier than Mac had anticipated. This was thanks to a surprise and, in retrospect, inspired communication. The idea was Helen's. On the ride home they were discussing old friends and also brainstorming on how they might use the tactics of the opposition against them.

For Mac to complete the task that he had undertaken would require several elements working together. First he needed an event, next he needed a 'book' on that event, as well as seed money, and third he needed to make sure that he had wagered on a winning position. It was clear that the opposition was confident in the political arena. Mac struggled with his conscience. He struggled for about three seconds, about the morality of rigging a political election. Actually he preferred to think that he would not be helping rig an election but that they were ensuring that a legitimate candidate was elected. The 'book' should be easy, as Hal in Las Vegas was happy to hold the money.

"Hal would hold both coats if there were a scrap in an alley," Mac speculated.

"Likely rifle through the coat pockets too," said Helen. "Well, the loser's pockets anyway."

The biggest question, as usual, was money. Mac had some in Vegas, but even at the five-to-one odds that a confident bettor might play, it was hardly going to put a dent in the money chest accumulated by the opposition from the last election.

"Who would benefit from Anders defeat?" asked Helen.

"Who hurt after he was elected?" Mac asked, and then answered. "Other than everyone."

"The defense industry disappeared; poor Mark lost everything," said Helen.

"Poor Mark was making a fortune on the inside and parlayed influence into pockets that we are better off not knowing about," said Mac.

"So he was a little gray," said Helen defensively.

"Jane Fonda pink and McCarthy light blue."

"Okay, Mac, you're right. But he was always close to the honey pot."

"He's probably on the most wanted list, right under the two of us. I'd be surprised if he is not in a group similar to ours, but you're right, we should approach him."

They were stopped due to the late hour and searched. Again they were saved by the smell and sight of chicken excretion on the load and the fact that the fertilizer, on top of the feed, was not edible.

Everyone was improvising; farmers had cut down on fertilizer by using chicken waste on the fields that were dormant and manure on the vegetable fields. It was more work, but it was necessary as other commodities, if available, were expensive. Mac was therefore carrying only what was absolutely impossible to substitute.

Mark was in hiding; Helen found him. It was difficult to talk so they arranged to meet in Las Vegas in ten days time.

Mac contacted Sean at his office.

"Mr. Lynch, that case we had discussed, seems that a witness has surfaced and we are meeting soon. Can we postpone our meeting of next Thursday until three weeks later?"

"Yes, sir, I believe we can. Thank you for calling and we shall see you on January 10th."

"God willing."

"God speed," whispered Sean.

Mac and Helen left in the afternoon, saying that they were headed home for Christmas. No one bothered to ask where they were going or when they might be back.

The pickup was stocked with everything that they might need for the whole trip, except diesel. There was even a cage with live chickens: a source of eggs, then meat.

Driving north, then east, the idea was to cross the border from Maine into Canada, hopefully unnoticed, on one of the many logging trails that seemed to ignore international treaties.

A problem in Canada was solved in a town near the border which had a money changing store. It appeared that many people went back and forth across the border on 'cash only' business.

Mac and Helen needed to drive over five hundred miles a day. It was grueling, even with two drivers. The good news was that Canada did not have road blocks. The other good news was the lack of traffic; drafting behind a large rig ensured no hassle with the police. The bad news was that they added a thousand miles to their trip. The other bad news was the weather which kept them off the road for hours and then meant driving through the day. It was already day eight when they reached Moose Jaw and prepared to reenter the U.S. into Montana. The plan was to stay on the Western side of the mountains for as long as they could to avoid the majority of precipitation which fell on the Rockies.

"How far?" asked Helen.

"Fifteen hundred miles," Mac sighed. "Fifteen hundred tough miles. A storm forecast tonight, then clearing."

"So we rest tomorrow?"

"No, we make the crossing in the storm."

Helen groaned.

"I'll drive, Helen. We need to carry as much fuel as we can. Get rid of the chickens and the cage."

She was crying, mostly from exhaustion, as she expertly dispatched the chickens, dunked them in hot water and started plucking.

Las Vegas was nothing like the last time that Mac had seen it. There were no lights on the signs. No sign of the palpable excitement of earlier days. People walked without laughter. It could have been almost any town. Driving down the street in a filthy pickup truck elicited no glances, no interest at all.

"We'll park at the first place that looks busy, then walk," said Mac.

"Anything you say, as long as there's a hot bath at the end of the walk."

Even in these austere times, when guests were scarce, there was concern at the desk when the check-in clerk looked out at the disheveled, hollow-eyed individuals. A call was made and, after a few minutes Mac was given the keys to a room and an extension number on a piece of paper.

"Please call this number and have a pleasant stay."

Helen was running a bath. Mac called the number.

"You're late."

"Bad weather, detours."

"Everything all right?"

"Nothing that twelve hours sleep won't cure."

"Eight. At exactly midnight go to the security desk alone. Do not speak. Got it?"

"Okay."

"Sweet dreams," Hal said as he severed the connection.

When Helen has vacated the bath, Mac showered and then joined the already sleeping Helen.

At eleven-thirty the alarm that he had set woke him. He reluctantly and swiftly got ready. He dressed and picked up one of the card keys then left the room without Helen showing any signs of waking.

The security man nodded and headed toward a wall behind him. The wall turned out to be an electronic door which opened as they approached. There was an elevator. Mac got in; the security guard reached over and pressed a number then stepped out, leaving Mac to ascend alone.

When the door opened in the penthouse there were several men waiting. Hal was there, as was Mark. The man seated at a large table was stereotypical and looked as if he headed a large illegal operation; the other men, all wearing dark clothes, were standing at the sides of the room. Hal stood and greeted Mac but made no attempt to introduce him to any of the other people. This was a meeting which would be private, conducted on a need to know basis.

"Mac, we understand the care that you took to get here. Since you called the meeting, perhaps you had better lay out the plan, the players, and the end game."

"Thanks, Hal, for setting up this meeting, and thanks for your hospitality."

"Not my doing." Hal waved across the table. "We go back some years, Mac, and you are a straight shooter which is the reason that we are here. It has also come to our attention that you are actually doing something about the crisis in this country."

"Not enough," said Mac. "The plan is simple in concept. We need to be able to trust everyone involved, therefore the principals are all present." He continued, "The Muslim Brotherhood funded a raid on our government with federal funds. In other words we the taxpayers paid for our own overthrow. What I propose is to reverse the money flow." Mac paused to allow what he had said to settle in.

He looked at the faces of the men in the room and was very glad they were not playing poker. "We identify events that will draw them in; since they have had success in politics, that will be our arena. We need to create a book that is attractive and believable; funding from Mark and his contacts will be necessary and then a proper conclusion that will be the responsibility of the Sons of Liberty. Questions?"

Hal received a nod from the table and asked, "How much?"

"Up to a billion dollars at five-to-one," said Mac.

"Do you have that? Do they have that?" asked Hal.

"Mark?"

"I think that I can raise a billion for this cause. My people have been hard hit. Very hard."

"Can we be quiet about it? Remember that the new political spending bill makes it illegal to use any but your own money," Hal stated looking at Mark.

"This is America. We can do it."

"Mac, do you trust this man?"

"Yes, I don't believe in what he does, but if he says a billion, then there will be a billion dollars to book our wager. We know that the brotherhood took three billion out of Vegas two years ago and spent it. We need to shake them and hit them where it hurts."

"Where do we come in?" asked Hal.

"If you can create and keep an active book, there is your 'vig', but we would like it if you could frame the president, maybe vice president, even the head of the militia."

The man at the desk gestured for Hal to come to him. There was a whispered conversation.

"It is believed that you have personal issues with these men. Do you want them dead?" asked Hal.

Mac glanced across the desk. This was a test of some kind. He was too tired to think it through.

"Yes, but I want the Brotherhood to do it after they have been humiliated. We want the frame to be airtight."

It appeared to be a good answer as the next question was asked after an imperceptible nod.

"What event?"

"The presidency, but as a trial we believe that they murdered the mayor of New York City in order to put their man in. The Sons of Liberty will run a candidate and protect her. We need 'dirt' on their candidate and support from any friends that you might have in the area."

Hal looked down the table; there was no movement.

"Enjoy your stay. Let's meet again tomorrow: same time, same place," said Hal standing.

The meeting was over.

Mac woke just before noon. He could not believe that he had slept so well. Disoriented, it took a while to get focused. Helen was singing in the shower and he was hungry. She came to the door with a towel around her body.

"Finally awake, let's go; we're meeting Mark for lunch."

"First things first," said Mac, pulling the towel away from her.

Mark, in the light of day, looked pretty good. He had lost about forty pounds, looked rested, and was clearly not eating and drinking on an expense account.

"Good of you to come," said Mac.

"What else have I to do? Do you think that your plan will work, and who gets to split the winnings?"

"Mark, the idea is that the Sons of Liberty need the funds. Your friends can either fund them directly or leverage through the plan."

"No problem, Mac. It's hard to remember that the good times may never return and then be reminded that there is a price on your head. Who were you planning to run for president?"

"We've talked about that, and I think Ellie May Joseph may be persuaded," said Mac.

"I, of course, think that Marjorie White would make the ideal president," said Helen.

"But she'd need to win a place on the ballot," argued Mac.

The meeting at midnight was more formality than informative.

"We've contacted New York and they will be in touch. The usual vigorish will be charged on the 'book', so that there is no suspicion. You'll receive irrefutable evidence that a certain 'gang' in

Washington have been meeting and plotting to make a lot of money and to create a dictatorship."

"Thank you," said Mac, nodding to the men who sat at the table.

"Thank you," said Hal. "There's no evidence of this meeting or that you have been in Las Vegas in the last two years. We've opened an account for Mark and set it up with firewalls."

Mac and Helen left the next morning, heading toward Texas. They were encouraged, as opposition to the President seemed to be growing everywhere.

Getting into Texas was a challenge. The militia had covered the major roads, but the pressure of blockade runners still making it through was enormous and increasing.

The Joseph ranch was an armed encampment. Mac asked for Bobby and was ushered through. They met with Ellie May Joseph and outlined the plan for the Sons of Liberty to help her run for President. Mac left out the details of his meetings in Las Vegas.

Ellie May asked about funding; she was assured that Mark Hughes was on board and could be trusted.

It was a long ride back to New England. They were passed from group to group, gathering and dispensing information. The Sons of Liberty were everywhere, but, unarmed, they felt impotent. Mac gave them encouragement and explained that their opposition to candidates supported by the new regime and support and supply of candidates was important.

In Boston, they reported at length and met Joseph Lloyd. A great deal was happening and fast. Still there was a difference of opinion, even with the positive news of solidarity across the country. Some were shocked that a list of weapons was being made, that an inventory of weapons and their location was being compiled.

It was getting more dangerous.

Chapter Six

Back in New Hampshire, Helen and Mac were both relieved to be home for a while. They had been gone for more than four weeks. There was evidence that there had been visitors. There were footprints in the snow around the house which showed no attempt had been made to disguise the intrusion. Mac recognized a set of prints as those made by Chuck Hamilton since there was a furrow on the left side of the footprint from his slight limp. The other two sets led up to and into the house. Mac checked the mail box, just junk mail, started a fire, and brought in their gear.

After a quick bite Mac went over to see his neighbor.

"Chuck, how are you and Elizabeth?"

"Both well thanks. You're back," he said redundantly

"Yes, about an hour ago."

"Is the rest of the country feeling poorer?"

"Worse than here in some places," said Mac noncommittally.

"Mother can't find stuff for knitting or some of the baking stuff she wants."

"Make a list. If I go down to Boston I'll pick it up for her."

"That'll make her happy, thanks."

"Thanks for checking on the house while we were gone."

"No problem."

"Did you see other folk around? There are lots of footprints."

"Yeah, I saw that too. Just once; I saw someone come in close on a snowmobile. Don't see many around, what with the price of gas. Noisy, so I noticed."

"What did they look like?"

"Big! Well, what with the snow suits, they looked big."

"Recognize them? Locals?"

"One, I think I've seen him around. Down in the store and in the bar there."

"Thanks."

"They take anything?"

"No, just looking, I guess." Mac wanted to change the subject. He knew all that he needed to know and more questions would make it a big deal. The information, in which they might have been interested, had been with Mac in the pick-up truck. He was now forewarned and would put anything sensitive where it would not be found.

Settling back into their home was easier. Helen was much more relaxed, perhaps even relieved after the tension of their cross-country trip. Mac was splitting wood, ice fishing, and hunting. Whenever he went out now, he was aware of noises, conscious of changes, wary of approaching people.

Mac and Helen went down to the pub.

Upon entering they were greeted with, "Been away have you?" in the rhetorical questioning way that New Englanders have of speaking.

"Yeah." The one word evasive answer was enough to suffice.

"Go far?"

Most people were listening as it was the only conversation different from the weather and fishing that had been started. Mac suspiciously looked to see who was paying attention. They all were. Mac saw that Joe Sykes was sitting with his back to the wall. Joe had asked the question at Randy Scott's party that had been personal. Looking at him now, with a halfsmile, Mac was convinced that he was looking at the man who had visited their house while they were gone.

"We've family near Albany," said Mac.

"That's where you were from, right?"

"Yes. Can I have the lamb steak and another beer?"

"Nice weather?"

"Same as here."

As the conversation was returning to the weather, some of the regulars returned to their predictions of the weather for the ice fishing tournament.

"We're out of lamb," said the waitress with a resigned gesture. She made no attempt to erase it from the 'special' board.

"Do you want a burger?" the waitress asked.

"Sure, medium rare and cheese."

"Same?"

"Why not?" Helen gave the resigned gesture of a native.

They were left alone to eat and headed home soon afterwards.

"Do you think that Joe Sykes was at the house?" asked Helen as they walked home.

"What makes you ask?"

"He was watching."

"Yes, I think he was in the house, looking around."

"But found nothing," Helen stated.

"I hope only the things that we wanted found," said Mac. "We need to be careful."

"No more dining out?" asked Helen jocularly.

Mac grunted his reply as he was worried and thinking.

The weather was cold, with snow most days, which made travel difficult; even leaving the house was a challenge. Mac trekked to the farm for eggs and chickens.

"Can you do a run to Boston for me?" asked Randy.

"When the weather lifts."

"Primary is coming up in a couple of weeks. Not much point in voting. Nobody on the Republican ballot."

"We still have an obligation to vote. It's the one right that we can exercise," said Mac.

"Who for? Nobody running against Anders or Serat or whatever he calls himself."

"I wouldn't say that," said Mac. "Ellie May Joseph is opposing him in Texas."

"I suppose. So, are you suggesting writing her name in?"

"Think of it this way, if you're the only write in for a Republican candidate, she would win in New Hampshire with one vote and she'll be 'so beholden' that she will invite you to be Secretary of Agriculture," said Mac laughing.

They were both laughing and it was obvious that this story would quickly pass through the community and result in a groundswell for Ellie May. Mac now needed to plant the story in the Union Leader.

Mac and Helen were writing articles. The story of writing in Ellie May Joseph on the Republican ballot, as a defiant gesture, was written, eliminating the names. Still, they were aggravating each other. Cabin fever was a local term, where long stretches of forced close quarters, indoors, made people long for outside personal contact.

They argued over little things, over big things, over everything.

"If Joseph Lloyd gets the weapons, are you going to storm the federal troops on Bunker Hill?" asked Helen.

"Breeds Hill."

"What?"

"It was Breeds Hill, not Bunker Hill," said Mac.

"Who cares? It was euphuism. There are probably too many abandoned cars on Bunker Hill and Breeds Hill to march up anyway!"

"No federal troops stationed there either."

"So?"

"So what?"

"Will you fight with Lloyd?" asked Helen

"I'm sure that there are several good responses to that, but, no, I'm a lover, not a fighter."

"I hadn't noticed."

"I think that the Sons of Liberty have it right, that we are writers. Propaganda is just as important as firing a gun. Besides which, I think that their aim is defensive."

"Isn't that what every crackpot in history said?" asked Helen.

"The ones in Ireland anyway."

"They were right."

"Maybe, but it took a hundred years."

After a silence, a truce had almost been declared.

"Weather should improve tomorrow," said Mac.

"Says who?" Helen asked dubiously

"Randy. He asked me to schedule a trip south."

"I need to come. Mum wasn't well before Christmas."

"We'll see."

"We'll see?" Helen asked petulantly. "Who's the 'we'?"

"It's just an expression."

"No it isn't! It's that bloody male aggression."

"What do you mean?"

"You can't wait to get your hands on Lloyd's bazooka." She was furious.

Mac looked at her and laughed. "Get my hands on his bazooka?"

Helen laughed too and the argument ended.

The weather was better, but the roads were still impassible by truck. Plowing by the town had been almost non-existent. The main route in and out of town for supplies had been cleared. In other populated areas residents had used shovels to clear paths. Other residents, further out, had to walk through snow two feet deep and avoid drifts that were deeper.

Helen and Mac trudged to the store, pulling a toboggan. Chuck and Elizabeth had gone to their daughter's house for the weekend and had not yet returned even though it had been more than a week. It was deep virgin snow, just about all the way. They shopped for a few necessities, staying longer just to hear different voices. There was a television with a very poor picture. The news showed the weather likely to clear; then the wind would drop, though the occasional snow shower could be expected. The meteorologist suggested that it may impact voter turnout in the primary, to which the anchor had rejoined, "Who cares?"

The next day Mac shoveled out the wood pile and began splitting and stacking wood. Helen came out and said that she had forgotten something at the store and was going to pick it up.

By the time she had returned it had begun to snow.

Chapter Seven

Mac had been looking north without noticing the passage of time. Now he turned away and back toward the solitary light that would be coming from the house.

A mistake. They would come tonight.

He knew it with a certainty, with the same clarity of vision that earlier, before the snow; he had when Helen came in from the store. Splitting and stacking he had looked up.

"Did you get everything? Pate de foie gras, caviar?"

Today there was no acknowledgement, no flippant reply.

"What is it?" he asked with that foreboding that came from interpreting body language.

"Nothing," she said going into the house.

The screen door gave a now familiar 'smack'. He could see her move toward the kitchen area, towards the heat, shedding her down coat as she went. He looked at the smoke leaving the chimney; he breathed the air embellished by the wood fire. Although he knew that there was plenty of wood stacked, he took what he could carry from the woodpile and carried it indoors.

"What is it?" he repeated.

"It's a New Year for crying out loud," Helen spoke defiantly. Everything is going to be different."

"You called your mother?"

"Mac…." Her voice trailed, "I know you said….."

It was done.

"What happened?"

"She asked where we were, as she usually does. They must be under tremendous pressure."

"And you said?"

"The usual, that we were somewhere warm. Then that guy at Randy's party, Joe, came in and shouted to Bobby that anyone at the Lyons Den tonight would need to ski down Gunstock."

"Your mother heard?"

Helen turned away and started to stack the groceries.

"Maybe she won't say anything," Helen said hopefully.

"Maybe," Mac rejoined, without conviction.

He had spent the next hour putting together anything that might be incriminating. Papers of little consequence he fed into the fire. The evidence on the President and their current writings he put into a large envelope. Sealing the envelope, he put his neighbor's name as the sender and addressed it to Professor Sanderson at Harvard University.

The snow was falling heavily as he left with the envelope and trudged next door. When he arrived at the entrance to the Hamilton's house he put the envelope into their mailbox and lifted the flag. It would be safe until delivery tomorrow, if the mailman made it through the snow. If he changed his mind overnight, then he would retrieve it; otherwise it would be on its way to Cambridge.

Mac walked back and noted with satisfaction that snow had already obliterated his boots tracks of just fifteen minutes earlier.

Mac and Helen had talked quietly over a venison steak. The subject that they wanted to talk about was not mentioned, but it was clearly at the front of their minds.

It was still snowing. They washed the dishes, cleaned up, and made love; gently, quietly, and passionately.

"What can we do, Mac?"

"With this storm? Nothing. I love you, always have, and always will."

"I'm so selfish. I'm so sorry. I just wanted to wish my mother a Happy New Year. Julie, my nephews."

"Nothing wrong with that, darling. It was a normal thing to do."

"Will anything ever be normal again?"

"Yes." Mac said it to satisfy Helen but without believing it himself. "Look at all the good things that will happen this year."

"And all of the potentially bad things." Helen had recognized that he was being optimistic for her sake.

Helen fell asleep early. Mac lay looking at the ceiling, listening to the crack of wood in the stove. He carefully left her sleeping, put a log on the fire, dressed in his winter gear, and went out. It had stopped snowing and stars had started to show through the clouds and the trees. He was reminded of how Martin Luther, coming home from midnight services, had seen the stars through the fir trees and had started the tradition of putting lights on trees at Christmas.

The magic and mystery of the universe stretched before him; here Mac could think. He was used to writing things down, making lists. Now the choices were not on a shopping list: they were life and death. The death, of the most wonderful thing to come into his life, made the decision harder. Helen was not his only concern. They knew things, people's names, meeting places, the plan for raising monies, the plans for acquiring arms; they were probably the most knowledgeable individuals in the Sons of Liberty movement.

Flight or fight?

The phrases occurred to him so many times that he realized that these were the only two alternatives.

Flight: Canada. Fight: here or in Massachusetts?

Helen had made the mistake today, but the reality was that they had evaded capture several times by sheer luck or timing.

Timing was everything.

The silence was broken, first by the crunch of his boots, then by a distant whine, and then, sounding like an owl in flight, a faint whop, whop.

They were coming, by snowmobile and helicopter.

Mac hurried into the house, the screen door smacking the frame woke Helen.

"What is it?"

"They're here."

"You're sure?"

Mac took down his rifle and a box of ammunition. Together they crawled under the house. It was at first deceptively peaceful, then the 'whopping' crescendo above them and a giant spotlight obliterated anything beyond the house. Snowmobiles came across the frozen lake and down the road.

"How many?" asked Helen.

"Too many."

"Jes come to visit little ol' me?" asked Helen with an attempt to lighten the mood. "Shucks, and me right out of cherry pie."

"Helen, we know too much. Capture is not an option. It's fight or flight; unless we outrun a small army then it is fight. Trouble is these boys are innocent; I can't shoot them."

"Matthew McDougal, Helen Harvey, surrender. We have you surrounded. Come out peacefully and no one gets hurt."

The loud speaker had been set up at the top edge of the trees, towards the lake. The speaker was standing just behind the nearest tree, about fifty yards away, and Mac could see that he was in full SWAT gear with helmet, visor, and body armor.

"This is Chief Milan. You have my word that we are here to escort you both back to Washington, to clear up some questions regarding the death of David White."

"Son of a bitch murders David and then wants to pin it on us; I take back the last remark about shooting anyone. He has murdered and tortured with impunity."

"Mac, there are so many of them. Maybe we should surrender."

"Helen, sweetheart, they are in body armor. It is not their intention that we reach Washington. A vigorous questioning, then disappearing without a trace – that is our fate."

"Then shoot the bastard."

"What happened to Scarlett O Hara? Now it's Rambo?"

Milan repeated his request that they surrender. Mac, who had been shooting deer from twice the distance to the speaker, was concentrating on his actions. Melvin Milan also made a mistake this day. He adjusted the microphone under his visor. The six inch gap of only a few seconds was all Mac needed to put a bullet into his neck.

There was a second of silence, and then the twenty men accompanying Chief Milan opened fire on the house. The firepower was out of all proportion to the single shot fired. All the participants would later swear that they had come under intense fire.

One heavy round hit the stove, then another as it exploded, causing the dried out timbers of the old house to burn in a conflagration that could be seen for miles.

No fire truck came, and the next morning there was nothing but smoldering embers.